AN EMBER IN THE WIND

STAGE TWO OF
AN ORTHOGONAL UNIVERSE

AN EMBER IN THE WIND

ROBERT LOYD WATSON

2013
MOUNT OLIVE, NORTH CAROLINA

Published in the United States by The Flying Wiener Dog Studio, LLC, Mount Olive, North Carolina, USA

Version D9 R83 FP
Digital File Compilation Date: May 15, 2014

ISBN: 978-0-9889572-2-0

Disclaimer: All characters in this book are fictitious. I think that pretty much goes without saying. If you want to believe they're real, then, well, I'm not one to criticize your lifestyle. Just keep doing your thing, and don't sue me. Also, I'm not omniscient. That means any resemblance to real persons is entirely coincidental, and not because I'm a passive-aggressive jackass. Honest.

For Elizabeth

STAGE II

I
The Well of Enlightenment

1. A Little Bit Higher

A swirling gray mass of clouds encompassed the car as we ascended the final mountain pass. Its finger-like tentacles weaved through the crevices of the vehicle–between the windshield and the wipers, the gap between the door and the mirror, and any other space it could. The road slowly disappeared. Little lights flashed all around us. I wondered if they were reflections from the headlights. They seemed brighter. Can reflections reflect a light brighter than its source?

"A little bit higher . . . " Sheridan said. He bit his lip. "Is all it would take."

I didn't know what he meant by that, and I didn't care to contemplate. The lights flashed brighter, with more contrast, like the static of a TV tuned to a channel that didn't exist. The noise, seemingly random, may very well have been *pseudo-random*. I wouldn't know, but Sheridan seemed to. He watched the lights with a wonderstruck eye.

This is it, I thought. *This is the end of the world Sheridan predicted.*

Ever since I'd plucked him off the side of the road, he'd insisted the world was going to end. And now, the clouds, the looming demons that had hung ominously over us since we'd left Raleigh, had finally caught us.

The sound of rushing air also tuned in and out. For a moment, it sounded like we were driving in a vacuum. Then the air returned. The lights grew brighter. Sheridan's shadow flickered all around the cabin. The light became so bright I could hardly see the steering wheel.

I closed my eyes and pushed harder on the accelerator.

After a while, I opened my eyes and saw nothing. I could hear the familiar sound of rushing air, steady as it should be. My eyes adjusted to the darkness, and I could see the dash panel lights. There was a low rumble, and I realized I was driving with the right side of the car on the shoulder. Just like that–the lights were gone.

We stopped at a diner at the bottom of the pass, near the Virginia-Tennessee border. I looked up at the top of the road, the clouds swirling around the peak like vultures. "Swirling" was Sheridan's description. I said they were chewing.

Sheridan stood with his face pressed against the door, staring inside. The lights were off.

"There's no use," I said.

I glanced at the sky again. There was no sign of the sun. The clock in the car was perpetually stuck at one in the morning, but it couldn't have been later than three or four. A thin, white light emitted from the bottom of the clouds–most likely the moon. A single yellow parking lot light hummed above me. It cast my shadow so long and deep that my head disappeared under a bush. My alter-ego had a bad afro.

Sheridan's shadow lurched at mine. I jumped back, and Sheridan laughed. "You're awfully jumpy tonight."

In actuality, Sheridan was several feet behind me–still at the door. The light's angle was playing tricks. "Well hell, Sheridan!" I yelled. "What do you expect?"

Sheridan knew exactly what I was talking about. He looked up at the pass. The thin light still glowed, but was slowly dimming.

"Could be the moon," Sheridan said.

I sighed and walked up to the door. I couldn't blame Sheridan for not giving up on it. I was *hungry*. But it was totally dark inside. The chairs were scattered haphazardly about the floor. There was a mural against the back wall of the New York City skyline. The artist had run out of room painting the Twin Towers, and had had to continue the top twenty or so floors on the ceiling.

"It's odd," Sheridan said.

"Tell me about it. It's been six months already, but that skyline still looks strange."

Sheridan shook his head. "No. I meant the chairs."

I shrugged. "It's closed. What do you expect?"

"Exactly!" Sheridan exclaimed. "Which is why the chairs should be neatly stored, upside down, on the tables."

I looked inside again. Sheridan was right. It was like people suddenly got up and left.

Sheridan tried the door handle. It opened without a fight. *They never even locked it!*

"We shouldn't be here," I said.

Sheridan had already made his way into the kitchen. I could hear him rummaging. "They must have forgotten," I called.

I stole quick glances between the kitchen door and the front. I just knew someone would walk in. But nobody did. Sheridan emerged from the kitchen with a couple bags in hand. "You're not going to just take that, are you?" I asked.

"Oh, no," Sheridan shook his head. He pulled a tiny roll of bills from his pocket. They were twenties. He had about eight of them, and he left them all on the counter.

I let out a "whoa!" which I did not mean for Sheridan to hear. He laughed. I was more surprised by the fact he even had money than the amount itself. When I'd first picked him up, I thought he was a bum. I realized just how much I liked that explanation, and why. If he wasn't, why was he here with me? The world made sense when he was a bum, and not a mathematician.

I regretted picking him up. If my Duke University *Changing Faces of American History* seminar had not gone so horribly wrong, I wouldn't have. I looked up at the sky again. Oklahoma City was a long way off, and I didn't need more of this.

He was staring at me.

"You know, you could give me some gas money," I said.

He handed me his last twenty on his way out the door. I looked around the diner one last time, then ran to catch up to him.

It started to rain again as we walked through the lot, distorting our shadows. The thin, white light below the clouds had disappeared. Only the yellow parking lot light lit our way. "Who are you?" I asked.

Sheridan laughed. "I'm me, of course. Who else would I be?"

"Don't give me that," I said. "You know exactly what I mean."

We reached the car. Sheridan stood in front of the door for a moment, looking up, into the rain. "I suppose I am, as we all are, just a traveler on the highway."

We pulled away from the diner and resumed our journey. Sheridan took very small bites out of a breadstick. "How did you end up on the side of the road?" I asked.

Sheridan hurried to chew his food before replying. He then cracked his usual, odd smile. "Well, I was telling you the story of Marcus and his quest to learn the foundation of wisdom."

"Yeah, yeah. Wisdom is a journey. But that was what ... nineteen hundred years ago? What happened between then and now?"

Sheridan smiled. "Well! Before, when we were up in the mountains, you asked me to tell you about the world."

I nodded. "And why you said it was ending."

Sheridan continued, "Are you sure you want me to?"

"I ... uh?" The way he phrased the question, it sounded like a warning. That smile made me nervous. He remembered my words. I still remembered *his* words: "12 March is the date the world will end."

"Don't let me keep you hanging, then," Sheridan said. "The tale resumes in the forests of Northern Italy, 1427. It was the year Mara Sanghid was born. Eight years later, she was about to make a discovery."

"Of what?"

"You'll see," Sheridan said. He flashed a quick grin.

I looked at the car clock. It was still frozen at one in the morning. But I knew time hadn't frozen. The twelfth was quickly approaching, and I could only think of the lights in the pass. Sheridan knew what they were. And I had a bad feeling he was about to share what they meant.

2. For Your Silence

Mara admired the sky. When hard times had struck her family's farm, her mother had told her to look up. So she did. She soon convinced herself that simply looking up solved nothing, but nevertheless, she found the sky fascinating. Gray skies were her favorite. Cold, gray days were frequently peculiar days, and life was always more fun when odd things were about and ready to be explored. She pondered the behavior of the sky. It so frequently changed colors, but always in a particular order: blue, gray, white, gray, orange, white, black ...

What controls the sky? she thought. *As it would certainly seem that if it were free, it could choose to be any color it wished to be!*

Indeed, the sky was never red, pink, or aquamarine.

"Don't fret, Sky," she would say. "You can be aquamarine if you wish. There are rules of etiquette dictating how one should present themselves, and I understand that. But we're friends, and friends should encourage each other to explore and become better people."

Of course, the sky didn't respond. But Mara laughed and danced through the field, occasionally looking upward and calling to the above. *How grand it would be to see a green sky!*

To see a free sky ... free to be any color it wished to be. And I could fly up and introduce myself. The sky would not have to feel shy, I hope. For I would think the sky would be friendly.

It would say ... hello, Neece Louise! It is so lovely to see you! And I would have to correct it and tell it my name is not Neece Louise. It is Mara! But skies have not much in the way of memory, and so I could not blame it for having not remembered my name. And of course, I would forgive it. I like to think of myself as a kind person, and forgiving is the sort of thing kind people do.

Oh, how wonderful it would be if people could talk to the sky!

Mara laughed as she spun herself, arms stretched, in the field. Her long, black hair whipped around her, cutting through the dust she kicked up.

She plucked a daisy from the grasses, smiled, and exclaimed, "Oh! And how wonderful it would be if people could talk to flowers!"

But the daisy did not have any words for Mara. It drooped in her hand. She studied it carefully, pondering how it got onto the field in the first place. "Are you a visitor? Don't be shy."

Her attention was seized by a loud *snap*.

The field was a small clearing, just a few yards away from her father's house. It was too small and full of rocks to farm, and on too much of a slope to build a decent house. Indeed, it was of no use at all to anyone except Mara. It was *her* field, an empty canvas on which to paint a grand world for herself.

Today, though, there was an intruder in the field. Mara watched with curious eyes as a man cut across it. He wore all black, and was too far for her to make out any more detail than that. He didn't see her. He marched straight toward the house, crunching twigs, branches, and any other debris without notice.

The man stopped at the door for a moment to inspect his satchel. He knocked thrice with a calculated motion. Mara stood in the field, still and silent with great curiosity, as she watched the man enter the house.

Visitors on the farm were rare. When they did come, they were usually couriers, bringing goods from the market. Such days, spread very far apart, were happy occasions, if only for the adventure of seeing a new face.

Yet, Mara was not eager to greet this man. She continued to watch the house in silence, and stood *very* still. He did not look like the other couriers. He gave her an uneasy feeling.

But Mara, like the cat, was curious. And often, like the cat, curiosity got the better of her. She slowly made her way through the field, careful not to make a sound, and approached the house.

- 2 -

By the side of the house was a small pile of firewood. The pile was always lopsided. The bottom logs had long since rotted, and nobody had bothered to remove them. It was the log pile where, last year, Mara had thought she saw a fairy. She'd been so excited, she'd run to her father, who had immediately scolded her. "Stop being silly!" he'd sneered. "Go help your mother."

Mara had never seen the fairy again, but she was always careful when she climbed on its home.

The log pile afforded her a view of the main room of the house. She was seldom allowed inside when visitors arrived, but demanded to know all the happenings. So she carefully climbed to the window and peeked inside.

The man and her father were talking. Like always, Mara was too far to hear what was going on. It seemed nothing interesting was going to happen. She began to grow bored, and her mind wandered back to the daisy. It was just a moment later when she saw the man look to the left, look to the right, and hand her father a small envelope. It was ivory, with a wax seal that bore the initials "AQ". It was bulky, perhaps full of coins, and had some writing on the cover which Mara couldn't read from her distance.

Mara loved to read. It was rare for commoner's children to read, much less a girl. But her father, a tradesman of a trade she didn't quite understand, frequently brought home books and pamphlets and other materials produced from the recently devised printing press. But as much as she loved to read, she loved to imagine more, and what she read often was not what the text said.

This time, though, she focused very carefully on the envelope's label. Soon, her father placed it flat on the table and disappeared into the back room.

Mara stared into the sky for a moment. She couldn't shake the horrible feel of unease, nor determine why she felt it. She shook her head and scolded herself. *Acting silly will not help anything at all!*

She took a deep breath and wandered to the front door. As hard as she tried, she could not bring her hand to turn the latch.

Suddenly, she heard a *click*. The door swung open. She looked up, and her heart leapt out of her chest. The man in black stared down at her.

Mara gulped. The man had a crooked nose and aged skin that had been tortured by the sun. He flashed a grin that was missing several teeth.

Mara turned around and ran off into the woods.

- 3 -

Mara ran further and further into Carrboro Forest. Whenever she stopped, thinking she had run far enough, a creak or snap would echo down the trail. She couldn't shake the feeling that the man was following her. His image burned in her mind, and she ran further down the trail.

She couldn't recall ever having trekked so far into the woods. None of her surroundings looked familiar.

The forest canopy was thick, cutting out nearly all of the sun. Mara's eyes grew wide at every creak and snap. *Reason,* she told herself. *He wouldn't have followed so far.*

She heard a loud *pop* behind her. She quickly spun around and found herself staring face-to-face with *it*:

Nothing.

She shook her head and scolded herself for acting silly. She then wondered if, perhaps, *nothing* was the greatest thing to be afraid of. *Certainly people have been afraid of nothing more often than something,* she thought. She scratched her head and took another look at her surroundings with focused eyes.

For the most part, nothing struck her as unusual. She had seen flowers and shrubs and tree trunks before. But there was a path, obscured slightly by a bush. The path led through a little tunnel formed by thick foliage. From where she stood, she couldn't see what was at the other end. But something cast a soft, bright blue glow.

The light ricocheted off the wet leaves and danced through the dust like little trapeze artists, beckoning Mara to admire their show. She stuck her hand through the bush and watched her hand glow.

Mara heard another *snap* and quickly backed away. She shook her head again and scolded herself for worrying about the squirrels, skunks, and other forest creatures scurrying behind the shrubs.

She sighed and turned back to the tunnel. The light at the other end soothed her. It called her to come closer. She carefully pushed the foliage aside, closed her eyes, and poked her head through the leaves. When she opened them, she found two black dots staring at her. She was just pondering how much they resembled eyes when the rest of the face came into focus. It was a dark face–a shadow, with barely noticeable features. When it suddenly thrust itself at her, she shrieked and pulled her head out of the foliage.

Mara did not immediately run. She gazed into the bushes. The face stared back. She could feel her breath tightening, and a sharp chill ran down her back. The face stared calmly, silently, and without motion.

Mara breathed harder. When she stepped back onto a branch and nearly fell over, she quickly regained her composure. She let out a tight scream, turned, and ran further into the woods.

- 4 -

Mara ran out of breath. She fell to the floor and gasped for air. Not very far in the distance was a small house. It stood in a clearing, underneath a beam of light. A neat little fence circled it, built at the very edge of the shadows, so that it separated the light and dark.

Mara tried to climb to her feet, but her body did not listen. She tried to crawl to the light side of the fence, but fell back down. She closed her eyes and rested.

She heard a subtle *crack*. Her eyes shot open. She held her breath, glanced up, and saw a man standing by her. He was old, with a beard that glowed silver in the shards of light. His eyes squinted, and he seemed to lean at a slight angle. He had a friendly, but concerned, smile.

"My dear!" the man said. He sat next to her on a small log that had fallen. "What has you so distraught?"

Mara looked up at the man for a moment, then closed her eyes. She tried to recall the events that had brought her here. *Did I really see a ghost? It* must *be the woods playing tricks on me.*

What would father say if he saw me? How odd they would think me back home!

She shook her head. "Nothing. I'm just being silly."

"Nothing?" The man chuckled. "You seem a bit too worked up for one with no worries."

Mara climbed onto the log. She sat and stared into the woods as she took several deep breaths.

The man stroked his beard. "Well, then, perhaps you would be willing to listen to my worries? I could use a friend to share them with."

Mara tried to smile, but looked away. "I don't have any friends."

"That's too bad." The man shook his head. "Then, I suppose, you'll just miss out on hearing the worries of an old fool."

Mara looked up at the man again. "I wouldn't mind being friends with an old fool."

"I wouldn't mind being friends with a silly girl."

Mara smiled. "Well, then. You best start holding up your end of the arrangement."

"If we're going to be friends," the man said. "I think I ought to know your name."

Mara introduced herself as "Mara . . . Mara Sanghid, daughter of Amedean the Gypsy and Elise–"

The man laughed. He held his hand to his mouth and cleared his throat. "That's quite a long name."

Mara nodded. "I don't want to be confused with all the other Maras."

"Well, my name is Sylow," he said. "A distinctively shorter name. I do hope you're not terribly disappointed."

"Oh, no!" Mara said. "I shouldn't confuse you with all the other Sylows I don't know."

Sylow lifted an eyebrow, and shook his head. "I suppose you do have a good point," he said. "Perhaps I shall be *Sylow the Mathematician."*

"Oh!" Mara exclaimed. "I was not aware of scholars in these woods."

Sylow nodded. "Hence my worry. I had sat down earlier today to do some studying, but my vision ... it's cloudy."

"So, how do you study your books?"

"Well, I lost my patience. I threw the book in the water! Can you believe that?"

Mara giggled, then covered her mouth. "I'm sorry," she said. "I shouldn't laugh."

Sylow chuckled and shook his head. "That's okay. Sometimes a good laugh makes things feel right."

"My father is teaching me to read. He wants me to help him with his business."

"He sounds like a good man."

Mara stared into the shadows of the forest. "Sometimes." She bit her lip. "Once, he lost his patience, and tried to throw *me* into the water!" She forced a laugh. "Can you believe that?"

Sylow didn't laugh. He looked down at Mara, who fidgeted a bit and cleared her throat. "Maybe I could read them," she said.

"My books?"

Mara nodded. "I love to read. And I wouldn't mind reading aloud in the least."

Sylow smiled. "I think I would like that very much."

Mara stared down the trail. The sun was beginning to set, and deep shadows stretched across the clearing. "My worry is the man with the crooked nose."

"I'm not sure who that is."

"My father was making some arrangement with a dealer. And it was secret. I could tell by the way they looked at each other ... like they didn't like each other. Then, when he stepped out, he started chasing me."

"Is that why you were out of breath?"

"No. Well, yes. I mean, I don't *think* he was chasing me. Not then. But he was a mean man."

Sylow slowly nodded. "I see ... "

"But he didn't *do* anything mean! He just smiled. Maybe it was intuition?"

"Sometimes intuition lies," Sylow said. He then thought quietly for a moment. "Sometimes, though, it's your most trustworthy ally."

Mara sighed. "So ... which is it?"

"I think you'll know," Sylow said.

Mara nodded. "Can I ask you another question?"

"Sure."

"A *silly* question?"

Sylow chuckled. "Any question you wish, dear."

Mara thought carefully for a bit. "Have you seen a tunnel of leaves? With blue light?"

Sylow's smile dropped. "A tunnel?"

Mara nodded. "It's ... a bit of the way down the trail."

Sylow glanced at the path leading away from his house. He then looked down at Mara, who was staring at him. "No," he said. "Never seen it."

Mara continued to stare for a moment, before looking away. The sun was beginning to set. The beam of light shining on Sylow's house had disappeared, and the air had grown cold. "I think I should return home," she said. "Father will be *very* upset."

Sylow nodded. Mara bid him farewell. She promised to return and help him read his books. Sylow, in turn, promised to be her friend. "And friends," he said, "share the wisdom they've earned, so that each can be a better person."

Mara smiled and nodded. She then darted away. Sylow called out to her as she was about to disappear.

Mara turned around.

"Don't stop walking," he said.

- 5 -

Mara stood in front of the door to her house, contemplating the ramifications of going inside. She dreamt of a crackling fire, something to eat, and her warm bed. But she feared her father's reaction upon seeing her enter so late. She feared her mother's worried cry.

As she pondered, she heard laughter. She took a deep breath and opened the door.

Her father picked her up and spun her around. "Mara!" he exclaimed. He sat her down on the chair. "My dear. Do you know what has transpired?"

"What?" she whispered.

Her mother was laughing. Her father was *unusually* giddy. In fact, Mara could not recall ever seeing him happy at all. He waved a fistful of coins in her face. "We just bought ourselves a better life."

He then darted into the back room with her mother, laughing and calling to her the riches they would buy.

The front room was left eerily quiet. Mara stared at the table. The envelope was open. She peeked at the door to the back room once more, then carefully made her way to the table.

The envelope rested flat on the surface, backside up. Mara gently picked it up by a corner. She read the label. In very hurried script, the envelope read, "For your silence."

3. You Only Need to Be Willing to Listen

Earlier in the drive, shortly after I'd first picked Sheridan up, we'd run into a rain shower. As I'd watched the water streaks drift outward, for just a moment, I'd seen a face in the windshield. I could have *sworn* I saw it blink. Now, I couldn't help but wonder what lay behind the bushes Mara had looked into; where the blue light had come from.

I didn't want to let Sheridan know of my curiosity, though. Perhaps he was just making a game out of all this, and I didn't want to give him the satisfaction of knowing he had me intrigued. I stared *at* the windshield again, not through it. Part of me wondered if it had meant something–some sort of message. The rest of me knew I was acting foolish.

Curiosity eventually got the better of me. "What's at the end of the tunnel?"

Sheridan smiled his usual, odd smile. "Oh! Tickled your curiosity bone, eh?"

"It's just odd, that's all."

Sheridan shook his head and continued, "For the next eight years, Mara kept her word to Sylow. She visited him, read his books to him, and, in turn, attempted to satiate her growing curiosity of the world. But–"

Sheridan paused. He stared off into space, like he always did whenever he was stuck on a thought. His eyes then lit up. "She never did stop at the bush. She always walked right by it, just like Sylow had told her to. When she was feeling

17

brave, she'd look at it as she passed. But that face burned in her memory."

I focused on the windshield once more. It was starting to rain again. If I didn't have to drive, I wouldn't have paid it the least bit of attention.

Sheridan was staring at me. "Something bothering you, Bartlebee?"

"No."

Sheridan shrugged. "As I said, things continued more or less the same for eight years. Every so often, roughly once a month, Mara would see those envelopes ... they all read the same: 'For your silence'.

One day, roughly a couple months after her sixteenth birthday, her father sat Mara down. He wanted to have a talk with her ... "

- 6 -

Mara sat in a corner of her house and stared out the window. It was night, with a full moon. But she wasn't looking at the night. *She* was watching a vast expanse of ocean roll by.

She knew her father wouldn't see an explorer. Amedean never understood what she found so amusing about the field. Instead, he'd see a foolish girl wasting time she could spend studying. "Studying" was the word he used, along with "practices". Mara shuddered whenever he said it.

"Mara!" he exclaimed. "Get your head out of the clouds and back to your studies!"

The ocean disappeared. It was replaced by a boring field. Mara looked away and sighed.

"Now!" Amedean said. He clapped his hands.

Mara shook her head and cursed under her breath. When Amedean walked off, she closed her eyes and began to drown in a sea of memories.

"Isn't Baron Rutsan a pushover?" she had asked.

"Mara!" Amedean had exclaimed. "That is *no way* to talk about royalty!"

"But he is!" Mara had protested. "Besides, he's what ... *three* times my age?"

"That's why we've got to teach you proper etiquette!" her father had said. "I think he'd like you. You're very pretty."

She'd rolled her eyes. Amedean had slapped her. "You straighten those eyes out!"

Mara opened her eyes and rubbed her cheek. Months later, the wound still hurt.

One day, she'd worked up the courage to protest her father's wishes for her. "I want to leave!" she'd exclaimed. "Run and dance in the fields–"

Amedean had shook his head. "The meeting of the lesser lords is this summer. I think it would be a fine time ... "

Mara had tuned him out, and his voice had been carried away on the wind. He had left her a book, *The Finer Points in the Education of the Lady*, which had originally been a book on etiquette. *Originally*, because she'd made some revisions to it.

Books, and paper, were very expensive. But Mara had found that if she was very careful, she could rub some of the ink away so that it was blank. She then had a nice journal with which to record the things she learned from Sylow.

Today, she opened her book to a page toward the end, and began to carefully rub the light ink out. Her mind drifted in and out of the near past.

Not too long after she'd first met him, Mara had found out Sylow was a member of a group of scholars. She sometimes heard him tell the others about herself, and that he "saw something in her". He seemed to even brag about her, as if she was his pupil.

But whenever Mara asked to be considered a member,

Sylow was very adamant about declining her request.

"I beg of you!" she'd exclaim. "Please let me join your group! The world is amazing and full of curiosities, and I wish to know them all!"

And Sylow would reply, ever so faithfully, "My dear, you are not ready."

"When, then? When will I be ready? I wish to learn, and you have left me in the dark all this time!"

Sylow would simply shake his head. "In time, dear. In time."

Mara slammed her book shut. Amedean was standing over her shoulder. He took the book from her hand. "What's all this?"

Mara's heart froze. She stared straight ahead as she heard him open the book. He then handed it back to her, opened to the third page. He walked off.

She breathed a sigh of relief. She knew well enough not to erase *all* the pages. She kept the page on posture. It was a good page to keep because she could never quite walk "right". Amedean scolded her about it so frequently, he never thought it odd she studied those pages as much as she did.

Mara tucked the book away. She sighed and resumed her voyage across the sea. The wind had picked up, and a light breeze entered the house. She heard a rustle behind her. An empty envelope had fallen to the floor. Mara read it carefully: "For your silence". She chuckled to herself. As the years had passed, the handwriting had become increasingly illegible. She peeked inside. A small coin was still wedged between the flaps.

She tried to pull it out. Her fingers brushed the edge of the coin, and she marveled at its smoothness. She felt a sharp squeeze around her wrist.

"What are you doing?" Amedean demanded.

She jumped out of her seat and threw the envelope on the

floor. "Why do you insist on marrying me off to the baron? I'm not some bartering tool for your purse!"

He stared blankly and didn't move. Mara could see his anger boiling. When she saw him clench a fist, she screamed and pushed him away. He stepped back and bumped into the wall. While he was distracted, she quickly turned around, climbed on the table, and dove out the window into her ocean.

- 7 -

As she walked, Mara watched the shadows of the forest canopy flicker on her hands. She imagined the trees would not think twice about seeing a girl studying her hands as she walked. "I'm just trying to make your acquaintance," she said.

She stopped and watched a thin birch tree sway in the breeze. Its dance became rhythmic. She watched the directions it swayed, and soon realized she was telling the way it would go before it did: closer, closer, farther, closer, closer . . .

She rubbed her eyes. The pseudo-random sequence then became a random sequence. A small blue light reflected off the bark.

Her heart skipped a beat. She looked to the right and saw the tunnel. Its light soothed her and sang quietly for her to come. She was drawn to its sweet voice.

She only briefly wondered why light would sing before she realized she was kneeling by the bushes. Her hand trembled as she carefully pulled the branches aside. She closed her eyes as she pushed her head in. She opened them, and saw . . .

Nothing.

She saw an empty tunnel, with the same light, but no face.

The soft singing grew louder. She watched arcs of blue light swirl around the leaves and branches, almost like fingers, waving for her to follow. She wandered closer to its source. The light grew brighter, turning the leaves cyan. She heard a *snap*.

Mara stopped dead in her tracks. She closed her eyes and gulped. A quieter *snap* followed, and the light's hum faded away. She slowly turned around and opened her eyes.

Her heart froze solid. She was staring at the eyes of a face. The rest of the face soon faded into focus, along with the silhouette of a body.

The shadow didn't move. They stared at each other, silent and still. She could imagine the shadow scolding her: *Stop acting silly. Go on your way!*

Mara clenched her fists as she glared at the shadow. The shadow stared back without emotion. *Go on your way! It's not the proper behavior.*

She screamed at the shadow, lunged toward it, and swung her fist. She stopped abruptly; her eyes widened as she felt the shadow's cold hand enter her chest. She gasped for air as she felt it pull on her insides and fell to the floor.

- 8 -

Mara cracked her eyes open. She rubbed them, and the room came into focus. Sylow turned her way.

"Where am I?" Mara asked.

Sylow lowered his gaze. "My dear ... it's me."

Mara glanced around the room. She nodded. "I see. I mean ... I'm here."

"Yes."

"But I wasn't ..." Mara groaned and rubbed her head. Her forehead throbbed, and her vision blurred, then refocused. Her encounter with the shadow suddenly came back to her.

"I found you by the well." Sylow shook his head. "I told you never to stop there."

"Well ... I ... " Mara fumbled her words.

Sylow raised his voice. "I *told* you to keep walking."

"Wait," Mara said. She sat up and glared at Sylow. "You *know* what is down that way."

"I–" Sylow said.

"You *know*, and won't tell me!" Mara interrupted. "What is it? You know something I don't."

Sylow sighed. "I know several things you don't."

"We're friends," Mara said. "We're supposed to share wisdom. Remember?"

Sylow stared out his window for several moments. He sighed again. "Fine, Mara. It's fine."

"What's fine?"

"I'll preface by saying I don't entirely believe everything I'm about to tell you."

Mara raised an eyebrow. Sylow continued, "But I don't have a better explanation. So here goes. Do you remember the day we met?"

Mara nodded. "You told me to keep walking."

"Not too long before, I'd met a woman. I don't remember her name. She may not have even said. But she told me the story of an idol that grants infinite wisdom, and a man who retrieved it."

"Infinite wisdom? Like, knowledge of everything?"

Sylow nodded. He walked over to the bookshelves and rummaged for a minute. He then handed Mara a small book. "She gave me that," he said. "The journal of Marcus, translated from the days of the Romans."

Mara flipped through the pages. One page, in particular, caught her eye–a note about lights dancing in the forest. She thought about the patterns she'd seen before running into the tunnel. She then looked up at Sylow. "I don't understand. Is there an idol in the water?"

"If you read the book, you'll see the idol was destroyed. But the woman told me about the Well of Enlightenment. The water supposedly grants infinite wisdom. Just like the lost idol."

"And it's at the end of the tunnel?"

Sylow nodded. "It's guarded by Anadaku, Demon of Ignorance. At least, that's what she told me."

Mara walked over to the window and looked down Sylow's path. She tried to remember the details of when they'd first met. "Why didn't you want to tell me any of this?"

Sylow put his arm around her. "The woman told me to look after you. That you were special."

Mara scratched her head. "But you met her *before* me."

Sylow nodded.

- 9 -

Left, right, up, right, right …; dim, bright, bright, bright, very bright… Mara flipped through Marcus's journal as she walked through the woods. She studied the movements of the leaves and grasses in the wind, but could not fathom any pattern.

What am I missing? She plucked a daisy and studied the formation of its petals. *Big, big, big …* She shook her head.

Mara tossed the daisy into the air and plucked another one. One by one she tore off the petals. *Big, small, or is it medium?* She picked a few more daisies, then sighed.

A shadow overcame Mara as a cloud drifted in front of the sun. A light breeze caught her hair and blew strands in her eyes. As she pulled her hair behind her head, she noticed a daisy dancing slightly. She focused entirely on its motions and tried to block all other thoughts.

West, north, south, north, pause, south ... Mara thought carefully about the pattern. Soon, she realized she was no longer observing the motions of the daisy, but stating in which direction it would go

Suddenly, the world came into focus. Her eyes grew wide. *Is it intuition?* She then sang, "Oh! How I wonder what the flowers have to say!"

Mara laughed as she spun herself, arms stretched, in the field. She plucked the daisy from the grasses, smiled, and exclaimed, "Oh! How wonderful it would be if people could talk to flowers!"

The daisy responded, "Oh! How wonderful it would be if ... "

Mara shrieked.

The daisy chuckled. "What, dearie? Are you surprised I spoke? Or that you only need to be willing to listen?"

Mara did not immediately respond, for she had to take a moment or two to catch her breath. Finally, she replied, "Little of both, I believe."

The daisy continued its lecture, "And consider that I was just thinking ... how wonderful it would be if people would listen to us. For you would be surprised how easy it is to speak, and how difficult it is to listen."

"I will listen!" Mara exclaimed. She leaned the daisy a bit closer to her ear. "What is it you wish to say?"

"I was just wishing ... hoping, really, that if I asked you human types to stop plucking us ... you would hear," the daisy said. "For I am fairly certain you would find it disagreeable if I had plucked your body from your feet."

Mara shook her head. "I would not like that in the least."

"Then you should understand my position," the daisy said.

"Oh!" Mara said. "Oh, dear! I'm *so* sorry! I did not mean to be imposing ... "

"Well, next time ... " the daisy said. It paused briefly in honor of its plucked friends. "Next time, don't be such an ass-canker."

4. Dance in the Rain

"I was not aware that flowers were so vulgar," I said.

Sheridan snickered. "Oh! Flowers are the *worst*! You may think that the daffodil looks sweet, but it swears worse than a sailor."

"I suppose that would change my outlook on giving roses on Valentine's Day."

"That's why I say, give your lover potatoes." Sheridan nodded. "They're real sweet-talkers. Plus, they make good batteries."

"You said you were married, right?"

"Any healthy, long-term relationship begins with a gift from the great state of Idaho."

"You're a nut."

"I'm a *human*," Sheridan said.

"In that case, you can tell me what Amedean is trying to pull off."

"Oh, it's a simple plan. He will marry Mara off to the baron, and collect a bride price."

"Can he do that?"

Sheridan raised an eyebrow. "What do you mean?"

"Like, will he just walk up to the baron and say, 'here's my daughter. Would you like to marry her?' I didn't think it worked that way."

"Oh, You," Sheridan said. He laughed and shook his head. "Are you making the assumption Amedean was *sane*?"

- 10 -

Mara crept up to her house and slowly pulled the door open. The front room was empty. She breathed a sigh of relief and stepped inside. She shrieked when she looked up to a pair of eyes staring at her.

"You were out," Amedean said.

Mara stared blankly.

Amedean held up her journal, opened to one of the re-placed pages. "You don't have much respect, do you?"

Mara's heart fluttered. Amedean glanced at the book, then back to Mara. They stared at each other in silence for a moment. He then clenched his fist, screamed, and threw the book at her. She slid out of the way. The book flew through the doorway and landed in the field.

Mara could hear her mother sobbing in the next room. Amedean grabbed her arm, pulled her away from the door-way, and slammed the door. He took a deep breath, and resumed his glare. "You little . . . *miscreant.*"

She stood up straight and returned his stare. "No–"

Amedean interrupted her. "You . . . *filth.*"

When he raised his voice, Mara backed away. He contin-ued, "You're lucky. You'll be well off. But you don't appreci-ate it." He raised his fist. "You'll–"

Mara screamed, "No!"

Before Amedean could reply, she turned and ran toward the back room. She stopped at the ladder to the attic. Ame-dean came after her. She rushed up the steps and slammed the trapdoor shut.

The attic was dark, with no windows. Mara heard a rustling and the *click* of the lock.

Mara felt her eyes begin to water, but she held back. *I will not shed a single tear for that man.* She stood in silence, then screamed, picked up a chair, and threw it against the wall.

- 11 -

Through a few cracks in the roof, Mara could approximate the progress of time. She fashioned a makeshift sundial by marking the passage of a shadow across the floor.

She counted twelve hours, including the evening she returned and the following night, before the trapdoor creaked open.

"Mara," Amedean called gently. "I want you to come down."

Even if she wanted to reply, her throat was too dry to speak above a whisper. She turned away from the door while her eyes adjusted to the light. When she brought herself to face the opening, she saw her father's open hand. "Come down, please," he said.

Mara stared silently, then slowly took his hand. He helped her climb down.

"*Mara*," he said. He watched his daughter stand perfectly still. They traded empty stares, little knives cutting through the tension.

Amedean fished through his pocket. "Here." He pried open Mara's hand and pushed a small silver ring into it. He then wandered off.

Mara flipped the ring over in her hand, contemplating its implications. The emblem, "AQ," was embossed on the interior side. She slid it onto her finger and admired the light sparkling off the silver.

- 12 -

It means he cares for me, right? Mara asked herself. She examined the ring as she walked the trail to Sylow's house. *Perhaps I'm more than part of some scheme.*

She contemplated asking the flowers' opinions, but wondered if she would just be sworn at. *They look so pretty,* she thought. *Who knew they had such foul mouths?*

While she was in the attic, Mara had decided she would run away. She'd run to Sylow's cottage and never return. Although Amedean knew who Sylow was, he wouldn't know how to find him.

After her father had given her the ring, she'd changed her mind. Still, she wondered if he would run into Anadaku if he tried to find her.

Mara often found her thoughts bouncing as she walked. Perhaps it was her way of keeping Sylow's promise. She often didn't notice the tunnel. But she did today. She thought about the well, and what it would be like to have infinite wisdom.

A lonely daffodil grew near the tunnel entrance. Mara stared at it and spilled her thoughts. "Marcus," she said. "He found the Idol of Trey. But he lost it. Now, there's this well."

The daffodil nodded in the wind. Mara scratched her head. "What is it with the world and its dumping of these odd devices that grant wisdom? What does the well have in common with the idol?"

She stared through the leaves that blocked the tunnel. She admired the blue light, then looked back to the daffodil. "Who keeps making these things?"

Mara heard a twig snap. She shrieked and jumped back from the tunnel entrance. Without looking back, she quickly resumed her trek to Sylow's.

- 13 -

When Mara made it to Sylow's cottage, she begged him to let her join his circle of scholars. Once again, he declined her. She tried not to take it to heart, but she couldn't help but wonder about his motives. *He must be acting fairly,* she thought. *But then, that means he really doesn't think I could make it.*

"My dear," Sylow said. He glanced out the window. "Do not distress."

"Do not distress!" Mara exclaimed. "Is that your only response? What kind of answer is that?"

Sylow continued to stare silently. Mara sighed. "I don't think you're telling me the truth."

Sylow didn't say anything. Mara repeated, "I think you're hiding something. From *me.* And friends are supposed to share wisdom."

"Friends *are* supposed to share wisdom." Sylow closed his eyes as he thought.

Mara stomped her foot on the ground. "So, why won't you share with me? What is my failing? I think I deserve to know that much."

Sylow shook his head. "You have no failing, my dear."

Mara glared at him. "You're lying."

"There's just a certain risk–"

"I don't need your protection," Mara interrupted.

"I'm just worried," Sylow said. He bit his lip. "About you."

Mara pushed Sylow aside and stormed out of the house. "I can look after myself!" she shouted, and slammed the door behind her.

She leaned against the door and took a minute to stare at the forest path. She closed her eyes and swallowed her anger.

When she opened her eyes again, she took notice of the path leading home. *If he really doesn't find me worthy,* she thought. *There is only one thing to do.* She gulped, then scolded herself. *Feeling scared will do you no good at all!*

She began the hike to the Well of Enlightenment.

- 14 -

Mara wandered along the trail, stopping to smell the flowers and ask their advice. None of them responded, and she wondered why the daisy, who had spoken to her before, was so special. "I'm afraid you must think of me like the dog," she said. "Smelling is not the most polite way to make one's acquaintance, but I must confess, you do smell quite lovely."

She stopped and stared at a tulip. "But the Well!" She poked the flower. "And ... father and mother. What would you do?"

She shook her head and sighed. "Oh, never mind it all! What advice should I expect from the lover of a bumblebee?"

"Mara ... " someone whispered.

Mara froze. She quickly looked about, but decided she was most certainly alone. She heard her name whispered again.

"Who are you?" she whispered back.

"Down here."

Mara looked all around again. No one could be seen.

"Further down," she heard.

She looked down at a small brook which ran alongside the road. "Are you the brook?" she whispered.

"Indeed I am," the brook replied. "Nice to see you again."

"Excuse me?" Mara asked. "Have we met before?"

"You've walked alongside me many times," the brook answered. "How are you tonight?"

"I am ... fine ... " Mara said, trailing off.

"You seem a bit tense," the brook said. "Do I smell a bit too much like fish?"

Mara shook her head. "No, no. You smell quite lovely, babbling brook."

"I prefer *brook*," the brook said. "I don't babble. I always have meaningful things to say."

"Oh, I didn't mean to imply anything ... " Mara said.

"It's quite okay," the brook replied. "So, what is it you are tense about?"

Mara took a seat by the bank. "I'm a bit worried about my future."

"Oh? Why is that?"

"I don't want the life that is expected of me."

"What do you want?" the brook asked.

"I want to be free!" Mara said. "I want to run in the woods and fields, dance in the rain and float in the water! The world is a fascinating place, and I want to know all about it!"

"I hardly see anything wrong with that," the brook said. "Why, I do all those things."

"Well, you are a brook, and I am a person. We both have different natures," Mara replied. She sighed.

"We are both of the same nature," the brook objected. "If you want to be a brook, I would love some company."

"You are pleasant company," Mara said. "But I can't be a brook."

"Thank you," the brook replied. "And no, you can't physically. But I think it is in your nature to be curious, and you shouldn't deny your nature."

"Maybe Sylow will accept me as a scholar," Mara said. "It's my only hope."

"Does he live in the cottage down the road?"

"Yes."

"I remember him. He seems good and trustworthy," the brook said.

Mara stared down the trail. "Are you familiar with the Well of Enlightenment?"

"I hardly think wisdom comes from water."

Mara bit her lip as she thought. "Sylow said he'd be afraid for me if I joined them. But I suspect he just doesn't think I'm bright enough."

"And you think drinking from the well will change that?"

"Well ..." Mara said. "He seemed to make it sound like that. I think."

"Well ... *I* think you'll learn more from having figured out what to do on your own," the brook said. "Experience is, after all, the teacher of wisdom. I think you know that."

Mara smiled. "You are a kind brook."

"We brooks are very kind, indeed."

"But experience is a slow teacher. The foundation of wisdom is the journey. That's what Marcus said. But the journey takes time."

"Are you in a hurry?"

Mara looked toward home. She bit her lip. "I think I am."

- 15 -

"It's a shortcut," Mara said. She was thinking out loud, staring into the blue light at the tunnel's entrance. "There's nothing wrong with a shortcut."

She thought about entering. But every time she tried to go forward, her body just wouldn't obey.

"There's no use in standing here, feeling scared," Mara scolded herself.

The daffodil which grew near the entrance nodded in the breeze.

"The brook said wisdom doesn't come from water."

The daffodil stood completely still.

"*But* then the brook said experience taught wisdom, so the Idol of Trey couldn't have helped Marcus learn anything. But it did."

The daffodil resumed its nodding.

Mara scratched her head. She stared at her hands, then back toward the brook. She wondered if the brook she spoke to was the same one Marcus had. It seemed odd to think a brook could be so old, but she couldn't think of any other brooks that acted so peculiar about their fish.

"A shortcut," she repeated. "If it teaches me something, it may be worth it."

She snapped a large branch off a nearby bush, took a deep breath, and pushed her way into the tunnel.

- 16 -

Mara held her breath as she walked through the tunnel. She would pause every so often and breathe as quietly as she could. She'd slowly turn to look over her shoulder, check that the path was clear, then take a few more steps.

The blue light was brighter than it had ever been, and she knew she was getting close to the well. She also knew better than to think that Anadaku would give it up so easily, and she clutched her branch so hard the bark began to fall off.

The hum began to change into a slight buzz. Mara stopped to try and decipher it. The hum grew faint, then strong, and back and forth so fast it sounded like a thousand bees.

Mara realized the random change in tone was *pseudo*-random. *What is it trying to tell me?*

The sound wasn't the only such phenomenon. The flowers seemed to be vibrating too, as if nature were screaming some message.

Mara took another step, and the sound suddenly stopped. She looked at the flower by her foot. It stood still, like a corpse. She frowned at the dead flower.

When she looked back up, Anadaku pushed her against a tree. The demon's shadowy face faded into focus–first its mouth, then two hollow eye sockets. She let out a tight scream as he sunk his teeth into her neck. She felt her voice seep away. He stepped back and grinned as Mara tried to scream for help. Her heart sank as she realized she couldn't emit any sound at all.

The demon stepped forward again. Mara ducked and ran around him. She ran until her body began to give out. She ignored its cries and ran faster.

Mara burst out of the tunnel and onto the trail. She stopped and looked behind her. She could see Anadaku's face through the opening in the bushes. He stared silently, like a cat waiting to pounce. His open eye sockets seized her gaze. He stared deeply into her mind, and she could feel it begin to cloud.

When she looked away, Anadaku's face suddenly appeared before her. She tried once more to scream for help, but her voice wouldn't cooperate. She ran toward home.

Mara stopped after running after about a mile. She clutched her chest as her lungs tightened. She looked behind her. Anadaku wasn't to be seen. She looked ahead, then behind her again. He was gone.

She rested for a moment while she studied the path she'd just carved. Only her footsteps dotted the road. She was just thinking how peculiar that was when she turned forward and found herself staring into two dark eyes.

Anadaku grinned as she silently shrieked and stepped back. The grin began to burn into her memory. The demon thrust his hand into her throat. Mara cried out as she felt his translucent arm move through her body, sapping her strength.

Mara fell to her knees as Anadaku stepped forward. He raised his arm and struck her again.

Mara rolled onto her back and lay on the roadside. She held her throat tightly, trying to regain her breath. The harder she tried to breathe, the less air she could take. She began to feel dizzy, and her vision blurred. She thought she could make out a figure coming up the road. She wanted to cry for help, but her voice still wouldn't obey. Anadaku seemed to fade away as the figure neared.

Mara closed her eyes.

5. I Do Not Wish to Follow This Road

Sheridan smiled. "The end."

"What? *The end*?"

"Are you disappointed?"

"Well." I could see Sheridan grinning out of the corner of my eye. He was trying to prove something. I was sure of it. "No."

"I bet you are," Sheridan said.

I *knew* he was still grinning. "I know you're not telling the truth."

"I see," Sheridan said. "Entertain me."

"I, well, what? Never mind. I know Mara didn't die. You haven't finished the story yet. See, it's one of your so-called "proofs". Where you are in the story tells us whether or not the protagonist lives."

"You sound pretty confident," Sheridan said.

I nodded. "You sound pretty pleased, yourself."

"Honestly, I am," Sheridan said.

I flashed a quick smile, then turned back to the road. "Glad to hear it."

"But you're wrong," Sheridan said. "First, the word is *conjecture*, not *proof*. And 'Bartlebee's Storytelling Conjecture' is not a true one."

"Why not? Who'd listen to a story where the hero dies right off the bat?"

"The protagonist in *Psycho* was killed halfway through the movie. It's why Hitchcock didn't let people walk into the movie late."

"Oh, well, are you saying Mara is now dead?"

"I was just curious what your reaction would be," Sheridan said. He shook his head. "What happened next is ... "

- 17 -

Mara awoke to the sound of her mother sobbing in a distant room. She could hear her father shouting, but she couldn't make out the words. She tried to remember the previous night, or day. She scratched her head. *How long have I been here?*

She looked around, then jumped. Her father was standing in the doorway, glaring. "We discussed this," he said sternly. "Where were you?"

Mara looked down at her hands.

Amedean repeated, "Where *were* you?"

"I was–"

"Daydreaming again. Goofing around, right?"

"No, I mean–"

"Just imagine my reaction, trying to get to the market when I find my own daughter lying in the middle of the road–"

"But–"

"When you should've been here. I wasted my entire afternoon dragging you back here."

"Listen–"

Amedean slammed his fist on the table. "You disobeyed me! You don't take me seriously, do you?"

"But ... " Mara stumbled on her words.

"I want you–" Amedean stopped, took a deep breath, and shook his head. "Wait for me in the attic."

Mara closed her eyes and quietly walked past her father. As she walked, she looked behind herself. Amedean took a belt from the clothing rack and disappeared into the other room.

The attic door creaked as Mara pulled it open. She could hear her father shouting again. Then she heard a crash.

Her clothes were tattered and torn. She pulled up on her tunic and stared at her stomach. A large gash extended a few inches across. She touched it to see if it was still tender and winced.

Mara had to concentrate hard to not cry. She'd begun to recall her encounter with the demon when her father's footsteps interrupted. The *clack* of his heels echoed down the hall toward the ladder.

She closed her eyes and took a deep breath. When she opened them, the small chair in the corner caught her attention. She briefly contemplated bashing Amedean over the head.

The chair sat in a small sliver of light. Mara traded more glances between it and the attic door. She clenched her fists as she heard footsteps coming up the ladder.

The ring Amedean had given her sparkled in the slim light. Mara stared at it. *It means he cares for me, right?*

The footsteps drew closer. She reached for the chair, then stopped herself. She looked closer at the ring. *That's why he gave it to me.*

She heard the attic door click. More memories of previous nights in the attic filled her mind. She tried to push them away, but could not resist their flow. No food, no water. Only darkness would be her sentence for misbehaving. *Only darkness*, she thought. In her mind, she could hear the belt's whip.

As the attic door swung open, Mara picked up the chair. Without any thoughts at all, she screamed and slammed it over Amedean's head. He didn't have a chance to speak before he lay on the floor, below.

Mara stared blankly down the ladder. She could see him still breathing, but he didn't so much as twitch a limb. The belt lay on the other side of the hall.

She slowly climbed down, took a final glance at her father, then bolted out the door and into the night.

- 18 -

Mara pounded on Sylow's door. Shortly after she'd fled her home, rain began to pour. She was now drenched, her clothes torn. She pleaded with Sylow to allow her to stay. "I can't go home," she cried. "Not anymore."

Sylow stared blankly.

"He'll kill me!"

"But—I—" Sylow fumbled his words.

"You *have* to let me stay here."

"I'd like to, but—"

"Amedean ..." Mara said. She buried her head in her hands and sobbed. "He beats me."

"Come in," Sylow said quietly. "Come out of the rain."

He guided Mara through the door, looked cautiously behind him, and locked it.

- 19 -

Sylow looked her over, hummed, and nodded. He turned around and began to rummage through an old chest. He said, "Yes, yes. We must clean you up." He rambled further, but Mara was caught up in her own thoughts.

She played with the little silver ring her father had given her. She twisted it and stared at it from all sides. She began to feel homesick. The more she mulled it over, the worse she began to feel. She felt bad for abandoning her family, and wondered if they'd miss her. She wondered if she'd made a mistake.

Sylow hummed and rambled on. He shook his head occasionally. "You're such a tiny little thing. I suppose it wouldn't be too much to ask of you to grow a few inches?" When he turned to face Mara's way, she choked back tears and forced a smile.

Sylow said, "You do not look well." He pushed a wad of clothing into her arms. "Put on some dry clothes. You'll feel better."

He guided Mara into the back room and shut the door. She stood still for a few moments and tried to organize her thoughts. *I should be happy.*

She looked at the ring once more and sighed.

A few minutes later, Mara emerged from the back room. Sylow frowned. "I hope you're not still upset with me."

Mara shook her head. She looked down at herself. "Sylow," she said. "I don't think these clothes fit quite right."

Sylow had given her a largish red tunic and a pair of leather boots that were, arguably, a size too big. He looked her over and nodded. He hummed and nodded some more.

Mara glanced at her reflection in the window. She pulled her hair back and forced a smile.

"I didn't mean for you to get yourself in trouble," he said. "In the fountain."

Mara pulled the shades down over the window. "It seems like such a silly thing. A fountain that grants wisdom?"

"*Infinite* wisdom. But the price of such knowledge is to be outcast from the paradise of ignorance."

"But I want to hold the world!" Mara exclaimed. "Open it up. See inside. See what makes it tick. Why can't I do that?"

"You seem to have a rather blind desire." Sylow smiled

briefly. "Rather like myself, I suppose. But some people know the wrong things."

Mara stared at her feet. "Is that why you turned me away?"

Sylow nodded.

"But what are the right things? What are the wrong things?"

"You want to know why I think you're special?"

Mara nodded silently. Sylow lifted her chin and looked into her eyes. "Because I see it, in your heart. You don't care. There's no right wisdom or wrong wisdom. Just wisdom."

"Then why turn me away? Why can't I be a scholar?"

"In time, Mara," he said. "I can't–"

"You owe me this much. Why must I be consistently declined? Why am I unworthy?"

"You're more than worthy," Sylow said. "But–"

Mara crossed her arms in front of her chest. "You just don't want to admit it."

"No–" Sylow said.

"If that were true, I wouldn't have practically killed myself at that damn fountain." Mara hid her face in her hands and shook her head. "You're worse than all of them!"

Sylow breathed a deep sigh. "It's not all my decision. I'll talk to the other members."

"Why can't you tell me what they said? I'm tough. I can take it. Teach me!"

"Some things ... " Sylow said, "cannot be taught. And some people are willing to accept that, but others not."

Mara shook her head. She pushed the door open and stepped outside. The rain had stopped, and a gentle light broke through the clouds. "Then," she said, pausing long enough to watch the clouds open further, "I shall learn, anyway."

- 20 -

Mara stopped at the edge of the brook, at a particular section of road which twisted underneath a dense canopy. Cracks in the leaves above allowed the sun to break through in dozens of thin beams. The water shimmered in the light.

The water stretched as far as she could see in both directions. She sat down and ran her finger through the cool liquid, watching its ripples drape like silk. "Brook?" she asked. "Am I happy?"

"Why are you asking me?" the brook replied. "I'm just a brook. Perhaps you should ask yourself these things."

"I tried asking myself, and all I got were more questions."

"Then perhaps you should answer them."

"I do!" Mara exclaimed. "But they're hard."

The brook thought carefully. "Life's questions are never easy. One does not need to be as wise as water to know that."

"I want my life to have a purpose . . . to carry on a legacy," Mara said.

The brook thought some more. "Will that make you happy?"

"It will make me content," Mara answered. "Is that happiness?"

The brook chuckled. "Well, dear, if you do not know that, how will you answer the question?"

"Oh, I don't know anymore!" she cried. She picked up a smooth, flat rock and skipped it across the water.

"Don't do that!" the brook snapped. "That hurts!"

"Oh . . . sorry!" Mara frowned. "I didn't know."

The brook continued, "Let's say . . . to be happy is to be satiated with life."

"Full?" Mara asked.

"Exactly. You've lived life to its fullest," the brook replied. "You've made the most of your time, so to speak."

"But is that happiness?" Mara asked.

"As best as a brook can tell," the brook said.

Mara thought quietly. "Well, I've never had reason to believe water is unwise."

"Then you should accept my definition."

"I will!" Mara exclaimed.

"So, what will satiate you?"

"I want the world!" Mara said. She grinned.

The brook laughed. "Ah, don't you all. Silly humans."

"Well, no, not to rule it," Mara explained. "I want to hold it."

"It would be hard to hold the world with such small hands."

"I do not see why I couldn't open it up. It may be difficult, but I could!" Mara replied. "I want to see inside. I want to see all the mysteries and know all the wonderful secrets. I want to be a part of it all!"

"That is the difficulty," the brook said.

"Perhaps it would be easier if I had bigger hands," Mara said. She pouted as she examined her stubby fingers. "Then it would be easy to open it up! It would be easy to see inside."

"But hands sizeable enough to hold the world?" the brook asked.

Mara shook her head. "No. That would not work out at all. For then, there would be more hand than Mara. They would have to give my hands a name, and I would be merely an appendage. They would say, 'there goes such a lovely pair of hands attached to ... that nameless girl. What's her name? I think it starts with a Q.' That would make me rather sad."

"As it would me," the brook said. "For I would rather be known as a brook, than as the fish which protrude from my surfaces."

"But what of my difficulty?" Mara asked. "Perhaps I could go about it the other way. Perhaps I could shrink the world. Then it would be easy!"

"But how can you reduce the size of the world without diminishing all it is about?" the brook asked.

Mara bit her lip as she thought. "I don't know! Maybe I could find some representative of the world?"

"Why don't you look at nature?" the brook suggested. "I'm certain many clues lie there."

"I am!" Mara exclaimed. "It is quite fascinating."

"Well, look further then," the brook said. "You may find an entire world rests in a little sequence."

Mara thought about the patterns she'd seen, and those Marcus described. She wondered if the brook was right. "But what is the sequence?"

"Even if I knew, I think you'd learn more for having figured it out yourself."

"So, you don't know?"

"No."

Mara sighed. She stood, then looked down at the water. "Anything worth knowing is so hard to find."

The brook replied, "Anything worth knowing is worth it."

- 21 -

Mara continued down the trail. She stared at everything she passed, trying to figure out if there were some sequence or pattern to what she observed. The leaves, the clouds, the motion of the grasses swaying in the breeze–none of it made sense.

It made sense once, she thought. *What was different then?*

She stopped at the turnoff to the Well of Enlightenment. When she realized where she was, she stood very still.

The daffodil slowly nodded in the breeze. Mara looked toward home, then back to the tunnel. She snapped another large branch off the bushes and traded nervous glances between home and Sylcw's house.

She closed her eyes. Thoughts of being trapped in the attic flooded her mind. She stared at the branch in her hands, took a deep breath, and ducked though the bushes guarding the tunnel.

With cautious confidence, she marched down the tunnel. Every few feet, she'd stop and look behind her. Nothing.

Night had begun to fall and only the well's glow lit her way. The light cast low, deep shadows. Mara's own shadow stretched far down the pathway, disappearing into the darkness.

Mara clutched her branch, tightening her grip with every step. The hum of the light grew louder and higher-pitched. It began to resemble a choir's song.

She stopped and listened. The constant tone started to flutter. Then it buzzed. *It's saying something,* she thought, pondering the pseudo-random nature of the flickering.

"Who are you?" she whispered. "What are you saying?"

Mara gasped for air as she felt Anadaku's hand move through her back and pop out the front of her neck. His fingers danced before her eyes, then disappeared as he withdrew his arm.

She stumbled as she turned around. Two empty eye-sockets stared at her. The demon thrust his arm into her chest, gripped her heart, and squeezed.

Mara dropped her branch and fell to her knees. She clutched her chest as she felt her heart constrict and stop. The demon pulled his hand out and pushed her onto her back.

Anadaku stared silently as Mara looked up. He flashed a grin.

Mara closed her eyes and lay as still as she could. She felt her heart beating again, racing as she inched her hand toward the branch. She tightened her fingers around it. The grin faded off Anadaku's face as Mara climbed onto her feet and swung the branch.

It passed through Anadaku's body like a stone dropped in water–creating little ripples that soon faded and left Anadaku's form not altered in the least.

Anadaku grinned again. Mara screamed and ran toward the well.

The buzzing grew louder and the blue light brighter than Mara had ever seen it. Occasional rays burst through the brush and trunks.

The light disappeared as Anadaku wrapped himself around Mara's body. Mara shrieked and swung the branch hopelessly. She pushed herself faster and Anadaku slipped away.

The blue light suddenly blinded Mara. She stumbled and hit her head on something hard.

She moaned as her eyes adjusted to the light. She was facing a small stone staircase consisting of about four steps. It stopped at the lip of the well.

The well sat in a small alcove surrounded by tall bushes, shielded from the sky by a thick canopy. Sitting on the rim of the well was a small, iron cup, full of water.

Mara picked up the cup and gazed into the water it held. It glowed slightly. Her heart fluttered as she realized Anadaku must still be in pursuit. No sooner had she realized her mistake than she felt his hands slowly closing around her neck.

In a panic, she tore herself from his grasp and threw the cup at him.

Anadaku screamed as the water sliced through his body. His empty face dissolved into the air, and his hands, clenched tightly, fell to the Earth as his arms turned to vapor. What was left of the demon faded into the night sky.

Mara stared at the void in shock. She stood motionless for a while, then sat on the steps. No trace of Anadaku was left in the spot where he'd fallen.

Mara continued to watch the spot in silence. It slowly sank in–Anadaku was gone.

She crept to the edge of the well, holding her hand over its waters. Rays of blue light shone between her fingers like the sun through breaks in a cloud. She slowly dipped her finger into the water and watched the ripples trail behind it.

The hum grew louder as the ripples dissipated. She closed her eyes and let its song fill her mind.

When she opened her eyes, she noticed the small iron cup on the ground. It had rolled back toward the well when she threw it, and rested by the steps. She didn't think twice about taking the cup and dipping it into the well. But when she held the full cup in her hands, they began to tremble. The water in the cup seemed to glow brighter than in the well.

Mara glanced behind her, then at the cup. She held it to her lips and let its warm water drip into her mouth.

For a moment, Mara stared blankly into the forest, waiting for something to happen. She looked into the cup and took another sip. Except for the water's warmth, nothing seemed unusual. She shrugged, and was about to take a third sip when she suddenly felt her throat closing. She gagged and threw the cup down. She gasped for air as the leaves turned into little green lights swirling around the clearing. The fountain began to glow brighter, and soon, her vision whited out.

6. The Whispering Forest

"A fountain that grants wisdom," I said. "Sounds *vaguely* familiar."

Sheridan nodded and flashed a smile. "It's a curious thing, yes."

"What's it filled with? Whiskey?"

"Do you find wisdom at the bottom of a bottle?"

"Sometimes. Well, never mind."

I glanced at Sheridan. He was staring quietly. "What?"

"Nothing," Sheridan said. "I just find if I stare at you long enough, there's a little vein on your forehead that pops. I take it you don't prefer the company of cats."

"Wh–I don't–you're strange."

"Thank you."

"It wasn't a compliment," I mumbled. Then, louder, "And I've noticed a trend in your stories. There always seems to be some sort of magic, wisdom-granting thingy."

" 'Always' is a strong conclusion to draw from a sample size of two."

"I guess," I said with a slight shrug. "I just never understood what 'infinite wisdom' really meant. I mean, how could you know everything if there's infinitely many things to know?"

Sheridan grinned. "Perhaps the problem with the fountain is one could never stop drinking."

"Well, then, let's hope there's an infinite latrine."

I thought I saw Sheridan snicker.

- 22 -

Mara awoke surrounded by a dark blur. She shivered as a cold breeze grasped her body. Her head throbbed. She sat up and rubbed her eyes. Her vision came into focus as they adjusted to the dim light.

A tiny sliver of sunlight rose out of the horizon. The well, while still glowing, seemed darker than Mara remembered it. Her heart raced as she realized she was near Anadaku's grounds. She climbed onto her feet and glanced around, then remembered the previous night. She was standing over where he fell. She looked down and shifted away from the spot. It was slightly darker than the surrounding dirt.

As she bent down to look closer, a whisper broke the forest's silence. She shot back up. Another whisper sounded from a different direction.

"Who's there?" she said quietly.

She heard more whispers. They trickled into the clearing like a light rain; then the storm surge hit. The clearing erupted into a sea of whispers, growing louder with each passing moment.

Mara screamed and covered her ears. The whispers seemed to come from nowhere in particular. She looked around, but nobody could be seen. She realized the whispers weren't coming from behind the trees and shrubs; they were coming *from* the trees and shrubs.

The entire forest was talking. But Mara couldn't make out any of it. She was an observer in a crowded hall, where all conversations blended into one indecipherable roar.

"Quiet!" she exclaimed. She pressed her hands harder over her ears. "I'm trying to listen to you!"

The whispering grew louder.

"No!" She began to run from the well. "Shut up! You're of no use at all!"

- 23 -

Mara came to a bend in the trail, which slowed downward into the shadow of a tall boulder. The wind whooshed as it raced around the curve, and drowned out enough of the whispering that she could clear her mind. She paused for a minute to catch her breath and noticed a small leaf floating in her wake.

Curious little thing, she thought. Just like Marcus used to describe, she could see precisely where it would go. She blew lightly as it drifted by, and watched its trajectory change.

Mara tried to push the whispering aside as she took another look around. She could see falling leaves, dropping dew drops, branches tossed in the wind—she could see the trajectories for all of it.

She shook her head. This time, the visions did not go away.

Mara walked slower, ignoring the whispering as she watched her surroundings closely. She stopped at a small puddle, reached into the water, and waved droplets into the air. She shifted aside as a small breeze carried them into her original location.

"What have I done?" she whispered. The whispering came back into focus. "Who are you?" she yelled. "Why are you whispering, forest?"

The whispers briefly grew louder. *They're talking to me*, she thought. *I just can't listen.*

She then heard a recognizable word, "...City..."

Mara glanced all around, but could not tell from which direction the voice came.

"You're lost," she heard.

"Who are you?" she demanded.

" ...it to ... " she heard.

Mara stomped her foot on the ground. "No! Be quiet! I can't hear you at all and you're just frustrating me!"

She sat on the ground, buried her head between her knees, and covered her ears. "Just go away!" she exclaimed.

But the whispers grew louder. The dirt and grass began to speak; each blade cried for her attention. Mara shivered. She picked up a rock and was about to throw it into the bushes when the rock screamed. She shrieked, dropped it, and shot back up onto her feet.

As she looked up, the canopy leaves thrust themselves apart. The sunlight caught in her eyes. She looked away, but was no longer on the forest path.

Mara gasped in shock. She looked down at her feet and found herself standing on nothing at all. The world around her blurred. She could feel herself moving, but could only see unrecognizable blobs of dark color.

She wondered if the sun had damaged her eyes, but she couldn't feel the ground, either. Then, the world came slightly back into focus. It was dark, and she hovered a few feet above a quiet road. "Where am I?" she whispered.

Except for the road and a dark horizon, nothing else occupied the world. Mara found she could twirl herself, as if she were floating in water. She managed to turn around and a small, bright light caught her eye.

It's a city! she thought, but it was unlike any city she had ever seen. The buildings seemed unfathomably large. Bright arcs of light extended from the city in all directions along the ground. Little sparkles danced in the sky above it.

As she stared at the city, her heart began to sink. Her mind filled with memories she'd never had. She became homesick and nostalgic, and felt very alone. She wanted so much to walk into the city, but as she looked back down, she realized just how far she was from it.

The city seized her mind. She could no longer look away; everything in her world lost meaning. She began to sob as she started to drift further away from the city. The speck of light soon extinguished itself, and Mara opened her eyes to find herself back in the woods.

Mara stood silently. The whispering was gone. The forest seemed quiet—impossibly quiet, as if it had decided to go out of its way to let her think.

She ducked under the bushes and stepped back into the fork. To the right lay the path home. To the left was Sylow's house.

Visions of the city raced through her mind. She could not shake the feeling of homesickness. She stared at the ring her father had given her for a minute.

As she took the first step toward home, a branch of decaying oak dropped into her path. She jumped back. The tree screamed and swiped at her again. Mara shrieked and began running toward Sylow's house.

- 24 -

Mara pounded on Sylow's door, screaming to be let in. From her position in the clearing, the whispering trees were well out of reach. But the sound roared closer, like an ocean wave.

When the door finally swung open, Sylow hardly had a second to speak before Mara burst into the room. "What have I done?" she cried. "It's all—"

Sylow interrupted. "What, dear? What—"

"The noise!" Mara said. She held her ears briefly. "They won't shut up!"

"Who?" Sylow asked. "Who won't—"

Mara continued, "and then the light—and the city! And the trees. They scream so loud! What have I done?"

"Breathe, dear," Sylow said.

Mara took a deep breath. She leaned against the wall and buried her face in her hands for a moment. She then looked up and sighed. "I–"

Sylow tried to be patient. "You?"

"I took a drink from the well," Mara said. "The Well of Enlightenment."

Sylow's eyes grew wide. "You *did*? How?"

"I put the cup of water to my lips and–"

"No, no," Sylow said. "I mean–"

Mara interrupted. "I put it to my lips, and it tasted sweet. And then ... *pow!* A whirlwind of light and sound, and the trees and dirt and sky ... they all speak. At once. And I have no idea what they're saying."

When Sylow managed to calm Mara down enough to construct coherent sentences, she explained all about the whispering forest. She then stopped herself. "But, I imagine, you know all about it."

Sylow shook his head. "I wouldn't know."

"But ... why?" Mara asked. She stepped away from the wall. "What did it do for you?"

Sylow stared into the distance. "I wouldn't know ... " he said. He stood quiet while Mara gazed impatiently. "I've never taken a drink from the well."

7. The City Which Shone Brightly

I thought for a bit that Mara may be delusional. Perhaps that's why she saw and heard the things she did. Sheridan seemed reluctant to comment on her sanity, but he may not have seen the world any different than she did.

We rounded a curve and started to descend into a thicket of trees. I wondered what words they'd have for me.

Sheridan always mentioned the trees swaying when they spoke. Maybe that had something to do with it. It was hard to tell from a moving car, but the trees didn't seem to be swaying, which wouldn't have been surprising if there weren't a perpetual, looming storm above us. Call it intuition, but something didn't seem right about them.

"Cat got your tongue?" Sheridan said.

I snapped back to attention. "No, no," I said. "I was just thinking."

Sheridan raised his eyebrows, but I was hesitant to reveal my observations of the trees. I didn't want him thinking he'd gotten into my head. "I'd be pissed," I said.

Sheridan grinned. "Really, now?"

"He sent her to drink from the well!" I exclaimed. "And he didn't himself. And–"

Sheridan was still grinning.

"Not that I care or anything." I added.

"Oh no-o-o," Sheridan shook his head. "Not at all."

I stared quietly at the road.

Sheridan said, "It just so happens that Mara was a bit peeved as well. But she didn't have much of a leg to stand on–"

"Anadaku cut off her legs?" I asked. "That must've smarted."

"Yes . . . " Sheridan said slowly. "That would've . . . *smarted*."

"I was just trying to make a funny."

Sheridan smiled. "D+, for effort. Mara felt Sylow had sent her to drink from the well–"

"Did you just grade my joke?"

"But she realized Sylow never told her to, and in fact, had warned her against it. She was more scared than anything else, but she would never admit *that* . . . "

- 25 -

Mara stood in the doorway, playing with the door latch. Sylow leaned against the wall. "What is with the world?" Mara asked. "And these peculiar devices that grant wisdom?"

Sylow chuckled. "I wouldn't know."

Mara glanced at the window. She closed her eyes and tried to sort out the whispers. "I can still hear them," she said. "They don't shut up."

Sylow nodded.

"Why did you never try to drink from the well?"

"What makes you think I never tried?"

Mara shrugged. "It just seems . . . if *I* could do it . . . " She smiled.

"Well . . . you're special."

Mara laughed. "So you say."

"I mean it!" Sylow exclaimed.

The smile dropped off of Mara's face. She fidgeted with her father's ring for a bit. Light reflected off of its surface, which momentarily captured her attention, "That's what the woman said, wasn't it?"

Sylow raised an eyebrow. "What woman?"

"You once told me . . . " Mara twirled her hair around her finger as she paused to think. "She said to look after me or something like that. But you didn't even know me."

"Oh . . . " Sylow glanced at the ceiling and trailed off.

"You know something," Mara said. She pulled her hand out of her hair and lowered her gaze. "You know something, and you won't tell me!"

"You won't believe me."

Mara folded her arms in front of her chest and glared. "Try me. You *always* change the subject."

Sylow sighed. "It's not like there are many people living in this area. Everybody seems to know everyone. It's the curse of a small town. Everything is everyone's business."

"I thought as much."

"I never had any reason to visit your father. But I knew who you were when I first saw you. You were what, eight years old when we first met? Seven?"

"Something like that." Mara closed her eyes and tried to remember.

Sylow nodded. "We met eight years after, that woman came to my door, sobbing. She told me she'd left a little girl on a doorstep, but didn't know if anyone was home. She wanted me to check, since he was my neighbor."

Mara's eyes grew wide. She stared at her father's ring.

Sylow continued, "She said you were very special. I invited her in for a bite to eat, and that's when she told me about the fountain and the books I've given you over the years."

"No," Mara said. She shook her head. "Why would she leave me . . . I don't understand."

- 26 -

After Sylow's revelation, Mara tried to clear her mind by hiking through the forest. "Why was I never told?" she asked.

The trees whispered all at once.

"Sure, I wouldn't expect Father to say anything. But why not Mother?"

Mara tried to hear the trees' response, but they continued to drown each other out.

"Oh, you're no help at all!" she cried.

"Who's to say we owe you help?" she heard.

Mara screamed. "Who said that? Don't you know it's not nice to scare people?"

"You did ask a question. Would you have preferred not to receive an answer?"

"No, I mean, yes, I would have. Who are you?"

"Look deep below your sole."

"Are you my psyche?"

"No. I'm under your feet."

Mara stepped back and a blade of grass sprang up. "Thank you," it said. "You really should be careful where you step."

"Oh!" Mara gasped and covered her mouth. "I'm so sorry."

"Whatever," the grass said. "Now, what about my question? Why do you assume we should help you?"

"I was just frustrated," Mara said. "There's no need to jump all over me."

"I think you're spending too much time thinking about where you came from, and not enough about where you're going."

Mara nodded, then changed her mind and smirked. "But doesn't where I go depend on where I came from?"

The blade of grass gently swayed in the breeze without a response. Mara tapped her foot on the ground. "Well?"

"Don't ask me," the grass said. "I've been in one place all my life."

"Argh!" Mara cried and walked off. "Fine."

- 27 -

Mara returned to the cottage. She sat slumped in a chair, staring at her ring. She twirled it around her finger, her mind empty of thoughts. She tried to push memories of home away. *It doesn't make sense*, she told herself repeatedly. Try as she might, she couldn't remember being born, much less to whom. As far as she knew, she just always was. And that bothered her.

I have no reason to believe I'm here, she thought. *Or that anything is here, for that matter. After all, how can we be so sure the world exists if nobody was around to witness its creation?* She scratched her head.

"Mara," Sylow said as he walked slowly into the room.

Mara looked up. "I'm sorry I yelled at you." She closed her eyes. "I was just upset."

"It's not your fault."

"It just seems like the more I learn, the less I understand the world."

Sylow smiled. "Welcome to the world of the mathematician."

Mara forced a smile. "Sometimes . . . I want to go home."

Sylow stood quiet. Mara waited for him to speak. She realized that, for perhaps the first time, he was unable to think of what to say. "I'm sorry," she said. "I didn't mean that."

Memories of being in the woods rushed over her. She closed her eyes as her vision of the glowing city came back to her.

"Mara," Sylow said.

She felt a slight breeze as she opened her eyes and the room came into focus.

"Mara," Sylow repeated. "You're not falling asleep on me?"

"In the forest," she said. "I had a moment of clarity."

Sylow raised an eyebrow. "What do you mean?"

Mara closed her eyes. "I heard something during the whispers and screams–a small voice, that told me of a city. *The* city ... the city which shone brightly."

"I have never heard of such a place," Sylow said. "Although, I suppose all cities have lights. And knowledge. And, well, there are so many ways to think of 'shining'."

"It was a faintly glowing city, so far away," Mara said. She stared through the tiny window and smiled at the sky. "So far, but it would be wonderful to travel. Oh! I wish I could! The road was long, but it called to me, saying to follow it to the end of the world."

"I think the end of the world would be hard to find," Sylow said. "A sphere has no ends."

"I couldn't decipher anything else," Mara said. She sighed. "How silly you must think me to be talking to trees and twigs."

Sylow smiled. "No, dear. I don't think you're silly at all. Perhaps we're both finding out what the Well of Enlightenment means. It means you have learned to listen."

"Then, why can't I hear anything?" Mara threw her arms in frustration. "It's all noise! Like in a crowded hall."

"Perhaps," Sylow said. He thought for a minute. "A key. You need a key to pick apart the voices."

"Like a lock?" Mara stared blankly.

"Sometimes, you need something to help you focus," Sylow said. "If you step out of a cave into the daylight, you're suddenly seeing all light at once. But it is too bright! It is too much. But if you step out of the cave with a dark shade over your eyes, a filter, it helps you see clearly."

Mara looked out the window again. She was reminded of the brook's words from the previous day. *You may find an entire world rests in a little sequence.* She was reminded of the patterns Marcus described, and how they seemed to be everywhere.

"But where can I find such a thing?" she asked. "Do you think Marcus's patterns hold the answer?"

Sylow reached his hand out. "Come with me. I have something for you."

Mara's eyes grew as big as a cat's. She took his hand and stood. "Oh! What! What is it?"

Sylow led her to a curtain. He pulled it back, revealing a door Mara had never seen. "It leads to the lower floor," Sylow said.

"Another floor?" Mara raised an eyebrow. "What's down there?"

When Sylow opened the door and led Mara down the steps, she could see why he'd kept it hidden. Bright moonlight entered through the windows, illuminating a long shelf full of books. Mara gasped as she looked around. All the walls were lined with shelves. "I've never seen so many in all my life! I mean, I knew you had books upstairs. But, all this time, down here!"

"It's more than a lifetime's collection. Probably the biggest collection in all the nation."

"Why didn't you tell me you had such a library?"

Sylow straightened a couple of books. He looked around the room before speaking. "It's not my library."

"It's not? Then why is it here?"

"It's your library."

Mara's heart stood still. "Mine . . . ?"

Sylow nodded. "It is. It is now, I mean. I want you to have it."

"Does . . . this mean I can be a scholar?"

"Yes," Sylow said. "I didn't convince everyone, but I convinced the majority. They'll be here in about a week to meet you."

Mara choked back tears. "I . . . I don't know what to say."

"I thought you might like some good news."

Mara ran up to Sylow and hugged him. "Thank you," she whispered.

Sylow stepped back and smiled. "But you must promise me you'll take care of the library."

"Oh! Oh, I will!"

"I know you'll be happy here. Everything you need is on these shelves, a million little gateways to far-away worlds."

"It'd be so wonderful to go," Mara said.

"Then I'm glad to have provided."

Mara ran her fingers along the spines of a few books. "The answer is in one of these, I just know it. I'll find it. Then, perhaps, I'll go on a wonderful adventure. Maybe I'll learn more about the world than I'd ever care to know."

Sylow laughed. "More than you'd ever care to know? I believe that would be quite impossible."

8. Speak Less and Listen More

"It's about time," I said. "He seemed to be pushing her around quite a bit."

Sheridan looked up. "Sylow?"

"Yeah. What did she finally learn that got her in?"

"She didn't learn anything," Sheridan explained. "There wasn't anything to learn. Mara didn't know what had changed their minds. And if she didn't know, how could she have written it in her journal for *us* to know?"

"So, this is a real book?"

Sheridan cracked a slight smile. "Yes."

"But, then, how do you know things Mara didn't know?"

"It's a secret," Sheridan said. "You'll find out, in time."

The vast, unchanging landscape continued to roll by. Time, it seemed, was at a standstill. Maybe it wasn't four o'clock. Maybe it was one. I didn't know, and that startled me a bit. Something was wrong. Something had been wrong since I'd first picked Sheridan up. And as we drove on, I was becoming less convinced it was just me being tired.

"Mara," Sheridan said, "spent the next few days in the library. The odd thing was, she couldn't find any mention of Marcus's SanCullep Island in any history book. In fact, Marcus's strange journey did not make any sense. It was a journal, after all. What happened to Marcus, and what Marcus *thought* happened, could have been two entirely different things.

"But she became obsessed with the sequences Marcus had described. She decided that if anyone could crack the code, it'd be her.

"She couldn't help but think she had something in common with Marcus. They both made the world their own, and she was now determined to continue his journey."

- 28 -

Mara sat in the field outside Sylow's house, among the rocks. The small rocks were uncomfortable to sit on, but she found them much more pleasant company than the flowers that called her such vulgar names.

Far behind her, she could hear the whispering forest. She sat as far as she could from the edge of the clearing, but the noise was still almost intolerable. "What is it with these trees?" she said, not to anything in particular. "Why can I hear the flowers so clearly, but the trees not at all?"

A slight nudge against her arm startled her. She looked down to see a small cockroach scouting her elbow. "Yech!" she screamed. She jumped onto her feet and flung the roach across the field. She watched it disappear behind the brush, and sighed.

"Perhaps there is something you see in the flowers that you do not see in the trees."

"Who said that?" Mara exclaimed. She looked all around, but nobody was near. "Who are you? Show yourself!"

"I am already showing myself," she heard. "Perhaps you cannot see."

"I can see just fine. I have two eyes."

"Tulips."

Mara smirked. "Yes, I have lips, too. But I don't see with my mouth."

"No. Down here!"

Mara looked down at her feet, but still saw nothing. She lifted her tunic up and saw a tulip.

"There you go," it said.

"You've been there this whole time?"

"There's nothing up there I haven't seen before."

Mara shrieked and scooted over the rock. "You scoundrel! Do flowers not have any morals?"

"Morals!" the tulip exclaimed. "Like *you* can stand on such a high pedestal!"

Mara crossed her arms in front of her chest. "I think I practice proper manners, thank you very much."

"That wasn't nice in the least!" Mara heard a tiny voice. She looked behind the tulip. The roach she'd flung across the field had crawled back.

"Well, maybe you shouldn't be crawling on girls' arms, spreading disease!" Mara said.

"Maybe *you* shouldn't be parading around the field, spreading disease yourself," the roach said.

Mara's eyes grew wide. She then smirked and huffed, "I think I should bid good day to you. After all, I was minding my own business until you two Diddly-duds decided to pester me."

"Yes, leave us alone," the rock said.

Mara screamed and stepped back. She lost her balance and crashed to the ground. The roach, tulip, and rock laughed.

"Oh, damn it all!" Mara exclaimed. "I didn't ask for any of this!"

"I beg to differ," a sunflower said.

Mara looked up and shielded her eyes from the sun. She could make out the faint outline of the sunflower, leaning over her. "But ... " she said. "You're so pretty!"

"Flattery does not make friends with flowers," the sunflower said.

Mara glared at the sunflower. Her icy stare softened as the

breeze pushed the flower out of the sun's path. She looked into the swirl pattern in the seeds. For a brief moment, she felt the world was clear. She understood how everything came to be, and how everything fit into its place. The whispers of the forest broke into a thousand tiny voices–each in its own place in a larger conversation.

But before Mara could take in any of it, the feeling passed. She sat up and looked all around. Her company stood perfectly still. "I saw it," she whispered.

"It . . . " the rock said.

Mara nodded. She looked at the sunflower's center again, but the same feeling didn't return. She stared, concentrated with all her focus, but couldn't see the pattern. "Tell me," Mara said. "Tell me the sequence!"

The sunflower stood silent for a while, then asked, "What sequence?"

"You know!" Mara exclaimed. "You must know!"

"My dear," the sunflower said. "I cannot tell you any sequence."

Mara stared at her hands. "That's what the brook said. It said I would learn more for having figured it out myself."

The sunflower nodded in the breeze.

Mara said, "Marcus was told he was on a quest. He never found out what it was, but learned from the experience of searching for it. Perhaps that's what I need."

"A quest?"

Mara nodded.

"What makes you think you aren't already on one?"

"I suppose I am looking for a purpose. That's all any girl needs. My quest is to find my purpose."

The sunflower snickered.

Mara folded her arms in front of her chest and glared at the sunflower. "You think it's a silly quest? Perhaps I think *you* are silly!"

"I think you should speak less and listen more."

Mara smirked. She turned her back to the flower and walked off.

- 29 -

Mara contemplated her moment of insight as she ran toward Sylow's house. The sun had set before she realized, and she knew she was late for the meeting with the other scholars. She threw the cottage door open and called, "Sylow! Sylow! Let me share something with you!" But no answer came.

She looked around. Footsteps from the upper floor echoed through the room. The library door hung on one hinge, leaning partly against the wall. Mara carefully pulled it open and poked her head through. "There you are! Where are the scholars?"

Sylow, standing flat against the wall, whispered, "Close the door!"

Mara propped the door into its frame. "Why are we whispering?"

"Get over here!" Sylow motioned her to come closer.

Mara jumped as a loud crash rattled the cottage. Her eyes grew wider. "What is going on?"

Sylow's response was interrupted by cries and screams from the upper levels. Mara's hands began to tremble and her face grew pale. Screams continued to sound from above. "What's going on?" Mara repeated.

"Shhh!"

The cottage rattled under another crash. Dust rained down from the ceiling. "We're being attacked," Sylow said.

"By whom?" Mara asked. She pulled the door more tightly into its frame and wedged a pole through the handle.

"I don't know," Sylow replied. "I've never seen them around these parts. We've got to get you out of here."

Mara pushed a chest in front of the door. "But ... where will we go?"

The cottage rattled again. A crackling sound echoed from above as dense smoke seeped down from the ceiling. Sylow looked up toward a small window. "There," he said.

Mara grabbed his arm and started to pull him toward the window. When he resisted, she stepped back and eyed him.

Sylow shook his head. "You can fit through there. I cannot."

Mara's heart dropped. "What?" she asked. "What do you mean? I can't go alone!"

"You'll have to, my dear," Sylow said. He dropped his voice. "If we go out the door we will be slaughtered."

"I can't go alone!" Mara cried.

Sylow pushed her toward the window. "Go on. Run. And never look back."

Mara shook her head. "You have to come! I will be lost out there!"

Sylow sighed. "I wish ... I wish I could. But I am old. You are young and full of life. It would be foolish to sacrifice both of us in my name. Hurry!"

"But ... " Mara closed her eyes. "I'll miss you."

Sylow held her for a moment, until the house rattled and crashed again. A loud thud echoed through the room as the library door rattled. "Go," he said. "There isn't much time."

Sylow helped lift Mara through the window. She climbed through and poked her head back in. Sylow handed her Marcus's journal.

Mara shoved the book behind her. "Take this, too," Sylow said, handing her a ragged leather satchel. "It has food, and water."

Mara sighed as she took the satchel. "Mara," Sylow whispered. "Don't forget who you are. Don't let anyone kill your spark. You have too much to offer this world."

The library door rattled again. Mara said nothing, too choked up to speak. She simply nodded and turned away.

Carving a hasty path through the dense forests, Mara stole a quick glance at the massacre from which she ran. Sylow's cottage was completely engulfed in flames, and she was certain he had already perished. She held tightly onto her book and satchel. There was no time for sadness or fear, only time to run.

II
Dance of the Marionettes

9. A Bittersweet Dream

"It was Amedean," I said. "He raided the house."

Sheridan shook his head. "He had too many enemies to gather enough friends to pull that off."

"Well, then ... " I tapped the steering wheel with my finger. "Cue 'Reveille' for Sylow, I suppose."

"Reveille?" Sheridan raised an eyebrow. He tried to keep a straight face, but I could see the corner of his mouth turn up. "You mean ... 'Taps'?"

"Whatever," I said. "The flowers seem to have a knack for standoffish behavior."

"Who could blame them?" Sheridan asked. "I mean, if I were a tulip, each day, I'd have to worry about being snipped. And don't get me started on if I were a dandelion."

"You've thought about this a lot, haven't you?"

Sheridan beamed a wide smile and nodded. "Haven't you?"

"Well ... no. No, I haven't."

Sheridan shook his head. "That's a pity. You should have more understanding for the plight of flowers."

"Now, just a minute." I glanced at Sheridan out of the corner of my eye. I couldn't tell if he was smirking or not, but he *probably* was. "You're telling me I should sympathize with flowers because they live their lives in mortal fear?"

"Yes."

"*Flowers.*"

"Yes."

"What about vases?"

Sheridan crossed his arms. "Now, what do you know about vases?"

"Why aren't they happy in vases? With their heads . . . you know what?"

"What," Sheridan huffed. I couldn't tell if he was really upset, or just faking it.

"I refuse to have this ridiculous conversation."

I thought I saw Sheridan hide a smirk.

"So, did the flowers tell Mara who the attackers were? Did they whisper sweet secrets?"

"Flowers don't know everything," Sheridan said. His eyes widened, and he looked straight at me. "Holly bushes, maybe." He shook his head. "But not flowers."

"You're nuts," I said. "Anyway who were they? The attackers? And wouldn't they have gone after Mara?"

"Well, Mara didn't know . . . and, no, they didn't chase after her. Mara and her book simply vanished . . ."

- 30 -

The stars began to slowly fade as daylight broke through the forest canopy. Beads of dew falling from the leaves above washed Mara's face of the soot collected from Sylow's cottage. She's woken up amongst a pile of wet leaves. The satchel Sylow had given her, once full of food, lay open, empty, and most likely picked clean overnight by some forest inhabitant. The highway glowed green as hints of sunlight reflected off the misty forest floor. There was a small stream nearby which splashed against aged and well-rounded rocks. *What a beautiful place*, Mara thought. For a moment, she forgot the circumstances which lead her here.

Her legs were still weak from running the previous night, and she struggled to climb her way to the brook for a drink of water. Her reflection caught her by surprise.

That's me, she thought, staring at the image. Her long, black hair appeared dark blue against the water. She reached into the liquid and ran her finger through it, watching the ripples distort her image. Her dark blue eyes so perfectly matched the shade of the water that it appeared as though it were moving through her. She backed away and looked up at the sky, but the sun hurt her eyes. Everything looked the same in all directions–trees. *Where am I? Where do I go from here?*

Mara wandered back to where she'd lain the night before, and gathered her book. She stared at them. Memories of the previous night rushed back. She struggled to grasp it all. What had happened? Who had attacked them? She closed her eyes and held the book to her heart. A tear rolled down her cheek as she recalled what she had once held, then lost. *I've never felt so alone in this world.*

High above, the bluebirds gathered, preparing to greet the morning with their song. *How wonderful it would be to be a bluebird.* Mara opened her eyes and gazed up. *I could soar high above this world and look down . . . look down upon it all.*

Mara shook her head. *There's no time to stand here feeling sad.* She looked around the clearing. The trail continued in two directions. One was where she'd come from; the other lead further into the forest. She struggled to remember which was which, but in the rush of the previous night, she had not thought much about it. Now, all she saw was one parallel to the brook, and the other surrounded by thick forest on both ends.

Taking a closer look at the trails, Mara thought how lovely the brook-bordered path was. It stood out more than the other. Above the trail, a constellation of stars was still visible.

The mist hovered, forming a green, glowing effect that encompassed the road. *This trail ... this one is calling to me.*

Mara thought about Sylow and the others. She thought about the library she'd left. *I don't think Sylow would have wanted me to stand around feeling sad,* she thought. *He wouldn't want me to stop looking. He would want me to go on. So I will resolve to do just that.*

Looking back the other direction, Mara whispered, "Goodbye, old friend. Be happy that I am going on, and I will not forget you."

Mara shoved the book in her ravaged satchel and staggered into the mist.

- 31 -

The thought that she was lost never occurred to Mara. Even as the sun reached its apex in the sky, she was entranced by the forest around her. *It's so beautiful,* she thought. The mist continued to hover over the roadway. *It's like a dream. A bittersweet dream.*

The brookside trail wound on and on. Every so often, Mara would catch a glimpse of her reflection in the water and think it was someone else. But each time she paused to look she was disappointed to find only herself.

After a mile or so, Mara reached a clearing. She stopped, stunned. The clearing glowed a brilliant gold in the sun. She gazed all around as she walked into it. She had never seen any place like it. Unusual flowers grew around the edges, showing off a vast array of colors. Above, the leaves of the forest canopy danced in the wind, making the sunlight flicker. Mara walked around the edges of the clearing, touching all the flowers as she absorbed their colors. The brook could still be heard as it passed the clearing.

To the right of where she'd entered lay another road. It started at a small bridge that crossed the brook. Mara crossed to the bridge and gazed across; the highway stretched away before her. She stepped onto the bridge and looked down at the brook. Her reflection greeted her yet again. "This is the way to go," her reflection said.

Mara looked all around her. "There is nowhere else to go!" she replied. "Except back."

"Well, then," her reflection said. "Don't go back."

Mara reached down into the brook, washed her face, and took another drink before heading down the highway.

After a while, she began to grow dazed. She was weak from hunger, and every step through the forest only lead to more forest. "Help me," she whispered to the wind. Her hands began to tremble.

A gust of wind charged through the woodlands, gently nudging her toward the right. "Follow the trail," it whispered.

Mara, weak and drained, sat down on a rock and looked around her. "Where am I?" she whispered back.

The leaves of the forest canopy rustled in the breeze. Mara felt the forest floor. It was soft and inviting. She arranged a small pillow out of nearby leaves and lay to rest. "Help me," she whispered. She closed her eyes.

- 32 -

Mara's eyes sprang open to the sound of footsteps rustling through the leaves. *It's the attackers! They've found me!* She leapt into the bushes as the footsteps neared.

Quiet murmurs and whispers from the forest canopy echoed. *The whispering forest!* Mara looked up. "Please tell me, forest," she whispered. "What do you see?"

Dozens of whispers came alive all at once, drowning each other out in a sea of chaotic noise. "Just one of you!" Mara whispered. "Who is there?"

The whispering grew so loud, Mara had to cover her ears. She closed her eyes and shook her head. "No! Shut up! You're no help! No help at all! Just be gone!"

She could make out the image of a man on the highway. He was quite tall, with wavy blond hair. As he neared, his amber eyes burned into her mind. He stopped in the road and looked around. Mara studied him carefully. He was armed. He slowly wandered toward the bush in which she hid.

She held her breath as the man took a closer look. *Can he see me?* she thought.

Mara screamed as the man opened the bush, revealing her. The man shrieked and jumped backward. The bushes snapped shut, slapping her in the face.

Mara breathed heavily as the man called out, "Oh dear! I am terribly sorry! *What* are you doing in the bushes?"

She dared not answer.

The man carefully approached again. "Don't be afraid," he said. "I won't bite."

Mara closed her eyes as the man opened the greenery once more. She felt his hand touch her shoulder. He smiled softly at her as she opened her eyes. "Hi," he said. "Who are you?"

Mara whispered, "Mara . . . Mara Sanghid."

The man smiled. "Hi, Mara," he said.

"Who are you?"

"I am Sanreils," he replied. "Don't worry. I won't hurt you."

"What guarantee do I have of that?" Mara asked.

Sanreils stepped back and hid a smirk. "Well, if I wanted to harm you, don't you think I could have easily done so by now?"

Mara rubbed her face. Sanreils frowned. "Besides that . . . I'm sorry! Such is not the best of introductions, I know. But I really meant no harm. I won't hurt you."

Mara climbed out of the bushes. "See?" Sanreils said. He smiled invitingly. "No harm done."

Mara sat down on a stump.

"Are you okay?" Sanreils asked. "You look a bit . . . well . . . quite frightened."

"I'm fine," Mara said. She shivered.

Sanreils shook his head. "Are you afraid of me?"

"No . . . no," Mara replied. "I'm just . . . lost. Can you tell me where I am?"

"You're in Fordham Forest," Sanreils replied. "Where did you think you were?"

"I don't know!" Mara cried.

"Where did you come from?"

Mara hid her face in her hands and cried.

"My dear," Sanreils spoke soothingly, "I did not mean to upset you. I was merely trying to help you find your way."

Mara abruptly stood and shook her head. "Feeling sad will not help anything at all."

"It's okay to feel sad," Sanreils said. He took a piece of bread out of his knapsack and handed it to her. "You look like you've had a hard time."

Mara nodded as she took the bread. "Thank you," she whispered.

Sanreils smiled. "Follow me," he said. "Let's find your way."

Mara followed Sanreils down the highway. Having now eaten and found some company, her thoughts of despair began to subside. "Tell me, Mara," Sanreils said. "How did you end up here, of all places?"

As they walked, Mara told Sanreils all about the previous night.

"I'm sorry to hear all that," Sanreils said.

"Who were they? Why did they come?" Mara cried.

"I wish I had answers for you," Sanreils said. "But I don't know."

Mara sighed. "I was so happy," she whispered.

She glanced up at Sanreils. He was watching her with a compassionate look on his face, so she continued, "I used to spend all my time curious about the world. I was fascinated by it. But no one seemed to care. They wanted a life for me that I didn't. So I ran away from home. I ran to Sylow's house. He, like several of his friends, loved the world for what it showed them rather than what they could force it to be. He taught me to embrace my curiosity . . . to keep seeking. But . . . I don't know why they killed him . . . maybe all of the scholars, too . . . And now, I'm here. Alone."

"Alone in the forest is not a nice place to be," Sanreils said.

Mara shook her head. "What do I do?"

"What do you mean?"

"I mean . . . where do I go? I don't think I can go home. Not after running away. Not after the things I said and the actions I took."

Sanreils thought a moment. "Perhaps there's something I can do . . . "

"You would help me?" Mara asked.

Sanreils smiled. "This is a very big forest. And it is not every day one stumbles upon someone as lovely as you."

Mara blushed profusely. Sanreils continued, "But alas, I am somewhat preoccupied with a job. I must be on my way soon."

"Can I come with you?"

"I wish you could. I really wish you could. But I work for

a courier service that is rather insistent I travel to where I'm going, alone."

"Oh," Mara replied. "I hope you won't get in trouble for having walked with me."

Sanreils shook his head. "I couldn't bear to think of you perishing," he said. He looked down the trail and thought carefully. "There's an inn ... in the Valley of Lennox. It's down the way. You could make it by nightfall. Easily."

Mara smiled. Sanreils fished around in his satchel and handed her a few coins. "Spend the night there. Then travel the rest of the way to the city of Locana tomorrow. I'll meet with you tomorrow night, if you wish."

"Oh!" Mara exclaimed. "That would be ... lovely."

"Please be safe."

"I'll try," Mara said.

"Good," Sanreils said. "Because I am hoping very much that our paths will cross again."

Mara smiled at Sanreils and replied, "Me too ... thank you for taking care of me out here."

Sanreils nodded. "Travel safe, and make it to Lennox before nightfall, okay?"

"I will."

"I'm really sorry about the bush," Sanreils said. "I still feel bad about that. Are you sure you're okay?"

Mara smiled and nodded.

"Good," Sanreils replied. He gently stroked her cheek. "Goodbye ... for now."

She smiled at him and whispered, "Goodbye."

Mara and Sanreils walked in separate directions. Mara headed forward along the highway, and Sanreils headed back in the opposite direction. She turned to watch him disappear into the horizon.

- 33 -

Mara continued her journey down the highway. It was mid-afternoon and the sun was beginning its trek back down to the horizon. The road wound deeper into the forest. "Please be kind to me, road," she said.

"I will," the highway replied.

Mara blinked, surprised by the highway's response. "You speak?" she whispered.

"Of course!" the highway replied. "You spoke to me, and it would be rude of me not to answer."

"True . . ." Mara said.

"Are you surprised?"

Mara shook her head. "Oh no, I talk to the world all the time. Just . . . this is my first time talking to a highway."

"Well, pleased to meet you, Mara."

"You know my name?"

"Of course! I've known you for many years. After all, how often have you traveled on a highway?"

"A lot."

"See . . ." the highway said. "Of course, I know you!"

Mara closed her eyes. "Please stay with me," she whispered.

"Just keep following," the highway replied. "Keep following, and I'll take you to the ones you loved. And I'll show you the world along the way."

10. That You're Happy

"I see it's back."

Sheridan looked my way and nodded. Once again I wondered how he knew what I was thinking. "Is it ... the same highway?" I asked.

"What do *you* think?" Sheridan asked.

"I have a feeling there's a trick here. But I can't put my finger on it."

"Of course, you can't put your finger on it," Sheridan said. "It's a thought. And thoughts aren't tangible."

"It's an expression." I briefly looked his way. He had that stupid smirk he always brandished. "Never mind."

"No trick."

"Then it must be the same one," I said. "It always seemed like that annoying lecturer who never wanted to answer your questions directly."

Sheridan smiled. "As long as there has been mankind, mankind has had roads."

"Apparently so."

I watched the divider lines scroll under the car. I thought of Sheridan's stupid patterns. The lines were evenly spaced. Maybe it was Morse Code.

"Have you ever spoken to the highway?" I asked.

Sheridan nodded. "But I was told not to tell anyone what it said."

"What–by who?"

"The highway."

I wondered if the highway was the one who'd told him the world was ending.

Sheridan said, "Mara felt a little better, having found someone to speak to . . . "

- 34 -

Mara sat on a small stone just off the trail. She leaned against a tree and stared at the sky. Thoughts flew through her mind, flickering on and off like a field full of fireflies. *Where is the highway going to take me?* she thought. *The shining city?*

The highway's words echoed in her mind. *Who are my loved ones?* she thought. She was sure the highway wasn't referring to Amedean. Perhaps it included her mother, and Sylow. *But the highway distinctly said loved 'ones', not 'one'. Maybe I'll fall in love with someone, but then lose them. That would make it plural.*

Mara grimaced at herself. *Wait–that's horrible!*

A breeze shook the forest canopy; the sun's rays broke and reunited with each gust. Mara eyed the light and leaves. *You may find the entire world rests in a little sequence.* She recalled the brook's words.

She traced the light to the ground and watched the leaves hop in the breeze. *Down, right, left, right, up, right . . .* she sat up. She watched the leaves closer. "It's like Marcus described," she thought aloud. "A little sequence. Could it have been repeating this whole time?"

"The world is full of mysteries," Mara heard a woman's voice behind her. She shrieked and jumped to her feet.

"Who are you?" Mara said as she turned around. "Don't do that!"

"Who am I?" the woman said. "I suppose we both are seeking an answer to *that* question."

When Mara glanced into the woman's eyes, she found she couldn't look away. They seized her attention, and her mind emptied of all other thoughts. The woman smiled. "I'm Aphrael."

Mara just stared. Aphrael was much taller than her. She had long, straight, black hair tied behind her back, and a maroon tunic with a tapered bottom that fell between her knees.

She said, "Speak."

Mara shook her head, and her thoughts came back to her. "Uh, I'm ... "

"Mara," Aphrael said.

"Thanks," Mara said. "Wait! How did you know that?"

"Who else would you be?"

"I suppose I could only be me," Mara said. "But ... now, *hold on!*" She crossed her arms in front of her chest. "You're trying to be tricky, aren't you?"

"Me?" Aphrael smiled innocently.

"Yes, *you*," Mara lowered her gaze. "Never mind it all. What do you want with me?"

She walked close to Mara and said, "Well ... I've been looking for you."

"Me?" Mara pointed to herself.

"Yes, my dear," Aphrael said. She slid a finger down Mara's cheek. "*You.*"

Mara blushed.

Aphrael grinned. "And I was wondering if, maybe, you could help me out."

"Oh ... " Mara said. She glanced off into the distance. "I don't know ... maybe ... "

"Of course, I would reward you," Aphrael said.

Mara hesitated, trying to look away from Aphrael's captivating gaze. "Maybe–"

Aphrael trickled her finger down Mara's chest. She whispered, "*Very* well."

Mara gulped.

Aphrael grinned slyly. She leaned closer. Mara shuddered as she felt Aphrael's cold lips touch her ear. Aphrael whispered, very softly, "*I* know who the attackers are. The ones who came after *you*, who killed Sylow."

Mara froze. Her heart nearly leapt out of her chest. She barely managed to collect herself enough to respond. "Wh–who?"

Aphrael shook her head. "It would do no good to tell you. No good at all!"

"What do you mean?" Mara exclaimed. She stomped her foot on the ground. "You can't tell me you know and not tell me!"

Aphrael held her finger to Mara's lips. "Shhh ... Shhhhh, my dear." She took a moment to think. "I'd like you to do something for me."

"Mmmph," Mara muttered. Aphrael removed her finger. Mara glared. "What?"

"There is a church ... *cult* in Locana," Aphrael said. "They are ... *trouble*."

"And?" Mara said. She continued to glare.

"My, my!" Aphrael exclaimed. She shook her head. "Aren't we the impatient one!"

"Sorry ... " Mara mumbled.

"La Nocturne," Aphrael said.

"Who?"

"Not 'who'," Aphrael said. "*What*."

"What?"

"Yes, that's the right question," Aphrael said. She flashed a brief smile. "It's a cult–a cult from a faraway place. You know what a cult is."

Mara nodded.

Aphrael placed her hand on Mara's forehead, stopping her. She explained, "That was a statement, not a question. You don't need to respond."

Mara stepped back and glared at Aphrael. Aphrael said, "They're not a church. They're a cult. There are many differences between churches and cults ... one notable are that cults tend to isolate their members from ... *others.*"

Aphrael paused a moment. Mara made neither motion nor response. Aphrael said, "My sister's name is Trisha. I miss her dearly ... so dearly."

"I'm sorry," Mara said quietly.

Aphrael sighed. She nodded. "La Nocturne is her show. It was a dead experiment of hers. She resurrected it, brought it back from a distant land."

Mara stared blankly. Aphrael continued, "She tasted power, and got herself caught up in it. I want her back. I need her."

Mara nodded shyly. "I ... " she hung her head slightly. "I think I know the feeling."

Aphrael said, "I knew you would, and I knew you would be a good person to talk to." She smiled gently. "I also know that you're probably one of ... well, *the only* one who can help me."

"I am?" Mara asked.

"I heard you've got quite a good head on your shoulders," Aphrael said. "And there's only one way to bring Trisha back. I want you to prove the world doesn't exist."

Mara scratched her head. "What do you mean, 'prove the world doesn't exist'?"

Aphrael shook her head. She explained, "A proof is–"

"I know what a proof is!" Mara said. "But you can't prove the world doesn't exist! Haven't you heard of–"

Aphrael sighed. She shook her head again. "I was afraid this would happen."

Mara lifted an eyebrow.

Aphrael said, "Mara . . . is that your name now?"

"We just talked about that *two minutes* ago!" Mara stepped back. "You're—"

"*Mara*," Aphrael interrupted. "It's a pretty name."

Mara smiled briefly. Aphrael said, "So, *Mara*, you of all people should've heard of Marcus and his quest to shed this reality."

"Of course," Mara said. "Sylow gave me this book—"

"I know." Aphrael smiled, then hid her grin. "So you know he failed. But *you* can do it."

"But that's silly! How does making the world disappear help you reunite with your sister—"

Aphrael held her finger to Mara's lips again. She shook her head. "That's not your concern," she said. "But I know *you* can do such a thing, because you can learn how it works, and then break it." Aphrael removed her finger.

"How can the world be broken?" Mara asked. "You can break a machine; you can't break a world."

"The world has patterns," Aphrael said. "You should know that. Learn them, and break them."

"I don't know," Mara said.

"Let's cut a deal. I have . . . a *proposition*."

Mara tilted her head and eyed Aphrael quizzically. "Agree to help me. In return, I'll tell you who the attackers are. In fact, I'll even help you get revenge."

Mara paused for a moment. She thought of the attack. She could feel rage boil inside her. But still, revenge wasn't in her character. She muttered, "Revenge . . ."

Aphrael lifted Mara's chin up with her finger. She said quietly, "I will see to it. See to your . . . justice. See to it . . . " She took a moment to brush Mara's hair out of her eyes. She then dropped her voice to almost a whisper. "That you're happy."

Mara stood frozen, stunned. Aphrael smiled. She said, "Think about it."

Before Mara could collect herself enough to respond, Aphrael disappeared.

11. Your Idea of Peace and Harmony

"She sounds familiar," I said.

"Aphrael?"

I nodded.

"How so?"

"Something about her demeanor. I can't quite put–"

Out of the corner of my eye, I could see Sheridan forming another stupid grin. "Never mind," I said.

"Fair enough."

I couldn't quite tell if Sheridan was still grinning. I didn't say anything for a while, just to see what he would do, but the silence began to grow awkward. "I have a sneaking feeling I've heard this story before," I said. "That–"

"Déjà vu."

"What?"

"Déjà vu," Sheridan said. "It's the feeling of already–"

"I know," I said, and raised my hand. "I've heard the definition before."

"Didn't you say history repeats itself?"

"Yeah, but that's not déjà vu."

"No," Sheridan said. He cracked a smile. "But a great historian once told me, 'history repeats itself,' and–"

"Flattery will get you nowhere."

Sheridan crossed his arms and smirked. "Boy, you're as snippy as a flower."

Sometimes, I wondered if Sheridan was telling his own version of *Groundhog Day*–history repeating itself until things are right.

The notion of a time loop bugged me, but only because it seemed like we were in a perpetual darkness. The car clock read "0:71," so it was clearly broken. The funny thing was that, without the clock, I seemed to have no ability to gauge time.

The scenery didn't help me get my bearings. I saw the same trees and the same road as I'd been staring at for the past few hours. The road kept bobbing up and down, brushing against the sky like a sine curve from Hell. The clouds were lowering, and memories of the flickering light haunted me. *Cloud-to-cloud lightning.* That must have been it.

Sheridan uncrossed his arms and set his annoyance aside, if he'd ever really been annoyed. He resumed prattling on about Mara.

- 35 -

I will see to it . . . that you're happy. Aphrael's words tumbled and turned in Mara's head.

She pulled a leaf from a branch and studied its veins. *I'll even help you get revenge.*

"Revenge," Mara said to the tree. "But I don't want to be a horrible person."

A small flock of birds passed overhead, following the breeze. Mara listened to the trees rustle. She closed her eyes and began to let the sound seep in. A shiver ran down her spine. "Why don't you say anything to me?"

She waited for the trees to speak up. But only the soft brush of wind sounded from the trail.

Mara ran down the trail with her hands cupped around her ears. "Speak! Where did you go?"

Out of breath, Mara stopped in the middle of the road. "Oh, why do I even bother?" she said. "You trees were all mouths and no ears!"

A voice piped up, "One must wonder why you talk to yourself. If it is not the trees who are listening, then your words fall onto only your own ears."

Mara froze. "Did I really hear that?"

"No. You must be insane."

"I was just thinking to myself that—"

"Who else would you be thinking to?" the voice interrupted.

Mara wondered how she could 'think to herself.' "How silly you must think me."

She then wondered if it would be possible to construct a language in which one could not express something that did not make sense—and what a horrible thing it would be if someone succeeded in doing so.

"Yes. Silly. That's what you are," the voice spoke with a slightly harsher tone.

Mara huffed, "I hardly see what is wrong with *that*. I do not believe you are one to judge, for you are a voice without a body, and, until I am convinced otherwise, I have no reason to believe you are anything but a figment of my own imagination."

The voice replied, "Is that a reason to ignore me? We've already established the merits of talking to one's own self. If I am your imagination, then I am you."

"I'd hardly think I would be such poor company. I happen to like me, and any good-mannered girl knows how to keep pleasant company."

"That's what you think, eh?"

"That's what the book or etiquette said. Before I made a paper crane out of the page."

"Well, maybe I don't want to talk to you, either. You seem

to be in a foul mood."

Mara lowered her gaze, but didn't know where to fire it. This only agitated her further, and her eye twitched a bit.

"Hey!" she exclaimed. "I was in a perfectly fine mood until you started picking on me! Thank you very much."

"Well, I am sorry if I spoiled your mood. But it's not every day you see a girl dancing down the trail talking to the trees. It's a rather odd circumstance."

Mara folded her arms and said, "Well, just because you happen to think it's *odd* doesn't give you reason to ruin my fun!"

The voice replied, "I apologize. But if I am your imagination, you have no one to blame but yourself."

"Who's to say you're my imagination?" Mara retorted.

"You said that yourself. Do you admit that I am not your doing?"

Mara looked around and replied, "Curses! Who are you then?"

"I . . . I am an omnipotent shrub."

"*Omnipotent!* Well, now, I hardly think a bush can do more than make a fool of itself to girls strolling in forests."

"*Strolling*, miss Fancy-pants?"

Mara glanced down at her bare legs. "Yes. *Strolling*. If you don't like my verbs, you can pick another and stick it up your vernacular. Whatever the case may be, it's still a lot more than you can do rooted in the ground."

She was starting to wish the trees could only whisper nonsense when she noticed the bush was wiggling. She picked up a rock and threw it as hard as she could. The rock bounced off a branch and hit the ground with a *thud*.

"Verbs and nouns may put me down, but stones will never hurt me," the bush said.

When it laughed and wiggled again, Mara glared and threw another rock. This time, the bush cried, "Ow!"

"Stones will never hurt, huh?"

Mara walked up to the bush. She carefully pulled the leaves aside. A young peasant girl with tattered clothes was squatting in the dirt. "You!" she exclaimed. "You're just having fun with me! You're not omnipotent! You probably can't do anything at all!"

The peasant rubbed her head and looked up. Mara stared into her hazel eyes. For a moment, she wondered if she had seen her before—perhaps in the fields by her old home.

The peasant interrupted her thoughts. She laughed. "I'm sorry!"

"Well, you should be! Aren't you a little old to be playing games with Maras?"

"Maras . . . your name's Mara? Just Mara? How can I tell you apart from all the other Maras?"

Mara cracked a slight smile, then hid it. "Sanghid. If you must know."

"I'm Matta." She smiled. "*Deis.* Matta Deis. But my friends call me Matta."

Mara replied, "Well, Matta Deis . . . I wish you good day."

"Wait!" Matta ran after Mara. "I really didn't mean to offend you. Why were you talking to the trees?"

Mara turned her back to Matta and began to walk off. "You wouldn't believe me, and I don't want to make more of a fool of myself. You'd just laugh at me with your friends, Matta Deis."

Matta watched Mara walk further. She then said, quietly, "I don't have any friends."

Mara stopped. She slowly turned around.

Matta added, "I ran away from home."

Mara nodded and turned away again. She started to walk away, then stopped and looked back. Matta sat on the forest floor with her face hidden in her arms. Mara sighed and walked back to her. The girl looked up. "I'm really sorry. I didn't mean to spoil your mood."

"Feeling sad will help nothing at all," Mara said.

Matta shook her head. Mara reached out and helped Matta to her feet. "Let's go. Before it gets dark."

"Together?" Matta asked.

Mara nodded. She cracked a slight smile. "Forgiving is the sort of thing kind people do."

"I could use a friend right now."

"I could, too," Mara said.

- 36 -

As they walked along the trail, Mara paused every so often to show Matta something she'd observed long ago. Matta often didn't know what Mara was talking about, but she tried to show interest in her new friend.

Mara's words bounced in Matta's head. *And friends share the wisdom they've earned, so they may both be better people.*

"The leaf," Mara held out a large, green leaf. "It has streets, doesn't it?"

"I see ... lines?" Matta wasn't sure what to say. She was nervous she would come across as not being interested, when, in fact, she just didn't understand.

Mara smiled. "Yes! They're streets. See, I grew up on a little farm. But I've read about towns. And roads. And the veins of the leaf don't seem any different."

"I suppose not," Matta said. "I've never been to a town, either. I lived in the fields all my life."

"But why are they the same?" Mara continued. "Surely, people are not flowers nor stems, nor even green!"

Matta laughed.

Mara giggled. "Such a thing would be silly, but I think it shouldn't matter. Green, purple, aquamarine, we all build our streets the same way."

"I suppose, someday, I would like to see a city." Matta's eyes lit up. "A whole city! Full of people and life."

"I'm on my way to Locana," Mara said. "Which, I've heard, is a pretty big city. In fact, it might even be–"

Matta waited for Mara to finish, but Mara cut herself off and stared into space. Matta poked her. "Even be, what?"

"Nothing," Mara said quietly.

"Nothing?" Matta poked her again. "I don't believe that!"

"You'll laugh at me. Or think I'm silly."

"Oh, I already think you're silly," Matta said. "But that's why I like you."

Mara smiled briefly. "Nothing." She held her hand out. "Come, explore the forest with me."

Matta took her hand, and Mara began to run through the trail. "Wait!" Matta exclaimed.

Mara led her around fallen trees, ducking under branches. Matta was about to stop when they burst through a thin veil of vines and into a vast clearing. The sun came out and the world lit up like somebody had just turned it on. Mara released Matta's hand and stretched her arms out, spinning, her hair flying in the wind.

"Where are we?" Matta asked.

Mara stopped, letting her hair drop in front of her face. She turned around and Matta laughed at her. Mara smiled. "Freedom," she said. "This is freedom. It's what you said you wanted, and what I want is to share it with you."

Matta watched the sunbeams in the horizon. "It's beautiful." She took Mara's hand and smiled at her. "Thank you," she whispered.

Mara smiled back and led her through the field.

- 37 -

Mara and Matta continued their way down the trail. Neither were sure what would be waiting at the end, but, for the time being, they didn't care. Matta, feeling quite liberated, danced circles around Mara, singing, "Free! How wonderful is it to be free?"

And Mara bounced about the trail, singing "Free! How wonderful it is to be free!"

Further down the road they heard an ominous moaning. Mara shrieked, "An enemy!"

"I'll protect you!" Matta exclaimed, and picked up the nearest large stick. She waved it around like a feather duster.

"Wait," Mara said.

Matta lowered her weapon.

"Look!" Mara exclaimed.

On the edge of the trail stood a fat little squirrel, opening and closing his mouth. The moaning continued.

"It's a squirrel!" Matta exclaimed.

"What do you think it's doing?" Mara asked.

Matta thought a moment. "Maybe he's hurt."

Mara stared at the squirrel. "No, I think it's . . . it's meditating."

The squirrel kept stretching its jaws, unaware of its company.

"It is!" Mara exclaimed. "It's a meditating squirrel. How exciting."

"I've never seen a squirrel do that," Matta replied.

"Neither have I!" Mara said, "But there he is just the same, achieving harmony. Listen!"

The moaning could still be heard.

Mara stared into the squirrel's beady little eyes. "It's beautiful," she said.

The moaning stopped abruptly. A faint voice sounded. "Morons."

Mara crossed her arms and scolded the squirrel. "If your idea of peace and harmony is to be a little twert, then I must protest!"

Matta swung her stick around. "You should be nice to those who are much larger than you!"

The voice moaned, "No, help."

Mara huffed, "If you want our help, then I suggest you first start by working on your manners."

The squirrel kept stretching its jaws. Mara bent down and tapped its back, after which, the squirrel immediately coughed up a small nut. It quickly scurried off without so much as a "thank you".

Mara said, "Oh dear. I think it was choking."

"I feel as though we've done a good deed, saving that squirrel."

The voice moaned, "How about helping me out?"

"What?" Mara asked. "You're not a squirrel?"

"Of course, I'm not a squirrel!" the voice exclaimed.

"Well, who are you then?" Matta asked.

Mara approached the edge of the road and looked down into the ditch. Inside lay an armor-clad man with blood and dirt smeared on his aging face and gray hair. "Oh, dear me!" Mara exclaimed. "Are you okay?"

The man moaned. "I am quite fine actually. I thought I'd just lie here in this ditch with pinecones shoved up my ass because it helps me contemplate nature."

Mara crossed her arms and stood up straight. "There is hardly any need for sarcasm or vulgarity!"

"Yeah!" Matta exclaimed. "Mara here can contemplate nature just fine without sticks jammed up her rear. I think you've been cheated!"

The man replied, "Will you *please* help me out of here? I think I've broken my arm."

Mara and Matta jumped down into the ditch and carefully helped the man out. Mara removed the pinecones as Matta collected his things from the ditch.

"Who are you?" Mara asked.

"You can call me Sid Strider," the man replied.

Mara began picking twigs and leaves out of his hair. "Sid, huh?"

Matta smiled. "That's what Sid said."

Mara nodded. "That's what Sid *Strider* said, silly."

Sid glared and exclaimed, "You two goof-knockers ball it off!"

Mara and Matta stared at each other silently for a moment, then burst out laughing. Sid continued to glare.

"That's okay," Mara said. "I sometimes have trouble with permutations, too."

Sid began to walk off. "Wait!" Mara called. "We didn't mean to make fun of you."

"Yes, we did," Matta said.

"Oh, well, yes," Mara said. She giggled. "But we didn't mean for you to care!"

"How did you mean for me to take it, then?" Sid asked. "This is very embarrassing!"

Mara smiled. "You're among friends, though! How did you get in the ditch, anyway?"

"If it's any of your business, which it's not, my horse threw me off and ran down the trail. So now, I have to deliver my message by foot."

"Oh!" Mara exclaimed. "*Another* courier!"

"*Knight*," Sid corrected her sternly.

"Sid, the permutatorically-challenged knight!" Matta exclaimed.

"Yes, well, I have business to attend to," Sid said. He gathered his satchels and other belongings with his good arm. "I have a very important message to deliver to the *baron*, thank you very much. I hardly have the time to breeze the shoot with a couple of silly girls."

Matta began to laugh, but Mara quickly put her hand over her mouth. "*Silly*! Silly, you say!"

"Sid *Strider* sternly said so," Matta replied.

As Sid began to fade into the shadows, Mara could hear him muttering words that, until now, she had only heard the flowers say.

12. The Pull of a Single Cord

"It's true," I said. "Those squirrels can be silly little things."

"They're fascinating creatures."

"More like annoying," I said. "When I was in college, some friends talked me into 'squirrel fishing'. You've never seen such a pissed off squirrel."

Sheridan snickered.

"It's not funny!" I protested. "That damned thing spent the rest of the semester throwing nuts at me."

"Sounds like college was the high point of your life."

"Don't go there."

"Oh?" Sheridan tried to hide a smile. "Why–"

"Just tell me about Mara."

Sheridan briefly sat quiet, then shrugged. "Well . . . "

- 38 -

Mara and Matta walked the last mile to the Valley of Lennox in the dark. "Sanreils said there would be an inn here," Mara said.

Matta poked her rib. "*Sanreils* said he'd take care of you."

Mara blushed. "Oh, hush!"

Matta giggled. They stopped in front of a large, dilapidated building. It stood just underneath a large pine tree, lit up by a broken moonbeam. Mara bit her lip. "This *must* be it."

"I don't know," Matta said. She coughed. "There's hardly a light on inside."

Indeed, it seemed like not a single light in the inn was lit. In fact, it didn't seem like anyone was home at all. Mara took a deep breath and knocked on the door. Dust and dirt fell off the cracked wood. She heard, *very* quietly, "Come in."

Mara pushed the door open with a loud creak. Moonlight fell onto a desk, lighting the boy who stood behind it. He watched the doorway with great curiosity, as if he hadn't seen a visitor in weeks.

"Why, *Sanreils* was right!" Matta exclaimed. She jabbed Mara.

Mara shook her head and ignored Matta. "Room, please!"

Matta laughed. "Enough business chit-chat." She stared the boy deep in the eyes. "Tell me. Do you always waddle about in the shadows? I bet you're hiding! Are you homely?"

The boy shook his head. "No, ma'am."

"Be nice," Mara said. She smiled and dropped Sanreils's coins on the desk. "Just for tonight."

The boy stepped out from the shadows to fetch the key. Mara studied him carefully as he walked past. He was short, with light brown hair and eyes. She couldn't get over the feeling she'd seen him before.

"Ooh!" Matta exclaimed. "He's a *looker*!"

The boy blushed, and turned away. He fiddled with the key rack, paying no attention to Mara or Matta. He tossed the key onto the counter. "Here's your key."

"Dahes!" a loud voice sounded from the back room. "Stop fiddling around out there! The linens won't mend themselves!"

The boy turned away without saying another word to his guests. He disappeared into the darkness behind the door.

- 39 -

The room Mara had rented had a bed with a mattress leaking down feathers, and a dresser that was missing one leg and was propped against the wall. She sat down at a desk and studied the various large, unidentifiable stains on its surface. "A girl could really get some thinking done here."

Matta inspected the torn curtains. "*Deep* thoughts," she said, holding up a bit of burned fabric.

Mara stared at the bed, grimaced, and bit her lip.

"Oh, come now, it's not that bad," Matta replied, hopping onto the bed.

She shrieked as it immediately collapsed, exploding in a cloud of down. Mara laughed as Matta struggled to pull herself out of the ruined frame. Mara twirled through the rain of feathers. "Look! It's snowing!"

Matta pulled herself free of the collapsed bed. She looked down at it. "I hope what's-his-name doesn't think we were having a honeymoon up here."

Mara gazed at the feathers with wide eyes.

Matta poked her friend's arm. "Hey! You're supposed to laugh at my funnies. That's what friends *do*!"

"Where do you think the feathers are going?" Mara asked.

"I don't know. They're feathers. I don't think they're going anywhere."

"Sure they are," Mara said. "Feathers aren't alive, are they?"

"Certainly not," Matta replied. "It's probably just the draft from the window."

"Well," said Mara, "There must be some reason the draft shoves them along those exotic paths."

Matta stared at the feathers, humming to herself.

"What if we were all feathers?" Mara said.

"What?" Matta exclaimed.

"I mean, what if the wind was just pushing us along non-sensical paths," Mara explained.

"I don't think the wind can be that strong," Matta replied. "Unless there was some kind of storm."

"No, that's not what I mean!" Mara exclaimed. "I mean a ... a metaphorical wind. Oh, never mind."

Matta watched Mara lose her head in the clouds for a moment before she finally looked away. "Mara ... "

Mara broke her gaze. Matta smiled weakly. "We're friends, right?"

"I'd like to think so." Mara nodded.

"I won't laugh if you tell me why you were talking to the trees," Matta said. Mara frowned as Matta continued, "Or what you think is at end of the road."

"Oh." Mara closed her eyes.

"You can *trust* me," Matta said. "Friends are supposed to share wisdom of their knowledge, or whatever it was you told me."

Mara smiled briefly. "I suppose so." She looked away again. "But it's stupid."

"I'm sorry I made fun of you in the forest," Matta said. "If it's important to you, I want to hear it."

Mara nodded. "I met this woman ... Aphrael. She said her sister got caught up in a cult. So she asked me to prove the world didn't exist."

"What do you mean?" Matta laughed. "How do you prove the world doesn't exist?"

"I read a story about a man named Marcus who was told to do just that," Mara explained. "And for the very same reason. A priestess, Vasigari, wanted him to prove it didn't exist, so that she could be reunited with Ilia."

"Who?"

"Her sister. Marcus was told to travel to SanCullep Island to find her."

"I guess he failed," Matta said. She poked her belly a couple times. "It seems the world is still here."

"Vasigari swore she'd get her way, but she died," Mara said. "Now, Aphrael's asked me to do the same thing."

"If I suggest something, will you get mad at me?"

Mara bit her lip as she thought. "I'd like to think not. But I think it'd depend on what you have to say."

"It's ... " Matta paused. "Maybe this 'Sancullep Island' was just in Marcus's head. And Vasigari was as well."

"Do you think Aphrael is just a figment of my imagination?"

"You read Marcus's book," Matta said. She shrugged. "You got the idea put in your head."

"But Aphrael seemed so *real*."

"Or maybe she knew Sylow? And she's trying to exploit you."

"I think–" Mara sighed. "That's more likely. She knew I was studying nature. She knew I was looking for a sequence. Perhaps she asked one of the other scholars about me, read Marcus's book, and put the two together."

"So, was Marcus's story real? Did those things really happen?"

"It *was* a journal," Mara explained. "But it could be that of a mad man."

"I wish I could read it," Matta said. "I never learned how."

"Oh." Mara turned to her and smiled. "I'll read it to you."

- 40 -

Mara and Matta lay awake in the middle of the night. Every time they were about to nod off, the building creaked. Mara eventually decided she couldn't sleep, regardless. She couldn't push away the thoughts of the glowing city, nor her anticipation that Locana may be it.

"The highway said the ones I loved are at the end of the road," Mara had said earlier, as she'd longingly gazed out the window. "Perhaps the city is what's at the end. And they're there."

"The highway's never spoken to me. It sounds exciting, though! To see all the people you never thought you'd see again."

Matta's words bounced around in Mara's head as she stared into the darkness. She wondered if Sylow was there. She then realized she'd never made any other friends until now.

The ceiling creaked as a loud *thud* echoed through the room. Matta quickly sat up. "What was that?"

The building continued to creak under the sound of footsteps above. "It's the attic," Mara whispered. "Someone's up there."

"It's the wind," Matta said.

The room vibrated as another loud *thud* shook the ceiling. "No!" Mara protested. "There's definitely someone up there."

"Maybe *they're* having a honeymoon," Matta said.

Mara carefully opened the room's door as she forgot to laugh at Matta's funny.

- 41 -

Mara carefully opened the attic trapdoor and peeked inside. It was almost completely dark. Matta thrust her head through the opening. The door swung wildly and slammed into the floor.

"Careful!" Mara whispered.

"Is anything back there?" Matta whispered back. She grabbed a long piece of scrap wood that had fallen to the floor.

The creaks echoed through the attic, seemingly unaware of the girls' presence. Mara whispered, "I think I see something!"

"Behind us?" Matta exclaimed.

She hopped through the door. In the process, she lost her footing and collided with some unlit object.

The object swung down into the door frame just as Mara finished climbing. She looked up and screamed, "Monster!"

Matta, regaining her balance, turned around to stare into the face of a thin, man-like figure with deep red eyes. Mara quickly stepped backward. Unaware the attic door had shut itself, she bounced off the door, fell forward and tripped over Matta's foot.

A third startled scream sounded from the other side of the attic. Matta, in a panic, swung her board just over the top of the monster. She missed, as the monster mysteriously collapsed. The momentum of the heavy wood sent her spiraling. She tripped over Mara and knocked her into the floor.

Mara screamed again as the board barely missed her and landed on top of the monster's scrawny neck, severing its head.

The room suddenly lit up as a startled boy ignited his candles. Mara and Matta struggled to free themselves from the pile.

Mara opened her eyes to stare into the lifeless gaze of a marionette. "It's a puppet!" she exclaimed.

Matta turned to look at the mess. In a heap on the floor was a broken puppet. Its wooden head lay separated from its body among a mess of splinters. Its strings dangled from the ceiling, severed. The boy on the other side of the attic cried out, "Silverstein!"

"Silverstein?" Mara exclaimed.

Matta kicked the puppet's remains away from her. Bits of wood scattered over the floor. "It's you again! Dahes!"

The boy backed up to the wall. "I'm just toying around! Why did you barge in?"

Mara laughed. "You're building little men up here! That is a very peculiar thing to be doing in the middle of the night."

Indeed, the entire attic was full of similar little men. Mara gazed around in wonder at the sight. At least a dozen, maybe more, hung from the rafters below a tangle of strings and ropes. The ropes appeared to be hung from crude pulleys, suggesting there was some way to move the puppets about. Each puppet was built from scrap wood and knick-knacks: old barrel tops, twigs, branches, and even an old shield. Eyes and mouths were painted, showing various expressions. Silverstein, appropriately, was in a state of shock.

Matta explained, "We thought you were a monster."

"I'm sorry," Dahes said. "I'm just very bored, and when I can't sleep, I come up here and make puppets."

Matta said in a slow, deep voice, "You are a very strange individual."

"Oh, he's not strange," Mara said. She smiled and continued, "It is your nature. And one shouldn't deny their nature."

Dahes smiled. Mara looked down at the remains of Silverstein. Splinters and other bits of puppet littered the floor. "I'm terribly sorry we broke your little man."

"It's okay," Dahes said. "I didn't mean to keep you awake."

"I think you just wanted us to come up and play." Matta nodded to herself. "But you'd have to play with me. *Mara* is in lo-o-ove!"

Mara blushed and pushed Matta aside. Matta laughed and stepped into the doorway. "Well, *I'm* going to get some sleep." She winked at Dahes. "I'll see *you* in the morning."

Mara chuckled as she watched Dahes turn red.

"Coming?" Matta asked Mara.

Mara pulled a few of the dangling strings. On the other side of the room, a pulley creaked. "In a moment."

Matta disappeared.

"She's just having fun with you," Mara said. She smiled. "So, why puppets?"

"Uh ... I can't sleep," Dahes said. "I know it sounds strange, but when I can't sleep, I feel like I should be doing something productive. I suppose you could call it a hobby."

Mara pulled one of the ropes which dangled from the ceiling. The arms of a puppet on the other side of the room started to wiggle. "It's quite elaborate," she said.

Mara sat down on the broken puppet heap and twirled the strings around her fingers. Dahes tugged on a rope, which lifted her arms a bit. Mara stared up at the ceiling, which supported more pulleys and gears than she'd originally noticed. Mara gasped.

"Neat, isn't it?" Dahes asked.

"It's magnificent!" Mara exclaimed. "You have a regular army up here."

"That's nothing," Dahes boasted. He started pulling on a vast array of ropes and levers. A line of puppets along the wall started to kick up their feet and wave their arms in a dancing motion. The floor creaked under their rhythmic steps. Mara clapped her hands.

"So, you've been up here dancing puppets!" Mara exclaimed.

"I'm not sure what I'm going to do with them all," Dahes said. "It's just to pass the time."

Mara nodded.

"Who are you, anyway?" Dahes asked.

"Mara." She smiled. "Sanghid. And that was my friend, Matta."

"I see," said Dahes. "I must ask, why stay here, of all places? I don't see many guests."

"We're on an adventure!" Mara exclaimed. "A quest for knowledge and truth."

Dahes smiled. "Sounds noble. When I turn nineteen, I will go to the university." He spoke loudly, with determination, but then dropped his voice. "At least, I'd like to. I'm not allowed to leave."

Mara nodded enthusiastically. "I'm on my way to Locana," she said. "And from there, maybe the world."

"The world?" Dahes asked.

Mara swung around one of the puppets. "Ever wonder what it is all about?"

"Probably a little too often," Dahes said. He pulled on the various cords.

Mara smiled. She lay down on the floor and watched the puppets dance around the room. "This is a fascinating place."

Dahes pulled more cords. Mara gazed at the rhythmic dance.

"I think the whole world is full of puppets," Dahes said. "None of them have any true will. They just follow whoever controls the strings."

"It's still beautiful," Mara said. "The way they mingle together. Such simple actions make such intricate dances."

A gentle breeze pushed through the attic vent, knocking the marionette pieces into each other. Mara thought about how much their sound resembled the click-clack of the wagons on the road.

When the wind quieted down, Mara looked away and giggled. "If I could build anything, I would try ... well ... what would happen if I made all the puppets dance to the pull of a single cord?"

"That would be quite a feat," Dahes said. "But amazing to watch."

"It would require quite a few pulleys," Mara said. She looked up at the roof again. "It'd have to be *very* complex. Or else you wouldn't get a very interesting show out of these little fellows."

"I suppose not," Dahes said. "The way I have it . . . each cord doesn't do much."

Mara nodded. She turned around and, having bumped into another puppet, jumped. "Do you ever get scared up here?" she asked. "These things are creepy in the dark."

"I do not," Dahes said, shaking his head. "They're all strung, anyway."

"But what if one broke free?" Mara asked. She looked toward the fallen puppet.

"I would kill it!" Dahes said.

"Why?" Mara asked. "A living puppet! Wouldn't that be a grand sight?"

"Well, I suppose, it would try to free its fellow puppets," Dahes said.

Mara sat up. "What's so bad about that?"

"The other puppets would fall because they'd no longer be strung," Dahes replied. "That, and I would no longer be able to make them dance."

Mara frowned. "That would be sad. It is a lovely show."

Dahes nodded.

Mara and Dahes sat on the floor, watching the puppets swing and sway.

"Dahes," Mara said. "You're very strange . . . making all these puppets."

"Mara," Dahes replied. "You've very unusual . . . sitting here, thinking about the puppets."

Mara smiled. "I just find it curious and wondrous. I love nature, and how the world just seems to work so brilliantly."

"Puppets can hardly be found in nature," Dahes said.

Mara jumped up and tugged at one of the puppets. "I disagree!" she proclaimed. She hoisted herself with the cord and started swinging around. "What if it were all clockwork?"

"What?" Dahes asked.

Mara danced around the puppets, pulling their cords and swinging and twirling around the moving limbs. "There's such a perfect ... beautiful harmony in the world! Wouldn't it be a grand thing to find the cord, and give it a tug? To watch it all unfold and explode in a brilliant cast of rays?"

Dahes protested, "I'd be afraid."

Mara climbed up on one of the cords and swung. Her weight on the vast maze of lines caused the other puppets to move in bizarre patterns. "Afraid of what?" she asked.

"Well ... I don't believe that there's anything resembling a 'cord' in nature," Dahes said. "But if there were, I would be hesitant not to leave it be."

Mara laughed, forcing herself to swing higher and making the puppets spin and dance in complex patterns. She sang, "Wouldn't it be amazing to open up the world and see what is inside? To dance in its rays and hold it in your palm? Wouldn't it be wonderful ... to be a part of it all?"

"Mara! Watch out " Dahes exclaimed.

The puppets, dancing in increasingly complex patterns, had begun to tangle with each other. As Mara began to hoist herself higher, the line snapped. She screamed as she crashed to the floor.

Dahes ran over to her. "Are you okay?" he asked repeatedly.

Mara sat up and studied the lines above her, attempting to put together the latest chain of events. "What happened?" she asked.

Dahes sighed. "You broke the line."

"Oh," Mara said quietly. "I'm sorry. I don't seem to be successful at staying out of mischief."

"It's fine," Dahes said.

"No," Mara sighed, shaking her head. "I feel really bad."

Dahes looked up at the lines. "The owner tears them down every few days, anyway."

"What?" Mara asked. "Why?"

"I live here in return for working downstairs during the day," Dahes said. "I'm an orphan. This is my only home."

"Oh," Mara said, not quite sure what else to say.

Dahes added, "But I want to leave! Like you said, be free! And that means, I need to go to the university."

"Oh! I'm sure *Matta* would love for you to join us. You're interesting."

Dahes laughed. "No one has called me 'interesting' before. Eccentric, maybe."

Mara shook her head. "Anyone who builds puppets for fun is most definitely interesting."

"I'd love to join you," Dahes said. "But I'm obligated to work here. I can't just up and leave."

"Oh, sure you can!" Mara exclaimed.

Dahes shook his head. "Naomi, the owner–she'd have my head! She says I owe her for my lodging. But the more I work, the more I lodge! And the further I sink into debt."

Mara grinned. "Come find us in the morning. I think we can settle your debt."

"How?"

"Oh, I have my ways." Mara winked.

13. A Man Made of Wood

Sheridan smiled. "So. Mara learned her first great lesson!"

"Not to dangle from hanging ropes?" I said. "Does she desire to connect with her inner pancake?"

"Well ... maybe," Sheridan said. "But dangling is fun! And so is swinging. But, no. That's not what she learned."

"She's weird," I said.

Sheridan smiled. "She *learned* about the idea that everything is connected!"

I lifted an eyebrow. "Puppets ... you mean?"

"A device!" Sheridan exclaimed. "An underlying *something* that somehow gives rise to the harmony of nature."

I scratched my head. "A cord?"

"Sort of like an *Equation of Everything*," Sheridan said.

"I don't understand."

"The *Equation of Everything* is supposed to unify the four fundamental forces of nature," Sheridan said. "And if you could find the cord, and control it, you could be the master of nature."

"Sounds silly," I said. "If that were true ... I'm sure someone would have found it a long time ago."

Sheridan shook his head. "Nothing enters the world pre-discovered. *Someone* has to find it. So, why not Mara in the attic?"

"She's moody," I said.

"Oh . . . she's not moody," Sheridan protested. "You have to admit . . . she's had a rough time."

"Okay. I'll give her that," I said.

"Only a small bit of time had passed since she'd lost everything," Sheridan said. "In fact, she was a bit homesick . . . "

- 42 -

Early the next morning, Mara walked around the hotel grounds. She admired the sunrise and wondered where the sun disappeared to every night. Every so often, her thoughts turned toward home, and she wondered if her father and mother were watching the same sunrise. She wondered if her father missed her.

She stopped at the back edge of the inn, just before the clearing met the woods. The trees stood silent, but Mara was more in the mood to be listened to, than to listen herself. "A funny thing happened last night," she said. "I saw the most amazing machine. Dozens of puppets strung to pulleys and gears. And all of them moved in reaction to a single cord."

The trees continued to stand, silent and motionless. Mara shrugged. "It was just strange, that's all. Like Aphrael described, I learned how it worked, then broke it. But I don't think she was referring to puppets."

Mara waited, secretly hoping for a response. When she got none, she continued. "Do you think she was talking about people? Are people like puppets? Nobody I've met seems so predictable, or controllable."

A quiet voice whispered, "Hello . . . "

Mara froze. Her heart skipped a beat. She collected herself and looked around. A soft breeze blew across the land. Perhaps it was only the wind.

Mara's ears perked up. She heard it again. "Hello-o-o . . . "

She looked around again, just to make sure nobody was hiding. Her eyes stopped at a little wooden puppet. It sat still, slumped over a small woodpile, staring at her. The metal rims of its barrel body gleamed in the sunlight. "It's *you*, isn't it?"

The puppet smiled. "Did you not see me before?"

"I'm sorry," Mara said. She stared at the ground, feeling a bit ashamed. "I'm not used to talking to barrels. Usually, they're for storing things, not for making friends."

The puppet sat still for a moment, and Mara began to wonder if she'd offended it. It then said, "I think I love you."

Mara's eyes grew wide. She looked to her left and right. She pointed to herself and quietly asked, "Me?"

"I don't see anyone else here," the puppet replied.

"I ... don't know what to say," Mara said.

The puppet shook its head. "You don't love me."

Mara, still *very* shocked, could only bring herself to say, "I ... "

The puppet interrupted her. "You're very pretty."

Mara blushed. "But ... " she said. "You're a man made of wood!"

"You don't think you could love a man made out of wood?" the puppet asked. "Is it the leaf? Does the leaf turn you off?"

Indeed, growing upon the puppet's right arm was a small, green leaf. It flapped gently in the breeze, suggesting, like the cat's tail, it had a mind of its own. Mara stared at it and smiled briefly. She then bit her lip. "I'm not a bad person! Please don't think that! And I love your little leaf. It's cute! But ... "

The puppet raised an eyebrow. Mara said, "I don't think I could love a man who would give me termites."

The puppet folded its arms across its chest and glared at her. "And just *what* makes you think I'd give you termites?"

"I . . . " She paused, at a loss for words.

The puppet scolded her. "Perhaps it is I who should be afraid of you! For what if you gave me some kind of human-disease . . . like the flu! Can you imagine me, a man of wood, coughing up twigs and splinters? It's preposterous!"

Mara sighed. "What can I say? Love is a very complicated emotion."

"You know what *I* think?" the puppet said. "I think you already found a suitor."

"What? No." Mara stomped her foot on the ground. Her cheeks turned pink. "Not true!"

"Ah *ha*," the puppet said. Its leaf jiggled as it let out a hearty laugh. "Then, tell me why you're headed to Locana."

"I–" Mara stumbled on her words. "It's just–"

"There you are!" Matta exclaimed as she appeared from around the corner.

Mara shrieked and whirled around. "Oh! It's you."

"I thought you were going to distract Naomi!" Matta smirked. "*Remember*? Dahes and I were supposed to sneak out."

"I was at the side of the building, by the kitchen door, like we planned," Mara said. "But the puppet! It fell in love with me!"

Matta held her face in her hand and sighed.

"It's true!" Mara protested. She pointed to the puppet, which lay in a heap of angles most humans would find tremendously disagreeable. "But our children would have so many weird angles; I think birthing would be a bit unpleasant. Plus, I would have to remember to paint them every spring, and who has time for that?"

Matta took Mara's hand and led her away. "Come on," she said. "*I* will go haggle with Naomi over the price of the bread. You tell Dahes when she's away from the counter."

- 43 -

The breeze in the clearing gently rocked the tall grass back and forth. High above, the leaves played in the same breeze, running amok on their branches. Thick, gray clouds hung low, moving swiftly across the sky. Frequent breaks allowed white sunrays to poke through, forming spotlights across the green terrain.

"The clouds." Mara pointed upward as the she rested in the grass. "Have you ever noticed anything odd about them?"

Dahes squinted, trying not to look into the sun.

Matta laughed. "That cloud! It looks like a bunny!"

"Oh!" Dahes exclaimed. "With three ears?"

Matta nodded.

"No, no," Mara said. "Well, yes. I see the bunny! It's very cute. But that's not what *I* see."

"*I* think it's funny that we can all make different pictures out of the same thing," Dahes said. He smiled, pleased with himself.

"I see a pattern," Mara said. "See, the sizes of the clouds as they roll over the horizon . . . they're different. But they're a pattern just the same. Big, small, huge . . . "

"Bunny," Matta interrupted. Dahes laughed.

"I'm being serious!" Mara exclaimed. "It's very unsettling!"

"All right," Matta said. "What's so bad about it?"

Mara looked away. "They're hiding something. I just know it."

"Well, I'm going to go move our things out of the field before it starts to rain," Matta said. She stood up, winked at Dahes, and motioned for him to follow.

"You don't believe me!" Mara exclaimed. She sat up and stared at Matta. "That hurts."

Matta wasn't listening. She reached down and grabbed Dahes's hand, giggling as he blushed slightly. His face grew more red at her reaction. "Stop being so shy!" she said, and tugged at his hand.

Suddenly, Mara felt very alone. She lay back in the grass and watched the world unfold. She listened to the leaves' rustling as the trees swayed. Bluebirds and redbirds flapped and pecked at a nearby bush. *How silly are the birds,* Mara thought. *They squabble so much over a little bit of food.*

Mara sighed. *Oh, how I wish I could fly and see the world from above.*

Quiet thunder rolled over the field. The wind grew cooler and quicker, and the intensifying rustling of the trees scared the birds away.

"I wonder where the wind comes from?" Mara said, mostly to herself, but secretly hoping someone would overhear and join her. "And for what reason do the clouds follow their ways?"

The frequency of the sunrays began to decline as the sky darkened. The luscious, green glow of the forest began to dim.

"I wish Master Sylow could have seen this," Mara said. "He would have been interested."

Mara looked over at the nearby highway. "It is such a long road to travel."

"Just keep following," the highway said. "Keep following."

"I'm scared," Mara replied. "I'm scared of what lies between here and the end."

"No one blames you for feeling that way," the highway replied. "The world can be a scary place sometimes."

"I do," Mara sighed. "I blame myself because this world is so fascinating and beautiful, and I will miss that if I'm scared. Please tell me not to be scared."

"I can't tell you to not be scared," the highway said. "I can't tell you how to feel."

"I suppose not," Mara said.

"But what I can tell you ... " the highway said, pausing to think, "is that it's your choice, and the world is as you see it."

The sky darkened further. Rain sprinkled down, splashing the forest floor. Thunder echoed closer, roaring off the nearby mountains.

"I haven't much left, and I have nothing foreseeable awaiting me." Mara tried to hold back the flood of emotion, but the dam burst. She buried her face in her arms and cried.

"Just keep following the trail, and I'll take you where you need to go," the highway said. "I'll show you the world like you wanted. Isn't that what you still want?"

Mara looked up and was about to reply, but saw Matta and Dahes instead. They stood nearby, watching her. She would never forget that look–they clearly had no clue what to say or think of their new friend.

14. When There's Trouble Afoot

Sheridan paused for a moment.

"I can't say I'd disagree with Matta or Dahes," I said. "I'd be weirded out, too."

"Oh?" I thought I saw Sheridan crack a smile, then hide it. "Do you think it's weird that she's upset?"

"I think it's weird she was talking to a *highway*."

Sheridan hummed a bit, and traded glances between me and the road. "I don't think that's weird."

"And talking to puppets?"

"You think it's odd she turned down the puppet?"

"Well, okay. You got me there. I don't think I could love a man who would give me termites, either."

Sheridan smiled.

"*Woman!*" I said. "I don't think I could love a *woman* who would give me termites."

"It doesn't matter," Sheridan said. "Unlike other western languages, in English, there are no log men or log women. Only *logs*."

"Oh good. Because, when I'm asked to think of advocates for gender equality, the first thing that comes to my mind are medieval Germanic tribes."

Sheridan laughed. "So, despite the fact that the little wooden man was quite enamored with Mara, she had to bid it farewell."

"Well ... good," I said. "He's too good for her ... she's picky."

"Oh?" Sheridan asked. "Do you have an inclination toward the love of puppet-people?" He tilted his head the other way and lifted his other eyebrow.

I glared at him. "I *really* hate you."

Sheridan laughed again. He exclaimed, "The universe is old and, by comparison, mankind is quite young! There are always new discoveries to be made!"

Without anything to add to that, I let Sheridan continue his story ...

- 44 -

Mara walked the rest of the way to Locana feeling rather uneasy. Dahes, she decided, had only a fleeting curiosity in the world–a curiosity that was always cut off by Matta. Matta seemed to only care about teasing Dahes. She wondered if they felt sorry for her, and otherwise, wouldn't care for her companionship in the least.

The forest seemed to go on forever, growing denser and denser. The trail narrowed, and soon, was only slightly larger than the width of a carriage.

"It's like a tunnel," Matta said. She elbowed Dahes, and they both giggled at some joke that was part of their private world.

Mara rolled her eyes and let it go.

Then, almost instantly, the city came into view. Matta, who had been chatting with Dahes, suddenly became silent. "It's ... more than I ever thought I'd see," she said. She turned to Dahes, smiled, and took his hand.

They had stopped at the edge of a clearing, overlooking the City of Locana. Mara's heart froze with anticipation. Perhaps this was the city which shone brightly.

The buildings seemed larger than Mara thought man could ever build, with tall spires and arches extending into the sky.

"I think I see ... the university!" Dahes exclaimed. He pointed to a large structure just off the center of the city, on the southern side–a connected group of eight towers surrounding a large hall. "It looks just like I read."

"It's ... interesting," Mara said. She started to smile, but decided it would be best to keep it to herself.

She looked further down. Though they had a marvelous view from where they stood, they were still quite far. Between them and Locana, the clearing ended and another spot of forest rose. Mara estimated it would take an hour and a half, maybe two hours, to make the rest of the journey by foot.

Matta was the first to bring up an oversight–a practical matter all three of the adventurers had overlooked. "So ... it's a lovely city. But where are we going to stay?"

- 45 -

By dusk, they'd made it to another open field in the middle of the woodlands. The woods seemed to be full of clearings, like a slice of Swiss cheese. The field consisted of a single large hill that stood out like a camel hump in an otherwise flat land. Tall pine trees grew around the borders of the field in a nearly perfect circle, obscuring the view of the mountains. Standing at the center of the hill was a crumbling, dilapidated tower. The gray, cylindrical stone structure stood four stories high, with the top floor missing most of its rock wall. The rest of it was rebuilt out of half-rotten, wooden planks, with crude windows cut out. There were no windows on the bottom three floors.

A small sign read, "Thorn Tower."

"See!" Mara said. "It's an inn!"

Matta hummed quietly and stared at the building with a goofy grin. "Not a very romantic getaway."

"What? Who said anything about romance?" Dahes said.

Matta whispered something to him.

He whispered "Oh!" as Mara complained about being left out.

Matta burst out laughing. "It's Sid! Sid *Strider*!"

Indeed, Sid had just stepped out of the tower when he saw Mara and Matta. His face drooped.

"Sid!" Matta shouted. "Sid *Strider*! I see–"

Sid interrupted, "What? What is it! Are you following me?"

Mara laughed. "Coincidence! Tell us, how are the rooms?"

Matta elbowed Mara and was about to whisper, when Sid shouted back, "What rooms?"

"At the inn, silly!" Mara exclaimed. She pointed to the sign.

Sid pointed toward the trail. "I don't know about any inn. Whatever it was, Baron's turned it over to me."

Sid paused, stared at the tower for a moment, and made a disgusted face. "Lookout, is what he said. In any case, you two numb-duds need to scram."

"Numb-duds!" Mara exclaimed. "Wait. It's empty."

Sid pointed toward the trail again. Matta protested. "Oh! It'd be a terrible thing for you to get lonely."

"I can entertain myself just fine," Sid replied.

"Come on," Mara said. "We saved your life! Remember? How long would you have been in the ditch had it not been for us?"

Sid stared blankly for several moments, then sighed. He motioned for them to approach as he shook his head. "*Just* until the baron commissions the building for the guards. And don't you speak about it. To anyone."

"Who's he?" Dahes whispered. Matta could only bring herself to giggle and shake her head.

"So, did you get your message delivered?" Mara asked. "That was fast!"

"If it's any of your business, which it's not, I did." Sid smirked. "You three should be careful."

"Oh?" Dahes looked up, away from the surroundings. "Here?"

"In the woods," Sid replied. "That's what the message was. A couple days ago, there were two fires in the woods. It looks like murder."

"Oh dear," Matta said. Her usual menacing grin dropped. "Who would've thought Fordham Forest was such a dangerous place."

Mara's heart fluttered, then froze. She knew what Sid was about to say. "No. Carrboro Forest. It's further north, but you three be careful just the same. When there's trouble afoot–"

The next few moments passed at half-speed. Mara's world began to cloud, and her vision lost focus. She cut Sid off, stuttering, "T-two?"

"Two?" Sid asked. "Oh, yes. Off the old mill route; a cottage and a small farm a mile further back."

15. You're Real, Aren't You?

"Ho ho ho," I said. "It's a good thing she ran away from home."

"*Ho ho ho*," Sheridan repeated.

"Yes," I said. "Ho ho ho. Is that odd?"

"Are you Santa?"

"Never mind."

"A pirate?"

"No."

"A pirate Santa?"

"Just *continue*."

"Well, you're a mean one, Mr. Grinch," Sheridan said. "Maybe I don't want to talk to you if you're going to be a 'Sour Sally'."

"So I'm a 'Sour Sally', huh?"

"Certainly seems so—"

"Don't start that up again. I almost lost it with all of Matta's alliterations."

Sheridan laughed. "Don't blame me for that."

We rounded another corner as our descent from the hills of southwest Virginia continued. I was never quite sure what I'd find around each bend. I kept imaging running into a deer, but the cynical part of me said there weren't any. Sheridan and I were the last ones left in the world. And all I had to keep me occupied were his stupid jokes.

"Mara finally made it to Locana," Sheridan said. "For a while, she wondered if it was the glowing city she'd envisioned. While she investigated, she set off to find Sanreils ... "

- 46 -

Mara walked slowly through the streets of Locana. She wished Sanreils had told her where to meet him. The thought to ask had never crossed her mind; she'd never anticipated Locana would be so large.

As she explored, a hundred thoughts bounced in her head like bingo balls, the chosen one's moment in the spotlight fleeting.

She stopped in the middle a large square, the intersection of Franklin Road and Knights of Columbia Highway. Never in her life had she seen so many people. She couldn't get over the contrast to the forests she'd always been surrounded by.

Shops lined the streets, with signs full of vibrant colors. Buildings of various shapes and sizes crowded the thoroughfare. *This is a city,* she thought, and was immediately struck by the peculiarity of the crowd.

The people spoke all at once, their voices mingling and dancing as they stirred into a single unintelligible mass. *It's just like the whispering forest!* Mara thought. But something seemed different.

Thoughts of her ruined home, her new life, and her isolation in the world disappeared in a rush of noise. Mara was glad for that, but thoughts of the people left her feeling uneasy.

She shook her head, and scolded herself. "Thoughts don't leave like water from the body of a wet dog, silly!"

A passing citizen stopped and looked at her curiously. Mara blushed slightly and turned away. "I wasn't talking to you," she said, but the man paid her no attention as he went on his way.

A large fountain stood in the center of the square, adjoining a small, abandoned booth. The architecture struck her as odd. It looked like it had been repaired many times over the course of several centuries. She wondered if it dated back as far as the Romans.

Water sprayed from the top of an obelisk, set just far enough off center that the structure more or less failed to please the eye. Mara found it so peculiar, she stepped into the fountain to get a closer look. The water was only an inch deep.

She moved further into the fountain and discovered the most wonderful feature. The water spray formed a little curtain, hiding her from the people in the square. Nobody walking past seemed to find it odd that a girl was standing in the fountain, not caring about getting wet. She concluded that they must not be able to see her at all, at least, not when looking casually.

But Mara could see the streets quite clearly. She watched the square with a close eye as the uneasy feeling that something was amiss returned. As she observed the townspeople's motions, she realized why the voices were different than that of the whispering forest.

She thought of the "No People" Marcus had described. *They walk with their eyes shaded and their ears plugged*, Mara thought, *as if they were fixed on a course.*

The voices of the people were more systematic than the voices of the forest. She no longer saw a thousand individual people; she saw a thousand gears in one machine. Mara realized the Locanans were quickly gliding along a set track, like the mechanisms of a finely tuned pocket watch. She looked down at herself. She studied her hands and felt her face. A chill ran down her back. *Am I the only real person here?*

She thought of Dahes's puppets. Aphrael's words, "Find them, and break them," ricocheted in her mind.

The Locanans moved, guided by an invisible cord. Her heart sank as a sudden loneliness set in. There were no souls to connect with here.

Mara hopped out of the fountain and ran up to a man, a trader pulling a cart into town. She touched his face. "You're real, aren't you?"

The man didn't respond. Mara shook him. "Answer me!" she exclaimed.

The man stopped when she blocked his way, but he remained silent, frozen in place. "Answer me, damn it!" Mara exclaimed.

She hopped into his cart, picked up the contents, and threw them in the air. When the man didn't respond, only resuming his silent march, Mara screamed and jumped out of the cart. She ran through the square, shouting, in tears, "Someone answer me! Someone! Help me!"

She fell to her knees in the center of the square. She hunched over and sobbed.

"Mara?" she heard.

She looked up. Sanreils stood above her, staring with a concerned gaze. Mara glanced around. The entire square had stopped, and all the townspeople were watching her. The man by the cart gaped at her, bewildered, among the pile of what she'd thrown from his cart.

Sanreils reached out and helped Mara to her feet. He held her face and wiped the dirt away from her eyes. "Mara, dear," he spoke softly. "What happened?"

Mara looked behind her. She suddenly felt very embarrassed and confused. She closed her eyes and shook her head.

"Mara," Sanreils said. He put his arm around her and began leading her away. "You're safe, now."

As Mara stepped out of the square, she quickly looked

behind her. The townspeople had resumed their business. As she studied them one last time, she realized she knew where they would go.

The trader, she thought, *will turn left onto Rosemary Road.*

When the trader did, indeed, turn left, Mara faced forward and walked as close to Sanreils as she could.

III
See Yourself

16. Don't Talk to Her

Sheridan stopped his story as I began to pull off the highway. "Where are we going?" he asked.

"Bathroom," I said.

"Say no more."

He remained quiet as we drove through the streets of the quaint little side-town. Without his story to tell, he seemed quite fidgety. "You can continue," I said.

Sheridan shook his head. "I'll wait until we can go uninterrupted."

I watched him out of the corner of my eye. For a while, I debated with myself over whether he was over-caffeinated, or whether he just really needed a bathroom break as well.

We entered an intersection as the signal light turned yellow. Sheridan nearly flew out of his seat.

"Yikes!" I exclaimed. "Calm down!"

"Sorry," Sheridan said.

"No more coffee for you," I said. "There wasn't a cop around ... was there?"

Sheridan was already looking behind, out the back window. "No," he said. "There's nobody. Why? Are you on the run from the law?"

"Nobody?" I noticed he was right. Being the middle of the night, I wouldn't really expect anyone to be about. But now that he'd pointed it out, I realized we hadn't passed a single soul since leaving North Carolina. I tried to shrug it off. "I just have five points on my license already."

"My, my," Sheridan exclaimed. "Lead-foot Bartlebee."

"Actually, the last two were from running red lights."

"You shouldn't run red lights," Sheridan said. "When the road wants you to stop, you should."

"Yes, I know," I said. "We've all seen *Wheels of Tragedy*."

I pulled around to the side of a gas station. The lights were off. At least the bathroom was left unlocked.

I watched myself in the mirror as I cleaned up. There was something odd about my reflection that I couldn't put my finger on, like it wasn't me. I shook my head and cursed Sheridan. I stepped out.

"*Boo!*"

I jumped back and hit the wall. "What did you do *that* for?"

"Sorry," Sheridan smiled. "I had to go, too."

I returned to the car and contemplated driving off without him.

While I waited, I mulled over the last installment of Sheridan's tale, and how much Aphrael resembled Vasigari. When I thought about it, it made sense to think that Aphrael *was* Vasigari. Marcus's tale had ended with Vasigari swearing she'd get her way. And the Locanans seemed very much like the No People. Maybe La Nocturne was Ilia's cult.

Sheridan ran up to the car and hopped in, grinning and laughing to himself.

"Do you think it's weird," I said, "that Vasigari swore death wouldn't get in her way, and then Aphrael–will you wipe that stupid grin off your face?"

Sheridan laughed and shook his head.

"What?" I asked. "You're up to something."

Sheridan shook his head again. "So," he said, still grinning. "You're one of *those* people."

"Huh?"

"You're one of those people who makes toilet seat protectors out of strips of toilet paper," Sheridan cackled.

"What's wrong with that?" I asked. "I'm health conscious."

Sheridan argued, "Inevitably, someone will miss. Then *bam*! No more toilet seat for the rest of the day."

"Well, I, for one, can't be blamed for the nature of human behavior."

"You could clean it up! Push the paper into the bowl. And flush. It's not too hard."

"Ewww! I don't want to touch that. My butt's been on it."

"Yes," Sheridan muttered. "Well, let's get back on the road, then. Get your rear in gear."

"I suppose I'll now have to hear every possible joke on the matter," I said.

"Unless, of course, you agree to help me wipe out this problem," Sheridan said. "We can put an end to it."

"Okay, okay. What about the Locanans?"

"Do you have concerns that need to be flushed out?"

"Never mind," I said. "Just go on."

- 47 -

Mara lay on her back in the grass outside Thorn Tower. She watched the clouds roll slowly over the horizon and disappear behind the tree-tops. They were very small clouds, numerous and scattered like ants. "Hello, clouds!" she exclaimed. "I trust you're doing well, today."

But the clouds seemed not to hear her. *How fascinating it would be to live like a cloud!* Mara thought. *Except, I don't think I'd care too much for feeling bloated all day, nor the feeling of birds flying in my tummy.*

Her thoughts then diverted to food, and the empty pantry in the tower. She stood and was about to go looking for some berry bushes when she heard a voice from behind: "Hello."

Mara shrieked. She spun around, let out a second scream, and, before she'd identified her, punched Aphrael square in the nose. After she realized what she'd done, she screamed again. "I'm sorry! I'm sorry!"

"Mara!" Sanreils exclaimed. He came running from the tower. "Dear! Are you okay?"

Mara looked around. Aphrael had disappeared. She caught her breath. "Yes ... "

"You were screaming bloody murder!" Sanreils exclaimed. He caught up to her and slowed down. "I thought you were dying or something."

Mara rubbed her eyes and looked about again. No Aphrael. "Sorry," she said. "Aphrael ... erm, this woman, snuck up on me and–"

"Oh!" Sanreils exclaimed.

"Aphrael? Do you know her?"

He nodded. "Don't talk to her! She's trouble."

"Trouble ... " Mara said.

"Yes."

Mara stared blankly into the woods. Her fingers tingled with a slight pain. She glanced down and flexed them, then wondered if Aphrael would be mad.

"Why are you staring at your hand?" Sanreils asked. He took Mara's hand and looked closely at her fingers. He raised his voice slightly. "Did she hurt you?"

"No," Mara said quietly. "I punched her."

Sanreils began to laugh. "You *punched* her?"

"I didn't mean to! She sort of snuck up on me."

Sanreils laughed harder. "Oh! I wish I could have seen that."

Mara cracked a forced smile and laughed hesitantly. *"Pow!* Right in the, um, nose."

Sanreils put his arm around her. "Oh, Mara, dear. You are one of a kind."

"I try to be," she nodded. "That way you won't confuse me with all the other Maras."

"Well, I'm glad to see you're feeling better." Sanreils took her hand and motioned for her to follow.

Mara's heart skipped a beat as she felt her hand in his. She didn't speak as he quietly led her to the edge of the clearing, where he'd tied his horse. He kissed her hand and hopped onto the animal. "Mara, dear," he said.

Mara looked up, but couldn't bring herself to speak.

"The baron is hosting a banquet; a rather exquisite affair, I believe."

Mara nodded.

"I want you to accompany me."

Mara nodded her head again, vigorously, although she wished she could hide her excitement.

Sanreils looked toward the trail briefly, then back. "And I was thinking, perhaps, I'd like to begin a courtship."

Mara's heart fluttered. "Oh?" she whispered. "Of whom?"

Sanreils smiled gently. He bent down, brushed fallen strands of hair out of her eyes, and stroked her cheek. "I think you know who."

Mara closed her eyes and whispered, "I would like that very much."

"I thought as such."

Mara smiled.

"Then, the banquet?" Sanreils asked. "You shall accompany me?"

Mara could only bring herself to nod once more.

"Very well, then," Sanreils said. He tipped his hat and charged down the trail.

After he left, Mara whispered, "I wouldn't miss it for the world."

17. It's Fine, Now

"Wait," I said. "Did you mean the same baron Mara's father wanted her to marry?"

"Caraloni Rutsan," Sheridan smiled and nodded. "After Sanreils had left, that thought crossed Mara's mind."

"And she wouldn't be weirded out?"

"Well, it's not like her father ever introduced them. It was an idea, that's all. He was full of them and hardly any really made sense."

"Mara is weird," I said.

"We're all weird," Sheridan answered. He leaned his seat back a bit and crossed his arms behind his head. "If you think about it, that is."

"I don't think I'm weird," I said.

"You think there are numerous *traveling professors* in this world?"

"What? It's a *great* job," I said. "How is it any different than a traveling motivational speaker?"

"Do you ever get lonely being on the road all the time?"

"No," I said. "Definitely–"

"I disagree." Sheridan cackled, very slightly. "And I think that's why you picked me up off the side of the road."

"What? No–"

"Yes, yes," Sheridan said. He sat up straight and tugged at a loose corner of the ceiling's fabric.

"Just go on," I said. "What happened to Mara?"

137

"You can admit it," he said. "I was lonely, too, thinking about heading on such a long journey. It's okay to–"

"*Just* go on," I repeated.

Sheridan didn't say anything, which was fine by me. I gripped the steering wheel and tried to focus on the road. I heard a subtle *scratch*, and out of the corner of my eye, I saw Sheridan still tugging at the lining.

"And stop playing with the ceiling!" I snapped.

Sheridan shrugged. "Mara was elated when Sanreils asked to start a courtship–"

"Oh, I bet she was on top of the world."

"No, she didn't go to Greenland," Sheridan said. "She stayed in Locana."

"What I meant was . . ." I said. Sheridan was smirking. "Never mind."

"Mara went on a brief walk. As she was enjoying the greenery, she realized someone had been following her . . ."

- 48 -

"*Damn*, lady!" Aphrael exclaimed.

Mara blinked and stared at her. "I'm sorry!" she exclaimed. "But . . . you look okay?"

Aphrael threw her arms in the air. "You broke my bloody nose!"

"I'm sorry!" Mara exclaimed again. "You startled–"

Aphrael held her finger to Mara's lips. She smiled gently. "Shhhh, my dear," she said. "It's fine."

Mara took a close look at Aphrael's face. Nothing seemed wrong. Aphrael brushed Mara's hair out of her eyes and grinned. "You've got quite a little fist there . . ."

Mara stared at her hands. Aphrael twirled strands of Mara's hair around her finger. "So, my dear, have you considered my proposition?"

Mara looked up. Aphrael's eyes began to seize her mind. She stepped back and shook her hair free of Aphrael's grasp. "What? No!"

Aphrael frowned. "That's disappointing ..."

"It's the silliest thing I've heard in all my life!" Mara exclaimed. "Where would we go?"

"... pathetic, too."

"Well, I'm sorry," Mara said. "Matta said you're exploiting me. How did you know I was looking for a sequence?"

"I know things," Aphrael said. " 'How' is not your concern."

Mara crossed her arms and lowered her gaze.

Aphrael stared at the woods for several moments, long enough that Mara began to grow nervous. She then smiled. "Mara, dear. What is it you want? What do you want more than anything else in the world?"

"More than anything?" Mara shifted her gaze. "Are you a genie?"

Aphrael chuckled. "Not of that sort."

Mara closed her eyes and thought for a while. "I want ... I want to be back in Carrboro forest."

"At home? You hated it there."

"No, wait," Mara stepped back. "How did you know that?"

Aphrael stepped forward, lifted Mara's chin with her finger, and stole her gaze. "Like I said, I know things."

Mara shook her head and stepped back again. She glared at Aphrael. "Well, then! You shouldn't need to ask me what I want."

"My, my, aren't you the impetuous type!" Aphrael shook her head. "You'll hardly get anywhere with such a short temper."

"Sorry," Mara mumbled quietly.

"Besides, who's to say I asked that question for my purposes?" Aphrael said. "Perhaps I asked it for yours, as I don't believe you know the answer."

"I know!" Mara exclaimed. "I know exactly what I want, thank you very much."

"Sylow's library was a means to an end," Aphrael said. "And not the *only*."

Mara stared blankly. Aphrael continued, "You want to see the world again, like you did, briefly, in the sunflower field by Sylow's cottage."

"I . . . " Mara closed her eyes and stood silent. "You were there?"

"Are you familiar with the University of Locana?"

"The one Dahes talks about?"

Aphrael nodded. "I want you to go talk to the Ori."

"The *what*?" Mara exclaimed. "What is an ori?"

"He's the wisest teacher in the university," Aphrael said. "He'll help you see the world clearly. He'll teach you the nature of reality."

Mara stared at her feet. "I . . . "

"Will," Aphrael answered for her. "You *will* find the Ori and learn. Because you want to be happy."

Mara nodded hesitantly. She then stepped further back. Aphrael grinned and moved closer. She whispered in Mara's ear, "I make you nervous, don't I?"

"Sanreils said you were trouble." Mara immediately regretted saying it. What if she were trouble? What good would it do to inform her what Sanreils believed?

"I think you made a new friend."

Mara shifted uncomfortably. She looked down. Aphrael lifted her chin back up with her finger. She gazed into Mara's eyes, and smiled as she realized Mara could no longer look away. "I think you made a new friend," she repeated. "And he seems to have you rather hypnotized."

Mara continued to stare into Aphrael's eyes, stunned. Aphrael waited for a moment, then said, "Speak."

"I . . ." Mara muttered. She shook her head and stepped back. She glared at Aphrael. "You told me you knew who raided Sylow's house. Who was it?"

Aphrael shook her head. "Oh, dear. Dear, dear, dear. You think I would so easily let that go? What assurance do I have I will see my sister again?"

Mara closed her eyes. Thoughts of her last night in Carrboro Forest rushed through her mind. She remembered Sylow pushing her out the window. She tried to stop the flood of memories, but the dam burst. She remembered looking behind her, seeing the flames rise above the tree tops. She felt anger taking over her body. Her eyes shot open.

Aphrael grinned slyly.

Mara said, "You *will* see your sister again."

"You're the only one who can help me," Aphrael said.

Mara stood silent. Aphrael began to gaze into her eyes. Mara froze, then stepped back yet again. "Stop that!" she screamed.

Aphrael grasped both of Mara's cheeks in her hands and seized her attention. "I want your word," she said sternly. "Give me your word I'll see my sister again."

Mara thought in silence for a minute, then slowly nodded. She whispered, "You have my word."

Aphrael slid her fingers into Mara's hair and wrapped her hand around her head, holding it steady. Mara closed her eyes tightly as Aphrael once more touched her ice-cold lips to her ear. "You want to know, don't you?" she whispered. "You want to know who killed your friend?"

Mara squirmed as Aphrael tightened her grasp. She shivered as she felt Aphrael's breath wrap its fingers around her neck. Aphrael then whispered, very softly, "Sanreils."

18. Many Other Maras

"I really shouldn't be surprised," I said. "He seemed like such a fishy character."

"You think so?"

"Well, where was he going in such secrecy? In the woods?"

Sheridan shrugged and smiled. It wasn't his usual stupid grin; more of a mischievous smirk, like that of the Cheshire Cat. "Never mind," I said. "I'm sure I don't want to know the answer."

"That's a funny thing to say. Like you're personally invested in the outcome."

"No, no," I shook my head. "Never mind it all."

"You say 'never mind' a lot. I think you should tell me. Your tone of voice suggests I should mind."

"*Never* mind," I said.

"Well, okay. So, Mara wasn't too sure what to make of it either. And she had enough to think about with the business of the Ori. She was afraid the Locanans would make a fuss about her being on university property. But Dahes had arranged to meet with the scholars about his enrollment, and offered to escort Mara to the grounds the next day ... "

- 49 -

Mara watched the trees sway in the gentle breeze. Every so often, a leaf would break loose and tumble through the air. She could hear the occasional "*wheeee*" as the leaves tumbled together like newborn kittens at play.

"What do you think?" she asked, and biting lip as she waited for a reply. "I mean, Aphrael doesn't seem like the most trustworthy person. But why would she make up something like that?"

The leaves continued to float and somersault, hardly even acknowledging Mara's presence.

"Oh, you're no help at all!"

"Who are you talking to?" Matta asked.

Mara screamed and turned around. Matta chuckled.

"Don't you know it's not nice to sneak up on people like that?" Mara scolded. She crossed her arms and huffed.

"Silly," Matta said.

"I ran into Aphrael earlier. Or she ran into me. Or ... " Mara tried to think of how to explain it. She realized she didn't really know how. "I don't know. She seems to just pop in."

"Pop? How peculiar."

"And she said ... I don't know. I think I'm losing my mind."

"That's a terrible thing to lose," Matta said. She shook her head. "I'll go organize a search party."

Mara laughed. "Oh, shut up. I wish, though ... " she sighed.

"What?"

"She said Sanreils was the one that killed Sylow. But ... "

Matta raised an eyebrow as Mara stared into space. Mara continued, "I don't know. It doesn't make sense."

"That Sanreils could do that?"

Mara closed her eyes and tried to remember the night the raiders had come. "I could just kick myself for not studying the scene."

"Well, you were scared. And in danger. Nobody would blame you for running."

"But maybe I could have *done* something. Maybe I could've killed them. Sometimes, adrenaline helps you."

Mara faced away and wiped her eyes. Matta took her hand. "Mara, you know I think you're nuts." She smiled. "But I've never had reason to think you didn't know how to handle yourself. Trust your intuition. What does it say?"

Mara took a deep breath. "I think . . . I think there was more than one raider. But Sanreils was alone. He had to have been. And what reason would he have to do that? But then what reason does Aphrael have to lie?"

"Maybe this Aphrael character has something against *Sanreils*. Did you ever think of that?"

"She doesn't like La Nocturne. Maybe Sanreils has something to do with them?"

Matta shrugged. "Maybe you should ask Sanreils who he works for. If it's La Nocturne, you may have your answer."

- 50 -

Mara walked with Dahes through the streets just past the fountain square. The fountain seemed to glow slightly in the crisp, cool morning air. The city had just woken up, but the streets were still relatively peaceful.

"I must admit, I am a bit nervous," Dahes said. He carried a small piece of bread, from which he had been picking bits.

Mara, her mouth full of bread, made little humming sounds. Despite her best efforts, a few crumbs flew out.

"I'm still not quite sure how to introduce myself," Dahes said. "I'm Dahes! I want to study here?"

"Ooo joos ..." Mara hastily swallowed her breakfast and tried again, "You just tell them you want to join their following! You have quite a head. They'll be sure to accept you!"

"But what if they say I'm too young? Too old? Not smart enough?"

"Too smart?" Mara asked. She smiled.

Dahes chuckled as he threw his crust on the street. "Maybe I just need to clear my mind."

"So," Mara said quietly. She smiled mischievously. "I ran into Matta yesterday."

"Hmmm?"

Mara nodded solemnly. Her eyes lit up. "I bet you two are an *item!*"

Dahes blushed profusely and nearly choked on his last bite of bread. Mara laughed as he fought to keep it in his mouth. Dahes exclaimed, "Who told you?"

Mara answered, "I've got eyes!" She winked. "And ears! And enough matter in between to put two and two together."

Dahes blushed again.

"That's quite a hue you've got going there."

"And you're not helping!"

They stopped at the university's gate. The entire university stood behind a tall, thick wall. From further away, only the peaks of the tallest buildings, painted in Locana light blue, could be seen. A large, iron door provided the only entrance. It was propped open so visitors could freely come and go. Dahes gulped at the sight.

"Oh, come on!" Mara patted his back. "You're a brave soul!"

"Yes," Dahes muttered. "Thanks for keeping me company, I suppose."

Mara smiled. "Well, I have an appointment, too."

She looked through the gate. Despite the prison-like appearance from the outside, the university was really quite elegant. The gate opened up onto a large courtyard, into which most of the buildings spilled. In the center was a fountain, much larger than the one in the square. On one end, a narrow bridge connected the edge to a small island in the center. Nothing was on the island except a small, stone base, which Mara figured had to have once held a statue.

"Oh, yes," Dahes said. "The Ori, right?"

Mara nodded. She wondered what had happened to the statue.

"I've never heard of a position like an 'ori'," Dahes said. "I suppose I could ask."

Mara looked further up. Towering above the roofs of the nearby buildings were the roofs of even more buildings. She wondered just how far back they went. "There must be a hundred thousand people here," she said quietly.

"Eh?" Dahes asked.

"Nothing." Mara smiled gently. "I'll figure out where he is. You have things to do."

- 51 -

Mara sighed. From the grounds, the university looked like it was the nexus of all knowledge. Once inside, though, all she found were twisty, dark passages. Servants' chambers, scholars' chambers, boarding rooms, and the like were all mixed together like cherry blossoms in spaghetti.

Even worse, not only did nobody know where the Ori was, nobody seemed to know *who* he was.

Every time Mara burst into somebody's room and asked, she was met with either confusion or annoyance. *It must be a closely guarded secret,* she thought. After all, it would make sense to restrict access to someone so knowledgeable.

She began to grow nervous, though. *If these scholars don't care for me, what hope do I have with the Ori?*

As she walked the halls, she noticed that every so often, a tiny hole had been cut in the ceiling to let light through. Whenever she passed under one, she would stare at the sky. Sometimes, she could see the tops of buildings. She stopped under a skylight at the end of one corridor, staring at a peculiar sight. Every roof in the university was painted Locana Blue, except for one—a little, gray peak.

A small door to her left led to a side yard. When Mara stepped out, she paused for a moment to take in the fresh air. She wondered how anyone could accomplish anything in such a stuffy place.

The yard bordered the edge of Fordham Forest. There was no fence, but the trees were so thick she couldn't imagine anyone carving through them. A small hill ran right up to the forest.

Mara hiked up the hill. It ended in a cliff that dropped down into a dark abyss, sandwiched between the hill and the treeline. She couldn't see how deep it was, and thought, *this must be the edge of the world!*

The peak stood in the shadow of a tall, obelisk-shaped building bearing the gray roof she'd seen from the skylight. It was much taller than it had seemed from the hall, at least a hundred feet high. And from where she stood, it sat perfectly in front of the setting sun's path.

It struck Mara as such a peculiar building; she spent a long time studying it. The structure was dilapidated, with vines growing up the sides and into the mortar. There was no door.

The Ori has to be here, she thought. *Where else could he be?*

She leaned against the wall and scrutinized her surroundings. Near the edge of the hall she'd emerged from sat a young man, playing with marbles. Mara crept up to him and asked if he had seen the Ori.

The man jumped and looked up at her. "Don't sneak up

on people like that! It's not nice!"

"Sorry," Mara said quietly. "I thought you would know."

The man looked her over. "I didn't mean to scold you," he said. "Who are you?"

"Frustrated" Mara said. "I was told to come and find the Ori. But nobody seems to know where, or who, he is."

"Frustrated is a very peculiar name, as is Ori."

"Oh, it's Mara. My name's Mara," she said, and smiled slightly. "*Sanghid.*"

"I'm afraid I've never heard of an Ori. Admittedly, though, I don't know many people here."

Mara looked down at the marbles. They sat inside a circle drawn in chalk, bordered by eight little circles which were tangent to the larger and each other. The man motioned for Mara to join him. "Come, sit down."

Mara sat. The man introduced himself as a new scholar. "I'm a philosopher, but I have yet to prove myself to the others. So, for now, I am sitting in this field waiting to be accepted."

The scholar handed Mara a large marble. "Take this," he said. He placed eight little marbles into a pile in the center.

Mara carefully inspected the marble in her hand. "What do I do with it?"

"Toss it."

Mara turned around and threw the marble as far as she could into the courtyard. It clinked as it hit the stone walkway and shattered into a thousand pieces. The scholar stared in disbelief. "I meant, toss it into the circle."

"Oops," Mara said. "I'm really sorry!"

"It's okay." The scholar handed her another marble. "This time, just toss it ... lightly ... into the circle. Try to knock one of the little ones. You want one to lie in each of the outer circles. The idea is to study the patterns in the arrangement of the marbles and take advantage of it."

Mara studied the circle carefully. "I'm good at patterns," she said. "Seems simple enough."

The scholar nodded. Mara stood a bit back from the circle and slid the large marble along the ground. It bounced off a little marble and rolled away.

The scholar scratched his head. "Eh, maybe next time."

"Wait, I can get this!" Mara brushed her hair out of her eyes and knelt beside the circle. The marbles sat in a distorted ring. She squinted as she studied it. "If I hit the little one on the edge, like so, then it will roll into the others."

"You think so?" the scholar asked. He grinned and handed Mara the larger marble.

"I *know* so," Mara beamed a smile as she nodded.

She tossed the marble into the ring. The scholar laughed, then stared silently as all the little marbles slowly rolled away. Mara poked his rib. "Told you so."

"Well," the scholar said. "What was your name again? I think I will make a point to remember it."

"Of course. I'm such a delightful, unforgettable person."

The scholar chuckled. "I'm Master Joseph, by the way. Though, I suppose the *master* part comes after the others take me in."

Mara smiled back at him. "I'm sure you'll get there."

- 52 -

After leaving the scholar, Mara spent half an hour walking all around the obelisk. Something about the structure piqued her curiosity. None of the passerby seemed to know what it was. Everyone just knew it had always been there.

There just had to be an entrance somewhere. She was sure of it.

Then, Mara found it. The faint outline of a large door stood behind a thick tangle of vines. She had to pull very hard to break them away from the wall. Little bits of the door peeled away with the greenery. When it was fully revealed, she slowly pushed it open.

The mighty door swung inward with only a whisper. Inside, the obelisk was deathly silent. When she stepped into the room, the click of her heels darted between the walls and floors, cutting the silence into little pieces. Her heart stood still, and she heard a deep voice: "Enter."

The door closed itself as Mara stepped further inside. The chamber was huge, with high windows on all sides. Something about the windows struck her as odd.

Beams of sunlight reflected off ornate glass circles, presumably for the letter 'O', which hung from the ceiling. The room's size shrank toward the back, almost as if it were a cone. A man sat at the end. He was small, and looked to be very old. Mara assumed he was the Ori. For such a tiny man, he had a very thunderous voice. The little alcove acted as a megaphone.

"What's your name?" the voice boomed.

Mara spoke sheepishly. "Uh . . . Mara."

"Why do you come before the Ori, Amara?"

Mara crossed her arms in front of her chest. "I am not *a* Mara! There may be many other Maras, but as far as I am concerned, I'm *the* Mara!"

"*The* Mara . . . "

"Of course. My identity must be unique," Mara smiled and nodded to herself. "That's what Sylow taught me."

"But there are many Maras! It seems to me that a mathematician should have a better handle on things like notation and naming."

Mara stared blanky. "Uh . . . "

"Never mind. Why do you come before me, *The* Mara?"

"She, um," Mara fumbled her words. "Aphrael! Aphrael sent me. She said to ask you about reality."

The Ori stared at Mara for several moments as he twisted his beard around his finger. "Well, *The* Mara. The first step to understanding reality is to understand one's own self. I don't believe you do."

"What makes you say that?" Mara asked. "I think I know my own self fairly well."

"Explain. How many fingers do you have?"

"I have ten fingers!" Mara nodded and beamed a proud smile.

The Ori took another moment to think quietly. "I'm not convinced."

"You don't believe me?" Mara held up her hands. "I can assure you, they're all real fingers!"

"We'll get to *that* later," the Ori said. "But first, we must establish what *ten* is. People assume numbers have always been around. But they haven't! Numbers are a man-made construction, and these things must be defined."

"Are you telling me I don't know what ten is?"

"You know what it is, but not what it's not. I'm not sure if your understanding *ten* is sufficient for us to continue."

Mara stared at her hands. "Do I need to know the ins and outs of ten? There's only *one* of me!"

"Everyone has to start somewhere," the Ori said. "The road to self-actualization and discovery is a long and treacherous one. If you don't even know how many fingers you have, you haven't much hope of getting very far."

"Oh, please let me continue!" Mara exclaimed. "Aphrael would be very disappointed if you failed me."

"And you wouldn't be?"

"See, I used to have a master tutor. And a library. But–"

The Ori held up his hand. "I don't care about your life story." He stroked his long, white beard as he thought. "You may do, though. I have an assignment for you."

"Oh!" Mara exclaimed. "That would be lovely!"

"Study yourself," the Ori said. He then waved his hand to shoo her out the door.

"But–"

The Ori waved his hand again. "No further questions. You have your assignment."

"Oh–" Mara stopped herself. She slowly backed out the door.

When Mara stepped outside the chamber, she glanced once more at the obelisk. *Something is wrong with it,* she thought, but couldn't put her finger on what.

19. Various Combinations

"That is weird," I said. "Why didn't the obelisk have windows?"

"What's weird about that?" Sheridan asked.

"You don't think it's strange? The obelisk had windows inside, but not out? How could she not notice?"

"Maybe she did," Sheridan said. He smiled and faced away.

"You know, you claim this is an historical account," I said, "but what are your sources?"

"If I show you, will you believe me?"

"Just the fact you felt the need to ask that makes me doubt I would."

Sheridan nodded. He reached into his pocket and shuffled a bit. I watched from the corner of my eye to see what he would pull out, but he remained empty-handed.

"I guess that means I won't see it," I said.

"Nope."

"Well ..." I tapped my fingers on the steering wheel. "What then?"

"Mara wasted no time venturing into Locana the next morning," Sheridan said. "She strolled down the streets of the awakening city, the Ori's instructions bouncing in her head. *Study yourself.* It seemed like the most impossible task she had ever been assigned. Partly because she could not see her own eyes ..."

- 53 -

You can learn a lot about a person by looking into their eyes, Mara used to say. But when she looked at her own reflection, her eyes seemed to be studying *her* as well–a matter she found distracting.

She happened upon the city square with its generous fountain. It seemed much friendlier than when she first met it; its waters sprayed straight up from the center, spread out, then trickled down in various patterns. Their paths and shapes varied by the wind.

Mara studied the patterns for a long time, and noticed the same peculiarities she'd noticed in the clouds and leaves. *Left, left, right, left, left, left,* she watched the droplets float in the breeze. High above, the sunlight fiercely battled the quickly shifting clouds. In the flickering rays, the droplets sparkled: dim, bright, dim . . .

Mara watched the falling water closely. The water droplets swayed right and dimmed, left and dimmed, left and bright, left and dimmed, stood still, right and glittered . . .

She laughed, wondering if anyone had ever bothered to look at such a thing. For a moment, she wondered if she watched closely enough, if she could predict the next movement. She recalled how Marcus had watched the falling water. She wondered why he'd never thought about it more than he had.

From the fountain, Mara also had a generous view of the square. She perched herself on the low stone wall of the fountain in the manner of a cat: curious, big-eyed. Her tail twitched with excitement as she watched in silence, ready to pounce on some new discovery.

The fountain spray continued to sway left and right in the breeze. Every so often, a bit of water would tap Mara's shoulder and beckon her to come play. She stood up, laughed, and wove between the streams. As she danced, she gazed at the world around her. *It's hard to study one's self when there are so many other magical—*

Her thoughts were interrupted by the faint melody of a song. She cupped her ear to hear better. "Are you the water?" she whispered.

But the water had nothing to say. Rather, a passing boy, with several large pieces of lumber on his shoulder, hummed a tune as he walked along the street. Mara focused on it, trying to decipher its hidden message. He seemed to be singing the same five words in various combinations. He caught Mara out of the corner of his eye and stopped.

The boy tilted his head curiously. "Why do you dance in the fountain?"

"It's a wonderful thing."

"I must admit, I find it strange."

"I find it strange to see someone carrying timber on his head."

The boy smiled. "It's for my master. One day, I'll be the master and have an apprentice of my own. But I don't think I'd make him do such silly things."

"Well, I'm my own master, I suppose. And my own apprentice." Mara beamed a proud smile and nodded. "And I make myself do silly things."

"Is that why you're in the fountain?"

"I'm studying myself," Mara said.

"And what have you learned?"

"I'm wet," Mara said. "And a bit cold. And I think I shall get out soon, because Maras are adverse to such nuances."

"I take it you're Mara?"

Mara nodded.

"And you refer to yourself in the third person?"

"Every so often; it's helpful to establish who I am. I refer to myself as *I*, but there are many other people who refer to themselves as *I*. It can be a bit confusing."

"But what if there are multiple Maras?"

"*Sanghid*," Mara smiled. "The only fountain-Mara in the square."

"You're silly," the boy said. "Not that it's a bad thing."

"That's very sweet of you to say. I'd kiss your cheek if I were down there."

"I–" The boy looked down and blushed slightly. "I think if you were down here, you'd be a different Mara. Not a fountain-Mara."

"I suppose you're right," Mara said. She bit her lip and stared into the sky. "In fact, perhaps it is so. Who I am is where I am? Or–"

Mara spent the next several moments contemplating, so much so that she missed the boy's departure. She looked down to see him disappearing into the horizon. When he was out of sight, his five-word tune lodged itself in her mind.

20. Unpleasant Trees

"Again with the sequences," I said. "I could swear I've heard about that song before."

"Oh?" Sheridan grinned.

"Aren't there a hundred verses?"

"One hundred-twenty," Sheridan said. "All unique."

"I remember your lesson in combinatorics," I said. "And not much seems to have changed since. It's still dark, and the same stupid trees keep repeating."

"Maybe you're seeing what Mara is learning," Sheridan said. "Nature is a big, repeating sequence."

The landscape was the same as always–trees, and none all that remarkable. The problem wasn't that the landscape was repetitive, though. I imagine it always was. No, the problem was that Sheridan had convinced me that that meant something was wrong.

"And she didn't recognize the pattern?" I asked. "Didn't she read Marcus's book?"

"Mara didn't contemplate it for long," Sheridan said. "For the next couple days, all Mara could think about was the banquet. Sanreils told her to meet him at the baron's manor."

"Ah, yes, the infamous Baron. That should be interesting."

Sheridan snickered. "Perhaps. She held on tight to Matta's words, and was determined to learn Sanreils's occupation. The funny thing, though, was that she wasn't quite sure which outcome she wanted to hear.

"If he *was* part of La Nocturne, she could feel fairly confident Aphrael was lying to her. But La Nocturne gave her an uneasy feeling. She tried to keep an open mind, but sometimes, wanting something makes it hard to see what is really there ... "

- 54 -

Mara's stomach growled; she was especially hungry. Typically, Dahes would have cooked enough for everybody, but he was now studying at the university, and Matta had a way of setting all her food on fire.

It was a cool autumn day—a gray day with a certain peculiarity in the air. Mara hadn't slept a wink, having stayed up all night stressing about Sanreils. The sun had not yet risen, and she stumbled around in the dark, losing her way in the tower. With her stomach rumbling, she fumbled her way into an isolated cellar chamber. As she meandered about the dimly lit room, she crossed paths with a cellar monster. She closed her eyes and let out a little scream before realizing her foolishness. *It is highly silly to think the act of closing my eyes will shoo the monster away.*

Upon opening her eyes, she saw that the monster was merely the reflection in an old, forgotten mirror. She took a moment to take in her appearance and frowned. *One does not look their best in the morning,* she thought, and felt even more silly for having been afraid.

She stared at her reflection. Her reflection wiggled its fingers when she wiggled hers, wobbled its head when she wobbled hers. *How much more is there to know about one's self?*

"Who are you?" The reflection spoke up.

"I am me," Mara replied. "At least, I should hope so. The Ori did instruct me to study myself."

"Then, why are you looking at me?"

"Well, you seem like such a good approximation. You don't agree?"

Her reflection crossed its arms as it thought, and Mara hoped she didn't look that silly when she was in contemplation. "No, I do not," it said. "Not if I arrived here from a different way."

"From the door on the left?"

"On the right."

"But you look like me. And you sound like me. Although, you smell like glass, and I'm not quite so shiny. So, I must be me and you're you."

"I am afraid you must be mistaken, for I am me, and I find it improbable that there are two of us," her reflection replied.

Mara thought about the proposition long and hard. "If you are me, then who am I?"

Only silence followed. Several moments passed, and Mara grew impatient. "Well?" she asked.

"One must take time to reflect on these things before answering," the reflection replied.

"Oh . . . no rush," Mara said. "I don't mean to be pushy. But clearly, we must determine which one of us is me, or else neither of us can go about our day."

"And that would be a shame, as it is looking to be such a lovely day."

Mara was quite joyous to learn her reflection shared the same interest in peculiar, gray days. "Indeed!"

"Okay. Let's say I am me. Then you must be someone, too."

Mara poked herself in her rib. "I feel real. I must be. If I'm not then I must be someone, as clearly I exist."

Her reflection poked itself in its rib. "I feel real. I must be. If I am not, then I must be someone, as clearly I exist."

Mara folded her arms and sternly replied, "This is no time

for childish copy-cat games! We have a serious matter to attend to!"

Her reflection grinned, "Sorry. But I feel quite trapped inside this mirror, and a bit of amusement is hard to come by."

"Well, I *could* let you out. But who would greet me at the glass? I'd hate for people to think I'm a vampire. They'd probably jab a stake through my heart, and I can't imagine a piece of wood that has been lying around would be all that sanitary."

"I wish you would let me out. It's unfair that, given I am me, I should be the one in here."

"Well, that is the hand which you were dealt," Mara replied sternly. "Because I am me, and there is only one of me, which means me cannot be you!"

"I won't live in here anymore!" her reflection exclaimed. "I want to see the world! I want to dance in the rain and leaves!"

Mara's reflection immediately darted from the glass and out of the cellar. Mara called out after it. "Hey! That's my line!" she exclaimed. "Hey! Come back here!"

As Mara darted out the door and into the woods, her stomach rumbled. She muttered to herself, "The last thing I need to deal with right now is an identity crisis."

Mara had only taken a few steps into the woods when she lost sight of her reflection. *I can't believe this . . . I will smash that mirror when I return home,* she thought. *There can only be one of me! I have but one identity, and it can't take on two different beings! It is a violation!*

- 55 -

Mara had run for nearly half a mile before kicking herself for looking in the mirror. *I'll never find my reflection now,* she thought. *It could be anywhere in the world!*

She stopped for a moment to catch her breath. *Maybe it won't be so bad being a vampire,* she thought. Her mind then turned to steaks, and how tasty one would be.

A small tree spoke up. "It's you again!"

Mara's heart skipped a beat. "What? You ... you speak!"

The fern spoke with an irritated tone. "Don't get smart."

"Oh, I've longed to hear the sweet song of the forest again. Please–"

"Dumbass."

"What?" Mara folded her arms and glared downward. "There is hardly a need for vulgarity!"

A neighboring oak tree spoke up. "Why have you returned?"

Mara stood silent for a moment. She scratched her head. Then it dawned on her that, perhaps, her reflection had come through here. "You've seen someone like me?"

"*Like* you?" the fern said. "There are *two* of you?"

"There is only one me," Mara said. "But ... you see ... "

Another tree, a tall pine, interrupted her. "There! You see! Don't play dumb!"

"But I don't understand!" Mara exclaimed. "What did I do?"

"Like you don't know!" the pine scoffed. "You were quite rude to the fern."

"You hurt my feelings!" the fern whined, its voice slightly quivering.

"Oh dear!" Mara said. "Let me explain ... "

Once again, she was interrupted by the pine. "All the fern wanted to do was wish you a nice day. You didn't have to make such a fuss about its grammar."

"We trees are very sensitive about our speech," the oak explained. "Grammar, in particular. That you had to make such a big deal about a small grammatical slip was ... well ... quite uncalled for."

"Yeah!" the fern exclaimed. "Why don't you pick on someone your own size?"

"Aren't you about her size?" the oak tree asked.

"Why don't you pick on someone bigger!" the fern immediately exclaimed.

"You look like you could use a challenge, anyway," the oak said.

"But you don't understand!" Mara exclaimed. "My reflection has gotten away from me!"

"Should we believe her?" The oak tree asked hesitantly.

"I'm pretty sure she just split an infinitive," the fern said.

"Then, maybe she's telling the truth," the pine said. "If her own grammar is so shoddy, she would have no business correcting others!"

Mara folded her arms and glared at the trees. "Now who's correcting whose grammar?" she asked, impatiently tapping her foot on the ground.

The trees said nothing. "Well?" Mara asked.

"That way," the fern said, its fronds waving toward one of the forest trails. "Your reflection went that way."

"Okay," Mara said. "Fine."

She left without saying goodbye, as she had no use for anyone with such manners. For the rest of her life, she would always look down on ferns as the most hypocritical of all the flora.

"I would hate to think there is some instance of myself parading around, correcting people's grammar," Mara muttered. "It's the most deplorable behavior! I simply must find my reflection."

She stopped briefly and gasped. *What if my reflection finds Sanreils before I do?*

Before she could dwell on that thought further, she ran toward the baron's manor.

- 56 -

Mara walked down the trail, closely investigating each crevice and alcove she found. However, none of them contained a reflection of herself. The chief difficulty she found in searching for her reflection was that her shadow made quite a game of it, popping up in unexpected places.

"Now, Shadow!" she sternly exclaimed, tapping her foot impatiently as she scolded. "That will be quite enough of you! If you can't be of service, the least you could do is not act like a little twert!"

Her shadow would simply laugh and continue to dance about, as shadows often like to do.

After half an hour or so, Mara grew quite irritated. She was about to protest when a sweet smell wafted her way. *Someone must be cooking!* she thought. As she walked closer to the source of the aroma, she could hear music playing. *It's the banquet!*

Mara drew close to the bushes and peeked through to the other side. She shuddered at the thought of Sanreils seeing her sans-reflection. A large gathering of minor lords had already arrived. Light blue tents were set up all around the edges of the clearing. A large tent at the front held a podium, along with the banner of Locana.

Despite concerns Sanreils might spot her, Mara pushed through the bushes and walked up to the banquet's chef. His cooking smelled very tempting. "My! What *is* that delightful delicacy you're preparing?"

"Revenge!" the chef exclaimed, grinning ever so eagerly.

"Revenge?"

"Revenge!" the chef repeated. "I hardly need to explain, it is a *very* tasty dish."

Mara watched the oven for a moment, its fire cracking and popping. She thought about what she knew of such a dish. "Correct me if I am wrong, but isn't that best served cold?"

The chef laughed. "No! You must cook it up first! Then let it cool!"

Mara's eyes lit up. "Like gelatin!" she exclaimed.

"It was the baron's special request for this great feast," the chef explained. "The flavor of revenge!"

The chef pulled a pan out of the oven. Mara stole a peek at its contents. The pan contained some kind of custard. "Revenge?"

"Revenge!" the chef exclaimed as the baron walked in. "It's done!"

Mara froze. Until now, she had never considered the possibility that her father had actually spoken with the baron. She wondered if he'd recognize her. But he didn't seem to. He hardly paid any attention to her at all. She looked him up and down, and tried not to laugh.

The baron was rather portly. He wore the Locana Blue robes that the rest of the dignitaries wore—but was hardly regal despite that fact. Perhaps it was his smile—or his voice. The careful observer could pick up on a wavering that hinted at nervousness. Mara recalled what Matta had said about intuition. He was scared, but she wasn't sure of what.

The baron immediately took a sniff of the custard. "Ah! Well done! Revenge has never smelled so sweet!"

"Thank you, sir! I have done my best."

The baron wandered off to check up on the rest of the preparations, leaving the chef to tidy up and prepare the rest of the meal.

Mara was still quite curious about the flavor of revenge, but decided it would do her more good to find her reflection.

- 57 -

Mara came to a long table, lined with all sorts of delicacies. Her stomach rumbled as she gazed at the food. Piles of bread, meats, and cheeses occupied the center, with fruits scattered about the edges.

As Mara reached for a pear, someone interrupted: "Excuse me."

Mara froze.

"Who are you?" a woman asked.

"I wasn't stealing!"

"Why not?" the woman said as she took several pieces of fruit. She pushed them into her satchel. "Baron Rutsan can be so wasteful sometimes. I doubt he'd miss half of this."

Mara smiled. "What is all this about?"

As Mara bit ferociously into a pear, the woman explained. "You're not from around here, are you?"

"Mmmhph ought," Mara shook her head as little bits of pear flew out her mouth.

"Culatan is the region to the east. We've had a spat with them since, well, the dawn of time, I suppose."

Mara nodded as the woman thought. "The violence has escalated recently. It certainly has my people, well, everyone's, on edge."

As the woman continued, Mara's mind began to drift. She thought of the attack on Sylow's house, and what Aphrael had told her. Maybe it was Culatan that had attacked Sylow. It seemed more plausible than Sanreils having a hand in it. *Unless La Nocturne wanted Culatan to do these things. But that doesn't make sense.* Suddenly, she didn't know what to believe.

"So then, there's La Nocturne," the woman said. "Promising peace, I suppose."

"I eard 'em!" Mara exclaimed, her mouth still full of pear.

The woman nodded. "See, everyone thinks the high

priestess, Trisha, and Baron Rutsan are all buddy-buddy. And *that's* why La Nocturne has been grabbing power from 'ole Rutsy." She stopped to glance behind her, then went on. She dropped her voice to a near whisper. "But *I* suspect the whole kerfuffle with Culatan has been engineered by the apprentice priests."

Mara shivered as the woman's words bounced in her mind. *So it is possible Sanreils could be responsible, even if he works for La Nocturne.* She had to concentrate hard not to cry.

The woman was staring at her. Mara took a deep breath. "Hence the custard? Revenge?" she said. "I suppose?"

The woman laughed. "The baron's idea of a celebration. A *revenge* flavored pie. I'd suspect it's just sugar and cream, but I've heard it leaves a bitter aftertaste."

Mara wondered why sweet revenge would leave a sour aftertaste, and began to think about how good a tart would be right now. The woman continued, "The only reason I'm here is because one of the apprentices is supposed to be giving a speech about La Nocturne and Rutsan's latest pact. I *should* be worried I'd lose my position, but–" She shrugged.

Mara reached behind her and grabbed a few berries. The woman chuckled again. "Who are you, anyway?"

"My name is Mara," she said. "*Sanghid*, so you don't confuse me with all the other Maras."

"You don't look like a Mara," the woman said. "The name *Mara* means 'bitter' in Hebrew. Or, it's a Hungarian variation of *Mary*."

Mara thought a moment. "Well, I am hungry ... which might give me reason to be bitter. But I like to think I am a pleasant sort."

The woman smiled. "I'm Lady Carlm. But, if you wish, you can call me Sanna."

Mara returned her smile. "*Sanna.* Can I ask you a question?"

"I'm all ears."

"No, you're not. You only have two ears, and the rest of you is other body parts," Mara said. "But that's beside the point. Have you seen me anywhere?"

Sanna stared blankly for a moment. "Hmm ... I suppose you're right in front of me."

"I mean, hmm ... " Mara pondered just how to word her predicament. "I'm looking for me, but she is not me. Rather, she is like me, but has a penchant for correcting grammatical mistakes."

"I've always been a proponent of clear communication," Sanna said. "But I can see how that would be annoying."

"You don't have to tell me that!" Mara exclaimed.

Sanna smiled. She grabbed a few more pieces of fruit and bread, and stuffed them into her satchel. "I should go," she said. "Good luck finding your other you!"

Once Sanna disappeared, Mara turned her attention to the table. She stared longingly at the last remaining pear. After a quick glance around, she grabbed it. Cursing herself for forgetting her satchel, she stuffed the pear down into her boot, which gave her a subtle, but noticeable limp.

- 58 -

Mara shook her head as she walked. Surely Sanreils would arrive soon, and she was entirely unpresentable. She contemplated giving up, finding a nice, shady spot and eating her other pear. Then, she saw it in the corner of her eye–a figure who very much resembled herself. It danced and laughed. "You!" she exclaimed.

Her reflection laughed again and ran off. Mara quickly chased after it before it could disappear into the crowd. "Come back here!" she cried. "Have you any idea how ridiculous this is! You have no business out here!"

"If I am ridiculous, then so are you!" her reflection cried. "Whatever you say reflects off me and sticks to you!"

"I must warn you, I am losing my temper," Mara said.

"I must warn you, I am losing my temper," her reflection repeated.

"Stop copying me," Mara said.

"Stop copying me," her reflection replied.

Mara pondered the nuisances of her own reflection. "Stop this silliness at once!" she exclaimed.

"Stop this silliness at once!" her reflection replied, sticking its tongue out.

Mara thought about the ridiculousness of this little game. She decided she might as well play along. "Mara is great!" she shouted.

"Why, thank you," her reflection replied. "I do admit, I have an abundance of greatness."

"Hey!" Mara exclaimed. "I was referring to myself. You're not Mara. I'm Mara. I'm me."

"No . . . I'm me," her reflection replied.

"I am me. And don't *you* forget it!" Mara said.

Her reflection winked, turned around, and dashed into the crowd. Mara started to chase it. She'd only run a few steps before the pear, jammed into her calf, caused her to trip. She cried out as she hit the ground, and beat her fists on the grass in anger.

"My poor dear," someone said.

Mara sat up. Baron Rutsan stood above her with his hand held out. He helped her to her feet. "Dear, dear! Are you a poor farm girl? Crippled by Culatan?"

Mara glanced at her feet. Baron Rutsan shook his head. "My poor dear," he repeated. "What's your name?"

She couldn't help but feel a little annoyed by his assumptions, but she breathed a sigh of relief, knowing he must have never met her father.

"Mara," she said quietly. "It means 'bitter' in Hebrew, or it's a Hungarian–"

"You look very hungry, indeed," the baron said. "Famished, even!"

"Well, I just ate a–"

The baron seized her arm and tugged her toward the chef's station. "Let's get you some food! Now, who took all the fruit?"

As Mara stepped closer to the tent, the pear irritated her leg further. When the baron wasn't looking, she pulled the pear up and laid it on the table. A round of applause came from the stage. "Come with me," the baron said. "We'll make things right."

Before Mara could protest, or ask what the baron had in mind, he'd already seized her and led her toward the stage.

All of the nobility were standing in front of the podium, along with a number of citizens from the city and surrounding region. Altogether, there must have been at least two hundred people.

The baron stepped onto the platform and spoke loudly: "For too long now, Baron Castent and the lords of Culatan have been nipping at our backs."

Several members of the crowd nodded. "La Nocturne has the capability of bringing peace to our region," the baron said. "But, I feel that some of you are not convinced."

Murmurs and whispers sounded from the crowd. The baron waited for a moment before continuing. "The strength of our region lies in the backs of those who till our fields, forge our swords, and milk our cows." He motioned for Mara to step forward. "I have with me a representative of the commoners! This is Mara. She is a hungry and bitter Jewish farm girl, crippled by Culatan."

"Actually," Mara said. "I think–"

Mara spoke too quietly for the audience to hear. More

murmuring sounded, along with a few nods in agreement. Sanna held her face in her hand and shook her head.

The baron interrupted her. "Tell us, bitter Mara, what difficulties have you had?"

Mara thought about her difficulties. She could say how she'd been unfairly accused of heinous crimes by the grammatically incorrect trees. She could talk about her disruptive shadow, and her unruly reflection which acted half her age. But she didn't believe the crowd would understand. They waited impatiently for her to speak. "I like to think I'm a pleasant person. My father's name was Sanghid, so now you won't confuse me with all the bitter Maras."

She watched a man in the back of the crowd dash off, and wondered if she'd somehow offended him. The baron nudged her. "Who crippled you?"

Mara stared blankly. She realized the baron must have seen her limping earlier, and began to feel very embarrassed. She shook her head. The baron said, "It's okay. You can tell us. Where is your farm?"

Mara froze. She didn't want to spill her thoughts in front of the baron, much less the crowd. She turned her head toward the ground. Finally, the baron gave up and dismissed her. He pointed toward the banquet table and invited her to eat, although the table was mostly empty.

As Mara walked away from the stage, she could hear the baron going on about "the peasantry" and "grave threats". She sat on a tree stump at the edge of the clearing and buried her head in her arms. Nothing would've pleased her more than to just be back in bed.

She rested and listened to the other speakers–mostly local folk with anecdotes–another farmer, a mill operator, a trader. Then, she heard the baron announce the next speaker.

"The good Church of La Nocturne has promised us hope! They've come to our town and promised light! By their good graces, we will persevere! Allow me to introduce my good friend, Sanreils of Laraux!"

Mara froze and her heart skipped a beat. She promptly faced the stage. Sanreils looked tired and sounded out of breath, like he'd just arrived. But he spoke with a clear confidence. "My friends! I have traveled the region, and I have seen! I see you struggle. I struggle, too. I see you suffer. I suffer, too. For the good church and you are one, and we are in this together!"

That answers that question, she thought, and wished it had brought her some comfort.

Some of the crowd began to cheer. Others eyed Sanreils skeptically. "We will lead you! As promised on our triumphant entrance, we will not turn our backs on our good hosts. We will lead you away from the darkness!"

More of the crowd began to cheer. Sanreils smiled widely. "Now, I know there is talk of war, and I assure you, personally, if you, no, *we* defeat Culatan, we will be well on our way to better times. March! And bring glory to Locana!"

Mara couldn't push Sanna's words out of her mind. She shuddered, and walked off before Sanreils could notice her.

- 59 -

Mara lurked in the shadows at the side of the clearing. She had, until now, forgotten all about her lost reflection. *It must be all the way to Spain by now,* she thought. *I wonder if the Spaniards will think I'm bitter just because I correct their grammar?*

She found herself back at the chef's station. The baron held the chef by his shirt collar. "You're *supposed* to be providing for our guests! That's what I *hired* you to do, remember?"

"I'm terribly sorry, sir," the chef said as he shook his head.

"We're out of bread, there's no water, and the fruit!" The baron held up Mara's pear, from which he'd taken a bite. "It's bruised and tastes like sweat!"

"Terribly, terribly sorry," the chef repeated. "I'll go to the kitchen at once!"

The chef sighed as the baron stormed off, muttering about the next speech he was to give.

"My!" Mara exclaimed. "You certainly are busy today."

"Tell me about it," the chef said. "The dessert will be starting soon. Somehow, I need to make it to town and back in ten minutes."

Mara looked up toward the hill overlooking the banquet area. She thought she saw her reflection up there. She was about to take off after it when the chef stopped her. He picked up the custard. "Perhaps you can be of assistance?"

"Revenge?" Mara asked.

"Revenge," the chef said. He handed her the custard. "Do me a favor, dear. Run this up to the feast. The baron will have my porkchops if I don't gather more fruit."

Mara nodded as the chef hastily ran off. She wondered how she would sneak it in without being seen by Sanreils. She faced the banquet and saw her reflection standing at the top of the hill. It wiggled its ears and stuck out its tongue.

She forgot all about the dessert and ran toward her reflection. The top of the hill ended at a short cliff on the western edge of the clearing. It was an excellent vantage point, and she kicked herself for not finding it earlier.

But the top was bare. Mara kicked the grass and scouted the banquet below. It didn't take her long to see herself, standing just behind the stage. "You!" she shouted.

Her reflection danced a little jig, kicking bits of grass up as it shifted its feet. Mara folded her arms and exclaimed, "You! You inconsiderate little twert! You get over here, right now!"

But her reflection only laughed, stuck its tongue out, and wiggled about.

"You're asking for it, you know!"

Her reflection grinned, then turned its back to her. It promptly leaned forward and exposed its rear. Mara gasped. Her reflection turned back around and stuck its tongue out again.

Fuming, Mara looked at the custard she held. As her reflection began to take off into the crowd, she threw the custard as hard as she could. A brief moment later, she regained her temper and realized that, perhaps, that had been a mistake.

"The time has come for action!" the baron exclaimed, repeatedly slamming his fist into the podium.

Most of the crowd cheered and applauded. The baron grinned as he spoke. "For long enough now, the enemy has been poking and prodding us. We must show that we can bite back! We've been made fools of long enough!"

As the baron raised his fist again, a small shadow overcame him. With his fist still in the air, he glanced up as a flying custard hit him square in the face. No one in the crowd spoke even a whisper as they watched custard slowly drip off the stunned baron.

Most of the crowd stared, completely stripped of words. A few whispers started to sound from the back, and some people looked up at the hill. Mara had already run off. For years, everybody would talk about "the great flying custard," with their own theories concerning who had thrown it, and for what reason.

- 60 -

Mara ran through the grasses and woods as fast as she could. She dared not stop to look behind her. After half an hour, she realized she hadn't the slightest idea where she was.

"Mara!" someone exclaimed.

Mara jumped. She wondered if one of the guests had spotted her, but the voice sounded familiar. "I know your voice, but I do not see you!"

"Down here," the voice said.

Mara looked down the path. A long, winding brook ran parallel.

"Mara!" the brook exclaimed. "It's been a while!"

"Are you the same brook I met before?"

"Indeed."

"And you have stretched all this way?"

"We brooks are as long as we are wise."

"Then you must be very wise," Mara said. "I am a long way from home."

"Wisdom usually stretches far from home. How goes your quest?"

Mara found a soft place to sit on the bank. "Exhausting, to say the least. The Ori said I should learn about myself. So I looked in the mirror. But my reflection ran away!"

The brook laughed. "How did your reflection escape?"

Mara held her face in her hands and shook her head. "I don't know! I was wandering the halls, and then I found the cellar. If it weren't for the Ori, I probably wouldn't have paid any attention to the mirror at all."

"And if it weren't for Aphrael, you wouldn't have met the Ori."

"And if it weren't for . . . well," Mara paused. "Suddenly, it seems like the entire universe is like a little machine. All sorts of gears and pulleys working together to put me here. Pulling my hair out."

"If the decisions in life are the roads in the forest, then you are the result of your life's journeys," the brook said. "And also, the journeys of many others who came before you."

Mara stared into the brook. She found her reflection, wobbling in the waves guided by a gentle breeze. "Then, who would I be if I'd arrived from a different way?"

"Another Mara, I suppose."

"Bitter and hungry. Maybe that's what the Ori wanted me to learn. Had it not been for the wind, guiding me like a floating leaf–"

"Perhaps you'd be a different Mara."

"But where does the wind originate from?" Mara asked. "Where do the water's ripples come from?"

"Both good questions."

Mara closed her eyes and sighed. "I made such a mess of things today. I hope Sanreils didn't see me. Maybe I could change my name."

"I think he'd see right through that. Would a Mara, by any other name, get her breakfast?"

"Don't make me laugh." Mara forced a frown. "I'm trying to be upset here."

"Mathematicians have a nasty habit of reusing words, each defined differently."

"Then, why can't I change what my name means?" Mara asked. "After all, I see no reason why I should have to change my name when it would be just as easy to change its meaning."

"Appalling to think you would be locked into being bitter. No, that doesn't seem to be you at all."

"Just like two," Mara said. "Why, if I were the number two, I might enjoy that very much."

"Me, too."

"But why can't two be one?" Mara asked. "After all, if I *were* two for all my life, I might think that, perhaps, I would like to try being 'one' once in a while."

Mara thought that two could be anything she wanted it to be.

"And what a 'one' you would be!" the brook exclaimed.

Mara blushed. "You really think I would make a good 'one'?"

"I don't see why not."

Mara laughed and thought how wonderful it would be to be any number she wished. She danced in a ring around the highway and pronounced herself to be all the numbers. "One! Two! Ninety-seven! Yes! I will be Ninety-seven!"

"You know, I think I might like very much to be a street!" the brook said. "Yes. That does sound marvelous."

"You would make a lovely street," Ninety-seven said.

"I've always wanted to try being a street," the street said. "Why not?"

Ninety-seven gazed at the brook which was now a street. "My! What a lovely street! What a lovely street I see!"

The street laughed. "The highway will have a good laugh at all this. 'How did you become a street?' it will ask. But, no. I think I would rather be a brook again."

"Yes," Ninety-seven said. "And I miss being Mara Sanghid. As much fun as it was to try being an integer, I feel life is too boring when one limits oneself to only wholesome values."

21. Then Amedean Had a Daughter

"Who would I be," I repeated, "if I'd arrived from a different way?"

"That's the question," Sheridan said with a slight nod.

"What in the world does *that* mean?"

"A question is a statement in which–"

"No," I shook my head and smirked. "Nitwit. Why would Mara be someone else if she arrived from another road?"

Sheridan tapped his fingers on the dashboard as he thought. A moment later, his eyes lit up. "Do you think you'd be a different John Bartlebee if you had taken I-95 instead of I-40 home?"

"I-95 doesn't go my way," I said. "And why would that matter?"

"We wouldn't have met," Sheridan said. "And the world would've ended with you inside it."

I grumbled. I wanted to glare at him, but had to keep my eyes on the road. That only agitated me further. "Will you stop telling me the world is ending? It's not happening. Do you hear me?"

"I think it's interesting," Sheridan said, "that you only had one route."

"Really? And why is that?"

"It means you're not free to choose."

"What?"

Sheridan grinned his usual stupid grin, and dismissed my question.

- 61 -

Mara walked slower than usual down the forest path. Even when she wasn't excited from the sights and sounds, she walked at a brisk pace. Today, she dreaded meeting with the Ori. She stopped to contemplate turning around.

"Good afternoon, Mara."

"Good ... " Mara paused. She looked around, but didn't see anyone. "Afternoon?"

"How are you?"

"*Where* are you?" Mara asked.

"Does that matter? Does where I am affect your mood?"

"Well, if you're, say, a skunk, I don't think I'd be all that pleasant."

"Some things are right under your nose."

Mara looked down at her feet. "Are you the highway again?"

"Indeed. How are you?"

Mara found a soft spot in the grass to sit. She sat parallel to the road, so that her feet rested off the path, as she found it uncomfortable to be talking to something she was standing on. She told the highway about Aphrael and the Ori. "Do you think I learned anything about myself?"

The highway chuckled. "I think only you could answer such a thing. Do you feel so?"

"I don't know. I thought so." Mara bit her lip. "Sylow could be a tough teacher sometimes, but at least he seemed to like me. The Ori doesn't seem to care for me in the least."

"Do you want him to like you?"

"I suppose I don't care. It'd be nice," Mara said. She forced a smile. "Can I tell you a secret? And you won't tell anyone?"

"That's what a secret is. And I'm not inclined to gossip."

Mara nodded. "I wouldn't tell *anyone* this, except you. The Ori intimidates me."

"I think you should just tell the truth. He'll understand, I'm sure."

"Maybe," Mara said.

She leaned back in the grass and watched a single cloud sail across the sky. It reminded her of her childhood, playing by herself without any friends. She remembered how happy she'd been when she first met Sylow. He was not only a companion, he was hope for a real future. She closed her eyes and tried to step back into his library.

Mara snapped back into reality when the breeze rustled her hair.

"Are you there?" the highway asked.

"I read about you in a book, you know. If I'm thankful for anything my father provided me, it would be this gift of reading."

The highway smiled. "And what did you read about me?"

"About Marcus," Mara said. "And a quest. *The* quest. I never found out what it was."

"I see," the highway said.

"Am I on a quest?" Mara asked.

"You are on a very long quest," the highway said.

"But you won't tell me what it is either," Mara said.

"You will see, Mara," the highway said. "Yes, you will see."

Mara pondered for a moment. It had seemed like Marcus's quest was to travel the road. She tried to follow the highway up the horizon with her eyes, but it quickly blended in with the rest of the landscape.

She threw her arms in the air. "When? I don't see!"

"You will," the highway said. "You have eyes."

"Well, I do try to be an agreeable person," Mara said.

The highway paused for a second. "No, I said *'eyes'*, not *'ayes'*."

Mara smiled. The highway said, "Oh ... you made a funny."

Mara nodded. She then asked, "Are you the same highway?"

"For as long as man has trekked, I have been his path."

"That's a long time," Mara said. "And in all that time, you haven't figured out how to describe the quest?"

"You'll learn more for having figured it out for yourself."

Mara nodded. She sat on the roadside for quite some time, churning the thoughts in her mind. *Maybe my quest was to meet the Ori,* she thought. *Or to find the sequence.* She even considered the possibility the highway had never had a quest in mind—that she could just make up her own quest and do it.

The highway eventually interrupted her train of thought. "It is a lot to think through, I will give you that."

"But I was wondering, Highway," Mara said. "Because I need to know—"

"That's a good reason to wonder," the highway replied.

Mara smiled. "For how long has man trekked your path? How long have you curved from town to town?"

The highway thought for a moment as it calculated. Mara's ears perked as she anticipated its answer. It then replied, "Two minutes ... and thirty-four seconds."

- 62 -

Mara gulped as she stared at the Ori's obelisk. Her earlier confidence had waned as soon as she'd pulled the vines away from the door. Now, she stared at the handle, wondering if she'd really learned what she was supposed to.

When she stepped inside, the Ori greeted her. "Have you solved your problem?"

"Hello to you, too," Mara said.

The Ori lowered his gaze and waited quietly.

"No," Mara whispered. "I mean–"

She contemplated saying 'yes', because she was fairly confident that she had. But she also knew she would have to defend her answer, and she wasn't sure how much throwing pies demonstrated deep understanding of herself. The Ori continued to glare, and didn't stop when she finally answered. "Yes, I mean, Yes, I have not."

The Ori hummed and tapped his fingers on his armrest. "Yes," he repeated, "You have not."

"Are you, uh, mad?"

"I don't get mad," the Ori said. "*Disappointed*, yes. Mad, no."

"I'm sorry. I really am. But, I tried."

The Ori stared out the window as he thought. "Amara," he said. "*Tried* and *did not* both have one thing in common."

"What?"

"*Failure.*"

Mara whispered, "Oh."

The Ori shook his head. "I'm not sure you're ready."

"Oh, but I am!" Mara exclaimed. "I am ready! Why would Aphrael have sent me? And Sylow seemed to think I was."

"I think he was just being nice."

Mara diverted her gaze as tears welled in her eyes. "I think–" She closed her eyes and took a deep breath. "It's Mara. Not *Amara*."

"And how many fingers does Mara have?"

"Well, I looked in the mirror to see if I could count them. But my reflection ran away! Then, I threw a pie at the baron."

"I see."

"No, you don't," Mara said. She straightened her posture. "I chased it! All the way to the brook. Then I saw it–"

The Ori interrupted. "And how many fingers did it have?"

"Ten."

"Why?"

"Because two minutes and thirty-four seconds ago, the universe popped into existence. Then, some things happened, and Amedean had a daughter."

Mara clenched her fists as she began talking faster and faster. "But he didn't want her, so he tried to drown her in the lake. But somebody from the church said that was immoral, so he tried to sell her to the baron. She ran away, and for exactly twenty-five hours, she was happy. Now, she has no friends, no future, no hopes, nothing at all."

She buried her head in her hands and cried. The Ori waited in silence for her to calm down. "I'm sorry," she whispered.

"I have another assignment for you."

"What?"

"Follow Rosemary Road, just outside the city. There is a glass-blower. Tell him I sent you. He'll teach you about perspective."

Mara stared quietly, then whispered, "Thank you."

22. Time For Sarcasm and Vulgarity

"So, Mara got another chance," I said. "Well. Good for her. But why is the world only two minutes old?"

"The highway is a mysterious enigma, indeed," Sheridan said. He nodded.

"I don't follow."

"Neither did Mara," Sheridan said.

When I was little, the clerk in the Pump-N-Mart used to tell me the world was only 6,000 years old. I wondered how that could be, since the teachers told me dinosaurs and the like were much older. I didn't know the same world could be viewed in different ways. I just thought somebody was lying–and I didn't know who, or for what reason.

I asked Sheridan what he thought. "How old do you think Earth is?"

"I'm not interested in politics."

"It's not a political question," I said. "It's just a question about . . . well, I don't know how to put it."

"It just seems like a silly debate, that's all," Sheridan said. "Since the world will end soon, I can think of better ways to spend our time than quibbling over the age of some bones."

The landscape continued to roll by–the lifeless void that had haunted me since I first met Sheridan. Nobody was out there. I should have seen *somebody*. I was on the East Coast– the side of the country that never sleeps. I wasn't expecting traffic by any means. But I should've met at least one or two cars, a trucker, *something*.

I took a deep breath. "Sheridan . . . " His ears perked. "If you're right—*if*—where would we go?"

I could tell he was hiding a smile. "I thought you didn't want to talk about it," he said.

"Well, maybe just a little."

"A speckle of doomsday will do you? A pinch? A teaspoon?"

"Whatever, Emeril. Where will we go?"

"Look outside. What do you see?"

It was a pointless exercise, but I looked again. The usual ominous clouds continued to loom above. The horizon was barely visible, but wasn't worth looking at anyway. "I don't get it."

"It's a world winding down, like a clock with a dying battery, a wind-up doll with a weak spring, a Furby that's been short-circuited."

"You didn't answer my question."

"You need to believe me first."

"If I say I do, will you tell me?"

Sheridan shook his head. "It's okay if you don't. Perhaps you will, after having heard how it came to be. Mara hoped the Ori's lesson would help her uncover a few clues about the world, too . . . "

- 63 -

As Mara walked down the forest highway, she tried to think of what the glass-blower would have to say. *If one thing leads to another and leads to another, then the same must be true in reverse. So, maybe, if I can figure out where it all originated . . . maybe that's perspective?*

The more she thought about the idea, the less she wondered about where everything was going. She felt more compelled to figure out where everything started. It seemed like a much better question. She walked by the trees and shrubbery, gazing around her. *All this came from somewhere,* she thought.

Mara's thoughts were interrupted by a terse "You!"

Mara shrieked and stepped back. She frantically looked around. "Who said that?"

"You don't recognize me?"

"I don't *see* you!" Mara exclaimed. She scanned her surroundings, until her gaze landed on a squirrel. It fluttered its tail.

"Hi there," the squirrel said.

"Oh!" Mara clapped her hands and jumped. "You talk to me!"

"The highlight of my life, let me assure you."

"Well, there's no need to be rude," Mara said.

"I suppose I should be nice. You did save my life."

Mara laughed. "Really? Me?"

The squirrel began to moan, imitating meditation. Mara's eyes lit up. "You! Oh, I bet you're happy I happened to be about."

"A mostly satisfactory outcome."

"*Mostly*? not *completely*? Are you a crazy squirrel?"

"They say 'you are what you eat'."

"Well, I think I'd be rather happy being a squirrel. You get to eat acorns and jump in trees."

"But lately, I've been wrestling with the meaning of life, the purpose of existence."

Mara watched the squirrel's tail sway in the breeze, a smooth, rhythmic motion that all too easily distracted her. She snapped out of it. "I've never heard of a squirrel philosopher."

"What else am I going to do with my time?"

Mara hummed and nodded. "I suppose so. It just seems like a silly pursuit; for a squirrel, anyway."

The squirrel's beady eyes shone slightly, and Mara got the impression he was glaring at her. "Well, you tell me, little miss Smarty Big-hair–what does it mean 'to be'?"

Mara gazed at the clouds momentarily. She thought of all the words that *should* have simple definitions. After all, they're used every day. Her eyes lit up, and she smiled to herself. "Pursuing happiness." She nodded proudly. "It's the pursuit of happiness. What gives meaning to your life? What completes your soul?"

"I eat. I sleep. Sometimes, I sit in trees and throw nuts at people."

Mara folded her arms and glared. "That's a very mean thing to do, Mr. Squirrel!"

"Ry."

"Ry, that's horrible! Surely your life has more meaning than that."

"The best part is the reaction on their faces. They can't believe a squirrel would purposely do that."

"Well, I never. Fine. Can you, at least, teach me about perspective?"

Ry turned his head and fluffed his tail in the breeze. He let it dangle a bit, so that Mara could see he had one and she didn't. He then said, "From up here, your head is no bigger than an acorn."

Before Mara could reply, Ry scurried off, his little squirrel chuckle dissipating into the wind.

- 64 -

The glass-blower's house sat a short way into the woods, just outside the city. Aside from a couple of decorative lanterns, it didn't seem particularly special.

It looks like any other house, Mara thought. *Perhaps the person inside is whimsical. After all, he knows the Ori.*

When she knocked on the door, thrice, and received no answer, she wondered if he was there at all.

On the fourth knock, the door creaked open slightly.

"Hello?" she whispered as she carefully pushed it fully open. "The Ori sent me to learn about perspective."

Nobody seemed to be home. *This has to be the right address.*

She peeked outside. The glass-blower's sign swung in the breeze. *Who will teach me about perspective now?*

Mara entered the house. "Hello . . . " she called. "I don't mean to disturb you. But in your window–" She paused. The house was almost entirely deserted. There were no signs of an occupant, or even furnishings, except for a single table. Resting on its surface, perfectly centered, was a bottle.

From where she stood, Mara could see the bottle was rather peculiar. She stepped closer and inspected it. Its neck twisted and turned back *into* the bottle–through a joint in its side. The outside surface folded into the inside.

Mara picked it up. She studied it closer. *It's the most peculiar bottle I've seen in all my life.*

She felt it all over and when she set it down, she realized she couldn't. She was inside the bottle! *I came in, but now I'm out. In is out and out is in!*

To make matters worse, when she looked outside the bottle, she realized she was looking *into it.* The house, surrounding forests, and the rest of the world were also in the bottle.

How am I supposed to learn about perspective now? Mara thought. *What utter ridiculousness!*

If the rest of the world hadn't also been inside the bottle, she would have felt safer. She thought how living in a glass bottle wouldn't be all that bad if she were alone. *I could read my books, and nobody would bother me!*

Mara stepped out of the house and closed the door behind

her. The world inside the bottle seemed just like that of the outside, except for the impending doom that surely would follow the bottle breaking.

Maybe it's a lesson, she thought. *Like in the mirror. Perspective is fluid, or something like that.*

Mara nodded to herself and decided she was the sharpest knife in the drawer. It was then that she looked down and realized the world was slightly amiss. She wasn't sure what it was; she called it *intuition.*

She stopped, leaned against a branch, and shrieked. Twigs jabbed into her hair, and she shrieked again when the branches pulled it as she hopped away. She looked down again, and figured out what was wrong. She was at least two feet taller than she'd been in the morning.

I'm fairly certain I should have stopped growing by now, she thought. *I'm 16 years of age, last time I counted. It's that cursed bottle! Maybe if I retrace my steps.*

I stepped out of the house, then complimented myself on figuring out the Ori's lesson. Then ...

When she glanced downward again, she screamed. She was now an additional foot taller. *What is going on? All I thought was how clever I was and -*

Mara had grown another foot. *Is one's ego in proportion to their height?*

"It's you again!" the fern exclaimed.

Mara jumped and stepped back. "You! It's you, little twiddley-dums."

"We don't like you," the oak tree said. "Why don't you make like your infinitives, and split."

"Well," Mara huffed. "I was just minding my own business, thank you very much."

"Is that her?" the pine tree asked. "The little snot-rocket? Oh! How gracious of you to accompany us."

Mara folded her arms in front of her chest and glared. "I

think this is hardly the time for sarcasm and vulgarity."

"On the contrary, my dear," the fern said, "this is precisely the time for sarcasm and vulgarity."

The pine and oak laughed. Mara was at a loss for what to say, and began to feel something shrink inside her. "Oh, look," the pine said. "She's shrinking!"

Indeed, as Mara's ego began to deflate, her body shrank in turn. "Oh, I'm sorry," the fern said. "We didn't mean to belittle you."

The trees laughed harder. Mara waved her arms, pulling the fronds away from her face. When she was able to see, she shrieked and jumped back. "What'd you do to me?"

"I think you did it to yourself," the fern said. "Serves you right."

Mara had shrunk to about one inch in height, and was still shrinking. *Oh, this is no good at all*, she thought. *But I can't tell if I'm shrinking, or if the world is growing. I still seem to be the same Mara.*

She wondered just how much she would shrink. Two minutes ago she'd been eight foot-seven, four more feet than her usual height. A minute later, she had shrunk to one foot, and half a minute later, the height of a thimble. *At this rate*, she thought, *it will never stop.*

Eventually, she shrank so small that she slipped between the cracks in the ground. Bits of soil tumbled along with her as she bounced down the canyon slopes. She was thankful she couldn't hear the fern anymore.

Mara landed on a soft spot of mud adjacent to a large water droplet. A couple of ants were drinking from it. When she sat up and moaned, they looked up, opened their mandibles, and approached.

"Oh! Please don't eat me," Mara said. She held out her arm. "See, I'm all stringy!"

The ants stopped briefly and looked at each other. Mara

scooted backward as they approached.

With each step, they grew larger. Mara backed up against the wall. As the mandibles came down, she closed her eyes and screamed.

The mandibles closed as tightly as they could. For a second, Mara found herself wedged between them. She then slipped through them and landed on the floor. The ants were now more than ten times her height.

Mara opened her eyes and looked up at the towering beasts. She had shrunk so much that they couldn't grab hold of her. Soon, they couldn't even see her, and went back to their business.

"Take that, foul vermin!" Mara exclaimed. She laughed.

Mara didn't notice the ants suddenly shifting closer. She continued to laugh at their plight. She felt something grow inside her. *This is certainly a morale boost,* she thought, and realized she was now growing.

The ants turned back her way. *Compliment yourself!* she thought.

Mara pointed to the ants and laughed, although they were now her size. "Fools! I scoff in your general direction!"

Soon, the ants were no larger than her toe. She immediately squashed them, and grew another ten times.

Her new height seemed to only feed her ego more, and with each passing moment, she doubled in size.

Feeling rather giddy, she began to laugh at the world below; the trees were now the size of her fingers. Eventually, the thought crossed her mind that her new size made her flaws rather easy to spot. *A 200-foot Mara is a peculiar enough sight. I wonder what the town would think of a 200-foot, naked Mara. It wouldn't be a pretty sight, now that my moles are mountains.* At this point, she stopped growing.

Upon observing her new size, Mara began to panic. *Oh dear,* she thought. *This is certainly a displeasing situation. I won't be able to make friends in the town. It's hard to make friends with people by stomping on them.*

Mara looked down at the lake, which now seemed not much more than a puddle. *On the upside, I shall no longer need to worry about being run down by the wagon-carts in the roads.*

She looked into the lake and watched her reflection wiggle in the currents. Her new height pushed her up into the heavier winds, which gave her considerably poofier hair. She pulled it back down and smiled at her image, then quickly covered her mouth. *Oh no!* she thought, and scolded herself for not keeping her ego in check.

Mara screamed as she grew another fifty feet. She took a few steps back and heard a *crunch.* Her heart fluttered as she looked down in horror at the ground. She'd smashed Baron Rutsan's manor into little pieces. *What have I done?* she thought. *Surely, they'll tie me to a wagon and lock me up in a temple for safekeeping.*

As she stepped back, she saw there was nothing left of either the manor, or the banquet grounds. The little hill where, earlier, she'd caught her reflection, had been smashed under her heel.

The sound of hurried voices and commotion around the manor rose into the air. Mara thought herself such a horrible person that her ego began to deflate, and she shrank to normal size.

Mara stood in the trees, just outside the banquet yard. She couldn't see much of it, but could hear guards shouting. They cried something about the work of Culatan.

Soon, the guards noticed Mara's rustling in the greenery. She fought her way through the shrubs until she arrived back at the trail. "You, there! Halt!" someone shouted.

Mara's heart skipped a beat. She turned around. A couple figures charged down the trail, then slowed. "Mara!" one of them called.

The voice sounded familiar. When she squinted, she saw one of the watchmen was Sid. "This is a dangerous place," he yelled.

When they caught up to her, Sid's partner eyed her skeptically. "What are you doing here?" he said.

Sid shook his head. "Never mind her." He took Mara's arm and pulled her aside. "You're not safe here. Come, I'll walk you back home."

Mara reminded herself to breathe. As Sid guided her down the trail, she looked back. Smoke was rising from over the treetops, along with the tips of flames. She wondered how she could have started a blaze.

23. Almost Perfect

"Wait, did she really stomp on the house?" I asked. "Is she Gallant?"

Sheridan chuckled. "Gallant? As in Goofus and Gallant?"

"No, the giant."

"*Gulliver*," Sheridan said.

"Whatever. I have a hard time imagining she could've crushed it. Maybe if she were a T-Rex."

"This isn't *Dinosaur Comics*," Sheridan said. "Besides, what else matters than what Mara sees?"

I wasn't sure how to respond to that. In some ways, Mara reminded me of Calvin from *Calvin and Hobbes*. The idea made sense in light of the fact that Sheridan was pulling the story from her journal or something.

Perhaps Marcus's trip to SanCullep Island had also been just in his head. But, if that were the case, how did he get the idol?

The problem with historical accounts is that they're written by people–and some may not be reliable at all. I got the sense that was where Sheridan was heading, even if he didn't want to admit it. He was telling the story of a madman, or woman, whatever. She'd never lost her childish imagination. Come to think of it, maybe Sheridan had never lost his.

"You know," I said. "You and Mara have a lot in common."

Sheridan grinned. "Oh?"

After I started to make my comment, I regretted it. His ears sat perked.

"You're both annoying as hell."

"Is eternal damnation supposed to be *annoying*?" Sheridan asked. He was smiling, but I think he tried to hide it. "There are some interesting visuals there. Do you think devils will follow you around, flicking your ear? 'Does that hurt'? 'How about now'?"

"It's just an expression."

"There's a parking space in the tenth circle of Hell," Sheridan said. "But the car in the next space has one wheel over the line."

"So, what happened to Mara after she smashed the house?"

"Nothing." Sheridan smiled; it was just a tad sinister. "But, over the next few days, rapid changes took place in Locana. Among other things, the Church of La Nocturne ushered in their own guard, much to Sid's dismay. Mara, on the other hand, paid hardly any attention at all."

- 65 -

Mara admired the buzz of the city as she walked. She thought about how she'd never seen so many people in all her life. Drums and horns echoed between the buildings and over the crowd. Every so often, rounds of applause would erupt.

Perhaps Locana won that spat with Culatan, she thought. But there were a considerable number of disgruntled and worried faces. People eyed the background suspiciously, whispering to each other whenever a guard wasn't watching.

The town guards wore new uniforms. They were still Locana Blue, but much more ornate. They even had bits of lace laid over their heavy armor. Mara recognized the patterns. They matched the trim of La Nocturne's temple.

A particularly large crowd had assembled around Mara's fountain. They were facing the street, cheering and applauding. Drums and the march of hundreds of feet drew closer. Mara stood on her toes to see over the crowd. Someone tapped her shoulder, and she spun around.

"Sanreils?"

Sanreils took Mara's hand and kissed it.

"Greetings, beautiful," he said.

"Hi."

"Um." Sanreils blinked and paused briefly. "Come ... to watch the parade?"

"Yes ... no ... what is this all about?" Mara struggled to see over the heads in front of her.

"Have you not heard?" Sanreils replied.

"I haven't a clue."

Sanreils explained, "The baron and La Nocturne have finally signed a pact. It's a proud day for our region."

"A pact?" Mara raised her eyebrows.

"Yes," Sanreils said. "The baron has realized the plague on Locana. He has handed the governing of our region to La Nocturne."

"I thought they were already governing," Mara said.

"No, dear," Sanreils replied. "We had been trying to convince the baron of the wonderful gift of peace we can offer. I suppose the raid on his manor was the last straw."

Mara's heart skipped a beat. "Raid?"

Sanreils nodded. "I'm glad you were safe." He took her hand. "I was worried about you."

"Oh ..." Mara turned slightly pale.

"Are you okay, my dear? You look like you've seen a ghost."

Mara shook her head. "Nothing. It wasn't my fault."

Sanreils laughed. "Oh, imagine that. Mara, the great warrior!"

Mara forced a chuckle. Sanreils cleared his throat. "I was worried because you missed the banquet."

"Oh," Mara sighed. "I'm sorry. I lost–"

She paused briefly. *Surely, he wouldn't understand that I lost my reflection. Would he?*

"Lost what, my dear?"

"Nothing," she muttered. "It's silly and, well, never mind. I spent the next couple of days meeting with the Ori."

"What's an ori?"

"*The* Ori. You know, at the university."

Sanreils stroked his chin. "I've never heard of an 'ori'."

"You haven't?" Mara asked. "Aph–"

She stopped herself before saying *Aphrael*. Sanreils was eyeing her. She continued, "Aph've been wondering something. The day–"

Sanreils stared down the street. The drums were beginning to fade into the distance. Mara punched his arm. "Listen to me!"

"Whoa!" Sanreils jumped back. "What? Why–"

"I'm sorry," Mara said. She closed her eyes and sighed. "The day you met me–what was the message?"

"We need to discuss something. Would you accompany me to the gardens?"

"Oh?" Mara whispered. "What do you want to tell me?"

Sanreils smiled. He led her down the street. "Patience, my dear."

- 66 -

For the entire walk, Mara didn't say anything. A hundred thoughts bounced in her head all at once. *Why is he taking me away? What does he want to tell me? Why is it in secret? Does he think it's strange I'm not saying anything? Say something! What?*

Sanreils didn't seem to mind the silence. He hummed an unfamiliar tune, then stopped at the garden gate.

The city gardens were surrounded by a short wall, about three feet in height and made of a white stone that reflected the sunlight. At one point, the garden had been a conflagration of colors. Now, most of the flowers had wilted.

Sanreils led Mara to a quiet spot, under the shade of a tall oak. He sat on a bench, and invited her to join him.

Her heart began to race. She couldn't push Aphrael's words out of her mind. *"He seems to have you rather hypnotized." Why had she said that?*

He took her hand. "Do you remember when I said I'd like to begin a courtship?"

Mara nodded.

"La Nocturne is hosting a ball, a celebration of the pact. I'd like you to accompany me."

Mara nodded again. Sanreils chuckled. "I take that as a 'yes'?"

"I think . . . I would like that," Mara whispered.

"We'll get it right this time."

Mara forced a smile and looked up at the tree. They sat together for a moment. She eventually broke the silence. "But, the day you met me . . . "

"Oh, I wouldn't ever forget."

"Where were you going?"

"I've been sworn to secrecy, my dear. I wish I could tell you."

"What was the message?"

Sanreils laughed. "Oh, Mara. I–"

He stopped, catching a glimpse of her eyes. They glistened in the light, and he could see her gaze growing icy. "You don't seem like yourself," he said.

"Just tell me. It was about the forest, right? Culatan? Were they in the forest?"

Sanreils sighed. "Yes," he said. "They were in the forest."

Mara closed her eyes and began to feel a great weight lift off her shoulders. *It was Culatan! It couldn't have been Sanreils.*

At the same time, her stomach turned into a knot. "What ... do you know why?"

"Listen," Sanreils said. He gazed at the sky and contemplated too long for Mara's patience. "I spent a great deal of time worried sick about you when we parted that day. But I knew you were safer alone. I couldn't bear the thought of you being in danger ... "

Mara held her face in her hands and shook her head. "I'm sorry," she blurted.

"You're sorry?" Sanreils frowned and put his arm around her shoulder. "What's bothering you?"

"I ruined everything."

Sanreils raised her chin with his finger. All the words fell out of Mara's mouth, and they briefly stared at each other. She began to feel anxious when he guided her head closer, laid his hand on her cheek, and kissed her.

Mara closed her eyes as all her thoughts rushed away. Sanreils smiled gently, and said, "I do apologize, my dear. I hope I wasn't too forward."

"Not at all," Mara whispered. She blushed slightly as she returned his smile. "Everything is perfect."

Sanreils nodded and kissed her forehead. "I'm glad to hear that."

Mara wondered if he knew she had just lied. *Almost perfect,* she thought. *Why can't I tell him about my reflection? I should be able to.*

24. What Have I Done

"So, how *does* one thing lead to another?"

Sheridan smiled. "You're really curious, aren't you?"

I shrugged. "Not much else to do, except drive."

"It's not an easy question to answer," Sheridan said. "What is the root of all cause?"

"Like, cause and effect?" I asked. "That's easy. A pin clinks because it was dropped. A clock moves because the springs push the hands."

Sheridan shook his head. "You can ask yourself a million questions. How does X lead to Y? Mara wanted one answer for all of them."

"A single answer? Is that possible?"

Sheridan grinned. "Perhaps now, you can appreciate the difficulty of such a task. From where does the wind originate? From where do the water's ripples come?"

"One answer for both questions?"

"One answer for *all* such questions!" Sheridan exclaimed.

"Why?" I asked. "That's impossible. The world isn't built that way."

Sheridan folded his arms, and leaned back in his seat. "Prove it."

"Well," I stuttered. "Okay. I can't prove it."

"Unbelievability and falsehood are two different beasts," Sheridan said. "But I will grant you that such a prospect is hardly intuitive."

"Can *you* prove it?" I asked. "Or disprove it?"

Sheridan grinned. "It's an exercise for the reader."

"Is that *really* a common phrase in math texts? Or is it just your way of dismissing my questions?"

"It's there. Of course. Granted, it is an odd question," Sheridan said. "And the answers to the odd questions are always at the end of the book."

"Whenever I talk to you, why do I get the feeling I'm conversing with a math book?"

"Would you rather me be a dictionary?" Sheridan asked. "I'd imagine that could get rather annoying–which is an adjective, meaning to disturb or irritate."

"That is annoying," I said. "I'd rather you be a math text."

Sheridan nodded. "While I may have had only a brief stint as a dictionary, in many ways, it was my defining moment."

Sheridan smiled to himself, probably thinking about how funny he was.

"So," I said. "What's next?"

"Oh, yes," Sheridan said. "Well, while you think about your homework assignment, I'll start telling you how Mara worked on the answer. Let's see if you can get it before her. If she ever does."

- 67 -

Mara walked alone in the woods. The sun had just finished setting as she made her way through the twisty trails outside the tower. Every so often, a break in the canopy would reveal the stars. She thought of all the constellations she'd read about in Sylow's library.

"I shouldn't worry about Sanreils," she said, not to anyone in particular, but secretly hoping the trees would respond.

Indeed, the trees heard. But once again, the whispering was indecipherable.

"La Nocturne can't be that bad," she said. "Can it? They seem nice."

She felt a bit weary, and found a cool, dry spot of grass to lie in. The entire sky opened up for her. "There is Aries the lamb," she whispered to herself, "Taurus, the donut, and Trey, the flying wiener dog."

"I'm a ram!" Aries scolded. "Ram! Ram! Ram!"

"Sorry," Mara replied. "But it said lamb in the book."

"And I'm a bull! Not a donut!" Taurus added.

"Be nice to her!" Trey scolded Aries and Taurus. "She didn't know!"

"Sorry," Aries muttered.

Mara smiled at Trey. "Thank you," she whispered.

"Not all the stars are rude," Trey replied. "Dogs are always kind."

"Even a star-dog?" Mara asked.

Trey nodded.

"How wonderful it would be to be a star!" Mara exclaimed. "How wonderful it would be to see the entire world at once."

"It is actually quite sad," Trey replied, "To see the world and its state."

Mara frowned. "How so?"

"I worry what will come of it next."

Mara closed her eyes and nodded toward Trey. "Well, no matter what happens, I'll still be me."

Trey smiled. "I admire your spirit."

"I'm flattered," Mara said. "I'm just a person, and probably insignificant compared to what you can see from up there."

"Oh, no! I've watched over you for a while!"

Mara smiled. "Why me?"

"You're rare," Trey replied. "It's refreshing to see people who ponder the world, who are captivated by its mystery."

"Yes, well, it's a quality I don't think anyone cares for down here."

"I think you're wrong," Trey replied. "There are people who care for it. I can see."

Mara smiled. "You're probably right. You're a kind dog."

"I try to be."

"Even if you are a star-dog composed of many stars."

Trey laughed. "You, as well, are composed of many parts."

"I am?" Mara asked. She looked at her hands and feet, which seemed, to her, to be all part of the same body.

"The whole world is," Trey replied. "Why, even thoughts and ideas are!"

"So, what is thought? What are ideas?" Mara asked.

"They are as stars and constellations," Trey replied.

Mara thought about how the stars could be connected in different ways to form different images. She stared at her hands as she twiddled her fingers into various shapes. *Why couldn't letters and words behave the same? And if that was the case, ideas themselves could act similarly, as well.*

"The collective wisdom of the world must be a complex assortment of many ideas," Mara said.

When she didn't receive a reply, she looked back up. Trey was growling, chasing his tail and nipping at his rear as he ran in a tight circle.

"Trey!" Mara scolded.

Trey looked up, and his tailed fluttered.

"Were you *listening*?" She crossed her arms in front of her chest and glared.

"Sorry. If you had a tail, you'd understand."

"Ideas?" Mara asked.

"Yes! Exactly! So, you see, it follows that more diversity of thought means a greater pool of humanity's wisdom."

"And, the greater the wisdom of each individual man," Mara added. She paused briefly. "The brook once said it was the sum of mankind's wisdom."

"I've met the brook," Trey said.

"So, what are you?"

"A dog," Trey said. He smiled. "A *star*-dog. Like the constellations, I'm the sum of man's thoughts and ideas."

"Well, I'm Mara." She nodded. "The sum of, well, Mara's thoughts and ideas."

"Of course," Trey said. "*Sanghid*, so I won't confuse you with the other Maras."

Mara smiled. "You know!"

"I wouldn't confuse you, anyway. We dogs don't usually go by names," Trey explained. "We go by smell. But, as you can imagine, I would have a hard time smelling you from up here."

Mara nodded. "I try to keep good hygiene. I should hope you couldn't smell me from afar!"

"I can go by looks, though!" Trey said. "Eyes, hair. You can tell a lot about where a person has been from their eyes."

Mara thought of her first morning in Fordham Forest. She'd crawled to the stream and glanced at her reflection, watching the water move through her eyes. "Trey," she said. "Can I ask you a question?"

Trey's ears lifted like little flags, flapping in the breeze. "What kind of question?"

"An *asking* question," Mara said. "What do you see in my eyes?"

"Love."

Mara smiled.

Trey then added, "And fear."

"What?" Mara lowered her gaze.

"You did ask," Trey said. "I didn't think you'd want me to be dishonest."

"Well, no. But, well, okay. Fine. I'm a scared little girl."

"Now, hold on! Don't get all defensive. Even the brave get scared. It's okay. It's called being *human–*"

"Something you dogs know *all-l-l* about."

"Well, we are man's best friend."

Mara smirked. "I see."

"No, you don't. But one day, you will."

Mara placed her hands on her hips and tapped her foot on the ground. "Are you suggesting I don't understand my-self?"

"Yes."

"Well! You're–"

Trey lowered his ears to half-mast in anticipation of Mara's answer. She lowered her voice and sighed. "Right."

"I'm sorry," Trey said. "I didn't mean to upset you."

"I saw the water move through my eyes. Why?"

Trey thought for several moments before returning with a quick, "I don't know."

Mara nodded again.

"Anyway ... it is late! You should go sleep!" Trey said.

"I should," Mara replied. "Thank you for keeping me company."

Trey smiled. "Anytime."

- 68 -

Mara began her walk home. Usually, the woods made her nervous at night, but the star-dog comforted her. Every few steps, she would look up. Trey smiled back down.

Mara rounded a dark corner, and stopped. She tried to raise her ears like Trey would. She heard a very faint crying. *Perhaps it's the wind,* she thought. But as she hiked further, the crying became clearer.

Then, she spotted the source. A woman sat in a small, moonlit clearing. Her face was buried in her hands, and she seemed not to notice Mara.

Mara recognized her from Aphrael's description. It was Trisha. She was adorned with the delicate Locana Blue, lace robes, torn from her trek in the forest.

Trisha looked up, wide-eyed and breathing heavily.

"I didn't mean to startle you," Mara said.

Trisha wiped her cheeks. "Who are you?" she whispered.

"Mara." She smiled gently and sat down next to her. "Don't worry. I won't bite. Aphrael told me all about you."

"Oh, no no no!" Trisha sighed. "Life was so simple when we were young. I fear what she thinks of me now."

"She misses you."

"She wouldn't forgive me. Not after what I've done."

"What did you do?" Mara asked. Trisha stared at her as Mara fidgeted. "If you don't mind me asking, that is."

Trisha waved her hand at her robes. "This! La Nocturne. It's my doing."

Mara raised an eyebrow.

Trisha continued, "I brought it to life, resurrected it from the universe's jail over a troubling sea. Aphrael warned me, but I ignored her. I made a world. And I joined it. Then it spread like an unattended fire in a camp."

"Aphrael didn't tell me much."

"It's out of my control, now. They took it over." Trisha buried her head again. "They're after me. You're not safe here. Go! Go!"

"But where did it come from? La Nocturne?"

"From where the wind originates. From where the water's ripples come."

"I don't understand!" Mara exclaimed. "But you have to come with me. Aphrael misses you terribly."

"I can't," Trisha blurted. Her words were muffled by her

hands, but Mara could still make them out. "La Nocturne will kill me. It has to be destroyed first."

"But why?" Mara asked. "How—"

She stopped herself and cycled through everything Aphrael had told her. *Find the sequence, and break it. But how? What does that even mean?*

Trisha raised her head. She looked up at Mara with tears streaming down her cheeks. "What have I done?"

Mara fidgeted and scraped the bottom of her brain for something to say. She diverted her gaze for a second, but Trisha took her hand and commanded, "Look at me."

"I—"

Trisha released her hand. "Leave this place. Leave Locana, and never come back."

- 69 -

Mara spent the next several hours wandering through the forest. The sun had long set, and only a sliver of moon had come out. She said nothing to the trees, but every few moments, they would whisper to each other.

Perhaps they're talking about me, she thought. *I'm an intruder in their home.*

Mara stopped. A faint, orange glow, partially obscured by vines and shrubs, had caught her attention. It vibrated slightly, and she could soon tell it was the glow of dancing flames. With her curiosity piqued, she edged closer.

The fire was too big to be from a camp. She wondered for a moment if the whole forest was going up in flames, but it did not appear to be growing. She heard faint chanting.

As she made her way closer to the light, she began to feel nervous. Something about it made her feel uneasy. The center was dark.

When she pushed even closer, she could see very clearly what the oddity was. She had to cover her mouth to keep from screaming and giving away her position.

In the center of the fire was a person, or the remains thereof. She, as Mara determined the figure to be female, had been tied to a post and lit aflame.

Mara shivered and felt weak, but curiosity drove her closer. The flames were surrounded by hooded figures with cloth draped over their faces. They stood perfectly still, chanting words she couldn't make out.

She dared not edge any closer, but squinted to see as best she could. The figure in the flames was undeniably that of Trisha.

One of the figures turned around and stared straight at Mara. Every muscle in her limbs froze. The figure lifted its hood partially, just enough to flash a wide grin.

Mara ran away.

IV
Eccentric, and Vastly Odd

25. Why Should I be Bound

"That turned nasty," I said. "And she still didn't answer the question. Where does the wind come from, or whatever?"

"Is there only a finite number of images which can be constructed out of the stars?" Sheridan countered.

"I have no clue. How does that answer the question?"

"Oh, take a guess," Sheridan said with a quick nod.

"Okay. I'm just going to take a shot in the dark–"

"You shouldn't drink and drive."

"Erm, I mean, answer the question," I said.

Sheridan smiled and tried to hide it.

"Well, there's only a hundred ways to combine the words in that song–"

"One hundred-twenty."

"Uh, yeah. The one Peoria sang," I said. " 'Close your sweet eyes, dreamer', or whatever. I guess it wouldn't be any different for the stars."

For the first time, but not the last, Sheridan's eyes lit up. "Ah!" he laughed. "Seems so, doesn't it?"

"Just a bigger number. Am I right?"

"The Ori's first lesson to Mara was for her to learn she is the product of a sequence of events, just like the variations of the song are products of a sequence."

"But what sequence?"

"That's what she needs to find. The Ori knows she'll need to know how to recognize it when she sees it, which is why he told her to learn about perspective ... "

- 70 -

Mara stood before the Ori's door, took a deep breath, and pushed it open. As soon as she stepped inside, the Ori greeted her. "Have you solved your problem?"

Mara bit her lip. "Yes. I mean, no. Maybe?"

The Ori stroked his beard. "Once again with the maybes. A little confidence goes a long way."

"Well, I grew really big. I stepped on the baron's manor."

"And you gained perspective?"

"I think so," Mara said. "Everyone thinks Culatan did it, and La Nocturne took over the government."

The Ori sat still, glared, and hummed. Mara stuttered. "But I ... I looked in the bottle! I think it flipped the world around. Then I got harassed by a fern."

"And what did the bottle teach you about the world?"

"I–" Mara stood up straight, then slouched a bit, "don't know. I guess I didn't get it."

"Failed."

Mara sighed. "I'm sorry I wasted your time."

"You were supposed to put the world in the bottle, and hold it."

"I tried!" Mara exclaimed. "I got sucked in with it! Believe me, I tried."

"But the outcome was failure. Come back in seven days. When you understand perspective, you can hold the world. It will fit between your thumb and fingers, and you'll be wise."

- 71 -

The following evening, Mara stood in front of Thorn Tower, staring into nothingness. She closed her eyes and dreamt of Carrboro Forest. She imagined herself back at Sylow's library. She imagined herself floating before the glowing city. *The city!* she thought, and kicked herself for having forgotten what she was after. *The highway said the people who loved me are there.*

She opened her eyes. She couldn't imagine who would be in the city.

"Mara!" Dahes exclaimed, interrupting her thoughts. He came running up the trail.

"Dahes!" Mara laughed. "I haven't seen you in a while!"

Dahes leaned against the tower door while he caught his breath. "I've been–studying!"

Mara nodded. Something about Dahes struck her as odd, but she couldn't figure out what. "I figured as such. Tell me! What have you learned?"

Dahes followed Mara into the tower foyer. He told her all about La Nocturne taking control of the university. Mara raised an eyebrow. "Why do they want it?"

Dahes shrugged. "They have good tutors."

Mara bit her lip. She wasn't sure what to think. She thought of Sanreils giving his speech at the banquet. It hadn't bothered her at first, but now, all she could think about was Trisha. She decided not to tell Dahes about what she'd seen, for fear of Aphrael overhearing.

"I suppose," she said. "They just make me a bit uneasy."

"Why?"

"They just *do*," Mara said. "It's just . . . intuition."

Dahes poked Mara's rib. "What about *Sanreils*?"

"Oh." Mara blushed. "I don't know."

"He's *something* at the church. And he seems to fancy you

well enough," Dahes said. "I don't see what you're worried about."

"Yes, well," Mara said. She glanced downward at Dahes's bare legs. "Where are your pants?"

"Matta ... " Dahes said.

Mara smiled. "You two have been seeing each other quite a bit. I think she has a little thing for you."

"I *thought* so!" Dahes exclaimed. "But she threw my pants off the top of the tower."

Mara laughed. She covered her mouth, trying to hide it. "I'm sorry," she blurted. She held her mouth for another moment. "I shouldn't laugh. But that's just really funny."

"Out the window! And now I can't find them."

"Dare I ask *how* she got them?"

"I don't know!" Dahes exclaimed. He buried his face in his hands. "We were on the top floor, and she was parading around with the pants, trying to keep me from catching them. Then she tossed them out the window!"

Mara laughed again.

"I think she was mad at me for refusing to leave the university."

"Why?"

"She's suspicious of La Nocturne, for the same reason you are, I suppose."

Mara folded her arms. "I'm not suspicious!"

Dahes shook his head. "You are, too! They're nice people, though. I've learned a lot."

Mara shrugged.

"You'll see," Dahes said. "One day I'll be a renown and distinguished scholar."

"On that note, there's still some daylight left." Mara put her arm over Dahes's shoulder and guided him back toward the door. "I'll help you find your pants."

- 72 -

The next day, Mara sat on the edge of the fountain, watching the streets. She stared, wonderstruck, as the people wove about each other. *They shift and twist in harmony,* she thought, *Just like the pulleys and gears of Dahes's puppets.*

She caught the attention of a wanderer, a boy slightly older than her. "It's you!" he exclaimed.

Mara looked around. "Me?"

"Yes."

Mara smiled. "Do you know me?"

"You're the peculiar one."

"We're all peculiar, if you think about it," Mara replied. "Why ... I wonder what the rest of Earth's creatures think. Here are these tall, lanky things wobbling around on only two legs ... with only a little blotch of hair on top! Clearly, we are in the minority!"

The wanderer smirked. "Why are you so different?"

"If I am not the same as you, then you are different, too."

"I just find it strange you don't follow the expected order of things."

Mara shrugged. "It's my nature ... and one shouldn't deny their nature."

"Here you are wandering the streets ... unescorted!" the wanderer exclaimed. "That should not be! I don't see why you have no suitor ... you're very pretty."

Mara blinked. *What kind of compliment was that?*

The wanderer continued, "Why ... if you're lucky, I might be willing to step in!"

"What?" Mara exclaimed. "You are a capital jerk!"

The wanderer bristled. "Who are you to insult me? You're just a weird fountain-head!"

Mara reached her hand into fountain stream and diverted its path onto the wanderer. He jumped back. "Hey!" he exclaimed. "Fine. So be it. Maybe, when you grow older you'll gain perspective!"

The wanderer huffed off down the street. Mara pondered the nature of perspective, and realized what the Ori must have wanted her to see. From where she stood, the wanderer appeared quite small in the distance. Should she hold up her hand, she could fit his head between her thumb and finger, and squeeze.

Mara contemplated the nature of the expected order. *All those puppets in the attic were bound to the expected order, and all they earned was a life under the control of the puppet master,* she thought. *I should be able to follow if I choose . . . but why should I be bound?*

26. One Shouldn't Deny Their Nature

"I don't see how learning to pinch heads will solve anything."

Sheridan laughed. "Oh, are you saying it wouldn't be a useful skill?"

"I can think of a few heads in that last audience I would've liked to have pinched."

After I said it, I immediately regretted it. I knew what Sheridan was going to ask next. "Oh? Whose?"

"Never mind."

"I think you're referring to your seminar," Sheridan said.

I glared at Sheridan with one eye squinted. "And just what drew you to that conclusion?"

"You said it went poorly," Sheridan said. "And you're upset about it."

"I didn't say it was your business."

"Aw, come on. You'll feel better. You should share! That's what friends do."

I laughed. "I'm not your friend."

Sheridan sat back without his usual goofy look. This time, he wore a blank face. I couldn't tell if he was genuinely hurt, or just pulling my leg. "You know," he said, somewhat sternly. "I know very well you're not driving me across the country because I can pay you."

"It's because Mara's just such a fascinating character," I said. "Go, go! Tell me more about her."

Sheridan put on a smile. "Oh! Well, *she*, unlike you, was quite cheerful and never sarcastic. She went on a walk ... "

- 73 -

Mara turned off Rosemary Road and walked down a small alley. The "Amber Alley," as it was called, ran between many pubs and eateries. She closed her eyes and took deep breaths, savoring the aromas.

Two Locana guardsmen stepped into the alley. Both were tall, stocky, and armed. She had run across their paths once before, outside the university. The left guard, Fepp Dows, had a moustache shaped like a tadpole. Berot Rehls, his colleague, usually smelled like dried onions.

"Mara!" Fepp exclaimed.

Mara groaned. "What now?"

Berot snickered. "Lovely to see you."

"Just here to wish you a happy morning," Fepp said.

Mara folded her arms. "I know very well you haven't stopped me just to wish me a happy morning. You've come to tease me."

Berot smiled. "No, no. We just saw you in the alley and I said to Fepp here, 'my, it's always a lovely day when we see Mara wandering around the town looking for her head.' "

Fepp laughed.

Mara growled. "If you have nothing better to do than act like a little twert, then I would suggest you have the intelligence of a mop."

Berot grinned and Fepp laughed again. "Look who's talking! It's Zombie-Mara, stomping about town!"

"Brains! Brains!" Berot moaned with his arms stretched forward.

"At least I have one!" Mara smirked and tapped her foot impatiently.

"We all do, dear," Berot said. He patted her head.

Mara replied, "Well, unlike yours, my head is not sore from having been sat on all day. Such are the merits of having the correct placement of my face and ass!"

Berot promptly slapped Mara across the face and forcefully shoved her against the wall, pinning her with one arm and drawing his sword with the other. Mara clenched her fists and choked back tears as she gazed angrily at the guard.

"Berot, Berot," Fepp said soothingly. "You don't want to do that."

"She insulted me!" Berot exclaimed. "A representative of Locana!"

Fepp shook his head. "You don't want to. Not to her."

Mara gazed icily at Fepp as he turned his attention to her. "Such a pretty face," he said as he stroked her cheek.

Mara closed her eyes tightly and turned her face away from Fepp and Berot. Tears ran down her cheeks as she wished to be out of the alley and back home, high above the town and out of its reach.

"Release her!" squeaked a voice at the end of the alley.

Berot released Mara, and Fepp drew his sword as they turned, facing the street. Mara looked up to see a scrawny figure. It was a boy she couldn't place, standing alone in the roadway. Mara began to think he looked familiar, but the guards soon seized her attention.

"Lookie here!" Fepp exclaimed. "We have a regular party!"

Berot snickered. "Why don't you come join the fun?" He tapped his weapon against his hand.

The boy stretched his hand out and curled his fingers, signaling "come here."

Fepp and Berot stared at each other a moment, then broke out in laughter.

"If that's what you wish!" Fepp cried.

The two guards slowly approached the boy, who stood

firm in the street. He waved his fingers even faster. Mara bolted toward him, past the guards, running as fast as she could. Fepp and Berot paused for a moment in confusion. Mara caught up with the boy and they both started running together. Fepp and Berot looked at each other, and followed.

Mara and the boy ran through the streets. Mara turned her head to look behind her. Fepp and Berot followed, but were not able to keep up.

"Just keep running," the boy said.

Mara looked behind her again. Fepp, moving too fast for his weight, lost his balance and fell flat on his face. Berot immediately tripped over him and crashed to the ground. Mara and the boy kept running until the town faded into forest, and it was all behind them.

They stopped when they reached a shaded spot in the forest, a bit away from the main road. Mara fell to her knees and collapsed to the ground, desperately trying to catch her breath. The boy lay on the soft forest floor, breathing heavily.

Several moments later, the boy sat up. Mara sat on a small rock, crying into her hands. The boy fumbled through his sack and pulled out a small tin cup. He filled it with cool water from a nearby spring. He walked to Mara and gently tapped her shoulder. Mara looked up at her rescuer. His dark, crimson hair and pale complexion burned in her mind.

Mara swallowed the water and stared at the boy. "Take your time" he said quietly. "We're safe here."

"Thank you," Mara whispered.

The boy nodded and walked back to his fallen pack.

For the first time since they'd stopped, Mara calmed herself down enough to look around. She was surrounded by unfamiliarity. The trees, the spring, the rocks were all unknown. *Where am I?* She looked to the boy. He had his back to her, watching the trail. As she struggled to climb to her feet, the boy turned and smiled softly at her.

"You're up," he said.

Mara stumbled a bit and fell against a nearby tree trunk. The boy rushed over to help her. "Who are you?" Mara whispered.

"My name is Theon," the boy replied. "Just Theon. I'm named after the old stoic."

Mara smiled slightly and started to introduce herself, but Theon interrupted, "I know who you are. You live in that tower down the other trail."

"Oh," Mara replied. She looked down.

Theon smiled. "I've seen you before. I always wanted to meet you properly."

Mara looked up and smiled at him.

"I wish the circumstances were better," Theon said. "Nevertheless, here we are."

Mara nodded. "Why did you want to meet me?"

Theon smiled nervously. "You're interesting. I see you in the streets, so preoccupied. I've always wanted to ask you over what. It must be fascinating."

Mara laughed. "Why did you never come and ask?"

Theon looked at his feet. "I'm shy, I suppose."

Suddenly, she realized where she had seen him. "I've seen you before, too!"

Theon smiled.

"You came by to talk to me one day," Mara said. "When I was standing in the fountain."

Theon laughed. "Am I that memorable?"

"You were singing a very peculiar song."

He hummed a short melody, followed by the lyrics. "Close your eyes, sweet dreamer."

Mara's eyes grew wide. "That's it! *What* is that song? It's haunting."

"It's a lullaby," he said. "I learned it when I was young, but I forgot all but the first five words."

"If you sing every possible combination of the words, you could get a full song!"

"How did you know that?"

Mara shrugged. "It just seemed like a natural thing to do."

Theon cleared his throat and flashed a smile. Mara stared into his eyes. They were a reddish-brown, almost the same shade as his hair. "Why do you look so familiar?"

"You mean, from the fountain?"

"No," Mara said. "I've met you before. But I don't know when."

Theon looked down and blushed slightly.

"It has to be," Mara said.

Theon looked up at her. "I have to know," he carefully formed each word, "what it is you're so lost in."

Mara started to speak, then stopped herself. Theon quickly reassured her, "I'm not planning to ridicule you. I just ... admire you."

Mara blushed. Theon smiled at her. "I'm really just curious," he said.

- 74 -

Mara and Theon walked down the trail to Thorn Tower. Along the way, she would stop and point out various wildflowers that grew in the dense woods. "I love this trail," she said. "It always puts me in a good mood."

"I don't spend much time out here." He plucked a flower and examined it. "It is quite scenic, though."

Mara stopped abruptly. "Here, let me show you something!" she called as she pulled apart a couple of bushes.

Theon looked into the opening Mara had exposed. The bushes hid a small, obscure trail leading into the darkness.

They followed it up a steep slope which ended at a cliff overlooking the town.

From the top of the cliff, the town was a tiny blotch on an intricately woven fabric of forests and fields. Little lines crossed through the buildings, barely discernible as streets. On them, people and carts moved between each other, like gear teeth on a finely set clock. Theon looked over the edge and gasped.

Mara smiled. She sat at the edge and motioned for Theon to join her.

"Look at everyone down there," Mara said, "going about their lives."

Theon squinted and tried to see the people. "They look like ants."

Mara pushed her hand into the grass, so that the blades poked up through her fingers. "It's calming."

Theon turned his head toward Mara. "Is that what you do all the time? Watch the city?"

Mara laughed. "Only sometimes. It helps me think."

"Oh? About what?"

"The Ori."

Theon raised an eyebrow. "I've never heard of an ori."

"Not *an* ori," Mara said. "*The* Ori. He's my tutor. He told me to learn about perspective."

"Did you?"

Mara leaned back. "Watch the clouds with me."

Theon lay back and stared up at the sky. Mara pointed to a long, stretched cloud. "What do you think that one is?"

"It looks like a dachshund," Theon replied.

Mara clapped her hands.

"Am I right?" Theon asked.

"Of course!" Mara exclaimed. "How could that be anything but a dachshund?"

Theon smiled. "I'm good," he said.

"And do you know how it got there?"

"Chasing cats?"

Mara giggled and shook her head. "Water! Clouds turn into rain, but the rain had to get up there somehow. And it grew into a blob. A big, puffy blob! But we see a dachshund. That's perspective."

"I always just assumed clouds were *there*."

Mara closed her eyes. Something about Theon's presence comforted her, and she tried to figure out what. "Can I tell you something?"

Theon sat up and nodded. He plucked a blade of grass and watched it drift in the wind.

"I'm scared," Mara said. "This city frightens me. But I don't want . . . I can't let them know it."

"Them? Who?"

Mara sighed. "La Nocturne." She sat up and watched Theon's blade of grass disappear below the ledge. "I don't want to lose what I have. I'm lucky."

"I miss the old city guards," Theon said.

Mara nodded and closed her eyes. She sat silent for several moments. Theon touched her shoulder and she looked up.

"But! *They* can just get used to me doing my thing, right?"

"Right," Theon said. He nodded and grinned.

Mara shook her head. "Most of *them* think I'm rather strange, anyway. It's not like I have many friends here."

"I'll be your friend," Theon said.

Mara laughed. She looked at him and smiled. "Thank you," she whispered. "I think I would like that very much."

Theon returned her smile. "Me, too."

"And friends," Mara said, "share the wisdom they've earned so that each may be a better person."

"I like that."

"I see things," Mara said. "The trees, the flowers, the clouds ... they all speak to me. They tell me where they're going and what they're doing."

Theon blinked. Mara turned around, so her back was to Theon. "Never mind," she said.

"No," Theon replied. "Tell me. I want to know. What do they say?"

"Mean things," Mara said. She turned back around to face Theon. "But I can read them. Sometimes. Sometimes, I can't."

"Like, you can predict the future?"

"Not reliably," Mara said. "I'm missing something. A sequence, I was told."

Theon stared up at the sky. The dachshund merrily scurried over the town, chasing the other clouds away. He wondered if Mara had known that was going to happen. "Who told you about the sequence?"

Mara told Theon about Sylow and everything that had happened since. It was the first time she'd told anyone the whole story. She could tell he didn't understand all of it, but he seemed interested. Mara couldn't recall anyone, other than Sylow, ever paying close attention.

"I was told to find the sequence," Mara said. "Maybe it'll help me get to the glowing city."

"They say history repeats itself. Maybe the sequence is there." Theon stared, then shook his head. "Scratch that. People aren't flowers or machines."

Mara's eyes lit up. "Oh! Maybe they *are*." She began to have flashbacks of her first day in Locana. This time, the thought didn't frighten her. "Maybe they're like Dahes's puppets, linked to some kind of vast array ... some kind of pattern ... of ropes and strings tied to a cord. Some kind of key. And what if you could find it? What if you could pull it? Wouldn't it be amazing to see what would happen?"

"How very complicated," Theon said.

Mara giggled. "Think about it!" she exclaimed. "Just a little tug; Just to see what happens. It would be so grand, to know what affects what. To see and hold the world in a way no one has held it before. To be one with the whole world ... to be a part of it all."

Theon stared at Mara.

"What?" she asked.

Theon replied, "I do believe you are the single most interesting person I've ever met."

Mara smiled. "Thank you."

Theon watched the sky begin to turn orange as the sun started its descent. "It's pretty."

Mara nodded. She turned her back to Theon and and watched the sky.

"I see why you come up here," Theon said. "You can see everything."

Theon and Mara peeked over the edge of the cliff.

"Look at the streets!" Mara exclaimed. "Look at the people. They're all just going about their lives, not even paying attention to this extraordinary evening."

Mara stood up, closed her eyes and opened her arms, inviting the breeze to rush over her.

A moment of silence passed. Mara opened one eye and found Theon gazing at her. He blushed. Mara smiled. She closed her eyes again and faced the wind. She dropped to her knees and took a deep breath as the wind brushed against her. "I think I know what the Ori wanted me to see." She opened her eyes, held her hand up, and "pinched" the city between her fingers. "I can hold the world. I can put it in that bottle, and then hold the bottle."

"You wouldn't be in it yourself? Wouldn't you, since you're in the world?"

Mara laughed. "Maybe I'm an exception!"

"You should be proud!"

"Yes! But it seems exceptions aren't welcome. I think that's the lesson I should take from this morning."

"Oh, Mara ... "

Mara closed her eyes and let the wind blow through her hair. Theon watched her for a moment. "Well, I shall proclaim you exceptional."

Mara smiled and laughed, climbing to her feet, stretching her arms again and feeling the world around her. "It is a wonderful thing!" she called into the wind. "It is a wonderful thing, indeed, to be part of this world, surrounded by curious and fascinating things. Mysteries abound, but I will be part of it all ... everything! I will see it and hold it."

Theon stood and opened his arms alongside Mara. She saw him, took his hands and exclaimed, "Let's dance!"

Mara, smiling and laughing, picked Theon up and swung him in a circle around her. "Cliff!" Theon shouted.

She put him down, opened her arms again, and ran up to the edge. "We're free up here, above it all."

Theon was still catching his breath when Mara turned around. She laughed when she saw him. "Don't be afraid, silly. It's just freedom."

"That's not–"

Mara ran toward him and took his hand. "It's a wonderful thing, and I want to share it with you."

Theon glanced down at his hand and gazed at her fingers interlocked with his. He then looked up and blushed slightly when his eyes met her's.

Mara swung around him and sang, "We are here, so high above! The world is ours below!"

Theon laughed. "We are! We are free!"

The sun had almost finished its trek down the horizon. From the city, the mountainside faded into a silhouette. Against the orange sun and dark blue sky, two figures danced, barely discernible. They were free from the world below as they stood in the sky, overseeing it all.

- 75 -

Mara led Theon back down the cliff trail, then walked with him the rest of the way to Thorn Tower. When they reached the yard gate, the moon bathed the dilapidated tower with a calm, silver light. Sid and Matta stood at the gateway.

"*There* you are!" Matta shouted.

Mara and Theon reached the gate. "Meet Theon. He says I'm interesting!"

"We all think you're *interesting*," Sid replied. He faced Theon. "And you ... Theon?"

Theon nodded. "After the old stoic," he added.

"Oh?" Sid asked. "Are you a philosopher?"

Theon shook his head. "That would be grand. But I'm a carpenter's apprentice."

"Perhaps you should be a philosopher!" Mara said.

Theon laughed. "I think that sounds like a better plan. But no ... not feasible."

Mara grinned, then frowned. She glanced at Matta, who had not said a word since they'd walked up and was gazing into the sky. Mara poked her in the rib. "Are you okay, dear?"

Matta shook her head. "I'm worried about Dahes. I told him, 'get out now!' " she explained. "But did he listen? No-o-o!"

"He never listens anymore," Sid said.

"I finally gave him an ultimatum," Matta said. "Leave. Now. La Nocturne has wrapped too many of its little fingers around the university. It's not the same place it used to be. And so many of the students are ... *weird*."

"Why would they want the university?" Theon asked.

"Same reason they replaced all the watchmen," Sid said. "It's a mystery."

Mara shuddered.

"I hate to just run off," Theon said. "But I worry that my master will give me a wallop if I'm tardy."

"Oh! Well, we don't want that," Mara said. She frowned, then wiped it off her face and waved cheerfully. "Please return!"

"Yes," Matta said, "Anyone who thinks Mara's *interesting* is certainly welcome here."

Theon smiled and nodded. Mara whispered, "Thank you again . . . for rescuing me this morning."

Sid's ears perked up as Theon waved goodbye. Mara and Matta waved back as he made his way across the fields and back into the woodlands.

"Thank you for . . . *what*?" Sid asked. "Are you okay, my dear?"

Mara nodded. "It . . . has been a trying morning."

"Have those two Locana guardsmen been giving you trouble again?" Sid asked.

Mara sighed.

"You've got to watch where you're going!" Sid exclaimed. "They'll keep giving you fits if you don't stay out of those alleys."

Mara shook her head. "They just want to intimidate me." She threw her arms in the air. "Why?"

"You shouldn't let them frighten you," Matta said.

Mara huffed, "And *who* says they frighten me?"

Matta stared at Mara. Mara sighed. "Okay! *Sometimes* . . . "

"What is a bird that cannot fly?" Sid asked.

Mara grumbled. "One held down by Fepp and Berot."

Matta grabbed a thin tree branch and frantically waved it around. "If I see those two, I'll . . . I'll give them what's coming!" she proclaimed.

Sid shook his head. "Now, don't you go getting yourself killed. Or getting us in trouble!" he said.

"I don't know what I've done to them!" Mara cried. "Really! Explain!"

"They're wary of you," Sid explained. "Now, I don't know why, but the church ... this whole New Locana ... they're wary of you. And they'll strike if they ever snatch an opportunity to."

"Why? I won't do them harm!"

"Consider the way you think," Sid said. "What you believe. First, they'll embrace you. Accept you like a true friend. Then, they'll wrap their own doctrine around yours, and you'll be assimilated."

"It's true," Matta said. She stood straight, with a defiant gaze–but tears began to well in her eyes. "Dahes is different. He's no longer curious, no longer embracing the world."

"Is that why they're shutting down the university?" Mara asked.

"They're not shutting it down," Matta explained. "Just taking control of it."

"He who controls access to knowledge controls the world," Sid replied. "Nobody stays in power for long if they have to answer questions."

"They're changing Dahes," Matta said. "And intimidating *you*."

"I won't let them." Mara folded her arms in front of her chest and glared.

"*That's* why they're wary of you," Sid said. "The next step, if they can't succeed, is to extinguish you. Put you out like a doused flame."

Mara shuddered. "But, why me? Why am I so special? I'm harmless!"

Sid replied, "Don't ask me why, but they must disagree."

Matta said, "Some people are just cruel."

Mara sighed and walked into the tower. Sid and Matta looked at each other. "I don't think she gets it," Sid remarked.

"What?" Matta asked.

"Nothing," Sid replied, shaking his head. "I'm just afraid, one of these days, she's going to get hurt badly by this world she claims to love so dearly."

"I knew you cared about us," Matta said. She grinned.

Sid smirked. "She's a *tenant*, which reminds me why I came in the first place. I'm going to have to start asking for rent money, or move in here, seeing as I've been stripped of my title."

Matta frowned, and revealed her empty pockets. Sid exposed his in turn.

27. June Bugs

" 'People are like machines'," I said. "That seems like an odd thing to say."

"You think so, huh?"

"What? You think it's true?"

Sheridan cracked his usual stupid smile. "Does it matter what I think?"

"I'm just curious," I said. "You don't have to turn it into a puzzle."

"Puzzles are fun," Sheridan said.

The storm clouds still loomed above. Though we were safely out of their reach, I began to have flashbacks to the start of our trip. Out of the blue, I remembered the billboards we'd passed, where the telephone numbers had formed the Fibonacci sequence. Who'd put those billboards up? I shook my head free of the thoughts.

"Am I a machine?"

"A marionette? I don't see any strings," Sheridan said. "But who's to say I'm the best judge of these things."

"Well, I have free will."

Sheridan stroked his chin and hummed–a rumbling tone surely meant to irritate.

"What?" I asked. "Why are you doing that?"

Sheridan chuckled. "I'm just wondering, that's all."

"Well, I do. You don't think so?"

"I don't think it really matters," Sheridan said. "Tell me, which way do you intend to drive?"

"Straight ahead?"

"You don't sound so confident."

"Okay. Straight ahead. Why?"

"I just find it amusing," Sheridan said, "that it's the *only* way you could choose to go. After all, when was the last time we passed an exit?"

"I don't know. I've been paying attention to the *road*."

"Drive straight, or ... you don't really have any other options."

"I could always drive off the road," I said. "But I won't, because you're such a pleasure to talk to, and never a downer."

"I suppose only a free-thinking being would have the ability to purposefully terminate its own life," Sheridan said. "And, on that upbeat note, Mara pressed on ... "

- 76 -

Unable to sleep, Mara wandered through the forest. She stopped every so often to take in the scenery. "Why won't you talk to me?" she asked the trees, which replied with the usual tangle of whispers.

She sighed and shook her head. A few moments later, she came to a break in the tree line. She watched the clouds roll away and reveal the moon. "Tell me, mountains, are there any secrets you keep?"

No answer came. "Mountains? Surely you speak, too."

"Just a moment," the mountain replied. "We were all huddled together, deciding whether or not to let you in on the big secret we've been keeping from you all this time."

"Oh," Mara said. "Really?"

"No! Silly!" the mountain replied. "We don't have any secrets. I wish we did. Maybe more people would find us interesting."

"You're back!" the Trey constellation said.

"Star-dog!" Mara exclaimed.

"Lovely to see you again," Trey said.

"Do you keep any secrets?" Mara asked. "Why is the world so complex?"

"Would you want it any other way?"

Mara shook her head. "I suppose not. It would be too boring!"

Trey smiled. "See, that's why I like you. I think everyone else just wants it to be easy. But when it's easy, you miss out on all the good smells."

Mara grinned. "It's all about smells for you dogs, isn't it?"

"Not really. I do enjoy dead June bugs. They're fun to roll in."

"I wasn't aware of any June bugs up there," Mara replied. She searched the sky for blotches of stars that might look like bugs.

"You can create anything up here if you change the order you connect the stars in."

Mara pondered the nature of connecting. "It's a sequence," she said. "The order you connect the stars in. Are you just a permutation of that sequence?"

"Well, I like to think I'm more," Trey said. "But if you think about it, aren't we all?"

Mara held her hand up and wiggled her fingers. She carefully examined how the various bones moved. "It would appear so."

"Remember what we talked about before? About ideas?" Trey asked.

Mara nodded. "Ideas are combinations of other ideas. I suppose, in a way, grand memories are composed of smaller ones, all forming an intricate web."

"Well, perhaps the whole world is a combination of smaller elements," Trey said.

"Of course!" Mara exclaimed. "The wind, the leaves, the people."

"The mountains!" the mountain added.

"They all compose the world," Trey said.

"Everything in nature is a combination of smaller elements," Mara said.

Trey nodded. "Like ideas. Like everything."

"I heard a song in the city," she said. "Close your eyes, sweet dreamer."

"Oh! That's a lovely song!" Trey exclaimed.

"But only five words were known," Mara explained. "I'm pretty sure there are more. But, if you don't know them, you can still go on. Just take the same five words and re-arrange them to get a new verse!"

"And if you connect the stars in a different way, you can get delicious, delicious June bugs," Trey replied. He licked his lips. "Mmmm, Mmmm!"

"I don't see any June bugs," the mountain said.

"We all see the stars in a different way," Trey replied.

The mountain chewed on that thought for a moment.

Mara smiled. "Here's a question for you, Trey. Is there a finite number of images which can be constructed from connecting the stars in different ways?"

Trey smacked his lips as he debated with himself. After a moment, he answered, "Yes."

"No!" Mara exclaimed.

Trey laughed. "You seem quite confident. But there are a finite number of stars! There are six ways to connect three stars, twenty-four ways to connect four stars, and so on. Sure, the number is huge, but it is still finite."

"It's still *infinite*."

"Okay, I must know why," Trey replied. He flittered his tail.

Mara smiled slyly. "It's an 'exercise for the reader'."

"What does that mean?" the mountain asked.

"It's a common phrase in math texts, meaning, I'd learn more for having answered the question myself," Trey said. "But part of me wonders if our little human friend is just trying to dodge my request."

"Oh, no-o-o!" Mara exclaimed, drawing out the 'O'. "I know the answer! But I do feel bad that you have taught me so much, and I have not taught you anything at all."

Trey wagged his tail, slamming it against the moon. "What makes you think you've taught me nothing?"

"I don't get it," the mountain complained. "What's the business with connecting stars in a different way?"

"It's like taking the same five words of that song and singing them in a different order to get a new verse," Trey explained.

Mara sang, "Your sweet close eyes dreamer."

"That makes no sense!" the mountain protested.

Mara thought for a moment. She studied her hand again, pondering how her own components were assembled. "I suppose not. Neither would it make sense if I had two heads, one attached to each arm ... and one hand upon my neck."

Trey tilted his head. "What's wrong with that?"

"It'd be hideous!" Mara exclaimed. "Wouldn't it?"

"Not if it loved me," Trey replied. "We dogs don't mind two-headed hand beasts by their nature."

Mara sighed. "I guess that's why you're man's best friend, because you never judge like we do."

Trey looked up as a shooting star passed over his head, pondering the merits of chasing it.

"You're quite full of questions," the mountain said. "What is it you're seeking?"

"I want the world!" Mara exclaimed. "I want to see it and know what it's all about! I want to hold it in my hand, to see the whole universe. I want to be a part of it all!"

"That's a pretty tall order," the mountain said.

"Agreed," Trey said. "But you can decipher it. Just assemble the pieces one by one."

"I've been trying to do that," Mara said. "It's hard. The world is complicated."

"Well, you said the world is a combination of smaller elements," the mountain said. "And each piece composed of even more pieces. Where does it begin?"

Mara thought a moment. "Where does the wind originate from? Where do the water's ripples come from?"

"I don't know," Trey replied.

"Me, neither," the mountain added.

"The brook told me to ask nature," Mara explained. "It said the world would tell me what I need to know."

"I don't think that means the world will simply tell you the answers. It might not have them," Trey explained.

"That's what I figured," Mara said. "Still, I didn't think it would hurt to ask."

"I'd love to know where the wind comes from," the mountain said. "I'm fairly certain that arrogant blow-hard has been slowly carving down my size. And every time I try to confront it, it just blows me off."

Mara frowned sympathetically. "Poor mountain."

The mountain nodded. "Several of us have had the same issue. In fact, we were thinking of taking civil action."

"Well, I don't know about the law. But I know the patterns on the forest's roads come from the falling leaves," Mara said. "And the leaves fall the way they do because of the wind. So one follows the other. But from where does the wind come? What controls it?"

"I don't know what controls the wind," Trey said. "But I

certainly can see how it would matter to our little mountain friend, or to the pattern of leaves."

"I resent the term 'little'," the mountain protested.

Trey thought a moment. "If, in any given span of time, the wind was strong, then weak, then average, you would get one kind of pattern on the floor."

"But if it were strong, then average, then weak, you would get another," Mara said.

"Exactly," Trey said. "So see, there's a permutation of a sequence."

"So, what if there's a central pattern?" Mara asked. "A perfect harmony to nature, like the marionettes' cords?"

Trey perked his ears. "Marionettes? Like . . . puppets?"

"Oh, yes," Mara said. She quickly told Trey all about Dahes's attic. "They danced with such harmony."

"There is quite a harmony to us," the mountain replied. "Wouldn't you agree?"

"Indeed," Trey said.

"So, what the pattern must do is . . . " Mara thought out loud as she worked through the mental jigsaw pieces. Both Trey and the mountain watched her think. Mara's eyes lit up. "The pattern must rule the permutations."

"How so?" the mountain asked.

"If everything in nature is some combination of ideas, a main pattern can exist only if its job is to shift the combinations around to form new things at specific times," Mara eagerly explained. "It must be! It has to be! Because that would give rise to a beautiful symphony in nature! It's a conductor."

Trey smiled. "It's a wonderful thought."

Mara laughed to herself and spun around, caught in the rush of revelation. "It has to be, and now, I must prove it is so!"

"Well, then there are more clues to gather," Trey said. "But I have no reason to doubt you."

"How does it work?" the mountain asked. "Nothing shifts me."

"Oh … really?" Mara objected. "The wind shifts you by moving your dirt piece by piece."

"That blasted wind," the mountain said. "I bet it's sitting there, laughing to itself. Twerty show-off."

"So, what controls the wind? The thing that controls the wind is something, and that something is controlled by something else," Mara said. "It's a big chain. And it must originate from somewhere. It has to."

"Well, you go find it," Trey said. "If anyone can find it, it would be you."

- 77 -

Mara continued to wander through the woods, alone, carefully examining her surroundings. She stumbled upon a field, littered with scraps of food and other waste. A few tents were still standing, and little burgundy papers floated about in the wind.

She wondered what she had missed out on as she picked a paper off the ground. Someone had written an agenda and a menu. *Perhaps I missed another banquet*, she thought.

She folded the paper into a little diamond shape. Her mind wandered between thoughts of her reflection, La Nocturne, and her perspective of the city from the cliff. *If one were to know the purpose of the world, it would end*, she thought. *Because then, there wouldn't be a goal. Someone would have obtained it, and there would be no reason for the world to exist anymore.*

Mara laughed to herself. She spent the next hour drawing little doodles of the surrounding woods. From time to time, she thought of the whispering forest. She realized she never consciously thought of it anymore. Like the sound of the breeze or breathing, it just always was.

She never had figured out what the trees were saying. *Everything comes from something, which comes from something else. But how? In what manner?* She thought that, perhaps, the key was related to what she'd discussed with Trey–that the world's components were governed by a sequence.

Mara picked up a clean piece of paper from the ground. While humming the little five-note lullaby, she carefully wrote "I, II, III, IV, V" in a column on the left side. She drew an arrow pointing to a small box filled with arrows. They pointed in seemingly random directions.

"A cord," she said to herself. "It will form some sequence of the five numbers."

She spent the next several moments drawing various icons, showing what was related to what else. The cord pointed to the wind, depicted by clouds. The wind pointed to the leaves and seeds. Seeds pointed to the forests and the placement of trees. The cord also pointed to the water's ripples, which, in turn, also pointed to the seeds. Mara smiled. *Water tells the trees where to be planted as well, as some seeds do fall into the waters.*

Mara contemplated just how complicated the world must be. She thought of her puppets and what she'd thought of the town. She connected the cord to an icon depicting a figure. *A puppet. Its thoughts are determined by the sequence.* The figure was shown thinking, but its thought clouds contained only a question mark. This icon pointed to another, showing the figure thinking about which of two paths to choose. *Everyone goes about their business. The town is like clockwork.*

A flock of birds passed overhead, on their exodus from the cooling landscape. She watched them disappear over the horizon. *The sequence. What is it? It can't just be 1-2-3-4-5. That's too simple.*

It was at this point she noticed the whispering trees. "You know," she said. "Maybe you're all trying to tell me at once. If all but one of you would be quiet, we could go about the business. Don't you know it's rude to interrupt?"

She waited for at least one of the trees to quiet down. When none did, she sighed. "Come on, now. One at a time. Don't you understand me?"

Her eyes widened. She set her pencil down and stared at the trees. "You *don't* understand me. And I don't understand you. You're not all talking at once, are you?" She studied their motion in the breeze. Autumn was in full swing, and the leaves had begun to change color. "You're speaking another language, aren't you? And I don't know it."

- 78 -

The next morning, Mara wandered toward the town, burgundy paper in hand. She contemplated making her way to the Ori. It wasn't time for her usual appointment, but she wondered if she finally understood perspective. *Maybe he'll be proud,* she thought. *Or, at least, think of me as less of a fool. Then again, he may not want to see me at all.*

The roadway grew narrow. As Mara walked further along, continuing to debate making the trek into the university, a figure came into view. It stood still, as though it were defying her wish to pass. She paused, staring at it. It began to move toward her.

Mara fidgeted and glanced back over her shoulder. Another figure had cropped up behind her, and was approaching as well. Her heart skipped a beat. *Fepp and Berot?*

As they grew closer, she recognized who they actually were: Enton and Dimitry, two of La Nocturne's temple apprentices. The presence of the two priests did not comfort her in the least.

Enton and Dimitry each stopped a few feet from Mara. She backed herself into a slight indentation in the trees, feeling slightly safer in the tiny alcove. Enton spoke slowly, "We're here to warn you."

Dimitry added, "You are too inquisitive for your own good."

Mara stepped back into the middle of the roadway. She folded her arms and glared at Dimitry. "On the contrary, I have just the right amount of inquisitiveness. When you stop asking questions, it's like holding your hands over your eyes and living under a rock."

"So be it," Enton said.

Mara quickly turned around to face him. He stood only an arm's length away. She turned about again and watched Dimitry approach. He stopped about an arm's length away, as well. Mara returned to the tiny alcove on the side of the road. She continuously and nervously turned her head side-to-side, watching both of them. Dimitry cracked a grin. "So be it," he said.

"Pardon me," someone said, followed by the clip-clop of horse hooves. Mara and the two priests faced the passing merchant, who struggled to squeeze by Dimitry without running into him with his cart. As he squeezed by Enton as well, he tipped his hat. "Pleasant day to you three."

Dimitry looked behind him. A second cart, far in the distance, was approaching. Enton looked at Dimitry and nodded. He motioned with his head for Dimitry to come. Dimitry walked past Mara, turning around for a second to remind her, "We are watching."

The two priests disappeared down the trail. As soon as they could no longer be seen, Mara resumed breathing. A moment later, the second cart passed. The merchant smiled at her and waved as he rolled by.

Mara sighed and shook her head. She shuddered, and

scolded herself for letting the priests rattle her. She promptly turned around, and headed toward home.

28. Paths to Their Destinies

"How do you get June Bugs in the sky?" I asked. I leaned close to the windshield and tried to sneak a few peeks at the stars. Unfortunately, it was much too cloudy to see any of them.

"They're simple," Sheridan said. "Just about any little blob will do."

"There are thousands of blobs!" I exclaimed.

"Are there?"

I looked again. Every so often, when there *were* breaks in the clouds, I distinctly remembered seeing no stars. It was unsettling, to say the least. I tried to shrug it off. "Well, usually there are."

Sheridan smiled. "So, you can see how Trey is so upbeat and happy most of the time."

"Rolling in June bugs?" I asked. "Doubtful."

"So often do we overlook the simple pleasures of life," Sheridan said. "Nothing better than the feel of a good June bug on your back to brighten your day, eh?"

"I, umm, will let you be the judge there," I said. "Never mind that I don't see how Trey could have *gotten* them in the first place."

Sheridan tilted his head. "What do you mean?"

"How would he get all those June bugs if he can't move?" I asked.

Sheridan grinned. "Who says he can't move? But ... regardless, Trey had a *hypothesis*."

"Oh?" I asked.

Sheridan nodded. "If you stare at something long enough, it will slowly gravitate toward your mouth."

"Only a dog would come up with something like that," I said.

Sheridan smiled. "Dogs are very wise, aren't they?"

"If that were true," I said. "I'd stare at something more worthwhile than table scraps."

"What would you stare at?" Sheridan asked.

"I don't know."

"That's the hardest part," Sheridan said. "Figuring out what you want. The easy part is getting it."

"I don't know about that," I repeated. "I want money. But it sure isn't easy to get."

"Is that what you really want?" Sheridan asked. "Or just the means by which to obtain what you really want."

I had to think for a while about that one. I shrugged.

Sheridan grinned again. "See, now what would you do if you suddenly had all the money in the world?"

"It'd be nice to not worry so much. To have security, I suppose."

"You're a funny one, John Bartlebee," Sheridan said. "Most people go into the humanities fully aware of the low pay, and the competition, but they don't care because they love their studies. You, on the other hand–"

"On the other hand, what?"

"Do you like history?"

"I have a relationship with history that, for the most part, is agreeable. But why are we talking about me all of a sudden? What about Mara?"

"You know, I don't feel like I know you very well."

"Well, what about *you*?" I asked. "Who are you? Why were you on the side of the road? And don't tell me it's the point of the story."

"Well, it *is*," Sheridan said.

"I'll make you a deal," I said. "I'll tell you something about me, if you tell me something about you. Fair enough?"

Sheridan considered the proposition all too long, staring into the sky like it was his mentor. "Fair enough," he said quietly.

"I suppose I'll go first, then. Let's see . . . "

"What were you doing in Raleigh?"

"I hosted a seminar at Duke."

"But that's in Durham."

"I . . . okay. But you'll laugh."

Sheridan hid a smirk. "Oh, I won't."

"I went to the Carolina-State tailgate party. You know, support the team."

"So, you're a–"

"Tarheel."

"I don't believe you," Sheridan said.

"What? I am! I can show you my diploma."

"No," Sheridan shook his head. "I don't believe that's the reason you went."

"How would you know?"

"Your tone of voice. You sounded upset."

"UNC lost. They'd had a winning streak until *I* came. Of course."

"You don't care that much about sports," Sheridan said. He stroked his chin and hummed as he thought, pretending he had psychic powers or something. "I think you were after something else."

I glanced at Sheridan and glared. He smiled. "Or, *someone* else."

"Enough about me," I said. "What about you?"

"Me."

"Yes. Tell me, where is Mingo?"

"Mingo ... "

"Is she at the end of the road?"

"Yes," Sheridan said, and before I could protest, he resumed his story.

- 79 -

As time progressed, the leaves continued to change color. Mara became fascinated with the reason why some turned red, some orange, and some yellow.

She accompanied Dahes on his walk to the university. It had been a while since they'd walked together. Before the night Mara had witnessed Trisha's execution, they'd walked together every morning. Mara would point out different leaves as Dahes talked about the machines he'd build next.

But lately, he wasn't interested in either. Mara pushed a red leaf with a hole at the top in his face. "It looks like a little man, don't you think?"

Dahes shrugged.

Mara wiggled the leaf-man a bit, so that it looked like it was dancing. "La de da, I have a hole in my head," she sang.

Dahes kept walking without comment. Mara sighed and stopped, just to see if he'd keep walking without her. He kept going for a few steps, then turned around. "I thought you wanted to walk with me?"

"I see why Matta is upset," she muttered.

"What?"

Mara shook her head. "Nothing."

"I'm sorry," Dahes said. "I've just been up all night reading."

"And all day," Mara said. "All the time. You don't seem like yourself."

"Who do I seem like?"

"Let's build a machine!" Mara exclaimed. "A big one. In the tower. Maybe we can make it think."

"Uh . . . "

"Wouldn't that be grand? A machine that makes *decisions*! It'd be . . . "

Mara trailed off when she thought she saw Dahes roll his eyes, but she couldn't tell for sure. Dahes turned away and resumed walking. She didn't bother keeping up with him.

"He's a jerk, isn't he?" Mara asked.

She held up her leaf-man, but it didn't feel like talking.

"Well," she said. "We'll just have to go find a friend for you. One who's interested in your leafy veins."

Mara let the leaf-man float to the ground. A few trees grew over the road, and she thought about the trees near Sylow's house. She had gotten so used to the whispering that she hardly noticed it at all any more. Every so often, though, she remembered they were saying *something*. She hoisted herself up the trunk.

"Tell me," she asked the leaves. "What secrets do you keep?"

"Yes," Aphrael said. "I'm very curious to know if you've found that sequence."

Mara screamed and looked over her shoulder. Aphrael was sitting beside her, carefully perched on a branch. She winked and asked, "Have you had any revelations?"

"Don't sneak up on me!" Mara exclaimed. "You could've made me fall and break my neck."

Aphrael smiled innocently. "Don't worry. I'd never harm you."

Aphrael repositioned herself so that the branches formed a crude throne. "Have you met the Ori yet?"

"He's . . . interesting," Mara said.

"I was just wondering and all, how you were doing with our deal?"

"Our deal ... " Mara trailed off.

"Yes," Aphrael said. "I fulfilled my end. I told you who the attackers were."

Mara bit her lip and tried hard not to look into Aphrael's eyes.

"I haven't heard of Trisha in a while," Aphrael said. She cupped her hand around Mara's cheek and turned her face so that their eyes locked. "And you know I miss her so badly."

A shiver ran down Mara's spine. The events of that night in the woods came back to her. She tried to look away, but Aphrael kept her head locked in place, looking toward her.

"You *do* remember our deal, right?"

Mara nodded.

Aphrael released her. She lowered her gaze. "You're hiding something from me."

"The Ori ... " Mara stumbled on her words. "She's–I mean he, is intimidating. That's all."

"I see," Aphrael said. She tapped her fingers on the side of the tree. "I don't believe you."

Mara scooted back. She tried to move slowly, hoping Aphrael wouldn't notice. But Aphrael slid forward, glaring, and raised her voice. "There's something you're not telling me."

"No, no," Mara said. She shook her head and pushed herself further back. "Just nerves."

Aphrael seized Mara's hand and held it tightly. Mara winced as her grip tightened. Aphrael then wiped the glare off her face and put on a gentle smile. "It's okay. You know I'll find out, anyway. So you might as well tell me."

Mara shook her head and scooted back once more. She screamed as the branch gave way, and tumbled onto the ground.

"My dear!" she heard.

Mara tried to pull herself out of the bushes, but slipped and fell back down. Sanreils ran up to her. His concern dropped when he saw she looked unhurt. "Oh, Mara," he said and shook his head. "What were you doing in the trees?"

"I–" She took a moment to catch her breath. "I was just–"

"Are you okay?" He took Mara's hand and helped her to her feet. "You look like you've seen a ghost."

"Just Aph–" Mara stopped herself, but Sanreils finished her thought.

"Aphrael?"

Mara nodded.

"Oh, Mara," he said. "She's dangerous. Don't you know?"

"I know you told me to stay away from her," Mara said. "She's creepy. But . . . she does seem somewhat harmless."

"She's spiteful," Sanreils said. "A deceitful, nasty woman. She lies."

"Sometimes, I get the feeling–"

"She has an agenda, you know," Sanreils continued. He lowered his voice and leaned close to her ear. "I think she's a spy . . . for Culatan."

"A spy?"

Sanreils nodded. "Not that I know for sure. But I've traveled up and down these roads enough to know very well who's to be trusted. And Aphrael, well, it seems whenever she's around, death always follows."

Mara shivered. "I know. Sometimes, she finds me, though. I just climbed the tree to look at the leaves."

Sanreils laughed and shook his head. "Silly. Why would you do something like that?"

Mara smiled. "Well, before the whole mess with Aphrael, I saw the most wonderful thing. I saw–"

Sanreils held up his finger. "I do apologize, dear, but I was headed . . . somewhere. I'm afraid I need to be on my way."

"Oh," Mara frowned. "But–"

"Some other time?"

Mara sighed and nodded. "Okay ..."

She stopped herself. "No," she said and crossed her arms. "You're *always* running off when I want to share something with you. Aren't you the least bit curious about what I have to say?"

"Of course," Sanreils said. He kissed her cheek. "But I've been called, and I can't very well refuse."

Mara closed her eyes. "Very well. Maybe ... later."

She opened her eyes and saw Sanreils had already left. The leaf-man still rested by the base of the tree. She kicked it, and watched its decapitated head float down the road.

- 80 -

Mara spent the rest of the morning wandering through the town. She forced her frustrations with Sanreils to the back of her mind and enjoyed the scenery instead. Eventually, she came to Theon's shop.

On cold Autumn days, Theon worked hard in the lumber shop, stocking various stacks of cut wood for his master. Often, he would see Mara walk by, and listen to her talk all about her thoughts on the world. He'd listen to her for hours, and hung on her every word. She wondered if he was just bored. He never seemed to understand what she described, but she was glad someone was willing to listen to her rambling.

He was in the store, preparing for the day, when he heard a tapping on the window. He turned around to see Mara's face smooshed into the glass. She breathed on it to fog it up. She wrote "Hello!" on the fog patch with her finger, writing the 'E' backward.

"Hey! Hi! Hello!" Theon called out, setting his lumber aside.

Mara waved and eagerly hopped inside. "Hi!" she exclaimed.

Theon smiled at her. "How are you?" he asked.

"Oh . . . fine!" she replied. "I was just on a stroll. I saw you working in here and thought to myself: it is just too lovely of a day for you to spend inside!"

"I'm getting the store ready," he said. "I take care of the place while the master is away. Not terribly exciting, but it needs to be done."

Mara shook her head. "You should come with me!" she exclaimed.

"But I can't just leave! The master would not approve!"

But despite his objection, Mara seized Theon's hand and pulled him out of the shop. "Come! It'll be fun!" she said.

- 81 -

Mara and Theon walked through the forest, watching the leaves changing colors and falling to the ground. Mara picked up a leaf and turned it over in her hand. "Why do you think the leaves change color?"

"Maybe they're embarrassed," Theon said.

Mara giggled. "What?"

"In ancient times, people had all these stories for the way things were in nature," Theon said. "Perhaps there's a story there. People turn red when they're embarrassed."

"But why would a leaf be embarrassed?"

"Wouldn't you be embarrassed if you took a great fall in front of all those other leaves?" Theon suggested. "I would be."

"They're blushing!" Mara exclaimed. She picked up a yellow leaf.

"Why are they blushing?"

"Because they're in lo-o-o-ove!" Mara exclaimed. She smooshed the two leaves together as if they were kissing.

"Awww ... how sweet."

Mara picked up a couple more leaves. "And they're mad ... because as they fall, they're kissing other leaves."

"Scandalous!"

"Yes," Mara nodded. "Autumn is a very randy season."

"So, why is the sky blue?"

"It's cold," Mara suggested. "Up there, all alone ... without clothes on."

Theon shook his head. "I think it's sad."

"Why?"

"It's sad because it was falling in love with one of the leaves, but the leaf was in love with one of the others," Theon said. "The sky gets so sad from time to time, watching the leaves, that it cries, and we get rain."

Mara frowned. "That is sad," she said.

"Sometimes, the world is a sad place."

"It's sometimes good, though!" Mara said, looking at Theon.

Theon smiled at her and nodded. "I suppose you're right."

"I mean ... just look at where we are!" Mara said. She opened her arms as she danced through the falling leaves.

Theon watched Mara twirl through the wind. She stopped, laughed, and took his hands. "Come!" Mara said. "Come dance with me!"

Mara spun Theon around through the falling leaves. "All the leaves!" she exclaimed. "They're amazing ... how each one follows their little paths to their destinies."

"Their destiny must be to be stomped on by us, then!" Theon exclaimed, kicking a pile of leaves up.

Mara laughed. "Exactly! We rain death and doom upon the leaves!" she exclaimed. She kicked leaves high into the air. As they showered down, she ran through them, emerging from the cloud with leaves plastered all over herself.

Theon walked up to Mara with his hands behind his back, smiling slightly.

"Oh!" Mara eyed him. "Did you find something neat?"

Theon nodded. "It's very . . . amazing!"

"Oh! What?"

"Destiny!" Theon exclaimed as he brought his hands forward and threw his hidden pile of leaves at her.

"Hey!" Mara laughed. "If destiny is you being a little twert, then it must be a destiny we all share." She quickly kicked a pile of leaves at Theon's face, turned, and ran down the trail.

Mara stuck her tongue out at Theon, who immediately chased her down the road. They ran for a while, until Theon lost sight of her.

"Where'd you go?" he called as he paused to look around. "Mara?"

He felt someone carefully open the back of his shirt collar. "Destiny!" Mara exclaimed as she swiftly stuffed several dozen leaves down his back.

Theon turned around to find Mara had fallen over into the leaves, laughing.

"You twert!" he exclaimed.

Mara was still laughing when Theon took the opportunity to shove leaves over her, burying her in the pile. "Hey!" she screamed as leaves continued to cover her.

Theon knelt beside the moving pile of leaves and uncovered just enough of them to expose Mara's face. She opened her eyes and blew a couple leaves out of her mouth. "That wasn't nice," she said.

"Sorry." Theon grinned.

Mara smiled. "I guess, this time, my destiny was to be buried by the leaves."

Theon chuckled and picked a couple leaves out of her hair. "Maybe, in another life, you'll be more fortunate."

Mara sighed happily as she gazed at the leaves continuing to rain down. "Each one follows their own intricate path, guided by the wind," she said. "There must be a way to know where they'll land."

"You'd have to know how the wind blows," Theon said. He stared at the trees. "And what controls the wind?"

"Something . . . " Mara said. "There is something! Something from which it all originates."

"Well . . . if anyone will find it, it'll be you."

"I hope so. I have to meet the Ori soon, and I'm afraid he'll fail me again."

Theon nodded. "To be honest, I don't think I understand what you told me about your adventure in the bottle."

"Me neither," Mara said. She laughed. "And I'm the one that had it! It's like I entered the bottle, and the world was left outside."

"If you put the world in the bottle, and can see it all at once, maybe you could see your sequence that way."

"Oh!" Mara exclaimed. "There's a thought. I just wish I understood how the bottle worked."

Mara watched a leaf drift down. She carefully blew it and giggled when it landed on Theon's nose. Theon smiled at her. "I should go before I get into trouble with my master."

Theon helped Mara climb out of the leaf pile. She smiled at him. "Thank you for coming with me," she said. "Aren't you glad you spent the day out here with me, instead of in that stuffy shop?"

Theon nodded enthusiastically.

"Good!" Mara said.

Mara leaned very close to Theon and whispered, "I have something for you before you go . . . "

As Mara leaned closer to him, Theon gulped. "What?" he asked quietly.

Mara swiftly opened the front of Theon's collar and stuffed a few more leaves down his shirt. "Destiny!" she exclaimed as she ran off, laughing.

29. You'll Figure it Out

Sanreils's dismissive answers made me think about Sheridan's. Was Mingo the mystery waiting at the end of the road? At the end of the story? I felt cheated. I already knew that, then.

"Something on your mind, Bartlebee?" Sheridan asked.

I shook my head, then changed my mind. "Yeah, actually. That was a pretty pathetic tidbit."

"A tidbit, eh?"

"Yes. We were trading *tidbits*. And I feel cheated."

Sheridan stroked his chin, as I suspected he usually did when he wanted to give the impression he was thinking.

"Tell me," I said. "Has the highway ever told you someone you loved was waiting for you?"

"Well, the thing about that is, it's a different question."

"So?"

"If you're unhappy with your answer, you should've asked a different question."

"Fine." I gave up. "Whatever. Just answer the question."

"You owe me a tidbit, first," Sheridan said. He crossed his arms defiantly and nodded. "One-to-one."

"I gave you one. You didn't pay in turn."

Sheridan smirked and shrugged. "I don't want to get into a 'is soup a meal?' thing here, so, okay. The answer's yes."

"It has?"

"Yes."

"Who?"

"That's a new question."

"Okay, okay, fine," I said. "What do *you* want to know?"

Sheridan cackled, although I was pretty sure he was faking it. Maybe he wasn't. He looked straight into my eye and asked, "Was someone *you* loved waiting for you at the end of the highway? In Raleigh?"

I watched the road scroll by for a bit, enough to realize just how pathetic it was in terms of entertainment. Sheridan waited for me to reply for what seemed like five minutes and forty-four seconds.

"So," I said. "Where did Mara go next?"

Sheridan wasted no time answering, as if he knew I wouldn't answer his question.

"She had her usual appointment with the Ori ... "

- 82 -

Once again, Mara stood before the Ori's door. She hesitated longer than usual. *A little confidence goes a long way,* she told herself. And, this time, she knew she had the answer. *Why am I so hesitant?*

She pushed the door a bit, letting it swing itself the rest of the way. As soon as she stepped inside, the Ori asked her, "Have you solved your problem?"

Mara stared at the Ori in silence. He stared back, then lowered his gaze.

"Yes," Mara said.

The Ori continued to stare in silence.

Mara fidgeted a bit, and repeated, "Yes."

"I see," the Ori said. He hummed and tapped his fingers on his armrest. "Go on."

"Well ... " Mara hesitated. She wasn't quite sure what the Ori wanted to hear. "I was standing on the cliff. You know, the one that overlooks the city?"

"I've never stepped outside," the Ori said.

"Oh, uh." Mara fumbled with her words. "Never?"

"Enough about me. You were on a cliff."

"And I saw I could hold the city," Mara said. "And maybe the world was in the bottle, after all."

"So, you see you can hold the world by putting it in the bottle?"

"Yeah." Mara chewed on her lip. "Which seems a bit strange. If I'm holding a model of the world, and I'm also *in* the model, then, uh ... "

"Uh," the Ori repeated.

"I guess, I don't know. Somehow, I'm both at once."

"In and out," the Ori said.

"Yes," Mara said. "In and out. At the same time."

The Ori sat still for what Mara felt was an eternity. He hummed every so often, but mostly just stared. Mara had finally worked up the nerve to speak, when the Ori spoke first. "I think you need to go find that sequence."

"But I already knew to find it!"

The Ori shook his head. "You thought you did. But now you know how. I think you see the world clearly enough to find it."

"I do?"

"Ask the other Mara. The one in the bottle."

"I–" Mara blinked. "I don't understand what that means."

"You'll figure it out."

"Do you think Aphrael will be upset?"

"I don't get involved in the personal affairs of others."

"But ... she sent me to you, to find the sequence so that she could free–"

The Ori held up his hand. "I know."

"Then, you know what happened to Trisha?"

"One day, Mara, you will find yourself at a crossroad. You'll find the sequence, and need to know what to do with it. Do you end the world? Do you use it for your own purposes?"

"Aphrael said to break it," Mara explained. "How do you break a sequence?"

"I see things," the Ori said. "But I don't *do* things. You'll have to ask her."

"Oh." Mara bit her lip. "I'm rather afraid of talking to her. I think she'll be upset Trisha died."

The Ori sat motionless, without response. Mara waited nervously. "Do you think I can find it?" she asked.

"Whether or not you pass the test is up to you ... and you alone."

"So, no."

"Incorrect," the Ori said. "The answer is not 'no'. It is 'don't ask me'."

Mara sulked back toward the door and sighed. She missed Sylow and his encouragement. The Ori had always encouraged her to observe, though, so she resolved to do just that. Though she would never be fully sure, she thought she saw the Ori crack a tiny smile.

30. Linear Dragon

"I don't get the bottle," I said. "How can the inside be the outside?"

"What Mara was probably describing was something like a *Klein Bottle*," Sheridan explained.

"Perfume?"

"No," Sheridan shook his head. "Not *Calvin* Klein. It's a bottle that sort of folds in on itself. Where's your car sketchbook?"

"Car *sketchbook*? Who do you think I am? Mark Kistler?"

He tried to draw a sketch for me on the back of an old receipt, but it didn't look special. It looked like a tall flask with a lip that folded around, poking into the base. He said the wall only had one side.

"You're nuts," I said. "Do you think the world is in a bottle?"

"I'll give you an answer," Sheridan said. "But you know the price."

"Oh, fine," I said. "What's your question?"

"Same as before," Sheridan said. "Was someone you loved waiting at the end of your highway, in Raleigh?"

"I've never loved anyone."

I *thought* I saw Sheridan look surprised, which would've been a first. He didn't seem to know what to say, but then, I wondered if he'd even bothered to listen to me at all. He seemed deep in thought.

Before I could ask if he was still on Earth, he replied, "It depends on which world you're talking about."

"Wh—what kind of answer is *that*?"

Sheridan smiled proudly. "One that'll make more sense in time," he said. "*And*, let me add that it doesn't count as a 'tidbit' if you lie."

Sheridan resumed his tale, after adding, "But I'll let it slide this time."

- 83 -

Matta stood in the tower corridor, fuming under her breath as she watched her feet. She looked up, nodded to Mara, then hung her head again.

"Matta!" Mara exclaimed. She put her arm around her. "What's wrong?"

Matta shook her head and sniffed. "It's Dahes! He's—" She closed her eyes and swallowed tears.

Mara frowned. "I've noticed he seemed *distant*."

"It's that damn cult!" Matta exclaimed. She shuddered and glared. "It's no church! It's a cult. That's what it is."

"What are you saying?" Mara asked.

"Dahes!" Matta exclaimed. "Those two *priests* . . . "

Mara froze. Sid walked in and eyed her, but hung back against the wall, waiting.

Mara asked, "The tall ones?"

Matta nodded. Sid glanced at both of them. "Who?"

Mara hung her head. "The two I told you about, it seems. Dimitry and Enton."

Matta said, "They've been after him, you know? Like we thought, because of his teachers and how those two got *them*. It's like ex-communication, but automatic."

"Ex-communication? How?" Sid asked.

Matta cried, "They got him. He's hardly speaking to me."

Sid shook his head. "*Dahes*, of all people!"

"Yes. We've got to get him back," Matta said.

"Now ... just one minute," Sid said.

"*How* can you be hesitant?" Matta exclaimed. "He's our *friend*! We've got to meet him. Persuade him to leave."

"Now, wait just one minute!" Sid repeated. "We can't just waddle on into the university and grab him! They'll kill you! *Us*!"

Mara nodded solemnly. "Sid is right. It's not that easy."

"If you protest, they'll silence you," Sid replied.

"Well, if you all don't care," Matta exclaimed. She grew silent, too choked up to speak. She shook her head and managed to say, "I do!"

"Now, don't you go do anything stupid!" Sid exclaimed. "You'll get yourself killed!"

Matta screamed, "How dare you! You've had it out for me since day one!"

"Hey! Hey!" Mara exclaimed. "We are *not* accomplishing anything!"

Sid nodded. "She's right. Come on. We need to rest our minds. Think clearly. Tomorrow morning, we'll discuss it again."

Matta shook her head and walked out of the tower. She slammed the door behind her.

Mara shook her head. "It's all falling apart," she cried.

Sid watched the dust near the door settle. "Don't worry. We'll think of something."

- 84 -

The next morning, Mara woke up early and a bit frazzled. *Sid's right*, she thought. *What does Matta want us to do? Just barge in and grab Dahes?*

She could imagine Matta's reaction, and tried to think of something encouraging she could say.

When neither Matta nor Sid woke up and joined her for breakfast, Mara slipped out of the tower and made her way toward the city.

I have my own problems to solve, she thought, but couldn't help but feel a bit guilty for not waiting longer for Matta. By the time she made it to town, she had pushed Sid and Matta to the back of her mind, and became lost in her own world.

Find the pattern, Mara reminded herself of the Ori's instructions. She wandered the streets, watching anything that moved.

Whenever her mind began to wander, she slapped herself and repeated the Ori's words. *But I already knew to look for the pattern. Maybe he thinks I've learned enough.*

As she walked, she tried to figure out how her lessons would help. *Is all this in the bottle? Am I in the bottle? Did the bottle not break when I grew obscenely large?*

Mara stepped close to a window and peeked inside. She laughed and clapped her hands, then tapped on the window and waved. Inside were several piles of lumber and wood. Theon was working inside, and didn't seem to notice her. She tapped the window harder.

Theon jumped, dropping the tools he held. He looked behind him and glared at the window. As soon as he saw who it was, he wiped the scowl off his face and smiled. Mara waved for him to come out.

"You!" Mara exclaimed as Theon stepped outside. "This isn't your usual shop. You must be hiding from me." She folded her arms and pretended to be mad.

"Well ... I ... " Theon stumbled on his words. Mara cracked a grin. She tried to hide it; she closed her eyes, raised her chin, and turned away from him. She exclaimed, "Hmph!"

Theon quietly snuck up on her and jabbed her in the rib. Mara screamed and faced him. "Evil! That was evil!"

Theon laughed. Mara shook her head, "Evil evil evil evil evil!"

"Sorry," he said quietly. He grinned.

Mara grabbed his arm and started to run, pulling him after her. Theon blinked and stumbled on his feet. "Hey! Where are you going?"

"*We* are going on an adventure!"

"But ... my work! The master would be *very* upset. I can't go."

"You can, too," Mara smiled. "No excuses. Think of it as penance. That's what you get for poking me!"

"That's *provoking*," Theon said. He then corrected himself, "Oh, wait ... "

"If you can't say something nice," Mara said, "the least you can do is not correct someone's grammar." She laughed. "You owe me another adventure now ... after this one. And don't think I will ever forget that you do!"

- 85 -

Mara and Theon sat on a grassy hill, watching the clouds and the sun rise. The stars were still visible, but fading. Theon asked where the *adventure* Mara had in mind was. She smiled and pointed up. "It's the sky!" she said. "Come, watch it with me."

They sat in silence for a while, until Mara broke it. "Where do you think words come from?"

"Words?" Theon asked. "I assume people just started using them."

"Someone had to point at, say, a rock, and say 'rock'! Language is a funny thing."

"Discovery is a funny thing."

"Do you think that someday, man will discover so many things that we run out of words?"

"How many words are there?" Theon asked. "I think we can just make more."

"Yes," Mara said. "But eventually, they'd get so long nobody could remember them!"

"I suppose people did point to something and choose a sound," Theon said.

"Who pointed to a leaf in the puddle and said 'float'?" Mara asked. "I could think of half a hundred better sounds."

Theon watched a leaf drift by. "When I was little, I wondered why some things floated . . . like ducks. And why some sank. My mother told me it was fairies."

Mara giggled. Theon continued, "I don't think she knew."

" 'I don't know', and 'I'm sorry' are the two most difficult sounds to utter," Mara said. "They're even more difficult when one tries to attach the proper meaning to them."

"Don't forget 'I'm wrong'," Theon added. "I think one customer at the shop keeps trying to pay my master with counterfeit gold. But he won't listen to me! *Clearly*, I'm the one in the wrong."

Mara smiled. "Drop the coins in a pool of water."

Theon raised an eyebrow.

Mara nodded. "There was a man who lived long ago. He figured out that if the item is really gold, it'll raise the water higher than another metal. Then, he ran through the streets naked. That's what smart people do."

"Should Locana expect a show when you find your sequence?" Theon asked. He immediately began to blush.

Mara laughed. "I don't think anyone wants to see me naked."

"You're probably right," Theon said. "I mean–eh–"

"Thank you," Mara said. "That's the nicest thing anyone's said to me all day."

"Oh, I didn't mean it like that. I'd love to see you naked," Theon said. "No! Wait!" He buried his face in his hands.

Mara winked. She looked away and whistled for a moment. The sun was showing its first hints of rising. The clouds faded away, revealing a final glimpse of the stars. "Make pictures in the sky with me."

"How do you make pictures up there?"

"Just connect the dots!"

"Okay," Theon said. "I see a line."

Mara laughed. "You can be more creative than that!"

"There's a ring around the moon, then," Theon said. He pointed to the moon and made a little loop with his finger. "And some dots around it."

Mara caught Theon's picture and stared at it for a moment. "Seven little dots. The little specks surrounding it can be the forest," she said. "And the loop of seven dots can be the fields of a clearing." She thought a bit more. "Yes. That ring can definitely be a field."

"I was going to suggest it was a pot," Theon said. "With specks of flame heating it."

Mara smiled. "I see that, too. Isn't it funny how the same stars can give birth to multiple images?"

"Many interpretations conceived from the same thing," Theon said.

"The entire world is a combination of the same elements," Mara said. "Think of words! How many words have multiple definitions?"

"True," Theon said.

Mara smiled. "I talked to the stars about it once."

Theon lifted an eyebrow. "You were talking to the stars?"

Mara looked away for a moment. "Umm, yes."

"They never talk to me," Theon said. "You must be special."

"You just have to listen," Mara said. She smiled. "We

talked about the way you can connect the stars in different ways to create different images, like we did."

"See that squiggly blotch to the right of the moon?" Theon pointed near the moon. It was full, and still clearly visible. "It's a little square-ish ring of about sixteen stars."

Mara thought for a moment. "I think I see it."

Theon grinned. "That's my nation! The land of–Theonland."

Mara laughed. "You can't be more creative?" She poked him in the rib.

"Hey! It's a great name! I would be proud to live there."

Mara pointed to Theonland. "See inside your ring? There is a smaller one. One of eight stars?"

"Yes, I see them."

"Those are the hordes of opposition," Mara said. "They think Theonland is a stupid name for a country and are planning to revolt."

"Hey! What are they going to change it to? Maraland?"

"That's the best name for a nation! They are going to take it over."

"Okay," Theon said. "Inside your ring of eight stars is one of four. They're the spies."

"Spies!" Mara exclaimed. "Well, my rebels are higher in number than your spies."

"But Theonland is bigger!" Theon said. "So, they will crush the rebels."

Mara studied the sky a bit more. "Okay. There is a line of stars outside of Theonland. Those are the armies of the Kingdom of Mara coming to take over Theonland!"

"Wait, *Kingdom of Mara*? Who says you can have two nations named after you?"

"They must know I am nothing less than stupendous."

"Okay, okay," Theon studied the sky some more. "See that 'S' shape above the line? That's the dragon coming to kill your armies!"

"An 'S' is a stupid shape for a dragon! The line next to it is the real dragon, coming to teach it a lesson. Teach it not to be stupid!"

"You can't have a linear dragon! The 'S' is for superior. Superior to your stupid line dragon!"

"The 'S' is for submission! Submission to the powers of the linear dragon!"

"If the line dragon is superior, then clearly, the laws of the world are in disarray." Theon said. "The blotch of stars above them are the judges, ruling that Maraland and the Kingdom of Mara are stupid nations and should be wiped off the face of the Earth."

Mara stuck her tongue out at Theon. "Take that!"

"Oh! A war!" Theon exclaimed. He retaliated by sticking his tongue out at Mara.

Mara opened her hands, touched her thumbs to her cheeks, and wiggled her fingers. "My nation's powers are superior to yours!"

"Okay, you made me bring out the secret weapon," Theon said. He copied Mara, and exclaimed, "Pfffffttttt!"

Mara gasped. "If it's a war you want, then it's a war you'll get!" She copied Theon, drawing out her "Pfffffffftttttt!" much longer.

For the next several moments, they both wiggled their fingers and spat at each other. Afterward, Mara stared up at the sky. "I think both of our nations have been decimated."

Theon frowned. "It appears so."

"The Kingdom of Mara blames you!" Mara pointed at Theon. "Your nation must pay!"

"Hey!" Theon exclaimed. "Well, Theonland blames you!"

Mara, on a whim, jabbed Theon in the rib as he stared at the sky. "Hey!" he exclaimed.

Mara smiled and looked a bit away. "It was a birdie,"

she said. She made a bird shadow-puppet with her fingers. "Look! There it goes!"

When Theon looked up, Mara jabbed him in the rib again. "Okay," he said. "You're going to get it now."

Mara whistled to herself. "Who said it was me? The Kingdom of Mara has ruled you are to blame!"

Theon repeatedly poked Mara's ribs. "No!" she exclaimed, laughing too hard to bring herself up. "Let me up!"

"Say it!" Theon exclaimed. "Theonland rules the sky!"

"Never!" Mara exclaimed between fits of laughter. She managed to bring herself up, tackled Theon, and struck back.

"No!" Theon exclaimed. Mara grinned. "Say it, now! The Kingdom of Mara rules the sky!"

"Never!" Theon exclaimed as he wiggled his way up and pinned Mara down. "Hah! Now you must admit it!"

The two continued this way for quite some time, until they were both out of breath. They lay on the grass, staring up at the sky again. "So, this is what the great conflict has brought us," Mara said. "Here we are, back at where we began!"

By this time, the sun was starting to climb out of the horizon. Theon, still lying in the grass, looked Mara's way. She lay there, catching her breath and staring up. He watched her for a few moments, until she looked his way. She smiled at him. "Hi."

"Hi," Theon said. "I like making dragons with you."

"Is that so?" Mara giggled. "We are very creative. Here we have an infinite palette of stars, we can connect them in any way we wish, and we make *dragons*. When I was little, I used to think the winds–that made the leaves dance and the trees sway–were wind-dragons. Oh, to tame them! You raise a wind-mill, and down the street, the wind would change."

"Maybe your sequence would tame them."

Mara's eyes shot wide open, and her jaw dropped. "Aphrael!"

"What?" Theon laughed. "Oh, the look on your face! What did I say?"

"*That's* what Aphrael must have meant."

"What? What? Tell me!"

"Find the sequence, and use it to break the world."

"You think the wind-dragons would crush the world if you could tame them?"

Mara watched a lone cloud soar across the sky. She imagined it was pushed by a wind-dragon. "Maybe," she said. "They're up in the sky, pushing the clouds. What if they pushed the sky downward and crushed the world?"

31. Out of Sounds Reach

"*Wind-dragons?*" I exclaimed, and looked up at the clouds. "That's your explanation?"

Sheridan laughed. "That's Mara's explanation. And you interrupted me."

"Well, I'm sorry," I said. "That just caught my attention."

"I'm glad you find my story intriguing," Sheridan said. He smiled.

"A little doomsday will get anyone's attention," I said. "So, okay, what did Mara figure out?"

"She was still discussing the sky with Theon," Sheridan said. "Turbulence is the word, but she wouldn't have known to call it that."

"So, the 'Butterfly Effect', basically?"

Sheridan nodded. "Mara was happy to have someone to help her sort all this out ... "

- 86 -

Mara grinned. "Aren't you so *very* glad I dragged you out here?"

Theon smiled. "Yes."

"Of course, you are!" Mara exclaimed. "Otherwise, you'd be in that stuffy shop, and we can't have that!"

Theon nodded. Mara grinned again. "You really don't like it much, do you?"

Theon looked confused. "What do you mean?"

"Because you never protest that it's something you'd *rather* be doing," Mara said. "It's always something you're *obligated* to do."

"Well ... I suppose," Theon said. "I think I'd rather ... "

Mara grinned. "You'd rather stall?"

"It's silly," Theon said.

Mara exclaimed, "Oh! How delightfully wonderful! Yes, we all must do silly things. It's what makes us happy!" Her eyes grew big. She leaned close to Theon, smiled, and said, "Do tell!"

"I wish I could study at the university," Theon said. "I think I'd much rather be a philosopher."

Mara smiled. "Why don't you? I think you'd be rather good at it. Imagine, thinking about the world all day."

"Well, I have to make a living somehow," Theon said. "I can make a better living this way, I suppose. I've been told I have pretty good hands. I can do the work. It's what I was raised to do."

Mara reached over and touched his chest. He stopped talking and stared at her hand. "But your heart's not in it. And *I* can tell."

Theon continued to stare at her hand. Mara smiled and said, "Oh, what great things you could do if you were not so tied to this silly, silly endeavor."

Theon exclaimed, "I could soar!"

Mara asked, "What is a bird that has no wings?"

"Am I that transparent?"

Mara grinned. "Maybe. But, see, you owe me one."

Theon tilted his head. "I do?"

"Of course, you do!" Mara exclaimed. "You must remember, I spared your pathetic little kingdom from my linear dragon."

Theon stuck his tongue out at her. Mara smiled proudly. "So, now, you have to promise me you'll do something that makes you happier!"

"If only it were that easy," Theon said.

"It *is* that easy!" Mara exclaimed. "Just go out and do it."

Theon thought for a moment and nodded. "Believe me, I'd like to. I don't know. Maybe we'll see."

"*We'll see?*" Mara asked. She jabbed his rib. "Come on, now!"

Theon sighed. "I don't know."

"We won't *see*. We'll *do* it!" Mara exclaimed.

"It's not that easy," Theon said. "I can't."

"You can!" Mara said.

He yelled, "I can't! The world is not that simple! You make it sound so easy. But it's not!"

Mara's eyes grew large as she leaned back. She sat quiet for a moment. "I'm sorry."

"No!" Theon said. "I didn't mean to yell." He sighed.

"I just–" Mara said.

Theon interrupted her, "I'm just frustrated. You're lucky, you know?"

"I know," she whispered. "I didn't mean . . . I just see you look so unhappy sometimes."

"Truth be told, I think I am," Theon said.

Mara sat quiet in an awkward silence. After some time, she managed something to say. "Thanks for coming out here with me. Not many people seem interested in my silly ideas."

Theon nodded and smiled. "Really, it is the highlight of my day."

Mara looked up and smiled. "Oh, is that so? Well. I simply *must* find us another adventure! Let's see . . . well, that is . . . if you want to go . . . "

"Of course," Theon said.

Mara looked up to the sky again, thinking of what might be the perfect adventure to set out on. "I think I would very much love to see the sea. I hear so much about it. But I've never been, much less seen it."

"Well, I will take you to the sea."

Mara's eyes grew large. "Really? You will take *me* on an adventure? Promise?"

"Promise," Theon said. "We'll go to the sea! And travel to faraway lands. Rolling plains and vast mountains ... "

Mara giggled. "Do you even know where all that is?"

"Well, no. But I promised! And good promises transcend rational thinking."

Mara laughed. She shook her head. "Well ... I'm sure you'll figure out a way."

Theon watched her for a few more moments. "Why do you ask me to come out here? On all these adventures?"

"Do you not want me to?" Mara asked.

"Oh, no!" Theon exclaimed. "I certainly do. I'm just ... a bit surprised you picked me"

Mara raised an eyebrow. "I thought you might like to hear about my conversation with the stars," she said. "You always seem interested in what I have to say."

Theon nodded. "I guess, I'm just a bit surprised you wouldn't seek out your suitor friend."

Mara blushed. "Oh. I guess."

"What?" Theon asked.

Mara sighed. "I don't know how interested he is in what I have to say. It's a bit frustrating, to tell you the truth. He always disappears."

"It doesn't sound like he appreciates you," Theon said.

Mara tried to think of why Sanreils had seemed so eager to pursue her. "I don't know," she said.

Mara stared blankly at the sky as she mentally questioned all the events that had taken place in the forest. "He tries so hard to take care of me, I think," she said. "He rescued me in the forest."

"Yes, he did," Theon said. "Why?"

"What?" Mara exclaimed.

"Nothing," Theon said.

Mara thought about the events since she'd fled Sylow's house. She wondered why some things failed to add up. *Why does he always disappear so suddenly?*

"I really was just curious," Theon said.

Mara closed her eyes. She said quietly, "I know."

"I just don't want you hurt, that's all," Theon said.

Mara shuddered. "I can look after myself. Okay!"

Theon quickly sat back. "I'm sorry," he said quietly.

He looked around the area and tried again to think of something to say.

"No! I didn't mean to yell," Mara said. "Not at you." She sighed.

Mara continued to stare at the sky. As she thought about it even more, she began to feel betrayed. "I just don't want to think about it right now."

"But he treats you like Dahes treats Matta."

"I *don't* want to think about it!"

"I . . ." Theon sighed. "I didn't mean to upset you. I need to go to the shop."

Mara frowned. "I should go home, too. Maybe I can try to sleep now."

Theon stood and tried to think of something to say, but couldn't. As Mara started to walk away, Theon called out, "Mara?"

Mara turned around. "Yes?"

Theon thought for a moment. "Never mind."

"I'll see you later," Mara said. "I'm going back to town in the evening."

Theon nodded.

As Mara walked away, he stood still. When she was safely out of sound's reach, he whispered, "I think I love you."

32. Eyes Without Squinting

I laughed. "Hey! You cheated!"

"Cheated?" Sheridan asked. "I did not cheat!"

"You said you were telling me a linear story," I said. "But Mara could not have heard that!"

Sheridan shook his head. "I did not mislinearize the story! I told it in perfect chronological order. I can give you information not available to the heroine. It's called *dramatic irony*. There's no rule against that."

I couldn't argue. But I had to ask, "Is *mislinearize* a word?"

"What do you think it means?" Sheridan asked.

"To . . . erm . . . not linearize something correctly?" I asked.

Sheridan nodded. "To be more precise: to attempt to organize things in a linear fashion, but fail."

"I suppose," I said.

Sheridan smiled. "Well. It has a meaning. It is clearly understood. I do say . . . it shall be a word!"

Now, I couldn't figure out if it really was a word or not. *Damn you, Sheridan!* He watched me struggle with the thought and laughed. I changed the subject. "Anyway . . . if this is some kind of history Mara wrote down . . . how did she hear *that*?"

Sheridan nodded. "Good question."

I nodded in turn. Sheridan sat silent. I asked, "Well?"

"Well, what?" Sheridan asked.

"Are you going to answer it?" I asked.

Sheridan grinned. "I will. But! It's a ..."

"Oh," I said. "I get it. It's coming later. Because it's a *linear* story."

Sheridan smiled slyly. "I wouldn't want to mislinearize it."

That said, he continued.

- 87 -

Mara stood in the fountain, trading glances between the Locanans and the water's ripples. *There is a pattern here; I just know it,* she told herself. It made sense when she saw it in nature. But she didn't see it in the movement of the people. *Could Theon have been wrong?* She shook her head, and decided she just wasn't looking hard enough.

Nearby, two Locanans were arguing.

"I'm telling you, the world *had* to have begun more than ten thousand years ago," the first Locanan said. "The sea, the mountains–they couldn't have formed in such a short time. What of the Greeks? And the Egyptians?"

"But you're wrong, my friend!" exclaimed the second. "They all have lived within a short time. Why have we not found any older history? If not ten thousand, how long?"

"A million," said the first. "At least."

The second Locanan laughed.

"Aye, I should be the one who laughs at you," the first Locanan said. "I laugh in your general direction."

"No, I laugh in *your* general direction."

By this time, Mara had poked her head from around the fountain pillar. The first Locanan pointed at her. "Perhaps she could break the tie."

"*Her*? The black-headed girl? She won't know anything."

Mara smirked. "I have a name, you know."

"She would, too," the first Locanan said. "I heard you're pretty bright."

"I'd like to think so." Mara smiled. "But, if you can cast your eyes upon me without squinting, perhaps it isn't so."

"Modest, too," said the second Locanan.

"Mara," said the first. "How old is our world? Tell us it's more than ten thousand years old."

"It is not older than ten thousand years," Mara said.

The second Locanan laughed. "Aye! She is a bright one!"

The first Locanan folded his arms across his chest. "But I can cast my eyes upon her without squinting."

"Tell us, fair lady. How old is it?"

"Oh, hush," said the first. "Stop boasting."

"The world?" Mara said. "It is about two minutes and thirty-four seconds old."

The first Locanan laughed and poked his friend. "There goes *your* theory."

His friend grumbled. "But I can cast my eyes upon her without squinting."

A few passing villagers had stopped to watch the argument. For the most part, they stood back and listened. A few snickers sounded from the back of the crowd. The first Locanan looked toward Mara. *"Two minutes?* I don't think that could be."

"She's a looney," said the second. "The world can't be that young. How would I have lived all these years if they were but two minutes?"

"Nobody said time was real," Mara said. "To us, it could feel like ten thousand or ten billion years."

"Well, the rest of us don't live on *Mara-time*," the first said.

"But it is!" Mara exclaimed. "It is two minutes! I asked the highway, how long man had trekked its path? How long had it curved from town to town? It said: 'two minutes, and thirty-four seconds.' "

Some of the bystanders chuckled. Mara shot a glare in their direction, and continued explaining. "I wouldn't think a road would have anything to gain from making something like that up. But, since then, maybe one or two seconds have passed."

A third Locanan laughed. "The highway?"

"She's a looney, all right," said a fourth. "Talking to roads and bridges, eh?"

"Must be a witch, I say," a fifth townsperson said.

To that statement, a few people stopped laughing. Mara stood up straight. "No, no, you're wrong! I'm no witch. There's a well. I drank from it, and the highway talked to me."

The first Locanan held back a snicker. "I think you made that up."

"It's true!" Mara exclaimed. "It was the *Well of Enlightenment*. In Carrboro Forest."

A lumberjack stepped up to the fountain. He held his arms up for a moment, quieting the crowd. Then, he faced Mara. "A well in Carrboro Forest? I think I know the one she's talking about."

Mara's heart skipped a beat. The chuckles and laughs in the audience quieted down. "Yes," Mara said.

"Eh, I seem to remember harvesting wood there," the lumberjack said. "A little tunnel?"

"Yes, yes!" Mara said.

"Some of the boys and I, we set up a latrine at the end of a little 'tunnel' of leaves."

The audience erupted in laughter. The lumberjack snorted, faced the crowd, and exclaimed, "Sure was private!"

"I didn't drink from a toilet!" Mara shouted, but could barely be heard over the crowd. "It was a magical fountain that grants wisdom!"

The lumberjack laughed as he pulled his pants higher.

"Oh, if you drank from *that*, I don't think it granted you enough!"

With the crowd in hysterics, Mara threw her arms in the air, lept off the fountain, and walked away. When she reached the end of the street, she looked one more time at the square. Everybody was talking among themselves and laughing, and nobody seemed to notice she'd left.

- 88 -

Mara tried her best to shrug off the lumberjack's comments. *Perhaps he thinks I'm a fool. Perhaps they all do. But they're wrong.* She looked up to the sky and forced a smile. *Theon will understand.*

Mara held her pieces of burgundy paper and read them as she walked. When she arrived at the shop, she tapped on the window and peeked inside. It looked quiet. *He's usually stocking the store by now. Where is he?*

Mara prodded the door and pushed it open. The wares had not been set up for the day. "Hello?" Mara yelled. "Anyone here?"

No answer came. Mara took a seat and waited. She counted the seconds to herself. "One, two, three, four ... "

Time continued to crawl, and still no one came. "One thousand nine hundred twenty-eight, one thousand nine hundred twenty-nine, one thousands nine hundred thirty, ... " she counted.

Finally, she heard the door swing open. "Hello?" she called out.

"Who's there?" Theon's master came hobbling into the room. "Oh, it's you."

Mara smiled. "Hi. Why is the store so empty?"

"Well, I can't stock the store alone, so I've been looking for help."

Mara raised an eyebrow. "Why didn't Theon do it? Is he sick?"

The master shook his head. "I hope you weren't waiting long for him, because he's not coming back."

"Why not?"

"He left town," the master said. He threw up his arms. "Don't ask me, because I have too much to do now to worry about figuring it out."

Mara's heart sank. "What do you mean he left town?"

"I mean, he thanked me for the opportunity to learn, but his heart was no longer in the craft," the master said. "Naturally, I asked him why, and if he'd thought this through. He said he was leaving town and didn't plan on returning."

"Why would he do that?"

"He insulted a customer! He wanted to do some stupid trick with the money. He says it's counterfeit. He started this big fight."

Mara bit her lip.

"Personally, I question whether or not he was ever really interested," the master said. "He said he was going to be a great philosopher. Imagine! Just like that!"

The master glared at Mara. "He always seemed to dart out of here when you came about. So, thank you very much."

"Sorry," Mara whispered.

"But, well, I don't care. It is what it is," the master said. "If I see him, I'll tell him you came by. After I chew him out, that is."

"Oh," Mara sighed. "Well, thank you."

Mara stared at the cold, gray sky as she wandered back into the street. She watched the swirling clouds mingle. It didn't add up. *He'd seemed somewhat distant earlier,* she thought. *I wonder if I did something wrong. I hope I didn't offend him. I really didn't mean to snap at him!*

The swirling clouds slowly tore apart and drifted away. Mara choked back tears. *He didn't even say goodbye.*

- 89 -

He didn't even say goodbye, the words bounced through Mara's head as she wandered down the streets. *Friends share wisdom so they may each be better people. Maybe he didn't care for me after all.*

Mara plunked down on the fountain lip. She was glad to see the crowd forgot about her, and watched people drift by like dead logs in a dirty river. She tried to put Theon's departure out of her mind, but it kept crawling back in. *It's not like we spent much time together. Why does it bug me so much?*

"Greetings, my lovely." Sanreils walked up, took her hand, and kissed it. "You seem a bit less cheery today."

Mara shrugged. "Just winter, I suppose."

"Well, we can take care of that." Sanreils smiled. "The church's ball is coming up. I trust you still plan to accompany me?"

"Oh," Mara said. She forced a smile. "Yes. I wouldn't miss it for the world."

"Good," Sanreils said. "I told the high priest all about you."

"What—" Mara's eyes widened. "Me?"

Sanreils stroked her cheek. "Yes, my lady. He seemed so eager to meet *us*. He even promised a blessing, and I think you know what may follow." He smiled gently.

"Wh–Well, I–" Mara stumbled on her words. "That sounds so, lovely."

"I do hope it's not too forward," Sanreils said. "But I knew when I first saw you, I'd ask for your hand in marriage one day."

Mara's heart skipped a beat. Sanreils said, "And the church ... well, now I feel I am being much too forward. But I asked for their permission, and they seemed so eager to grant it."

Mara lowered her head and watched the streets. "I don't know what to say."

"Well, the blessing first, my dear." Sanreils leaned down and kissed her cheek. "And before that, the ball."

"The ball–" Mara said quietly.

"I know you'll be lovely as always, and have a glamorous new outfit befitting the occasion."

Mara's thoughts turned to Sid and her empty purse. She flashed a brief, weak smile and nodded. "Of course."

"Then, I must be off," Sanreils said. "And–"

"So soon?"

Sanreils raised an eyebrow.

"You always seem to leave so–"

"I do beg your pardon," Sanreils said. "I am running late, and I fear I will be in trouble with my masters."

Mara closed her eyes and nodded. "I see. Well, I don't want that."

As Sanreils left, Mara glanced at herself. She rummaged through her empty satchel, glancing at the ring Amedean had given her, her only thing of value.

- 90 -

Mara fiddled with her ring as she walked down the street, pulling it off and slicing it back on. She hadn't thought about it in a long time, but suddenly, she felt homesick.

All the nights in the attic came back to her. *He didn't even say anything when he gave it to me.*

She closed her eyes and choked back tears. She then stood up straight and clenched her fist. "I will *not* shed a single tear for that man!"

She stopped before the jeweler's shop, a small house sandwiched in the shadow of two larger buildings. Mara contemplated the meaning of the name: "Aria Quineas." She wondered what it meant, deciding it must have been created to sound like Latin.

She shrugged and sauntered into the shop. "Excuse me," she said quietly.

The jeweler, a surly, gray old man turned around. "What?" he said with a slight scowl.

Mara removed her ring and placed it on the counter. "I'd like to sell this."

The jeweler eyed her suspiciously. He looked down at the ring, then back at her. "This is yours?"

"What do you mean?" Mara stepped back, folded her arms, and glared. "Do you think I *stole* it?"

The jeweler shook his head. He grinned slightly. "No, my dear. Not in the least."

He reached for the ring and studied the inside. "I haven't seen one of these in a long time."

"Oh?" Mara said. "It is valuable?"

The jeweler set the ring back on the counter. He snapped his fingers. A large man, cloaked in black, emerged from a side door. He quietly locked the front door. Mara fidgeted nervously. "Well ... I won't ask much."

"You won't ask anything at all," the jeweler said. He motioned for the other man to approach. "Consider it repayment for a foul deed."

"What deed?" Mara shook her head. "I don't understand."

Mara stepped backward into the waiting arms of the man in black. She cried out as he grabbed her wrist, twisted it, and pushed her into the counter. The jeweler pulled a dagger from behind the counter, walked to Mara, and held it to her throat. He looked up at the other man and grinned. "Like a fly, wandering into the spider's web."

When Mara tried to speak, the man in black twisted her wrist further. "I knew she wouldn't have wandered very far," he said. "Imagine our good fortune!"

Mara looked up at the jeweler. He covered her mouth and cracked a smile as he began to push the dagger into her throat.

She tried to scream, but the jeweler held her mouth tighter. She bit down on his fingers as hard as she could.

The jeweler cried out in pain as Mara wrestled herself free. As she turned around and lurched forward, she ran into the man in black. For the first time, she got a good look at him. Her heart raced. She immediately recognized his crooked nose and dilapidated smile as the man who'd left the envelopes for her father.

Before she could contemplate any further, the man in black lunged forward, grabbed her by the throat, and lifted her off the ground.

Mara gagged and kicked the air in vain as the man in black stared at her. "Understand," he said calmly. "We cannot have you spreading our secret."

She closed her eyes as the man held her higher. She swung her arms at him, to no avail.

"Very kind of you to finish the job for us," he said. "We had quite a time trying to find you in the woods. We found Amedean. We found Elise. We found that man who hid you from us."

Mara felt the room begin to slip away. She swung at the man one last time, but he held her too far. The room began to spin. She thought of kicking and swinging, but her body failed to react. His toothless smile burned in her mind as her vision began to fade.

33. Nothing to Experience

"You're not done with the story, though," I said.

Sheridan laughed. "Oh? You're that confident?"

"There's too many things unresolved," I said. "Bartlebee's Storytelling Conjecture, you called it."

"True, true," Sheridan hummed. "But–"

"*But* nothing. It's more evidence my theory was correct."

"But your *conjecture* was already disproved. It only takes one counter-example, and let's not forget Hitchcock."

"You're a tricky one, mister ... "

"Yes?"

For the first time, I realized I didn't know the most basic fact about Sheridan–the one thing someone should know about a person.

"Say ... what's your name?"

"Sheridan," he said, spoken clearly, without the least bit of surprise that I'd asked.

"No, no, no," I said. "And *don't* say it'll cost me a 'tidbit'. What's your first name? Or last? Or, whichever's the one that's not 'Sheridan'."

"Yes," Sheridan said. "That's an *interesting* question."

"You're dodging it," I said. "Don't try to fool me."

"Okay," Sheridan replied. "You got me. I just can't tell you."

"What? Why not?"

"Because," he said. "If I did, you'd know more about me than you need to know right now."

And since Sheridan couldn't fathom that I'd have a response to that, he immediately continued prattling on about Mara.

- 91 -

Mara opened her eyes, but saw nothing. Her head throbbed. She started to sit up, hit her head against something, and tried to scream. A sharp pain ran through her throat, and she made no sound. Her heart began to race. *Am I dead?*

She took a moment to catch her breath. A few memories began to trickle back to her. She remembered walking into the store, and the man in black.

She tried to call for help again, but her voice failed. She pounded on the barrier above her. She couldn't tell if she was blind, or in the dark. *I'm dead,* she thought. *This is Hell. No burning wall, or devils. Just nothing. Nothing to experience; nothing to do.*

She began to sob, then scolded herself. *Feeling sad will accomplish nothing at all, so stop that!*

For the next few moments, she felt around. Her hands touched a rough surface which could only be wood. *I'm in a box,* she thought. *I'm dead, and they buried me.*

Her heart raced again. *Or I'm alive, and they buried me by mistake!*

She pounded on the surface above. The rattle gave her some relief, as it wouldn't have budged at all if it was covered by dirt.

Whenever she pushed against the surface, a tiny, dim sliver of light became visible. *Or maybe they think I'm dead, and are about to bury me.*

Mara started to cry for help, but her throat burned. She pounded on the surface, then stopped herself. *Maybe I'm still in the shop. That makes sense. If they'd thought they killed me, they wouldn't turn me over to the town to deal with the body.*

She sat as silent as she could and listened to her surroundings. Nothing was audible. She wiggled around until she was lying on her stomach, then braced her back against the surface and pushed. The wood creaked and began to snap. When it gave way, she thrust herself to her feet and almost lost her balance.

The falling wood kicked up a thin cloud of dust. Mara looked around and saw she was in a cellar. She had correctly discerned she was in a crude casket.

One cellar wall was lined with shelves, holding bits of gold and silver. She walked over and took a few bits. *Repayment for a foul deed,* she thought. She heard footsteps above.

Mara held her breath as the footsteps inched closer to the cellar door, then stopped. Another set of footsteps entered, and she could hear faint voices.

Her first thought was that the footsteps were those of her assailants. When she heard a third set, she figured there must be at least one customer. She climbed onto the top of the casket and began to pound on the ceiling.

The footsteps started to scramble like disturbed hornets, and the ceiling shook. Mara pounded the ceiling again. She could hear faint grunting and a loud crash. Then silence.

Mara stood as still as she could. A single set of footsteps carefully trekked toward the cellar door. She could tell the person above was cautious.

The feet stopped just before the door. The handle jiggled a bit. Mara stepped off the casket and broke a large piece of wood from the cover. The sound of the snapping wood prompted the person on the other side of the door to stand still.

Mara slowly climbed the short staircase to the door, careful not to click her heels on the stone floor. She stood to the side of the door, and raised the beam.

The handle jiggled again, and the person pushed against the door. Mara saw it was locked. She couldn't figure out what to do. If she left it alone, the other person surely wouldn't forget about her. He'd be waiting for her whenever she came out.

Mara placed her finger under the latch and lifted it. The handle jiggled again She held her breath as the door began to open.

When it had opened an inch, Mara placed her fingers through the opening and swung it open. Before she could register the identity of the other person, she lifted the board and swiftly brought it down on his head.

With a clear *crack*, the man fell forward and dropped down the stairs, not even uttering a grunt or groan.

Mara closed her eyes as she caught her breath. Then, she looked down. She didn't recognize the man and froze in horror.

When the body had landed, he'd dropped a dagger and a small pouch. Her eyes widened when she noticed the dagger was coated with a thin film of blood. She traded glances between the door and the fallen man. *Is he alive?* she thought. *Was he a rescuer?*

She poked her head into the main floor. Suddenly, all the pieces of the puzzle fit together. The jeweler and the man in black lay on the floor, dead. Most of the contents of the shelves had been knocked over, and a few cabinets opened. Their contents must have been in the pouch the fallen man had dropped.

Mara threw her weapon into the cellar. She buried her head in her hands. *Stop that!* she scolded herself, and took a deep breath.

The front door flew open. Two guardsmen barged in. Mara recognized Fepp. The other guard demanded, "Halt!"

Fepp's eyes widened. Mara was standing in front of two dead men who were at least twice her size, with no weapon in hand. She lowered her gaze and smiled at Fepp.

34. It's What You Say

"See," I said. "Bartlebee's Storytelling Conjecture. Proved."

"The usual way to end a proof is 'Q.E.D.'." Sheridan said. "But, need I remind you–"

"Fine. Hitchcock."

Sheridan nodded.

"So, what's your name?"

Sheridan tried to look annoyed. I say *tried*, because he had his stupid grin hidden beneath a scowl. "I'll give you a hint," he said. "But only because it won't do you any good at all."

"Then, why bother?"

"I share a name with a North Carolina town."

"Charlotte?"

"Do I *look* like a 'Charlotte'?"

"It could be your last name." I shrugged.

"To be honest, I'm surprised you didn't ask me when you first pulled over," Sheridan said. "It's like that scene from *Seinfeld* where Jerry never asked his girlfriend's name."

"Boone," I suggested. "Wilmington? Mar-Mac? Mount Olive?"

Sheridan completely ignored me. I guess the name would cost me a 'tidbit' after all, but he didn't offer this time. He just continued his story, as if I didn't have more towns to suggest.

- 92 -

Nobody believed Mara could have killed the jeweler and his accomplice, which Mara was glad for after she'd set aside her feelings for Fepp. The two guards took Mara to the jail, where she sat for only a few minutes before Sanreils arrived to let her out.

She spent her time in jail feeling strangely immortal. When she saw Sanreils, though, she broke down in tears.

Sanreils demanded her release, and sat with her until she felt calm enough to walk. "Come with me," he said. "I'll take you to safety."

- 93 -

Sanreils took Mara's hand and led her through the corridors of the La Nocturne temple. He took her through the back entrance and side halls, where very few eyes watched them. During their walk to the temple, she'd managed to calm herself down. Her mind, once buzzing with a thousand thoughts at once, now sat dormant and dazed.

He stopped in a small annex, lit by moonlight shining through a small hole in the roof. "Are you with me, dear?"

Mara nodded and forced a smile. When Sanreils turned toward a door, she pulled the piece of burgundy paper out of her boot. She unfolded it and tried to read the writing that was distorted by the crumples.

Sanreils passively glanced at the paper, then pushed the door open behind him. Mara frowned. *He could at least be curious about it,* she thought. He motioned for her to join him through the door.

Mara stepped into Sanreils's chambers. He had led her into a private annex. It had a domed roof like the hallway, but with a bigger skylight. She could see the silhouettes of other nearby towers. Sanreils had his own fountain. A small, raised trench directed water out of the chamber.

"You'll be safe here," he said.

Mara nodded again. Sanreils laughed quietly and shook his head. "My dear! You need to regain your voice."

"Sorry," she mumbled.

Sanreils shook his head again. "Oh, Mara." He led her to the fountain and helped her sit down. "I'm so sorry for what you've been through."

Mara stared blankly at the wall as she thought. She'd initially been grateful when Sanreils had released her from the jail. But an uneasy feeling had soon overcome her. She'd tried to push it aside, but it kept returning. *Think!* she scolded herself.

Sanreils kissed her forehead. "Well, I'll be here whenever you come around."

Mara smiled. "Thank you," she whispered. "I'm sorry I don't sound more thankful. I really am."

"I know."

Think! Think! She shook her head clear. "You've always been so kind to me."

Sanreils brushed her hair out of her eyes and nodded. "Of course, my dear. Why would I not be?"

"Just seems like there aren't so many who are."

"Well," Sanreils said. "I just happen to know you're special."

Mara blushed. She turned away and tried to hide it, then laughed. "I'm glad at least one person thinks so!"

"Thinks? *Knows.*"

Mara closed her eyes. "I wish I could repay you."

Sanreils smiled gently. "I think you should stay the night."

Robbed of her speech, Mara just blinked. Sanreils chuckled, and took her hand again. "You'll be safe with me."

"I–" Mara stuttered. "I don't know what to say."

"Yes," Sanreils said. "Say you will."

"But," Mara said. She bit her lip. "Doesn't La Nocturne forbid it?"

"Well, maybe," Sanreils said. "There are rules. And '*rules*'."

"You're their spokesman," Mara said. "What would your people think?"

Sanreils briefly turned away, taking a moment to craft his words. "It's not what you do," he paused again. "It's what you say."

Mara stared blankly, then nodded and forced a smile. "But I'm not sleepy."

Sanreils laughed and shook his head. "Oh, Mara, my dear. What will I do with you?"

Mara realized she was still holding her paper. She looked at it all crumpled, and was suddenly struck by what bothered her. Her eyes widened, and she shifted away from Sanreils. "What is it?" he asked. "Do you see something?"

"You," Mara said, "lied to me."

"What? When?"

"You lied to me," Mara repeated. "Culatan wasn't responsible for the raid in Carrboro Forest. It was–"

"Well, uh . . . " Sanreils stumbled on his words. "I suppose. I did the best I could!"

"Did you know?"

Sanreils shook his head. "Honest!"

Mara unfolded her paper and glanced at her writing.

"It's true! I swear . . . " Sanreils started to speak.

Just like Dahes, Mara thought. She felt stupid for not seeing it before. Everything Matta had complained about seeing in Dahes, Mara now saw in Sanreils. *How could I have not seen it? It's so obvious, and I'm very stupid.*

She interrupted. "And whenever I start to talk about anything . . . you disappear! Why is that? What do you see in me? Why are you so eager to . . . "

"Here," Sanreils said. "I think we both know I'm quite infatuated with you ... and without being too presumptuous, I will say the feeling is mutual."

Mara smiled slightly. "You look out for me."

Sanreils smiled at her. Mara thought for a moment and sighed. "But who am I to you? Why have you pursued me?"

Sanreils thought a moment. "Look, I know you're going through this stage right now. But I know that when–"

"A stage?" Mara interrupted. "What?"

"I figured, when you'd settled down a bit ... "

"Settled down?" Mara stood up, gazing icily at Sanreils. "Settled down? Who am I to you?"

Sanreils stood. "I should think you would be happy that some in this world are willing to see through your eccentricities and appreciate the person underneath."

Mara clenched her fists as she choked back tears. "That is a horrible thing to say!" she exclaimed. "I am myself!"

Sanreils shook his head. "The town will eat you alive! I've seen you walk along the highway. I've seen you talk to the trees and the sky. You wander aimlessly through the streets ... doing who knows what. You dance in the fountains. You live in a dilapidated old tower amongst a bunch of misfits. I mean ... come on, now. You're lucky. The townsfolk are wary and not that tolerant."

Tears rolled down Mara's cheek as she crumpled her paper into a tight ball and hurled it at Sanreils. "I hate you!" she exclaimed. "You're worse than all of them!"

As Mara stormed out the door, Sanreils yelled, "They are wary! They'll kill you!"

Mara turned around and yelled across the hall, "You're wrong! You are cruel! You are the devil! Did you hear me? The devil!"

V
The Woods in Winter

35. With Every Winter Comes a Spring

"So, Mara threw her writing away," I said with a slight chuckle. "That wasn't too bright, was it?"

"Well," Sheridan said, "she *was* upset, no?"

"I don't get it."

"See, Sanreils–"

"No. The model. I don't get the model. A sequence? What's it do?"

Sheridan pondered the question, staring into space as his gears churned. "Did you ever see *Back to the Future*?"

"Do you think I can get this car up to 88 MPH?"

"I'll take that as a yes. And the kid, what's-his-name, alters the future by changing the events in the past."

"Yes."

"Suppose you had a map that could tell you the future that would result from the present you'd created." He smiled. "That's what Mara's Model is."

"Wait, so you can tell the future?"

"In a sense."

"But wouldn't . . . I don't understand how that would work. Are you telling me Mara could tell the future?"

"*She* didn't know that."

"That doesn't make sense," I said. "What if everyone could tell the future? Wouldn't there be conflict?"

"Of course. It's like the scenario of the time machine salesman."

"Wait. What?" I asked.

"The time machine salesman," Sheridan repeated. He straightened his posture and turned slightly. "How many time machines do you need to run a successful time machine dealership?"

"There's got to be a catch. Fifty."

Sheridan shook his head. "None. It's a trick question."

"Of course."

"Anyone in the business of selling time machines is probably not on top of their game. Obviously, more money could be made in selling one time machine to the same customer over and over again, as opposed to maintaining a big lot." Sheridan beamed a wide smile. "It's yet another scheme in *The Big Book of Time Travel Practical Jokes.*"

"That sounds . . . brilliant!"

"Ah! I knew it would be up your alley," Sheridan said with a slight chuckle. "Of course, if everyone knows that trick, then what you have is a big web of people selling time machines to each other, constantly trying to go further and further back in time to make the first sale. And, of course, prevent themselves from having been sold the time machine they currently own. This is the same problem with Mara's Model. If *everybody* knew it, then, well, it'd be like a million time machine salesmen trying to sell each other the same single time machine."

"Assuming Mara was correct."

"Assuming the model is real."

"Is it?"

"Perhaps," Sheridan said. "If such a sequence could be found. But as winter came—"

"Wait," I said.

It occurred to me that if Mara could predict the future, even if she didn't know it, then everyone else would be like those puppets. Once again, I got the feeling Sheridan viewed me as a puppet ... and not metaphorically, like a "puppet to society" or something like that. No, I wondered if he thought he could actually control me.

But it was a ridiculous thought.

"Never mind," I said.

"As I was saying," Sheridan continued, "as winter came, the trees and flowers had much less to say ... "

- 94 -

"Ass!" Matta's screams echoed down the corridor. "That's what he is–a total *ass*!"

On cold nights, the third floor of Thorn Tower provided the most warmth. The floor had eight fireplaces, spread fairly far apart. All the chimneys came together into a large shaft through the center of the ceiling. Cracks in the aging walls allowed traces of smoke and light to enter the room. Mara leaned against the shaft wall, staring at the edge of her shadow. Matta's voice reverberated up the stairwell.

Matta screamed and kicked the walls as she marched up the stairs to the floor. Mara heard her, but her mind immediately dropped the thought.

"Did you hear me?" She poked her head through the entryway. "I said it! He's a total–what's your problem?"

Mara briefly looked up, then back down at her shadow. Matta clenched her fists and shuddered. "You *won't* believe it. Well, you will. But I don't want to. Why are you staring at nothing?"

"It's cold."

Matta glanced around. "Yes, I'll give you that. Did you hear a thing I said? You don't seem like yourself."

Mara tossed a little pebble across the room. "Well, maybe it's better that I don't seem like myself."

"He was just so excited," Matta said. "The university, well, the *new* university of La-whatever, made him an apprentice."

Mara looked up, but stayed silent.

Matta took a deep breath. "I don't know. It's easier for the elite. I hear they're told who to marry."

Mara scooped up some pebbles and leaves and threw them into the fire. Sparks and embers flew from the fuel and spiraled up the chimney.

"You know what?" Matta said. "We should just go in there–right into the university–and kidnap him."

"Kidnap who?" Mara raised her head.

"Who do you think, numb-nut?"

"Never mind," Mara said. She looked back into the fire.

"Oh, I didn't mean that." Matta sat next to Mara and helped her throw pebbles in the fire. "You're lucky. You've never held love and thrown it away."

"That's not true," Mara said. "Sanreils. He behaved the same way, all the time. I feel so dumb for not seeing it."

"I don't want to let Dahes go," Matta said. "He once told me he loved me. I can't just forget that."

"But can we save him?"

"We should just march right in there and take him. Drag him away. Then, we'll leave Locana."

Mara closed her eyes and sat silent. "I'm starting to like the idea," she said quietly.

"Nothing," Matta said. "That's what we have."

Mara forced a slight smile. She reached into her satchel and removed a small handful of gems. "I wouldn't say that."

Matta's eyes bulged. "What? How? Wh-where?"

"Repayment for a foul deed."

"But–What–"

"We could all buy a piece of land. Live like lords and ladies."

"Wow," Matta gasped.

Mara diverted her gaze, staring blankly into the corridor. "I think I would like that very much. There's nothing here."

"But," Matta said. She bit her lip. "Well, how do we get Dahes?"

- 95 -

Mara braved the cold fourth floor to gaze out the window at the stars and mountains. She watched the stars of the Trey constellation twinkle. "Trey?"

The Trey constellation fluttered its tail. Trey faced away, providing Mara a generous view of his rear. While the tail acted on its own, Trey, himself, had his head down. He growled occasionally.

Mara scolded, "Trey! *What* are you chewing?"

Trey jumped and spun around. He held something in his mouth. Mara folded her arms over her chest and glared at the dog. She sternly commanded, "Drop it."

Trey wagged his tail.

Mara repeated, "Drop i-i-i-it."

Trey obliged. He opened his mouth. Venus fell out and rolled across the floor, leaving a small trail of drool along its path. Mara gasped. "Trey! You *ate* Venus."

Trey's tail dropped between his legs. He smiled innocently. "I didn't ... *eat* it."

"You did so!" Mara exclaimed. "Look, it's leaving a trail of spit. I bet it has teeth marks and all sorts of other dog-ly things in it."

Trey lowered his head. "I'm sorry. I am a dog, you know."

"Oh, Trey," Mara shook her head. "You know I love you."

The Trey constellation beat its tail against Mars. "Who wouldn't? So, tell me how you've been."

"You're interested?" Mara asked.

"Of course. We dogs are as nosy as we are good at smelling."

"If you really want to know, I'm pretty torn right now."

"Oh dear," Trey said, drooping his tail. "That's what I thought."

"*How* did you know?" Mara asked.

"We dogs are as perceptive as we are nosy," Trey explained. "Perhaps the two go hand-in-hand?"

"Why don't you dogs talk more often?" Mara asked. "I would imagine that you'd be good at it. You always seem to know the right things to say."

"What makes you think we don't speak?" Trey asked, fluttering his tail again. "Why, if I were an Earth-dog, I'd curl up in your lap and poke your face with my wet nose whenever I thought you were feeling down. And you could tell me anything, and I would listen!"

"I think that speaks volumes," Mara said.

Trey wagged his tail. "See! We do speak!"

"I feel like I'm losing the world again."

"Whenever I worry that I'm going to lose something, I pee on it. Then I'll be able to find it."

Mara laughed, shaking her head. "I don't think that will help."

"Maybe I can help you find the world," Trey said. His tail started to beat against the stars. "I have a pretty good view from up here."

"Can you see if it's safe for me to go into the university? To see the Ori?"

"You don't think you're ready to see the sequence?"

Mara closed her eyes and shook her head. "I think I need help. But I'm afraid to venture inside."

"That's not the Mara I know. There's no wall around the obelisk, remember? You can go around, through the woods."

"I know I shouldn't be afraid," Mara said, and sighed. "I wouldn't admit it to anyone but you."

"It's okay to be afraid sometimes," Trey said. "I'll look over you."

"Oh, that'd be lovely. I wish I could do you a favor in return."

"You don't have to."

"But I want to," Mara said. "Can I find you some June bugs?"

Trey smiled and wagged his tail vigorously. "Delicious ones?"

"Yes!"

Trey licked his lips. Mara spent the rest of the evening searching for June bugs in the stars.

36. A Filthy, Dirty Snow

"Again with the June bugs," I said. "Leave it to a dog to want *that*."

"Well, have you decided what you want the stars to contain?" Sheridan asked.

"Oh, no," I shook my head. "Not this again. We've been down this road."

"We could make another deal."

"Uh . . . no," I said. "You didn't hold up your end of the bargain last time."

"I did *too*," Sheridan said.

"The only tidbit I got that had any substance was where you're heading."

"The end of the road."

"Which," I said, "let me add, is rather obvious. Where does the road end?"

"At the end of the world."

I glanced at the sky. The ominous clouds still loomed above, continuing their slow descent. Every so often, I'd get another flashback from our ordeal in the mountains.

"So, let's assume you're right," I said. "At the end of the road, there's Mingo."

"Yes," Sheridan said.

"And you meet her, I assume."

Sheridan nodded.

"Then, what happens to *me*?"

Sheridan stared blankly for a long time–an unbearably uncomfortable pause that was broken by a declaration that wasn't any more comforting. "I don't know."

"You," I said, "don't know."

"I don't," Sheridan said. "Yet. But maybe, sometime soon, I might."

Before I could protest, Sheridan faced me, smiled, and said in an all too cheerful tone, "So. Your turn. Riddle me this. Were you going to Raleigh to meet a lover?"

"No."

"An old girlfriend?"

"No."

"Boyfriend?"

"*No.* Shut up," I said.

"Well, that's hardly a polite thing to say," Sheridan said. He frowned, but I knew he was faking it. "You *owe* me a tidbit. That was the deal."

"*Fine.* Later. Tell me about Mara."

Sheridan sat silent for a moment, then protested, "Oh no. I *never* learned what you were doing in Raleigh–"

"I was bored."

"Bored ... "

"Of life," I said. "There. Are you happy?"

"Maybe you should break out of your comfort zone," Sheridan said. "Take on new challenges."

"I didn't ask for advice," I said.

"Well, okay," Sheridan said. "I suppose, then, in the meantime, Mara set off to find the Ori ... "

- 96 -

Mara followed a band of merchants through Locana. It was time for her usual appointment with the Ori. She had missed the previous, and feared she'd miss today's if the guards spotted her.

As she ducked behind passing carts, she thought of how nice it'd be to leave the city. *Aphrael must know of more tutors,* she thought. *The Ori will be glad to be rid of me, I'm sure.*

Sometimes, she was forced to hide behind a cart that was moving *away* from the gate. She gritted her teeth whenever she took a step away.

When she was within eyesight of the university gate, the last cart turned away. Mara froze, then shifted her eyes. She thought she spotted a guard, and bolted into the neighboring woods. *I can't keep this up. I'm no better than an outlaw.*

She sighed, and waited for nearly an hour before the guard left. *I haven't even broken a law.*

But Mara feared that was wrong. Only Sanreils's good graces with the church had her freed from the jail.

"I know they don't believe I could've killed them," she'd told Matta about the incident the day she returned. "But they'd use any excuse to hang me."

When Mara finally mustered the courage to approach the gate, she found it was locked. *Here lies the tradition of open knowledge,* she thought, and ducked back into the woods.

Mara reminded herself of the knoll by the Ori's obelisk, and the break in the wall. With most of the leaves having fallen by now, and more paths open, she began her trek into the forest.

- 97 -

It seemed simple enough to trek around the wall. But in places, the only paths led deeper into the forest. It took Mara only a few minutes to get lost.

The sun flickered as harsh, cold winds bullied the tangles of branches. Whenever Mara faced away from the wind, it changed directions and punched her in the face. Her nose ran, and her eyes stung from the dryness.

The isolation of the woods provided little comfort from her concerns of the guards. Every errant snap sent her heart racing.

A particularly loud *snap* sent her flying into the air. She lost her footing and fell face-first into the cold, dried mud.

She cried out and rolled onto her back. The dried pit provided an odd comfort. She then noticed the silence.

The trees weren't whispering.

"Where did you go?" she asked, and received no reply.

Mara sat up and brushed the dust from her hair. She focused on the wind, ready to pounce on any sign of the woods' former life.

A subtle trinkle of water sounded from the other side of a small rise in the ground. She clamored to her feet and stumbled over to it. "Are you the same brook?" she asked the thin stream of water.

"Same as always. How are you, Mara?"

"What happened to you? You look so," she paused for a moment, "Thin."

"The ravages of winter," the brook said. "But, with every winter comes a spring."

Mara thought of sitting down, but she stood among pointy rocks. "I'd like to believe that," she said. "I think I'm in my own personal winter."

"Oh?" the brook asked.

She sighed. She told the brook all about her ordeal with the jeweler and Sanreils. She waited for the brook to respond. When it didn't, she sobbed. "Nothing is going right."

Mara let out a scream as she felt a sharp pain across her back. Her spine burned as she fell to her knees and into the water.

Icy liquid filled her lungs as she gasped for air. She

flipped onto her back and gagged. She opened her eyes as a second blow to her stomach stole what little breath she had left.

Her assailant removed their foot from her chest. She scooted backward through the mud as her eyes came into focus. A tall, wispy figure stood before her. It was slightly translucent; the world behind it distorted.

Mara tried to scream, but her voice failed. She climbed to her feet and ran.

The *ice demon* reminded her all too much of Anadaku. Her foot caught under a rock, and she fell.

She rolled down a small embankment and landed in a river. For all of two seconds, she felt safe in the ditch. Then the water's icy hand grasped her hair and pulled her under.

She gagged for air and flailed her arms for something to grasp. The chill raced down her back and sapped her strength. Just when she'd grabbed hold of a rock, the water sped up and she slipped.

The water carried her into a stone. She threw her arms around it and held tight. The water's cold hand punched her throat, and she let go of the stone.

The river carried her a few hundred feet more, then threw her onto the bank. She rolled several times before coming to a rest, face-up.

Mara sobbed quietly, then scolded herself and took a deep breath. She rested for a while, and opened her eyes.

Several spires shot up into the sky. As her vision regained its focus, she saw she was at the edge of the university. The familiarity provided some comfort.

Mara stumbled onto her feet and looked around. There was not a soul in sight. Just a few weeks ago, the grounds had been bustling with activity. Now, there was silence. *Just like in the woods,* she thought. *No life. Nothing.*

"Where did you all go?" she whispered.

The wind carried her voice away to join the other lost sounds.

Mara scanned the university grounds. Blanketed with snow and ice, she hardly recognized any of the familiar buildings. The plaza where she'd met the marbles-scholar had been buried. The once sky-blue towers were now gray. *It's a dirty snow,* she thought. *A filthy, dirty snow.*

She found the Ori's obelisk, which had been cleared of its vines. It, too, seemed bleak and lifeless. Mara ran her hands along the walls. *What happened here?* she thought as she wrapped her hand around the door handle and pushed it open. She fell to her knees and cried.

There was no chamber. Inside the obelisk was a tiny room which stored a few barrels. Before Mara could comprehend it, she felt a tap on her shoulder. She looked up. Dimitry glared down at her; Enton was behind him. "I think you need to come with us," he said.

37. It Had Your Name on It

"You think I'm a puppet," I blurted.

I had finally snapped. Maybe it was his tone of voice. He seemed to look down on me.

Sheridan gasped. "That was rather unexpected."

"Because my life is stale, or predictable, or something like that."

"Well, I do think your life *was* stale," Sheridan said. He smiled. "Then, you met me!"

"And how can you read my mind all the time?" I asked. "If you ... whatever."

Sheridan shrugged.

After I brought it up, I regretted it. I realized I'd learned nothing. Sheridan, after all, was most likely just having fun with me–a bored hitchhiker doesn't mesh well with a bored driver. I changed the subject.

"I knew something was off about the obelisk," I said.

Sheridan nodded. "Mara ran the scenario through her mind a dozen times, no round of which helped her sort it out ..."

- 98 -

Mara sat alone on a wooden chair in the center of a cold, dark room. A tiny slit just below the roof let a trickle of sunlight in, which disappeared somewhere behind her.

She had spent many hours on the knoll wondering what was in the university towers. When she was finally brought into one, she was unimpressed. They were bare, and more like prisons than the grand libraries she imagined. Enton and Dimitry had taken her to the top of a side tower and tied her to the chair. The seat was bolted to the floor. Mara wondered how many people had been tied to it before her.

The soft pat of footsteps echoed up the stairwell. Mara held her breath as the door creaked open.

Dimitry stepped inside and wasted no time. "We want to know why you keep poking your head into our business."

Mara lowered her gaze. "Whose business?"

"Ours," Enton said. He motioned toward the slit. "Our world."

"I wasn't aware you had it marked," Mara said. "Did you pee on it?"

"Well, it's certainly not *yours*," Enton said. "Haven't you heard, 'curiosity killed the cat'?"

"Getting into things it shouldn't," Dimitry added.

Mara wiggled her fingers as she tried to grasp the rope. Dimitry had tied her hands behind the chair and pulled the rope as tight as he could. She'd feigned discomfort, but her wrists were too thin and the rope too thick to lock them in place.

"Well," Enton said. "You haven't been charged. *Yet*. But know that we are discussing the matter with the judge."

"We were very clear about trespassing," Dimitry said. He looked Mara up and down. "You should know better. We don't want *your* kind in the church's university."

"And just what kind am I?" Mara glared.

Enton pulled the door open and held it for Dimitry. After Dimitry passed through, Enton shook his head. "Fool."

Once the door shut, Mara slipped her hand through the

knot. She stood up and looked at the slit. *Even if I could fit through there, who knows how long of a fall I'd be greeted with.*

She walked over to the door and tried the handle. It wouldn't budge. She sighed, and looked around the chamber. *This hasn't been my month.*

Just then, she heard footsteps. She froze solid as the latch clicked. The door began to swing open. Mara pressed herself flat against the wall.

Berot walked in. "Well, well, well," he said. "If it isn't–"

Berot looked around. "Now, where did you–"

When Berot faced Mara, she punched his face and kicked him in the groin. As he fell over, she barged through the door and ran down the stairs.

- 99 -

Mara fell over in the woods. She held her stomach tightly as she fought to regain her breath in the cold. She hadn't stop running for more than half an hour after she'd left the tower. She had climbed the knoll, jumped into the stream, and headed back into the woods.

She sat in the frozen mud, trying to hold back the pain of a hundred thoughts. For the first time, she realized the anamoly in the Ori's chamber. She thought of the dangling circles, catching the sunlight which beamed through the windows. *What windows?* she asked herself. The outside of the obelisk showed none.

A cold gust of wind lifted her hair and stung her neck. She stood and wrapped her arms around herself as tight as she could. *And the supposed Well of Enlightenment. What a fool the town must think I am.*

The whispering forest was gone. The Ori was gone. *But they seemed so real. Was it all imagined? Maybe I'm utterly alone in the world.*

Mara thought about the glowing city. Surely, there would be no way to visit it now. Nothing suggested she would even find out what it was.

Mara threw her arms in the air and screamed. Her voice echoed slightly before the wind muffled it.

38. It's Inevitable

"So, I was wondering," I said, "is the glowing city meant to be Heaven?"

Sheridan curled his eyebrow. "What do you mean by *'meant to be'*? I'm telling you Mara's historical account–not a literature class novel with symbolism."

I shook my head. "Don't get me started on literature classes."

"Well, you're supposed to use the Cliff's Notes to *supplement* the reading."

"I made 'D' on my *Great Gatsby* paper because I thought the green light meant envy! What's wrong with my interpretation? It's not *Family Feud*."

Sheridan was smiling. "You seem rather upset."

"Oh no, no, no," I protested. "You're not getting away this time. Answer the question."

"The glowing city?"

I nodded.

Sheridan hummed for a bit, then said, "It'll cost you a tidbit."

"Never mind," I said. "I'm not paying that toll right now."

"Okay," Sheridan said. "Maybe Mara's thoughts will shed some light on your question. She continued her run in the woods ... "

- 100 -

Mara ran through the woods, screaming at the trees. "Hello!" Her voice echoed, and was met with only the wind.

Just like that. Where did it go? She kicked dirt from the road into the bushes. "Answer me!"

Maybe I hit my head. That's it. I hit my head and had all my good sense knocked out of me. She stopped before a large, decaying pine. *Or it's winter. Do trees hibernate like bears?*

A faint clicking sound emitted from the trunk. Her ears perked, and she leaned closer. A very subtle rustling could be heard inside. She reached into a small hole. When she removed a fistful of dying spiders, she screamed and shook her hand, sending them flying across the trail. She turned around, and ran straight into Aphrael.

Aphrael groaned as Mara pushed her off the trail. She fell backward, into a tree. Mara stumbled the other way.

"I suppose I had that coming," Aphrael muttered.

"You!" Mara exclaimed. "Just who I was looking for."

Aphrael briefly stared in silence, then smiled innocently. "Me?"

"Yes, you." Mara lowered her gaze. "You lied to me."

"Oh?"

"Sanreils."

"I heard you two had a falling out."

"Don't change the subject. He didn't have anything to do with the raid in Carrboro Forest."

Aphrael glanced upward, then forced a smile. "Oops."

"Oops?" Mara rolled her eyes. "*That's all?* If you knew it was the jeweler, why didn't you tell me? They almost killed me! Wait—" Mara stopped herself. "How did you know it happened in the first place? Were you there?"

"Well—"

"You were, weren't you?"

Aphrael's perpetual grin dropped. She let out a slight sigh. "Yes. I was there."

Mara stared at her. She watched every twitch of her face and movement of her eyes with scrutiny. "Who are you?"

"Sylow probably told you about a woman who'd left you on a doorstep. Am I right?"

Mara's eyes bulged, and she gasped. "You? You're—"

Aphrael shook her head. "No. That's what I told *him*."

Mara lowered her gaze and sneered. "What do you mean, 'that's what you told *him*?'"

"I told him I was your mother."

Mara thought she saw Aphrael giggle when she spoke. The thought burned in her mind, even though she wasn't quite sure. "Why did you tell him that?" She clenched her fists and shook with anger. "He told *me* that! And I spent my mother's remaining days thinking that."

"Oops."

"*Oops*? That's all you have to say? Do you tell anyone the truth?"

"You defeated my demon. You drank from my well."

"*Your* well?"

"The Well of Enlightenment." Aphrael laughed before she could cover her mouth.

"The well," Mara said. She bit her lip and shook her head. "It was a latrine. That's what the lumberjack said."

Aphrael smiled innocently. "It was not a toilet. It was a test."

"If your intent was to make a fool out of me in front of the whole town, I'd say I passed with flying colors."

"It was a test of your ability. I had to know it was you."

"My ability? Who am I?"

"Reality," Aphrael said, "is as you define it. *You* are as you define it."

"Where did the Ori go?"

Aphrael didn't respond.

"You lied about Sanreils," Mara said. "Why?"

Aphrael lifted Mara's chin and stared into her eyes. "Sanreils seemed to have you rather hypnotized. I was simply trying to protect–"

Mara stepped back and glared. "I can take care of myself!"

Aphrael took Mara's cheeks in her hands and seized her attention. "Now, you listen to me. A lot was riding on my sister being freed from that temple. One day, you'll understand. But you *failed*. Do you know what that means?"

Mara tried to shake her head within Aphrael's grasp. Aphrael continued, "It means you're going to die."

"No," Mara said. She winced as Aphrael's grip tightened, and her heart began to race. "That's not true."

Aphrael released her. She closed her eyes and shook her head. "It's inevitable. Believe me. I don't want it to happen."

Mara didn't dare admit Aphrael had scared her. Whenever tears began to form in her eyes, she looked away and stared at the sky. "I don't believe you."

"It's okay," Aphrael said. "We all die eventually. I'll die. You'll die. But there's always another chance. Until things are right."

"Until things are right? What happens then?"

"Then, there's no reason for the world to be here."

Mara felt a tear roll down her cheek. She stared straight up at the sky.

"I don't mean to scare you," Aphrael said.

"You don't scare me!" Mara screamed.

"Yes, I do," Aphrael said. "I feel bad about it, I really do."

"You don't scare me, and I don't believe you," Mara said. She pushed Aphrael away and shouted at her. "I don't believe you. I don't believe you even exist!"

Before Aphrael could respond, Mara turned and ran away.

39. Just a Bunch of Trees

I turned Aphrael's words over in my mind several times. I didn't want Sheridan to know it, but every so often, he said something that gave me pause. He was watching me stare at the highway, and smiling. He probably knew.

Sheridan said the world was ending, and Aphrael had said there was no need for it to exist once things were set right. That raised the obvious question.

"Are things right?"

Sheridan looked puzzled. "What things?"

"*Aphrael*'s things," I said. "This is an historical account, right? And the world is ending?"

Sheridan nodded. He eyed me curiously for a bit, but then the light bulb went off in his head. "Ah! Well ..."

"Well, what?"

"I'll tell you the answer," Sheridan said. "But you know the deal."

"Great."

That put me two in the hole, which seemed hopeless. So, I ignored Sheridan's offer. He waited for a minute or two, then started telling me more about Mara.

Mara ran through the woods, screaming as she swung at twigs and branches. It had started snowing when she ran from Aphrael. Thousands of unique snowflakes that all looked alike as Mara swiped the air.

She stopped at the edge of a trail, screamed again, and kicked a stone. "Nothing," she said, looking up toward the treetops. "That's what you are. Just a bunch of trees!"

The forest said nothing. Mara ran forward, stopping where the brook usually met with the road. Its bed had almost completely dried, and what water was left had frozen. "You're just a brook!" she screamed. "Nothing more."

She picked up a rock and threw it into the brook bed. It bounced on the ice and rolled a bit. "Talk to me," she said.

A quick, cold burst of wind raced down the trail, lifting her hair and biting at her neck. She shivered, and threw another stone into the brook. "Talk to me!"

Mara kicked the remains of a bush. Little bits of twig flew off into the air, quickly coming to a rest without so much as a hint of life. She screamed at the brook again, picked up the largest boulder she could, and dropped it into the frozen water. The ice shattered in a dozen directions. Only the sound of the wind followed.

"Please talk to me," she whispered, then fell to her knees and sobbed.

A moment later, she looked up, wiped her eyes, and glared at the highway. "You're just a road," she said. "Nothing more. Did you hear?"

She scooped up a bit of dirt from the trail and tossed it into the wind. "Nothing more."

VI
Mara's Model

40. Why You Dislike Us

"Penny for your thoughts?" Sheridan asked. He was staring at me with his usual big eyes.

"You know, it *is* possible I was being quiet and attentive to your tale," I said. "Why do you always want to know what I'm thinking?"

Sheridan shrugged. "Why not?"

"Fine," I said. "'Well, I don't see how you can call Mara a mathematician when you've yet to tell me about a single equation or something like that."

Sheridan laughed. "I'd hate to think that someone put it in your head that mathematics is about equations."

Sheridan kept chuckling to himself for a moment. He then stretched and leaned back in his chair, letting the seatbelt dangle loosely. "It's about–"

"Don't say finding that silly sequence."

"Do you think such a thing is possible?"

Sheridan hung on my every word, possibly looking for something to poke fun at. I glanced at him. "You owe me a penny."

"I take it you and mathematics don't get along well."

"In third grade I got stuck on 'four times seven' playing 'around the world'," I explained. "I suppose I started hating math, then."

"You seem to hate a lot of things," Sheridan said. He hummed quietly for a bit, then asked, "Is there something you like?"

"Can the answer count as a 'tidbit'?"

"Sure," he said. "I suppose I should tell you, then, my thoughts on the glowing city."

He contemplated for a few minutes before saying, "I'm hoping to find out if there is such a place." He stared out the window again, looking down at the highway. "But I suppose, I already know the answer. At least, I should. But you can hope and know at the same time, you know?"

"I suppose."

"So, what do you like?"

"Money," I said.

Sheridan chuckled and nodded. "I figured as much."

"But not because I want to buy things," I said. "It just helps me quantify success, I suppose."

"Don't you have anybody to cheer you on?"

"Tell me if things are right," I said. "That's the other question you left hanging."

Sheridan looked my way, raised one eyebrow, then looked back to the road. "Not yet."

I wasn't sure what to make of that. Sheridan quickly asked, "So . . . what's my answer?"

"No."

"I–"

"You left me hanging," I said. "What happened to Mara?"

"She made it back home," Sheridan said. "But she was in no mood to speak to anyone. Matta was still distraught, and her grief only added more stress to Mara's life. Unable to sleep, she slipped out early the next morning . . . "

- 102 -

The following day, Mara returned to the forest, found a large, flat rock to lie on, and stared up at the trees. She kicked

herself for throwing the burgundy paper at Sanreils and cursing the highway.

With winter in full force, there were only a few leaves left
to view. They danced wildly in the wind. *If the leaves are
like people, then they all fall a certain way to their destiny*, she
thought. *I wish Theon was here.*

High above, thick clouds drifted by, each a swirling mass
of gray, white, and gray-blue. She watched the colors fade
into each other; a sign written in a language she couldn't
fathom. *Just like the whispering forest*, she thought as her mind
wandered back to her days in Sylow's clearing. *The trees, the
fountain, the clouds, they all have something in common. Maybe
the Mara-in-the-bottle knows.*

Mara glanced toward the highway. "Do you see it?"

She tried to wait patiently for a response and pushed
away the thought that one wouldn't come.

"Please talk to me," Mara said. "I didn't mean it."

"Well, well, who are we talking to?" someone from behind asked.

Mara froze. Someone else was laughing. That laugh
sounded familiar. And it didn't take very long for her to
figure out who it was. She turned around to see Fepp standing in the trail, smiling to himself. Berot stood behind him,
grinning.

"What do you two want?" Mara asked. She folded her
arms and stared them down.

"Why, we were just thinking what a dull day this has
been, having been assigned highway duty. But then we find
none other than Mara, chatting with the wind," Fepp said.
He nodded toward Berot.

Berot chuckled.

"We didn't mean to interrupt!" Fepp exclaimed. "Go on.
I'm sure you two have much to discuss."

"I hardly see the need for you to be a twert, but if you

must, then I will wish you both good riddance," Mara said. She turned her back to them and started to walk down the road.

Mara had walked only a few steps when she felt something sharp prick her back. Looking behind her, she saw Berot standing with a sharp dagger aimed at her. "Come with us."

What now? She closed her eyes and clenched her fists.

Berot opened a path through the shrubbery. "Through here," he said.

- 103 -

Fepp and Berot led the way down a small path, cutting through the bushes. Mara walked silently. Her heart raced as she thought of any possible scenario in which she could safely escape. *I could run*, she thought, *but they would surely catch up with me. And when they did, they'd probably kill me.*

The guardsmen stopped in a low clearing. "This will do," Fepp said. "Check for anyone who might be nearby."

As Berot finished checking the shrubbery and trees, Fepp shoved Mara against a trunk. He tore her coat off her back and tossed it over his shoulders. "Thank you," he said. "I was cold."

Mara shivered. Fepp chuckled. "So, I've heard you had a falling out with your little friend ... Sanreils." Mara glared icily at Fepp.

He added, "Who no longer seems to care for you in the least."

Berot laughed. "We want to know ... " He faked a frown. "Why you dislike us so much."

Mara continued to glare. Fepp, too, faked a frown. Mara clenched her fists. She attempted to move, but Fepp pushed her back into the trunk.

She said, "You're foul vermin. Last I checked, I had no interest in conducting business with disease-ridden rats."

Mara felt a sharp, cold pain race through her chest. She glanced down and gasped for air as Berot removed his dagger from her abdomen. She choked back tears as she felt her strength drain.

Berot raised his arm. Fepp stopped him from striking again. "Berot ... Berot ... You don't want to do that." He turned his eye to Mara and smiled deviously. He stroked her cheek. "Not to her."

"She insulted me!" Berot exclaimed. "A representative of Locana!"

As the guards bickered, Mara looked up. In the corner of her eye, she saw a small, brown blur. It was a squirrel. A small branch snapped under its feet. The *crack* startled both guards. During the brief moment the guards' attentions were stolen, Mara seized the dagger from Berot's hand. Fepp noticed first. He grinned for a moment.

Mara quickly thrust the weapon. Fepp immediately released his grip on her. She wasn't sure if she'd hit him, or just shocked him. She didn't take the time to assess her actions. She ran.

She carved through the snow as quickly as she could. Small patches of ice and fallen trunks and branches littered the highway, threatening to stop her in her tracks. Looking over her shoulder, she saw Berot beginning to catch up. The cold air invaded her lungs, and she could feel her body beginning to give out.

The air stung her eyes and invaded her wound. She stopped and gasped for air. "Just keep following," the highway said. "Keep going, and you'll see where to stop."

Mara took a deep breath and continued running. All she could focus on were Berot's footsteps.

She shrieked as her foot caught a root, and she crashed

face-first into the snow and ice. She rolled onto her back, held her chest, and sobbed. Berot's footsteps grew louder.

Mara closed her eyes. "Please stay with me."

"I have followed you all these years," the highway said. "Why would I leave you now? After you have come so far?"

Mara climbed to her feet. She pulled her hand away from her chest. Drops of blood littered the snow.

She wiped the ice out of her face and continued running.

"I must confess," Mara said. "I am a bit scared right now."

"Understandable," the highway said. "You don't have far to go."

The highway's words bounced around in her head, rattling with each footstep. She began to feel dizzy and nauseous. She closed her eyes once more as a cold gust rushed over her.

When she opened her eyes, she caught a sparkle of gold. A sunbeam shone through a slight break in the clouds. Its fingers caught a small tree, clinging to a few yellow leaves. Mara ran to them. For a moment, she fell into their trance. A *snap* startled her out of it. Berot was closing in.

Mara realized where she was. To the right, through the bushes, was the ledge she had taken Theon to. She slipped through and ran up to the cliff.

Frigid gusts of icy air blasted her face when she looked over. She could hear rustling from the bushes.

A second gust of wind caught her hair. She looked down to shield her face. Her hand was now entirely covered with blood. She glanced at the snow. Her footsteps led to the cliff's edge, suggesting she had jumped. She quickly ducked behind a rock.

Berot burst through the bushes. "Come out, come out, wherever you are!" he exclaimed. "I won't hurt you."

He looked at the footsteps and chuckled to himself. He walked up to the edge and peered down. "Mara?" he shouted.

His voice echoed slightly.

Mara carefully snuck up behind Berot. She broke a large branch off a nearby bush.

The snap echoed behind Berot's voice. When he turned around, Mara struck him in the face, shoving him over the edge. His scream was cut short by a soft *thud* as he landed on the rocks below.

Mara stood silently for a minute. She began to feel dizzy again, and stumbled her way toward the road.

She collapsed in the snow. She lay shivering by the side of the highway as the breeze picked up. As the twigs of nearby brush rustled, her pulse quickened. *Perhaps Fepp is still alive?*

She climbed to her feet, tightened her grip on her branch, and stared down the way. As her eyes focused, she let out a little gasp. Her heart beat faster. She dropped her branch and took a step backward. She stared face-to-face with the ice demon. Its cold wind whipped around it. It stood silently, grinning ever so slightly. Mara shook her head. She slowly backed away. The monster slowly approached. As it neared, the wind whipped violently around her.

Mara took another step back. In an instant, the ice demon laughed and lunged forward. Mara winced as it sunk its teeth into her chest. The force of the beast entering her lungs threw her back. With each breath she took, she felt weaker. She fell to her knees, too drained to stand.

She sat as tightly hunched as possible. She closed her eyes as she shivered uncontrollably. She heard the crunching sound of footsteps drawing near. She was too tired to open her eyes and see who was approaching. "Please ... don't let it be Fepp," she whispered. "Please ... help me."

Mara felt someone slip a blanket over her. She struggled to open her eyes, but failed. She was too tired to stay awake, or even think. She felt herself being lifted off the ground and carried away.

41. Magical Discovery

I noticed that for the past several dozen miles, we'd stopped ascending noticeably high. It seemed we were pulling out of the mountains. Then I noticed the sign–Memphis was right around the corner.

I squinted in an attempt to see the city lights on the horizon. I didn't see anything; we must have been too far still.

Sheridan watched me gaze into the horizon. He must have known I was thinking about *something*. But this time, he didn't seem interested. He leaned back in his seat and continued his story.

- 104 -

Mara's eyes shot open as she regained her breath. She screamed, coughed, and sat up. The cold had dissipated, along with the snow. The forest she sat in was green and full of life. The sun beat down on her through a tiny break in the clouds, and a cool breeze danced over the trail. High above, a voice whispered, "Wake up, Mara."

"Who? What?" Mara rubbed her eyes. Pieces of her memory came back. "Where did–" She looked up and the sun blinded her. "Where did winter go?"

"Wake up," another voice said. "You're safe."

"You're almost there," a third voice whispered.

"Who are you?" Mara looked all around. The tree leaves drifted slightly in the breeze.

"Stand," a fourth voice said. "Further down."

Mara obeyed the voice and stood with ease. Her injuries seemed to have disappeared. But, despite the return of summer, the whispering forest was still gone. Her heart skipped a beat. She looked up at the trees again. "You–you're–I can hear you."

"Had you not been able to before?"

"No." Mara shook her head. "Why all of a sudden? What have you been trying to say?"

"Look down."

Mara glanced toward her feet, and saw she stood by a small puddle. Her reflection wobbled in the weakening current, which quieted into a perfectly still image. The Ori's last instruction bounced in her mind. *Ask the other Mara. The one in the bottle.*

"Life brought me to this point," Mara said. "Did it not?"

Her reflection silently nodded.

"If I'd come from a different way, then I would be one of the other Maras. And if I find the sequence, I will know which path I am guided along."

Her reflection nodded again, and nudged its head toward the horizon. Mara turned her head to the right as a light rain began to fall. "But what lies at the end of the road?"

The leaves parted in the breeze, exposing a road bathed in glittering sunlight. The highway called to her. "Follow me."

"Follow you?"

"Follow me to the end of the world. I'll take you to the ones you loved. And I'll show you the world along the way."

Mara squinted to see through the light. She whispered, "Ohhh."

Far away, barely visible against the horizon, was the same city she'd seen after drinking from the well. "But ... it's so far."

Mara suddenly felt very warm. She glanced all around. Crackling, like that of a fire, was barely audible. She couldn't see anything that would produce such a sound. She tried to walk toward the city, but her feet wouldn't budge. They felt as if they were tied together. She tried to speak, but could only moan. The sound of the crackling grew louder, and the sky darkened.

- 105 -

Mara screamed as she sat up; she was drenched in sweat and burning up. She struggled to open her eyes, but her vision blurred. She could make out the glow of a fire, and a faint figure standing near it. "Who are you?" she whispered.

The figure continued working, giving little notice to Mara's attempts to move. Her head pounded, and she suddenly felt very nauseous.

She closed her eyes, and fell back asleep.

- 106 -

Mara woke a second time. Her headache had subsided, and her vision returned to normal. She found herself lying in the unknown bed of a humble cabin. A tiny window showcased a harsh winter evening, the wind beating on the trees and howling through the valley.

She rested under at least three or four blankets. The fire had nearly gone out, but she realized now why she'd been so warm before. She found she could sit up, but attempting to stand seemed to drain all her energy.

The cabin door opened with a burst of frigid air. The figure, shadowed by the darkness outside, stepped in with an armful of wood. Mara held her breath as she waited for them to step into the light.

"Well, look who's up," the figure said.

"I, yes, but–" Mara squinted. "Theon?"

Theon waved.

"Theon!" Mara exclaimed.

"I am me. Well, last time I checked."

Mara smiled. "You're still you. You were the one on the highway, weren't you?"

Theon nodded as he gently pushed Mara back onto the bed "I was trying to clear a path before the blizzard grew worse. Then I found this." He lifted her satchel off the floor, then carefully set it down.

"My satchel!" Mara exclaimed. "And my book?"

Theon nodded.

"Oh, Theon," she said. "I don't know what I'd do if I lost that."

"I recognized it," Theon said. "Then, after a short hike, I saw a figure on the road."

"Me."

"I tried to wake you up, but you looked sick. Then I saw you were injured so badly. I was scared you were gone."

"I think I'll be okay," Mara said. "The cold gave me such a terrible headache."

Theon hung his head. "During my struggle to carry you down the highway, I slipped on the ice, and you took . . . a fall."

Mara laughed. "It's okay," she said as she smiled warmly at him. "I probably wouldn't be here at all if it weren't for you."

She reached out of the blankets and held Theon's hand. "You saved my life," she whispered. "I guess I owe you one."

Theon lifted her satchel again.

"No, two," Mara said. "I owe you two."

Theon brushed fallen strands of hair out of her eyes. "You should get your rest."

Mara smiled at him and closed her eyes. She promptly fell back asleep.

- 107 -

The following morning greeted the small cabin room with an abundance of clear sunlight. Fresh snow glowed brightly as it began to melt. Its reflective light bathed the house and cast deep shadows across the room.

When Mara woke, she climbed out of bed and greeted the brilliant day. She pressed her face against the window and smiled to herself as she viewed the scene. The world was fresh and clean. She quickly turned around as Theon stepped into the room. "Look! Snow!"

"It looks a lot different than yesterday."

"Come here," Mara motioned for him to join her.

Theon pressed his face against the glass.

Mara looked his way and smiled at him. "The whole world has been given a breath of new life."

"Why do you suppose the snow is white?" Theon removed his face from the window, leaving a foggy spot where his nose had been. "If water is blue, and snow melts into water, shouldn't the snow be blue?"

"I missed you," Mara whispered. "Why did you leave town?"

Theon stared at Mara as his mind churned. She continued to watch him. Finally, he responded, "I had business to take care of. I decided my craft wasn't right for me."

Mara closed her eyes and nodded. "Fair enough."

They stood in silence, until Mara opened her eyes again and looked at Theon. "I want you to know, though, that I missed your company."

"I missed you, too."

"You hurt me," Mara whispered. "You didn't even say goodbye. Why?"

"I'm sorry," Theon whispered back. "I'm ... shy?"

Mara closed her eyes again and sighed. "I know."

"Will you forgive me?"

She smiled slightly at him, taking his hand. "Come with me," she said, tugging him away from the window.

"Where are we going?"

"Out into the world. It's a lovely winter day, perhaps the best of all the winter days we've had. I want to share it with you."

- 108 -

Mara and Theon walked slowly down the roadway outside the cabin. Over the morning, the sun had melted the snow on the nearby weeping willows. Soon afterward, the clouds had returned and the water had begun to freeze again, weighing down the thin branches with a coating of clear, bright ice. Now that the sun was emerging yet again, the ice glowed and sparkled. They walked through the glimmering archways. White sunlight blanketed the ice, casting the entire spectrum of colors in patches against the white. "It's our own crystal palace!" Mara exclaimed.

"We have captured all of the rainbows," Theon said.

Mara smiled and said, "They're ours. What should we do with them?"

"Hoard them!"

Mara reached down and tried to pick one up. She showed her snow-covered hand.

Theon frowned. "That's too bad."

"Not all is lost," Mara said. She packed more snow in her hand. "We still have plenty of snow."

"I suppose so," Theon said. "Still, what can we do with snow?"

Mara promptly hurled her snowball directly into Theon's face. "Splat!"

"You twert!" Theon called as he ran toward her.

Mara stuck her tongue out at him, and ducked behind a tree. She could no longer hear Theon, only the gentle wind and clatter of the ice. She explored the path, and came to a dead end in the maze of ice-covered trees. "Where'd you go?" she yelled.

Someone ran behind the trees, shaking them. As the branches shook, little bits of ice fell. The sun cast against the tiny shards, filling the alcove with a shower of sparkling light. Mara stood still and silent, gazing at the glimmering rain. She didn't notice as someone carefully approached until they pushed a small pile of snow down her back. Mara screamed. Theon exclaimed, "Destiny!" from behind.

Theon fell over laughing as she struggled to free her back from the cold snow. She grinned, and quickly shoveled snow over him.

"Mmmmph!"

Mara knelt beside the moving pile of snow and uncovered just enough of it to expose Theon's face. He opened his eyes and blew snow out of his mouth. "That wasn't nice!"

"Sorry." Mara smiled as she brushed flakes of snow off his face.

"Help me up." Theon stuck his hand out from the snow pile.

She took it and helped him sit up. "Better?"

"Quite," Theon said. He promptly sprang forward, pushed Mara over and pinned her to the ground.

Mara screamed and laughed as Theon sprinkled snow over her face.

"Okay! Okay!" she yelled. "You win!"

Theon helped her sit back up, and she stuck her tongue out at him. "Twert." She grinned.

"Admit it, though, you rather like it out here," Theon said.

"I do," she whispered. "This is a beautiful place."

Theon nodded and glanced around the ice cave. "The world is full of magical discoveries."

"Hey, you're taking my lines!" Mara said. She poked his rib. "Am I rubbing off on you?"

Theon laughed. "No, I'm not stealing your lines. I just remember saying that the first time I saw you."

Mara blinked and grew silent. Theon blushed. "Hey, let's go look around some more," he said abruptly as he climbed to his feet.

"No!" Mara stood and seized his hand. She looked into his eyes for a moment. "You really mean that, don't you?" she whispered. "I'm a magical discovery?"

Theon blushed again.

"You do!" Mara exclaimed. "It has to be true, because if it weren't, you wouldn't have said it without thinking about it first."

"The world seems ... like an entirely different place around you." Theon stumbled on his words. "It seems more ... alive?"

Mara smiled. "Alive is good."

"You open my eyes sometimes," Theon continued. "You make me think about ... things. Things I've never even dreamed of. The world just seems ... more ... "

She held him tightly and laid her head on his shoulder. "Don't you dare disappear again, okay?"

"Okay," Theon whispered.

"Good. Because if you do, I may just have to hunt you down." She jabbed his side. "And you know I will, too, because I'm stubborn enough to track you to the end of the world. And you should also know, if I have to go that far, I will have some words for you."

"Fair enough."

Mara smiled at him. "So, we're in agreement on the terms, then."

Theon nodded.

"Let's go exploring!" she exclaimed, seizing his hand and tugging him along.

42. You Must Be Floating, Too

The thought of Mara taking Theon for an adventure in the snow made me think of the last scene from *Calvin and Hobbes*–the one where they're sledding off on an adventure. Maybe Mara was a figment of Theon's imagination.

Then again, I realized that didn't make sense. Theon, like Peoria, hadn't shown up until the middle of the story.

I could feel the puzzle pieces clicking into place. Theon, like Peoria, had sung that stupid song with all the verses. And Mara had said he looked familiar. Suddenly, a light bulb turned on over my head.

"Sheridan," I said. "Would you turn off that map light? It's reflecting off the rear view mirror, and I can't use it."

"My leg brushed up against something."

"It's probably just paper, and you broke my concentration."

Sheridan squirmed around as he pushed his arm under the dash. He lifted a piece of paper, looked it over, and laughed.

"What?" I asked. "I hate that laugh. It's usually aimed at me."

Sheridan showed me the paper–a page of notes for my disastrous seminar at Duke. "What went wrong?"

"Give me that." I tore it from his hand and stuffed it between the door and the seat. He was still laughing.

"There's a story here. I just know it. What happened?"

"No," I said.

"Aw, come on." Sheridan's eyes lit up. "I'll even let you ask me a question."

"If I ask you a question, will you answer it?"

Sheridan nodded.

"It's like I found a genie," I said. "Now, I don't know what to wish for."

"I'm glad you find me intriguing."

"Well . . . there's just nothing else on."

"I see," Sheridan replied. He leaned back with his arms crossed behind his head, ready to tackle anything I could throw at him.

"Do you believe in reincarnation?"

"That's a random question," Sheridan said. "Not that there's anything wrong with that."

"I mean, can someone die and come back as the same person . . . but, like, also a different person?"

The funny thing was that Sheridan seemed to know what I meant, although he tried to look confused. At least, that's what I thought. It was hard to read his face.

He let some thoughts churn for a while. "Well, there's always the question of nature versus nurture."

"Like twins who were separated at birth, but grow up to be different people."

Sheridan shrugged. "Why do you ask?"

"I had a theory," I said. "*Conjecture*, rather. But I lost my train of thought when you shone the light right in my face."

Sheridan chuckled and turned the light off. I looked in the mirror and remembered that it probably didn't matter if I couldn't use it. Who would be behind us?

"I didn't mean to disrupt your study," he said. "So, what went wrong at the seminar?"

"Okay, fine. My specialty is mid to late twentieth century history," I explained. "So, I was giving a lecture on the

World Trade Center bombing, and the events that led up to it. Part way through the lecture, this guy stands up and starts preaching about how we're all going to–"

"*Hellfire!*" Sheridan exclaimed. He made a fist as he lowered his voice. "The pits of *Hellfire!*"

"*How* did you know that?"

Sheridan laughed. "His name is Kaldred. He's a preacher of sorts. Or, rather, *was* a preacher. He'd sit in the middle of the NCSU campus and tell everyone how they're going to Hell. I'm surprised you didn't run into him at the tailgate party."

I shook my head and mumbled, "What a world."

"It is a small one," he said. "Was, anyway."

"So, who is he?"

Sheridan turned and looked straight into my eye. I waited for a smile to crack, as it usually did when he pretended to be serious. But this time, he didn't smile. He just said, "In time, you'll see."

And, before I could ask a follow-up question, he said, "Let's continue working on just that."

- 109 -

Mara and Theon walked through the glimmering arches, gazing at the dances of light. Mara watched the willow leaves sway in the wind, and thought for a moment about Marcus's patterns. "Left, up, right, up, up ... " she muttered.

Theon poked her. "What was that?"

"The key," Mara said. "Or cord. Whatever you want to call it."

Theon watched the willow leaves sway. Little bits of ice dropped off, clinking as they hit the ground. "The one you're looking for?"

"Yes," Mara said. She pointed to the sky. "If you haven't noticed, the very same pattern is in the clouds. When the leaves sway toward us, the clouds drift west."

"But they're always drifting west," Theon said. "Aren't they?"

"When the wind dies down, the leaves fall as well. And if you didn't see, whenever that happens, the clouds change their trajectory. Slightly, but they do. And always in sync with the leaves."

"Like a clock," Theon said.

Mara laughed. "Yes! It's exactly like a clock. But what's driving it?"

"Wind?"

"Exactly. And where does the wind originate?"

"A giant," Theon said. "With a really big mouth. I hope he didn't have fish for dinner."

Mara giggled. She shook her head and smiled. "I'd like to think so. But I think the answer is only entertaining for those who find the matter of the wind worthy of discussion at all."

"Something even more peculiar," Theon said, "is the storm."

"Storm?"

On cue, a low rumble roared from the east. Mara jumped and eyed the horizon. A massive, anvil-shaped cloud loomed, like the dust from a herd of a hundred horses, galloping over the hills. "A thunderstorm? In winter?"

"Maybe we should go inside. I don't want to be hit by lightning."

Mara shook her head. "It's the most peculiar thing I've seen in the past five minutes! We should get a closer look."

"A closer look?"

Mara nodded and jumped excitedly. "Yes! It's a marvel of nature."

"That wasn't my objection," Theon said. "More like, well, how?"

"Oh," Mara said. "You're afraid of the height."

"What? No."

"It's okay to admit when you're scared."

"Well, I mean, okay," Theon said. "I am. I don't like heights. But that wasn't–"

Mara smiled. She took his hand and held it tight as the wind picked up. "I won't let you fall. You can trust me."

"What? You can't fly!"

Mara slung her satchel over her shoulder. "We're going on an adventure."

"Into the sky? How?"

"Just empty your mind, and let it take you there," she said.

Mara closed her eyes and spread her arms, inviting the breeze to race through her hair. Theon shrugged, closed his eyes, and lifted his other arm.

A sudden burst of wind raced through the trees, spraying the willow's ice into a sea of light. Its roar drowned out Theon's words. At that moment, he looked down to find that he and Mara had been carried forty feet above the ground. He let out a yelp and clung to Mara. She laughed.

"Now, really! If you just apply a bit of *reason*, you would know that you have no need to be afraid! You must be floating, too."

Theon stopped breathing quite so heavily. Mara smiled reassuringly at him. He closed his eyes, let go, and having realized he didn't fall, opened them again and laughed. By this time, they had risen nearly a thousand feet above the city, which now appeared as nothing but a tiny blur. Mara seized both Theon's hands and pulled him up higher, faster. "My dear, you dawdle much too often! Come soar with me!"

Thunder cracked as lightning bolts connected the clouds.

The people in the city could barely be seen, weaving through the streets without giving the storm so much as a glance. Each speck of a person acted as a tiny mechanism, its path through the streets precisely defined. Further lightning danced between the clouds, carving intricate routes as they arced across the sky. "They are one and the same," Mara said. "Aren't they?"

Before Theon could respond, a shimmering, translucent beast swooped down, thrusting Mara away from him. She screamed as she tumbled a few feet. Theon froze solid.

A second beast flew through the newly opened gap, then turned around and shot backward.

Mara regained her composure. The two beasts chased and tumbled through the sky like cats, playing with each other's tails. She laughed, but Theon kept his guard up. "What are they?" he asked.

"Perhaps, we'll call them wind-dragons," Mara said. She opened her arms and let them swirl around her. She grabbed Theon's hand as the wind-dragons pulled her further into the sky.

"Higher!" she exclaimed, and pointed to the storm.

The wind-dragons pulled them closer to the storm, higher, then above. Mara gasped as she saw a city unfold. "I've never seen such a peculiar sight in all my life."

"A city in the clouds?" Theon asked. "What–well–I've never seen the top of a storm."

Mara pulled Theon in the direction of the city. Tall buildings, much higher than any she had ever seen, towered into the sky. Arcs of lightning swirled around them, occasionally dropping to the earth below.

"This isn't real," Theon said. He shook his head. "It can't be. Can it?"

Mara smiled and pulled him close. "I don't see why not," she said. "Why shouldn't what we see exist?"

Theon fidgeted a bit, but Mara pulled him closer. "You're coming with me," she said. "I'll show you what it is to dream."

43. Dogs Never Judge

"I don't understand," I said. "Are they just imagining it?"

"That they're flying?" Sheridan asked. "What's there to not understand?"

"They're *people*! People can't fly."

"Airplanes, and–"

"You know what I mean."

Sheridan cleared his throat. I suspected he just hid a chuckle.

"Mara has a very active imagination," I said. "That must be it. A shared hallucination? A joint make-believe session?"

Reality is as you define it, or something like that, were the highway's words to Marcus. Or maybe they were the brook's words . . .

Sheridan smiled. He shook his head and laughed a little. "Fair enough, I suppose."

"You never answered my question. You're a *bad* storyteller."

"Perhaps there is no answer," Sheridan said. "Mara chose to see her world the way she wanted to, and her definition of reality made sense to her. What else would matter?"

I wasn't sure what to make of that response. For the second time, I wondered if Marcus's journey to SanCullep Island had been just a dream. His story would certainly make more sense that way. But The Temple of the Night Song that Vasigari had described still sounded a lot like La Nocturne, and the "No People" were a lot like the Locanans. Trisha's story about resurrecting the cult would then make sense as well. Trisha *was* Ilia, or related, and somehow moved the cult off the island.

Still, something wasn't adding up. But perhaps Sheridan was about to reveal the answers.

- 110 -

Mara held Theon's hand as they walked through the city gate, which consisted of a stone archway built at the edge of a platform. When their feet touched the floor, Theon resumed breathing. "It's odd," he said, after laughing it off. "I wasn't afraid until we got close enough to the city to see it was real."

"Silly." Mara giggled. "It's okay."

When they'd first seen the city, it was a uniform, dull gray. Now that they stood in its streets, the city appeared more of a vibrant silver, with subtle colors on the roofs and building supports. Windows were trimmed in gold and sapphire, with brass shutters and grilles. The entire city was polished to a high gloss.

"How," Mara gasped, "did they ever find the money to build such a place?"

Theon looked down at his feet and tapped the walkway with his toe. "Is that the *first* question that popped into your mind? The economics?"

Mara smiled. "You can't fault me for asking! It's a legitimate question."

Every so often, thunder's rumble would echo down the streets. The lightning rods they'd seen from the sky were only barely visible among the city towers, but when they flashed, their light filled every niche and crevice. The people walking around hardly paid any attention to it at all.

As they explored the city, the sun began its descent. The city began to turn a bright gold, then ruby red. Mara took Theon to a small courtyard off the main road. Its floor was polished to form a near perfect mirror. When the stars came out, they could see all the constellations.

"Oh!" Mara exclaimed. She pointed downward. "It's all the world's knowledge."

"In the floor?"

Mara took Theon's hand and led him into the courtyard. When they looked straight down, they were floating in the night heavens. She smiled at him and continued, "Everything in nature! The wind, the ripples, the leaves! They're all consequences of sequences. Even thoughts and ideas!"

"In the sky? Thoughts and ideas?"

Mara smiled again. "They are as the stars in the sky! All these little thoughts floating out there. You gather some by experience. You connect them to form little images."

"Constellations!" Theon said. "You make constellations!"

"How do you connect the stars?" Mara asked. "You pick somewhere and start drawing lines. You jump from one to another in a set order."

"A sequence," Theon said.

"Now, two people may do this from different starting points and arrive at the same picture. But there's only so many ways to get the same picture," Mara explained. "Remember sitting on the cliff that day? Watching the town below?"

Theon nodded. Mara continued, "They're all going about, thinking and such, and drawing little pictures. What if the pattern manifested itself in them?"

"Governing how they think?" Theon asked. "What ideas they arrive to?"

"Then, you collect all the people, and you have an immense array of thoughts!" Mara exclaimed. "Imagine! If you could find the pattern, it'd be like a skeleton key. It lets you unlock every door. There are millions of doors in the world ... and you couldn't possibly open them all ... but you have the key! So, you could go anywhere you pleased!"

"You could hold the entire world," Theon said.

Mara smiled. She closed her eyes and stretched her arms out, feeling the world around her. "Wouldn't it be something?" she asked. "To have the whole world at your fingertips?"

"Oh, do be careful flying like that. I fear you'll drop straight into the stars."

Mara laughed and shook her head. "I doubt–" She opened her eyes wide. "Trey?"

Theon stepped back. "Trey?"

"See the North Star?"

Theon nodded.

"Look just to the right. There is a line of four stars that form a little arch. See it?"

"Yes, I think so," Theon replied.

"Do you see two stars just below the arch? One to the left of the middle, and one to the right?"

"Maybe ... I'm not sure I'm seeing it," Theon said. "What is it?"

"To the right of the arch are three stars that form a small triangle."

"Yes," Theon said.

Mara added, "That's Trey."

"Trey?" Theon asked.

"The great flying dachshund!" Mara exclaimed. "You remember that story I told you, about Marcus? Well, he described a guardian spirit, a flying dachshund who watches over the interests of those who are curious about the world and nature."

Theon stared at the constellation.

"Dogs never judge," Mara said. "That's why they're man's best friend. They love you like a true friend should, without strings attached."

"Oh, Mara," Trey said. "You flatter me all too much."

Mara laughed and clapped her hands. "The star-dog!"

"What?" Theon asked. "Who's speaking?"

Mara pointed downward. Theon watched a small collection of stars slowly grow brighter. He jumped back as the shape of the dog became clearly defined. "I see it! It *is* a dog-shaped constellation."

"The brilliant philosopher of the skies," Mara said.

Theon let out a yelp as Trey jabbed his crotch with his nose. "Trey!" Mara scolded.

Trey stepped back and lowered his head. "Sorry. I am a dog, you know."

Mara giggled and scratched Trey's ears. "I don't think he minds."

"Nice to meet you, too," Theon said. "Do you live in the city?"

"I live in the skies," Trey said. "But it appears the sky is on the floor tonight! Upside-down, of course."

"I can't imagine living upside-down," Mara said. "It must give you such a headache."

"I was about to say the same of you, my lady," Trey said. He raised his ears and shook his head. "So, have you found the world again?"

"Oh!" Mara said. She eyed Theon and smiled. "I'd like to think so. We found this wonderful city. But ... "

"But?" Theon asked. "You sound disappointed."

Mara shook her head. "Oh, no. Well, I was hoping this was the city. *The* city, rather."

"The shining one?" Trey asked.

Mara nodded. "It's lovely, though."

"I think, if you keep looking, you'll find your city," Trey said.

"I know," Mara said. She closed her eyes and tried to imagine how wonderful it would be. "After my run-in with the guardsmen, I thought I'd found the sequence, the cord. And I pulled it. It opened a misty green highway that called me to follow.

"It was raining, not hard; the water sparkled on the ground and sprayed a fine haze that glowed a brilliant green. I followed the road. The forest was beautiful, and full of life. At the end, I found a clearing, glittering brilliant gold as stray rays of the sun, broken through the clouds, shone down ... the light flickering as the leaves danced in the wind."

Trey asked, "But why do you think finding the sequence will open the road to the city?"

"Because, for a second, I had a moment of clarity. After I drank from the well, I saw the sequence, and immediately, the city."

"So, you think by pulling this 'cord', you'll open up a road?" Trey asked.

"When I got to the clearing, I looked to my right and another road opened up," Mara said. "It looked so long. But that's when the highway told me the ones I loved lay at the end of it, in the city which calls me home."

"It's safer up here," Theon said. "I think so, anyway. Maybe she'll find it here."

"I do worry about you," Trey said. "I never felt you were safe down in Locana. Especially around that Sanfeyl guy."

"Sanreils," Mara said.

"Yeah," Theon murmured. "Me neither."

"Where did he disappear to all the time?" Mara asked. She sighed. "I feel so stupid. I should've seen it."

"It's not your fault," Trey said. "Sometimes, you have to be in the sky to see these things. See the camp for what it is."

"Camp?" Mara asked.

"That's where he was going," Trey said. "The apprentices all make a trip to some camp in the woods. Just once, each. It's an initiation of some sort. Dahes's turn is coming up, I believe."

Theon nodded. "Sounds–"

Mara held his mouth. "Wait. *Dahes*?"

Trey nodded. "One by one. And I know the order, because they always walk in the same order between the quarters and the dining hall."

Mara froze. She stood still and silent for several moments. Trey beat his tail against the floor. "Are you okay?"

"Maybe a wet nose to the crotch will wake her up," Theon said.

"My crotch is fine," Mara said. She glared at Theon. "But ... are you sure?"

Theon stepped back and wandered out of the courtyard while Mara and Trey continued talking. He watched them for a few minutes, then walked down the moonlit street. "Stupid," he muttered to himself. "Stupid, stupid, stupid."

- 111 -

Mara wandered the streets looking for Theon. Every so often, she would call his name, but passerby would turn and she'd feel embarrassed at making a scene.

As she turned the corner, her reflection caught her eye. She shuddered at the thought of it bolting away again, but it merely smiled and nodded. Mara crossed her arms and glared at it. "Now, you behave," she said. "No grammatical fusses. And have you seen Theon?"

Her reflection shrugged. Mara sighed and sat on a small bench at the edge of the road. She faced a large clock tower and listened to the gears click. "It's like a clock," she said, hoping Theon would pop out of nowhere and reply.

A gentle breeze blew through the streets, catching the leaves of nearby trees and pushing them into each other. *Like a clock,* she thought, and her eyes widened.

"It *is* a clock," she whispered. "That's the sequence. Someone, or something, is counting seconds. Or parts of seconds."

Her mind raced through every observation she could recall. One always stood in her mind, *dim, bright, bright, bright, very bright, dim,* which was the first pattern Marcus had ever written in his journal. It stood out to her because when she'd read it, she knew she was not alone in her observations.

She stared at the clock, watching its measure of time creep by, adding to an ever growing tally of ticks in the gears of the universe. *It's a tally. But it's divided into only three outcomes. The sequence is not 1–2–3. It's 1–2–2–2–3–2 . . . something*

Dim, bright, bright; 1, 2, 2. She watched the wind and the clouds for almost an hour, working through all the possibilities of what the sequence could be.

Ever since she'd first noticed the clouds, she'd known something was peculiar about the world. And now, it had finally clicked. *It's a clock. And it's winding down,* she thought as she hummed Theon's tune. *There are only so many possible combinations of positions for the clouds, leaves, and sunbeams, just like there's only 120 verses of the song. What happens when they've been exhausted? Does the world end, or does it repeat?*

- 112 -

Mara caught up to Theon a few blocks from the courtyard. She ran up to him and jabbed his rib. He cried a startled yelp. Mara smiled gently. "I'm sorry," she said. "I didn't mean to snap at you earlier."

"It's okay," Theon said. "I guess it wasn't the time for fun and games."

"At least I finally learned the truth," Mara said, "where Sanreils was going when I met him."

"So, he wasn't a courier, like you said—"

"*He* said." Mara sighed. "It's hard to imagine Dahes following in his footsteps. I don't want to see Matta's heart broken. But I don't know what to do."

"Maybe it'll solve itself," Theon said. "Can't you see the future?"

"You really think I'm some kind of crystal ball, don't you?" Mara poked him and giggled. "It doesn't work that way, I'm afraid."

"I thought—"

Mara shook her head. "Sometimes. I mean, I can. But I can't *always*. It's like being in the woods and every so often, a breeze pushes the canopy aside and the trail lights up. Then, I can see it."

"People, too?"

"People, too."

"What about me?"

"No," Mara said. "I've never seen it for you. Or Matta. Or Sid. Or, well, it's weird."

"So, you don't know if Matta will be safe."

"Did you ever ride a cart down the trail on a foggy day?" Mara asked.

"Not that I ... know of."

"Mother used to take me to a little market every so often," Mara said. "In the morning, when it was foggy. And every now and then, the fog would clear, and I could see. That's like the future."

Theon scratched his head. Mara continued, "But if you change course, then the future changes. You see a new one. And sometimes, I can see very, very far. But, it seems like there's a handful of ways it can change."

"So, what's our future?" Theon asked.

Mara closed her eyes. Theon watched her for a moment, and he could see she was holding back tears. His heart sank. She looked up and forced a smile. "I think . . . it will be okay."

Theon shook his head. "You're holding something back."

"I know," Mara said. She took a deep breath. "Aphrael, the priestess, she said I was going to die."

"But she can't tell the future."

"I don't know!" Mara exclaimed. "I mean, I don't think so. I don't exactly trust her. But she scared me. And then the guards came after me, and the world took a strange turn."

Theon took her hand and pulled her close. "I think a lot has happened in a very short time," he said. "But we're together now. And, for now, we're happy. At least, I'm happy."

Mara looked up at him and nodded. She whispered, "I'm happy, too."

"You don't look happy."

"Happiness is a fickle creature," Mara said.

"Yeah," Theon said. He sighed and nodded. "Its demands are so incontinent."

Mara laughed. *"Inconstant.* Oh, Theon. You're such a goof-knocker."

Theon blushed. Mara giggled again and kissed his cheek. "Come with me," she said. "Let's find a place to spend the night in this lovely city. There's something I want to show you."

44. It's What People Do

"I don't get it," I said. "1–2–2?"

"Well, there's only three states," Sheridan said. "If I propose a sequence, say, 1–2–3–4–5, and divide every number by 3, the remainders are 1–2–0–1–2."

"Dim, bright, uh, whatever came next."

Sheridan nodded.

"But what is *dim*? And *bright*? Those are just descriptions. What about in between?"

"Three is all Mara observed. If seven were possible, divide by seven instead of three."

"I don't buy it," I said. "Let's see the stars. They twinkle, don't they? And I bet I'll find an infinite spectrum of brightness."

Sheridan glanced upward, and I knew what he was looking at before I saw for myself. "Zero," he said. "Zero, zero, zero . . ."

"No stars," I muttered, and continued to watch the sky.

I suppose all zeroes was still a sequence. A dead one. I *knew* Sheridan had to be putting all these thoughts in my head. At least, I thought I did. I couldn't fathom why he would do such a thing. He was watching me. "So, what happens if the sequence, all the combinations, are exhausted?" I asked. "Does it terminate? Or repeat?"

"Well," Sheridan said, "what do you think?"

"I think you know, and just don't want to tell me."

354

Sheridan tried to hide a smile, I was sure of that. "I think history repeats itself," I said. "It's what I've always been told."

"In a sequence of random numbers, it's entirely possible to find repetition," Sheridan said. He paused a moment to stroke his chin and contemplate the void outside the car. "But that repetition may also come to an end."

- 113 -

Mara held onto Theon's hand and pulled him into the tower chamber. The walls of the top floor rose only a foot above the floor, above which were several pillars holding the roof. From above the storm, the stars were crisp and clear. Their silver glow sprinkled the room with light. Theon smiled nervously at Mara, who bounced around excitedly. She pulled a thick, leather-bound book out of her satchel. "This is it!"

"Your book?" Theon asked.

Mara nodded enthusiastically. Theon held it in his hands and scratched his head. "Etiquette?"

"No, silly. That's just the title."

Theon hummed a bit as he opened a marked page. "What's the sequence?"

"Oh! I think I found it."

"Really?" Theon asked. He forced a smile, hoping a lack of understanding wouldn't come across as disinterest. "What is it?"

"Well, see, I started working out what it was. Working backward, I suppose. I jotted some notes down and threw them out."

"But, what is it?"

Mara laughed. "Oh! You should've seen the clock! It was like ... whatever that word is, that means you should run naked through the streets."

"Did I miss it?"

Mara laughed again and shook her head. Theon held the book over his face in an attempt to hide his blushing. He flipped through the rest of the pages. There were 389 altogether, most of which consisted of handwriting he couldn't make out. He looked at the last two pages, which contained a scribbled, but barely readable entry: "The city which shone brightly."

"The city I saw," Mara said. "Sort of like a dream. I thought that, maybe, finding the cord would bring me to it. Somehow, open a path, like I told Trey."

"Did it?"

"I don't know." Mara sighed and glanced at the sky. "I don't know if I've really found it. I don't know how to use it. Aphrael said it'd show the world didn't exist, but we're still here."

"Well, maybe I can help you figure it out."

Mara stood still for a moment, then said quietly, "Listen." Theon looked up as Mara continued, "I . . . please don't show anyone else this. If the town found out . . . well, it's secret."

"Don't worry."

Mara added, "It's just, I've never shown anyone this before."

Theon looked up at Mara a second time. "Why me? I mean, I'm flattered that you trust me. But, why me?"

He stared at Mara for a moment and started to grow nervous when she didn't answer. She simply stood, waiting. Theon grew more nervous and started to speak when Mara took him in her arms and kissed him, slowly and longingly. Shocked and surprised, Theon nearly dropped her book on the floor. Mara took a step back and smiled at him. Theon blinked for a moment as he absorbed what had just happened. Then, he smiled back.

"Thank you for . . . " Mara said, pausing to think of the

right words, "helping me see the world again."

Theon stumbled for words, "I . . . uh . . . you're welcome?"

Mara smiled. "You're blushing."

Theon's face grew more red. Mara smiled and laughed. She took his hand and whispered, "Follow me."

She led him to the window and sat down on the edge. "Watch the night with me."

Theon sat next to her, smiling nervously.

"Look at the sky," she said. "Isn't it beautiful?"

He tried his best not to think of the possibility of falling from the tower. Mara's laughter didn't help. "You're not afraid of the height, are you?"

"Me?" Theon gasped. "Oh no-o-o."

"It's okay to be scared sometimes," Mara said.

"I'm not!"

"Can I tell you a secret?"

Theon stole another glance at the abyss, then quickly faced the inside. "S-sure."

"I feel like a fool," Mara said. "The well, the Ori. Have I been tricked?"

Theon fidgeted, afraid to speak and say the wrong thing. "I . . . you're not a fool."

"Theon," Mara whispered. Her eyes glistened as she looked up. "How do I know *you're* real?"

Theon tapped his forehead, which made a subtle *thunk* sound. "I'm pretty convinced I'm here."

"Maybe the sound is imagined, too."

"I . . ." Theon said. "I'm not sure what to say."

Mara took his hand and stared into his eyes. "Then, hold me?"

"Uh–" Theon muttered.

"You don't want to." Mara leaned back against the wall and crossed her arms.

"I . . ."

"You're afraid, then."

"No, I'm not."

"Yes, you are." Mara sighed. "You're afraid of what they might do to you."

Theon stared at the ground, saying nothing.

Mara said, "It's not like they're watching."

Theon looked up and forced a smile. "I suppose not."

Mara returned his smile and settled into his arms. "It's a natural thing. No 'proper code of conduct', or anything like that. It's what people do. It's called *affection*."

Theon's cheeks turned a slight pink.

Mara sat up and said, "Kiss me."

Theon's cheeks turned redder. He quickly eyed the window and half-expected someone to be watching. Mara sighed slightly. When Theon faced her again, she forced a reassuring smile. Theon lifted her chin and stared into her eyes. He couldn't shake the feeling of having seen them before. *Where have I–*

Mara interrupted his thought. She pulled his head closer and kissed him. She laughed to herself as she could see he was speechless, then leaned back and grinned. "Do you feel better now?"

"I ... " Theon paused, then smiled. "Do you think I'm real?"

"I'm not convinced," Mara said. She smiled suggestively.

"Well," Theon said. He tried to hide a grin. "I guess there's nothing I can do to convince you then."

Mara's face went blank. She closed her eyes for a moment, just long enough to worry Theon that he'd said something he shouldn't have.

"I'm sorry," Theon said. "Did I say something wrong?"

Mara took his hand and blushed.

"What is it?" Theon asked. "I–" He began to blush as well, but wasn't sure why.

"Nothing," Mara whispered. She opened her eyes and winked.

"That's not a 'nothing' face. What are you hiding? Are you going to stuff more leaves down my back?"

Mara giggled. She leaned close to his ear and whispered. Theon's eyes grew wider. "Oh."

- 114 -

Mara woke to the warmth of sunlight on her face. She sat up, pushed her hair out of her eyes, and looked around. A gentle breeze breathed life into the window curtains, which soon demanded their freedom from the rod. Theon sat along the wall, watching the clouds below. When he heard Mara rustle the sheets, he looked up and smiled. "I've never seen the clouds roll in from *under* before."

"Were you there all night?" Mara giggled. "Silly."

"Just for the past half hour or so."

Mara stretched and nodded. "I don't hear much thunder."

Theon pointed out the window. "I can see the men working on one of those rods. They look burnt, but they've been polishing them. Maybe I could find employment as a rod-polisher."

"Oh my. That sounds dangerous."

"I think it's safe. Besides, it'd only be for a while. Maybe I can study here."

"I thought you were afraid of falling through the clouds."

"Well," Theon said. "I think I'd be fine. I couldn't leave you."

Mara smiled. "I think it'd be a lovely place to live. But–"

"But?" Theon raised an eyebrow.

Mara closed her eyes and sighed. "I made a promise."

"Oh."

"And I can't break it."

"Could Matta live here with us?"

"I don't think she would be happy. She hates Dahes. But she loves him, too." Mara climbed out of bed and walked over to the window. She looked down and admired the formations of passing birds. "But, maybe, we can come back. I'd love to."

Theon nodded. He took Mara's hand and watched the birds with her. "I understand. But I'm afraid of what they might do to you."

"I know. I am, too." She turned toward Theon and smiled gently. "But we can come back. And be happy together. I'm not setting one foot in Locana ever again."

45. It Looks Different Now

"I still don't understand if their journey was some kind of make-believe thingy," I said. "I can't imagine they really flew."

"You can't, huh?" Sheridan asked.

"It's the journal of a madwoman. Isn't it?"

Sheridan said, "Pull over for a minute."

"What?"

"Just pull over."

I don't know why I bothered putting on the hazard lights, but I did. We stopped on the shoulder and Sheridan fished around in his pocket. He pulled out a small, beat-up book.

"Is that Mara's book?"

Sheridan shook his head and laughed. "Oh, no."

He showed me the cover, on which the word "JOURNAL" was written in small, faded letters.

"Whose book is it, then?" I asked.

"It belonged to an Italian professor," Sheridan explained. "He kept it in 1929."

"Did he find Mara's book, or something?"

"He did, and copied its entirety, including Mara's copy of Marcus's journal."

"It's a chain," I said, and put the car back in gear.

As we drove off, Sheridan pushed the book back into his pocket. "You asked me how I knew the world was going to end."

"Yes?"

"Because there aren't any more blank pages. Well, almost. There's one."

I wasn't sure what to think about that. "Assuming our existence is tied to a journal, you couldn't just buy another blank book?"

Sheridan chuckled. "No," he said. "It doesn't work like that."

"I don't get it."

"I know," he said. "This is why I didn't want to tell you, yet. It will make more sense when we get to that point in the story."

"I suppose. Let's go, then. What happened next?"

"Mara had made a promise to Matta. So, she left to keep her word ... "

- 115 -

Mara held Theon's hand and led him through the sky. They drifted in silence, admiring the view as the wind-dragons whipped by.

From their height, Locana was only a dot, partially obscured by passing clouds. The quiet hum of the wind carried the sounds of the city away.

Mara thought she could see her father's farm, a sight which brought the realities of her home back to her.

They fell through the clouds. The sky grew gray as her mind raced through memories of Locana.

Theon managed to stay calm throughout most of their flight, but as the city became well-defined, he clenched Mara's hand.

He landed on the snow first, catching Mara as she fell into his arms. She forced a gentle smile. "Home."

They'd landed by Theon's cabin, near the spot where they'd taken off.

"It looks different, now," Theon said.

Mara nodded. "I may have a future again. Maybe I'll find the Ori again. Maybe the shining city is not so far off."

Theon took Mara's hand and led her down the road toward Thorn Tower.

- 116 -

The gate to the tower yard had frozen shut during the late evening. Mara gazed at the tower as Theon pushed against the jammed latch.

"It's hard to believe this is my last night here," Mara said. "I remember when it was a place of dreams and hope–a home."

The latch gave way. Theon stumbled and caught himself on the fence. "I think we'll be happy in the thunderstorm city. Aren't there dreams and hope there?"

Mara took Theon's hand and smiled at him. "I'd like to think there are. It's just sad to see this place robbed of them."

Mara led Theon to the door.

"You!" Sid exclaimed. "Where *were* you?"

"You were worried about me?" Mara asked. She grinned. "I think you were."

"No, no," Sid replied. "Just . . . fine. Yes."

Mara smiled. "We're fine, now."

"Good."

"But . . . well . . . I think you should know."

"Yes?"

"I'm leaving."

"*Leaving*?"

Mara nodded. "Leaving the city. I just don't feel safe anymore."

"That's just like you!" Matta shouted. She stormed down the stairs. "Fine. Go. Leave me to my–"

"Just a moment!" Theon said. "We came back for you."

"And Dahes," Mara said.

"You mean the ass?" Matta asked.

"I think we can bring him out," Mara said. "Bring him back to us."

Matta folded her arms. "Yeah? How?"

"In Carrboro forest. The apprentices are sent there to a village near the Valley of Lennox. It's where Sanreils was headed."

"So?"

"I think I know," Sid replied. "You can't be serious?"

"He'll be alone," Mara said. "I know."

"And what?" Sid asked. "Kidnap him?"

"Well . . . yes. I think the four of us can take him."

"*Four*?" Sid raised his eyebrows.

"Yes," Mara said. "Because *you're* a friend, and I know you feel the same."

"You make it sound so simple," Matta said.

"It is." Mara nodded. "We'll go to the thunderstorm city."

"*Where*?" Matta asked.

"It's a city," Theon said, "in the sky."

Sid and Matta looked at each other. "Uh–" Sid muttered.

"Well," Mara said. "We can work on *that* later. Let's at least get Dahes back."

"You really think we can, huh?" Matta asked.

"Trust me," Mara said. "I *know* Dahes will be the next to make the journey."

Matta threw her arms in the air and marched off. "Whatever."

"Well, I think we could pull it off," Sid said. "But I don't want to get killed."

"We won't get caught!" Mara exclaimed. "It's safe! I know!"

"How?"

"Sanreils," Mara said. "The day I met Sanreils, he was alone. They send their apprentices on a trek through the woods to some temple or something. That's where he was going. It's a test, I suppose."

Sid scratched his chin and smirked. "This sounds like a fool's game. But, whatever."

Mara lowered her gaze and folded her arms. "Do you have a better idea?"

Sid grumbled and began to walk off. "We can discuss the details in the morning."

- 117 -

Mara sat with Theon on the top floor, watching the stars flicker. Neither of them could manage to sleep. Mara had spent the past hour describing all the places she had read about in Sylow's library.

"Have you heard of Athens?" Mara asked. "I think it'd be a neat place to see. And Rome."

"Rome, huh?" Theon asked. "Well, maybe we could travel together."

Mara smiled. "I think I'd like that very much."

"Strasbourg," Theon said. "Have you heard of Gutenberg? I think it'd be neat to see a printing press."

"There's one place I want to see more than any of them," Mara said. "*The* city."

"The one you saw in the forest?"

"I keep thinking about that road," Mara said. She sat still for a moment before continuing, "That highway to the glowing city. I want to go there with you."

Theon smiled. "I'd like that."

Mara closed her eyes. "But in the dream, I was alone. I was sad. And ... happy. But you can be happy and sad at the same time, can't you?"

Theon nodded.

"Happy because I was going there, but sad, too," Mara explained. "Someone I missed so much was there. I was happy to be going, but sad that they weren't here."

"Who was it?" Theon asked.

Mara opened her eyes and smiled at him. "I like to think it was you."

Theon returned her smile.

"But, the thing is ... " Mara said.

Theon stared at her. Mara continued, "I love you."

Theon blushed and grew very still.

Mara said, "And to think you're in another city, so far away, scares me. How did you get there? How did we get separated?"

Theon took her hand. "I don't know,' he said. "But I can't lose you! Not after I finally found you. Not after we've come so far together."

"I suppose," Mara said. She bit her lip and looked out the window. "If you're not there, if you're so far away, I'll just have to find happiness in knowing you're waiting for me." She then faced him. "Or, *hoping* you're waiting for me."

"I'll wait for you," Theon said.

Mara smiled at him. "It's not every day you find—"

"Someone to go on adventures with?" Theon asked.

Mara laughed. "Yes! Yes! You *owe* me an adventure, still."

Theon nodded. He poked her rib. "You make it sound like a chore."

The silver light of the Trey constellation shone into the tower, bathing the room with light. Mara and Theon looked out the window, thinking about everything that was out there. She closed her eyes and settled into his arms. She looked up at him and smiled. He returned her smile. She said, "Tell me everywhere you will take me."

46. Save Yourself

"I still don't know if I get this sequence," I said. "But, I have no proof, I suppose. Or disproof. I'm just not sure I buy it."

"Well, it's not for sale," Sheridan said.

"*What* does that mean?"

"Do you not understand, or do you not want to?"

"Why would I not want to?"

After I'd asked, I knew why I wouldn't. "You must think I'm one of those puppets," I said. "That's why you said I'm on a road with no branches, only able to go straight."

"Why would I think that?"

"Because you think you know what I'm about to say, before I say it."

Sheridan smiled, and turned away. "I think the road is getting to you."

"You think so, huh?"

"Perhaps," Sheridan said.

"Never mind," I said. "Just go on."

- 118 -

When day broke, Mara and Theon still sat at the window's edge, watching the sunrise. The commotion of the world below did not enter their minds as they enjoyed the morning. Neither of them spoke as the sky changed from shades of black to orange to blue. Sunrays broke through the clouds, shedding beams of colorful light into the mountains. Mara sighed happily and broke the silence. "I just love mornings like this."

"Me too," Theon replied. "But you do know what this means, don't you?"

"What?" Mara asked.

Theon answered, "It *is* morning. It's the sun! We've been up the whole night."

Mara smiled warmly at Theon and settled further into his arms, watching the sky. "The world is so beautiful," she said. "Just think. One moment it was dark and sparkled silver. Now, it's an explosion of blue and orange and red."

Theon smiled. "How quickly things change. It's amazing."

"I can't believe you would stay up with me to watch it all," Mara said.

"Count all the stars?" Theon asked.

Mara giggled. "Yes. And now, we know *precisely* how many are up there!"

"10,982," Theon said. He smiled. "Did you check my results?"

"Twice," Mara said. She laughed. "I've sat up here many times just watching the mountains light up. I've wanted someone to share it with for so long."

"I'll share it with you," Theon replied.

"Nothing would make me happier," Mara whispered.

Theon smiled nervously. "I wanted to ask you something."

"Oh?"

"But . . . " Theon took a deep breath. "Maybe this isn't the right place. Or the right time."

She took his hand and her eyes glistened. "Does it matter?"

The heavy wooden door to the chamber swung open as Sid charged into the room. "Mara! Theon! They killed Matta! They killed Matta!"

Mara and Theon sprang up from the window. "What?" Mara exclaimed. "What do you mean? Who?"

Sid ran frantically through the room to the window and looked down. "They killed her! I can't believe they killed her!"

Mara's face turned pale, and Theon shouted, "Calm down! What? What is going on?"

Sid replied, "The Locana guardsmen killed Matta! She went to the university, made *some* demand. I tried to stop her."

"But why didn't she wait?" Mara asked. "What about our plans?"

"They're coming for us! You! You've been sitting by the window, have you not noticed?"

Theon crept up to the window and looked down. Several guardsmen were charging toward them in the distance. "Mara!" Theon exclaimed. "It's the guardsmen!"

"Why?" Mara asked. "Why are they coming?"

"Sanreils!" Sid replied. "He's been telling people in town that you're a witch. They're coming to arrest you."

"How could he do that?" Mara cried. "What did I do to him?"

"I'm going to defend the doorway," Sid replied. "You two make an escape."

Mara approached the window and turned her attention from the sky to the ground. The guardsmen approached from all sides, closing in. "I'm scared," she said.

"We'll make it," Theon said.

Theon looked out the window again. Below, Dahes was running across the field toward the tower, calling for Matta.

"Dahes!" Theon shouted from the window. He called to him, trying to warn him to stay away and not look for her.

Mara looked outside toward the field. She watched Dahes take a few more steps before a guardsman's arrow pierced his chest. Theon cringed as Dahes fell to the ground. Mara stepped back from the window, her face white.

"Mara ... " Theon said.

Mara didn't speak as she backed further away from the window.

Theon looked down again. Sid stood near the yard gate, struggling with the guardsmen. "Sid!" Theon shouted out the window. "Save yourself! Run!"

Outnumbered, Sid fought fiercely before the guardsmen swarmed him. They swiftly beat him to the ground and kicked in the gate.

Theon bit his lip. The Locana guardsmen were moving in closer on all sides. "I don't know, Mara. I really do not know."

Mara stared at the floor for a moment. She breathed a heavy sigh as she walked over to the bookshelf. Her hands trembled as she rummaged through the shelves.

"What are you doing?" Theon asked.

Mara handed her book to Theon. "It's me they're after. Not you. Take it. Don't let it be destroyed. Carry it forward."

"No!" Theon exclaimed. "We can't give up!"

Mara cried in despair, "What else are we to do? They're all around and soon, there will be no escape. You can leave untouched. Sanreils never knew you. The Locana guardsmen probably don't even know who you are ... much less that you're here. Go!"

Theon took Mara's hand and pulled her to follow. "Not without you! We can make it! There's still time."

"No, there isn't!" Mara protested, though she allowed herself to be pulled out the door.

They both ran down the spiral staircase, taking the sharp turns as fast as their bodies would allow. At the bottom, they stopped just before the entry door.

Mara said, "You go out the back and run. I'll go out the front. We'll meet by the waterfall in the woodlands."

Theon replied, "No! We must stay together. Please! We'll be safer."

"Please! We will both be fine. I promise!"

Theon looked out the small, thin window which overlooked the woodlands. He turned his head toward Mara, who was waiting anxiously for his decision. He looked into Mara's eyes and clutched her book. "I couldn't bear it if anything happened to you, but if you're sure this will work out, I will take your word for it."

The moment Theon let go of Mara's hand the front door burst open. A split second afterward, the side door burst open as well and Locana guardsmen flooded the bottom level. They swarmed around Mara, casting Theon aside. "Mara!" Theon exclaimed, pushing into the huddle. Mara called out, "Run!"

Two of the guardsmen turned their attention to Theon, who struggled in a blind attempt to do anything.

Mara exclaimed again, "Run!"

Theon took off with Mara's book, two of the guardsmen in pursuit. The rest swiftly carried Mara away as she struggled to break free.

47. I Am Harmless

"Well," I said. "*Well*. Get a few townsfolk on the witch-wagon, and they sure follow it through."

Sheridan nodded. "Call it Sheridan's Lemma. *As the number of participants in a meeting or discussion group increases, the collective intelligence quotient of the mass approaches zero.*"

I watched the world slowly drift by. Sheridan was carefully chewing his lip and tapping the window-pane. I broke the silence. "Why didn't Theon rescue her?"

Sheridan replied, "He never knew where she was taken. History is not like in the movies. Sometimes, you do all you can, but it's not enough. It's a sad fact I've had to come to terms with many times ... sometimes, nothing can be done."

"I suppose so," I said. "I must wonder then, why she didn't try to fight her way out."

"What ... ninja-style?" Sheridan asked. "You *have* watched entirely too much TV."

"If she could figure out all she did about the world, you'd think she could have learned kung-fu."

Sheridan chuckled. "Yes. In fact, what I didn't tell you is that she and the brook would often hold secret martial arts lessons."

"Really?"

"No."

- 119 -

Mara sat in the dungeon cell, alone, with a tiny window to keep her company. The window sat about ten feet above the floor, and let a few select sunbeams pass through. It wasn't the jail she remembered. She wasn't sure exactly where the guards had taken her, but felt certain it was somewhere hidden, a rug they swept dust under.

The wait dragged for an eternity. A thousand thoughts raced through Mara's mind, too many for her to make sense of. She thought about Theon. She hoped he wasn't lying dead in the fields. Perhaps he was even on his way to free her, but she knew not to get her hopes up.

Two guards came and opened the cell door. One eyed her sternly.

"Come with us," the other said.

Mara complied. She didn't resist, nor was she angry. She moved silently and without emotion. The guards led her down a dimly lit hallway with no visible windows. They took her to a small room lined with chairs. A few were occupied by officials she had never met.

The events of the morning began to sink in. She felt a knot in her stomach as the guards sat her down in a lonely chair, tucked into a corner of the room. She hung her head and stared at the floor. The judge took his seat. He eyed the room, and said, "Let us begin."

"I think we all know why we're here, and what we're to do. Since the destruction of the baron's manor at the hand of Culatan, harder times have followed. But hope is not lost, and time has not run out. Now, we know! We know *why* we've all suffered so. A witch! A witch walks amongst us! And thanks to the good graces of La Nocturne, we know who."

Are they trying me? Mara thought.

Whispers from the witnesses grew to chatter as the judge

repositioned himself in his seat.

"Quiet," the court attendant announced.

"Mara Sanghid!" the judge exclaimed, pausing to look through his stack of papers. "You have been accused of witchcraft! Do you wish to plead guilt?"

Mara looked up at the judge, who stared coldly at her. He sat silent, glaring at her as he waited for an answer. She closed her eyes and hung her head as a single tear rolled down her cheek. She wanted nothing more than to be back in bed.

"Mara Sanghid!" the judge repeated. "You have been accused of witchcraft! Do you wish to plead guilt?"

Mara trembled. She clenched her fists, stood, and exclaimed, "I am not a witch!"

"So, that is a no," the judge said. "Very well. Let us read the accusations."

"I am not a witch!" Mara repeated.

"Your actions speak against you," the judge said. "You are eccentric and vastly odd. You wander the city, daydreaming. You dance in the fountains. You talk to the wind and trees."

As the judge continued to read from the list, Mara interrupted. "Stop! This is cruel!"

"No," the judge replied. "You are a threat to the innocence of our town and peace of the region."

"What? I am harmless! I have done nothing wrong!"

"Your behaviors and your practices contradict that. You talk to the roads and sky. You live in a dilapidated old tower with a bunch of misfits," the judge said. "Scheming, right?"

He once again eyed Mara. Her eyes grew large, and she was rendered speechless. "Are you going to confess, or not?" the judge asked.

"Confess to what?" Mara protested. "This is ridiculous! The townsfolk are just wary because someone told them to be! There is nothing real there. They're just blind followers!"

"Are you going to confess, or not?"

"There is no crime to confess to!"

"Are you going to confess, or not?" the judge repeated, speaking with growing impatience.

"No! I am not a witch!"

"Very well," the judge said. He gazed upon her as he rose from his seat and approached. He towered over her, glaring down. "Confess! Confess, my dear, and the church will take care of you. Confess, and we may show *some* mercy!"

"Confess to what?"

The judge stroked her cheek. "Such a pretty little face. I'd hate to see what will become of you."

Mara choked back tears. She clenched her fists tightly and shuddered with rage. She rose to her feet and spit on the judge.

The judge blinked, his demeanor faded and his face went blank. He collected his senses. "Kill her."

Mara stared blankly at the judge as he resumed his position at the head of the room. He faced the court, not her, when he read his decision. "You are hereby found guilty and sentenced to die."

48. That I Will Soar

"That was a dumb move." I shook my head. "Why would she confess? You're a terrible storyteller."

Sheridan chuckled. "Oh? I don't think I can do much about what Mara did."

"You could change it. Put a happy ending on it. She kung-fu-chops her way out of the jail."

"That would make for some interesting visuals," Sheridan said. He nodded. "Perhaps I should sell the story to Hollywood."

"I'll even split the profits with you."

Sheridan stroked his chin and nodded some more. "That sounds like a pretty good deal. Of course ... "

"Of course?"

"Well, half of zero is still zero."

"You're a killjoy."

Sheridan smiled, proudly. He then looked me straight in the eye. "So, tell me, Bartlebee. What would you have done? Would you have confessed?"

"You don't want to know my answer."

"That's the problem with having principles," Sheridan said. "It's–"

"Wait, wait, wait! Are you saying I have no principles?"

All I could think was, *Puppets have no principles*. It was true–that's how he saw me. I felt betrayed by sharing all those 'tidbits,' even if they were just payments to receive information myself.

"*Anyway*, Mara was in the jail ... "

- 120 -

Mara stared up at the window. Only the moon and a few stars could be seen. She thought about how the world she loved now lay obscured by the bars and spiders' webs.

She whispered at the stars, "Last night, I had a dream that I was back on the highway in Fordham Forest. The highway told me to keep following, to not stop, and everything would turn out fine.

"I told the highway, 'Please tell me that day will come. That I will soar out of this cell into the world obscured by the window-bars. I'm not ready to leave this world yet. The ones I love still remain, and I don't want to let go.'

"The highway replied, 'Just don't stop and you'll see. I'll show you the world along the way and, at the end, you'll be united with the ones you loved.'

"Please, stars, tell me that day will come."

She stared out the window, waiting for an answer. None came.

"Please," she whispered.

She curled into a tiny ball and cried herself to sleep.

- 121 -

A few hours later, Mara woke to the sound of footsteps and clanging. Guards entered her chamber, followed by a few witnesses and a hooded man. He was covered in black attire, with only fiery, amber eyes and a few stray strands of blond hair showing. The hooded man spoke with a familiar voice. "Mara, it's time."

Mara cried out, "No! You do not understand! How can you sentence me to my death?"

The hooded man calmly replied, "You have been charged with witchcraft. You know your punishment."

Mara clenched her fists and proclaimed, "I am not a witch!"

The witnesses shouted out, "Witch! Witch!"

The hooded man said, "You have had a fair trial. You have had your chance to confess. Your behaviors and actions stand and speak for themselves."

Mara replied, "They do not make me a witch!"

The witnesses shouted, "Witch! Witch!"

The hooded man grabbed a hold of Mara, held her firmly against the wall and took out his sword.

Mara looked up at the tiny window at the top of the wall. The moon shone brightly upon the world's brilliance, obscured by two bats watching the room silently. Her eyes filled with tears as she cried out, "You are wrong!"

The witnesses proclaimed, "Witch! Witch!'

The hooded man leaned in close and whispered, "You see and know too much for your own good. You are a threat to us. You are an enemy."

Mara's eyes grew wide as the hooded man pressed his lips close to her ear, and whispered, "You have figured out too much about this world, too much about its true nature, and we can't allow you to live any longer."

The executioner's voice tore into her mind. She closed her eyes tightly and whispered, "Sanreils?"

Before Mara could speak any more, the hooded man quickly raised his weapon and slit her throat. As she perished, the witnesses cheered at the justice they'd observed. The hooded man held his weapon to show the crowd, who continued to applaud. The bats in the window flew into the sky, screeching and crying under the moon.

For the public, Mara's body was burned at the stake. The hooded man watched silently. He looked down at several pieces of crumpled burgundy paper he held in his hand, grinning slightly. He threw them into the fire, turned his back to the crowd, and walked off into the darkness. The cries of "Witch!" dissipated into the night sky.

49. It's Not Your Fault

"That really sucks," I said, "Perhaps we can take comfort in the possibility Mara's child will live on."

Sheridan raised an eyebrow.

"You know, if Theon got pregnant?"

Sheridan raised his other eyebrow. We stared at each other in silence for a moment. "You must think I'm the world's biggest dumbass."

Sheridan flashed his usual, stupid grin. "What answer would you like me to give you?"

"It's a *rhetorical* question."

"I'm a mathematician," Sheridan said. "There are no rhetorical questions. Only Millennium Prize Problems."

I didn't know what that was supposed to mean, but it was probably some sort of insult. "You seem to have a *penchant*," I said, "for killing off the characters."

Sheridan smiled innocently.

I asked, "Can't you tell *happy* stories?"

"That's not how it happened."

"But there are still stones unturned," I said. "What about Aphrael? What about Trisha's cult? So much for *Bartlebee's Storytelling Conjecture*."

"A lot of great mathematicians have had their conjectures fall flat."

"Well, can you tell me *something* good?"

Sheridan stroked his chin and hummed. "Mara's *spirit* can live on."

"Like, as a ghost?"

"No, no," Sheridan shook his head. "Her ideas! All people expire someday, but their ideas can live on."

"I suppose that's some constellation."

"*Consolation.*" Sheridan nodded. "Ideas are like embers; they spark from some great fire, fly free, and glow for a while on their own. Some flicker out before they land. Others, though, ignite a new fire, which will cast a great light upon the world ... "

- 122 -

A few charred pieces of burgundy paper lay amongst a heap of spent wood and debris. A strengthening wind flirted with them a bit, then lifted them from the ground and whisked them away.

Ideas only die if they stand still. At some hour, when they seem almost faded, all it takes to breathe new life into them is to be carried away by some wind.

Theon held Mara's journal as he walked into the university. He stood in the entry-hall, looking down. Many doors branched off, and he wasn't sure where he wanted to go. He entered the first open door. A young master sat at his desk, tossing a few marbles around. He looked up as Theon entered.

"Hello?" the master asked.

"Hi ... " Theon said quietly. "I'm looking for someone."

The master looked at himself. "Me?"

"Not sure who," Theon said. He showed him the book. "Someone who might be interested in this."

The master looked at the cover. He chuckled. "A book on etiquette? This silly thing takes me back. My sister–"

Theon shook his head. He opened the book to one of the middle pages, where it was quite clear the contents had been changed.

The master looked closer. "Who is Mara Sanghid?"

"It's her journal," Theon said.

"Oh!" the master exclaimed. He glanced at one of his marbles. "Why, I think I know who that is! Very peculiar girl."

"You knew her?"

The master nodded. "If she is who I'm thinking of ... she said something along the lines of, 'my work wouldn't die if I shared it'. I've tried to keep good to those words. She had a curious knack for patterns."

"That's her!" Theon said. He smiled briefly and handed the book to the master. "Will you share this, too?"

The master flipped through the pages. "Quite curious, indeed. But, I'm afraid I'm not quite sure what I'm looking at." He laughed. "There's quite a bit here! Look, she even wrote about me!"

"She wrote about everything."

The master read the last page, " 'I found it,' I told him. 'The pattern. The key. It was so obvious.' Theon seemed doubtful–"

The master looked up at Theon, then back down to the book. " 'Marcus found it ... almost. But the key dates back to before him. Theon kept asking me what it was. He's so impatient. But I love him, anyway.' "

Theon stepped forward. "She–"

The master looked up again. "Yes?"

Theon stepped back. "Nothing. Go on."

" 'I threw my work at Sanreils,' " the master read aloud. " 'But, sometime I'll sit down and copy it again.' "

The master closed the book. "That's the last page."

"She didn't write it anywhere?"

The master looked closely at the back cover, then flipped through the book. He shook his head. "No. It doesn't look like a page was removed. It looks like she never got to it."

Theon stared blankly for a moment. "Well ...I don't know what to do."

The master flipped through more of the pages. "She should explain what the pattern is. I'd love to meet her again! You should send her."

"She died ... " Theon said quietly.

The master closed the book and looked up. "Oh dear," he said. "What a great shame. Whatever happened?"

"The town executed her," Theon explained.

The master blinked and shook his head. "What did she do? Kill someone?"

"Nothing!" Theon exclaimed. His voice began to crack. "Someone said she was a witch."

"Oh my," the master said. "I never really believed in such silliness. Fear does brew the worst in men."

Theon sighed and nodded.

"It's a sad state for the world," the master said. "I think La Nocturne builds its power by curing people of the fears they made up to begin with. I won't say anything, though. They'd probably kill me, too. I worry what the future has in store for Locana."

Theon didn't say anything. The master watched him for a moment. "*You're* Theon, aren't you? And she must have meant something to you. *That's* why you brought this book to me."

Theon choked back tears. Unable to bring himself to say anything, he simply nodded again. The master carefully set the book aside. "Well, I'll take good care of it," he said.

"Thank you," Theon said quietly.

- 123 -

By the time Theon left the university, night had fallen. He stopped at the fountain in the town square. The fountain sat dry, as the water had been shut off for the remainder of the winter. He closed his eyes. He could still remember her voice.

The silver light of the Trey constellation had shone into the tower, bathing the room in its glow.

Mara and Theon looked out the window, thinking about everything that was out there. She closed her eyes and settled further into his arms. She looked up at him and smiled. He returned her smile. She said, "Tell me ... everywhere you will take me."

Theon looked down at Mara and brushed the fallen strands of hair out of her eyes. "On our adventure?"

"Yes!" Mara exclaimed. "Do tell! I have been fully curious since you first mentioned it!"

"Oh ... lots of places!" Theon exclaimed. He paused for a moment to think. "Erm ... interesting, amazing places!"

Mara giggled. "You don't know, do you?"

"Oh! I promised you!" Theon exclaimed. "We'll go to the sea. Set sail! Trample the sea monsters!"

Mara then laughed. "Sea monsters, you say?"

Theon nodded enthusiastically. "Exotic islands! Vast mountainscapes! Rolling plains! We'll travel the lands. Be explorers! Epic heroes ... Slay monsters and battle injustice!" Mara continued laughing as Theon kept going, "Uncover all the world's great secrets! Unlock them all!"

Mara's eyes grew big. "It all sounds so lovely."

"It's a big world out there," Theon said.

"Promise me!" Mara exclaimed. "Promise me we'll go!"

Theon smiled. "Only if you promise me you'll come."

Mara closed her eyes and returned his smile. She looked up at him, took his hand, and replied, "Of course! Of course, I will come with you! If you take me. I wouldn't miss it for the world. I told you if you went away, I'd follow you to the end of the world. Don't you think you're going to escape!"

Theon opened his eyes and touched the fountain. He looked up toward the stars. "You promised you'd follow me to the end of the world!" he exclaimed. "That was our deal! We agreed! How can you follow through on that now?"

He glared at the sky. He shouted, "I was supposed to take you on an adventure!"

A cool breeze glazed over the fountain. He stood quiet for a moment, then said quietly, "You made me promise to take you on one. How will we do that now?"

A couple of townsfolk watched Theon from across the square. They whispered to each other. He looked their way and then back to the stars. He breathed a sigh. "It's not your fault," he said quietly.

Theon stood at the fountain, watching the constellations. He whispered, "I miss you."

High above, the stars of the Trey constellation twinkled. For a brief moment, they seemed to shine brighter than the other stars. Theon felt a tap on his shoulder. He turned around and found himself staring deep into the eyes of a woman he'd never met. "Who are you?"

The woman smiled reassuringly. "That's not important," she said, and handed him a piece of paper.

Theon traded glances between the paper and the woman. He carefully unfolded it, and read the first few words. "This is from Mara's book, isn't it?"

The woman nodded silently.

"How did you—what—*who* are you?"

The woman lifted Theon's chin with her finger. She looked straight into his eyes and sternly said, "Mara made a *promise* that I would see my sister again. Death is no excuse. I *will* get my way."

Theon stared blankly as the woman turned and marched away, disappearing into thin air. He read the rest of the page:

I saw in the forest that the trees whisper as the wind-dragons dance through their leaves. But what controls the wind?

The wind-dragons. They are the wind. But they don't play. Their movements are governed by the sequence. And through them, the sequence governs the world.

How to break it? The answer may lie with the whispering forest, whose language I never learned. Their language is that of the wind-dragons.

The wind-dragons don't touch me. And I don't know why. But that's why Aphrael chose me. It must be—and why Vasigari chose Marcus. Why were we exempt? How are we related? The highway has to know, but why is it so guarded with the secret? Am I being tested?

The Ori said that once I found the sequence, I'd find myself at a crossroad. Help Aphrael? It's too late for that. Help myself? I don't know how. But I found what Marcus missed. Marcus wrote 'Left, right, up, right, right . . . ,' the motions of the leaves. These motions are governed by the sequence. The sequence is π.

50. Road Without Branches

"*Pi*?" I asked. "How would Pi show the world doesn't exist?"

"Knowing the sequence is one thing," Sheridan said. "What to do with it is another."

"If Aphrael knew it, why didn't she use it?"

"For the same reason *you* can't 'use' it. You just have a number in your head. But Mara, like Marcus, could see patterns in nature. She just figured out what they were."

"So, now we'll never know. That's twice you've told a bomber." I glared at Sheridan.

Sheridan chuckled. "I'm just telling history the way it is. Or was."

"I wish you wouldn't keep putting me in a down mood," I said. "I mean, we're halfway to–"

I cut myself off. Memphis was rolling over the horizon. As soon as I saw them–lights–I did a little mental happy dance. The clouds still loomed above, but suddenly, I didn't care. Here we were! I wondered if this was Sheridan's glowing city, but he didn't seem impressed.

I breathed a sigh of relief. A great weight lifted off my shoulders, and the world felt real and alive.

For a minute.

Memphis isn't a little town. It's a large city. Even in the middle of the night, there should be *some* cars on the highway. But we were completely, totally alone.

"Where is everyone?" I asked.

"Well, it *is* the middle of the night," Sheridan said. "I think."

"You think?"

"It's usually dark at night," Sheridan said. "Except ... "

I looked down at the car's clock. It read 0:92.

"Interesting," Sheridan chuckled.

"We've been on the road for several hours," I said. "Where's the day?"

Sheridan looked up. He grinned. "Eaten by the clouds?"

"That's not funny," I said. "Really. Where is it?"

There were no cars on the road. There were no lights to the side. Memphis was a lit oasis in a black sea, but even the lights of the city seemed to be dying.

I considered the idea that I was in a hallucination or dream, like Mara's trip to the sky or Marcus's journey to SanCullep. The car, the landscape, the clouds, even Sheridan–none of them existed. I was in a dream.

But that *conjecture* didn't seem to hold up. My surroundings seemed too real. They were dying, but it was a real.

Why was it still dark? Where did time go? The world felt like a clock winding down. The highway spanned nothing, connecting two points in a plane devoid of a home or destination.

Sheridan stared quietly.

"The world really is ending?" I asked.

Sheridan nodded slowly.

I thought of earlier in our trip, before Sheridan had begun the story of Mara. I remembered the flashing lights in the mountain pass, when we'd briefly entered the clouds. The lights were like the static of a channel that didn't exist. The clouds had continued their descent. This time, the road wouldn't descend away from them.

For the first time, I believed Sheridan. Mara's Model implied that I, like the Locanans, was a gear in some grand clockwork. If the world ended, I'd surely be shut down.

Part of me wondered if Mara was *right*. Could I just be a marionette, like the Locanans in the fountain square, without a decision to make? I watched endless mile after mile of highway scroll by. No exits. I realized just how right he may be. I, like my life, was on a straight course, with no opportunity to turn.

A puppet on a set track? Is that all I am? Sheridan was staring at me, this time with a look of genuine concern.

"That's how you can read my mind," I said.

Sheridan stared blankly.

"You don't think I'm a real person," I said. "That's how you always know what I'm going to say."

Sheridan stared quietly. I could see it in his eyes. He wasn't amused, or joking around like he usually did. He was concerned. He said, "Even a free-willed individual is predictable when they're on a road without branches."

I wasn't sure what he meant by that, but I thought of Dahes's marionettes. Now I knew why Mara had annoyed me. Mara was Sheridan, at least in spirit. She, like him, professed to know all about me–like I was dangling from the ceiling.

As I watched yet another mile pass, I turned my eyes back to Sheridan, and the urge to prove him wrong overcame me.

Sheridan's words from earlier in the drive rolled through my mind. *I suppose only a free-thinking being would have the ability to purposefully terminate its own life.*

"Is this something a marionette would do?" I exclaimed, turning the steering wheel sharply to the right. The wheels screamed as the car burst through a guardrail. The engine revved loudly as we flew through the air and into the darkness below.

Did you miss Stage I?

History repeats itself. This is what I taught, and always believed. Then I met Sheridan, a man hitchhiking down the highway without a care in the world—a lonely figure who told me history, and the world, was ending. His evidence was the story of a mathematician who tried to prove the world didn't exist.

It was a silly proposition. Nobody can prove the world doesn't exist. But as I became more convinced Sheridan was right, that the proof lay at the edge of reality, I could only wonder, *where would we go?*

The first stage of *An Orthogonal Universe*:

A FOUNDATION IN WISDOM

Keep up to date by visiting the blog at:
http://www.anorthogonaluniverse.com

Find a copy of *A Foundation in Wisdom*:
http://www.afoundationinwisdom.com

Thanks for reading!

Robert L. Watson's current incarnation began on 9 April, 1983 in Fort Worth, Texas, USA.

During his stint as a daffodil in 1653, he had pondered a proof for Fermat's Little Theorem (daffodils, as we all should know, have ample time to themselves for thinking). Unfortunately, he was snipped before he could complete his work. During his next incarnation he was successful in proving the theorem. But alas! No reputable mathematics journals would accept manuscripts from basset hounds. Even to this day it is true. He is still bitter about it.

Today, Robert is a mathematics professor who enjoys crafting mathematical fantasies in his spare time. He lives in North Carolina with his wife, Elizabeth, and cats Milton, Spenser, and Euclid.

Acknowledgements

The production of this book has been helped along by many people over the years. My deepest gratitude is reserved for my wife, Elizabeth Watson, who has read each revision. (And there were many!) Also deserving of a "thank you" are ...

My family, for their encouragement and support. And, in particular:

My brother, Joe, who (unknowingly) provided the inspiration for the first revision.

The town of Chapel Hill, NC provided the scenery for Locana.

A special thanks goes to Kisa Whipkey of Nightwolf Art & Design, whose editorial guidance helped shape the original manuscript into the book you're holding.